D0052657

The Wicked Worthingtons Series

WITH THIS RING
AND THEN COMES MARRIAGE
WHEN SHE SAID I DO

I Thee Wed

The Wicked Worthingtons Series

CELESTE BRADLEY

A SIGNET SELECT BOOK

SIGNET SELECT
Published by New American Library,
an imprint of Penguin Random House LLC
375 Hudson Street, New York, New York 10014

This book is an original publication of New American Library.

First Printing, May 2016

For more information about Penguin Random House, visit penguin.com.

ISBN 978-0-451-47597-8

Printed in the United States of America
10 9 8 7 6 5 4 3 2 1

Penguin
Random
House

This book is dedicated to my dear friend and partner in crime, Susan Donovan. Welcome home!

Acknowledgments

I could not have completed this book without the help of Darbi Gill and Susan Donovan.

Thanks must also go to the Geek God, who is not only smart and funny but cooks like a five-star chef! I would live on scrambled eggs it if weren't for him.

Without the love and support (and food!) of my friends and family, I would be a useless pile of goo on the floor. I love you all.

Prologue

IN a large, previously luxurious but now-shabby house in London lived the spirited Worthington clan. More concerned with creativity and self-expression (and yes, the occasional victimless crime!) than with the opinions of Society, the Worthingtons lived in complete disregard of the rules of the land and the expectations of their fellow members of the aristocracy.

While their mysteriously high connections made them difficult to shun entirely, their irreverent opinions and outlandish actions alarmed and fascinated the upper crust of London Society. The dashing Worthington brothers and their stunning sisters were not the sort of company one hoped to keep—yet how could one bear to exclude them entirely from one's social agenda when they were just so bloody intriguing?

The eldest sister, Calliope Worthington, found herself compromised into marriage by a man so deeply in the shadows that Callie never saw him coming—which might be why she was caught pawing through his jewels.

The notorious Worthington twin brothers, Castor and

Pollux, also known as the Double Devils, kept Society's jaded wives and wicked widows sighing with satisfaction until the day the two brothers met shy widow Miranda Talbot. They both fell hard, and for the first time in their partners-in-crime existence, they had a falling-out.

With the Worthington name becoming more and more synonymous with scandal, and with the family coffers becoming ever emptier, family beauty Elektra formed a plan to save them all. Is it still kidnapping if one plans to marry the man in the end? Of course, if the Worthingtons hadn't had bad luck, they would have had no luck at all. When Elektra finally got her hands on a duke's heir, she discovered that she'd captured his sarcastic manservant in his place!

Which brings us to the present. Three Worthingtons married off, five to go—brilliant Orion, heartbroken Pollux, war-torn Lysander, steadfast Daedalus, and frighteningly precocious Atalanta. If we were to consider their long-lost cousin, Bliss, the total would rise to six.

It is bound to happen, isn't it, when untamed hearts fly free?

Another day, another Wicked Worthington in love . . .

Chapter 1

LONDON, ENGLAND
1818

"ARE ye sure that's all o' your luggage, sir?"

Orion Worthington, the future preeminent biologist in all of England, had never concerned himself much with material possessions. However, as he looked down at the sum total of his belongings resting in the entry hall of Worthington House, it occurred to him that perhaps he had rather little to show for his nearly thirty years of existence.

Of course, he hadn't packed many books, because his destination held a fully stocked library. And he hadn't packed any specimens, or his scientific equipment, or really anything from his study-laboratory-bedchamber except for several volumes of his notes, for Blayne House contained one of the finest laboratories in London. If he had brought all the notes from all his studies, perhaps then his pile of luggage would have filled the foyer. As it was, his few items of good clothing, a small selection of his collections he'd wished to have with him, and perhaps three or four tools from the laboratory fit into a large trunk, a medium-sized box, and a small valise.

What he left behind was far larger and far weightier. The

past fairly bowed his shoulders with the burden of Worthington House itself, and every Worthington still within it.

His family was disorganized, chaotic, and unpredictable. Worthington House shook with noise and theatrics all hours of the day and night. If Orion had not forced himself to be highly disciplined, to disassociate himself from the emotion-steeped chaos, to barricade himself behind the comfortingly solid walls of logic and reason, he doubted he would have finished a single experiment the past few years.

That would end now. His mind fairly itched to play freely in the well-stocked, well-ordered, expensively equipped facility of Sir Geoffrey Blayne, a renowned chemist, biologist, and widely published innovator who had been knighted for his discovery of manufacturing applications for rubber. Of course, as Sir Geoffrey's new assistant, he would be expected to pursue Sir Geoffrey's scientific goals as well as his own. No matter. Orion was interested in many things, and the search for a method to isolate rare compounds found in plants would do for now.

Orion didn't see any point in hiding his own ambitions. If he helped Sir Geoffrey, Sir Geoffrey would help him. While Orion's past work had earned him some grudging interest and admiration from scientific circles, he could never hope to be included in the highest and most exclusive order in the land, the Royal Fraternity of Life Sciences. That seat was reserved for those who not only served brilliantly in their fields of work, but maintained a most respectable and serious existence outside the lab. There was no room in the Fraternity for nonsense and notoriety.

Which meant that Orion was automatically excluded on the basis of being "one of those Worthingtons"—unless he could prove his merit to Sir Geoffrey, gain the man's sponsorship, and move out of the shadow of his outrageous family.

As much as Orion loved his family, for some time now he

had longed for the peace in which to truly work, to study, and to discover the secrets of the scientific world.

Peace in Worthington House was rather hard to come by.

Even as that thought crossed his mind, a crash came from somewhere within the upper story of the house. It was a thumping, tumbling sort of crash, not a shattering, incendiary sort of crash, so Orion saw no need to rush to the source to discover what had fallen.

Gravity was not a friend to the Worthington clan. Worthingtons tended to pile things up. Gravity tended to pull them back down. Looking up the staircase from his position in the entry hall, Orion saw his father, Archimedes Worthington, wild haired and disheveled, rush past at the top of the stairs, followed by his mother, Iris, her trailing lace sleeves fluttering like wings behind her.

It was good to see that his aging parents were still so spry. Furthermore, the house itself wasn't nearly as dangerous as it had once been. Castor's new bride, Miranda, had worked diligently to bring order to the chaos, until her advancing pregnancy had recently begun to sap her energy.

Orion had been mildly interested in monitoring Miranda's pregnancy. She'd been willing, but his brother Castor had threatened to take an ax to Orion's Cabinet of Curiosities the next time he came at Miranda with a measuring tape and a list of questions regarding her current state of nausea.

Cas had always been quite illogical on the topic of his lovely bride. The turmoil of their romance had already driven one brother from Worthington House. Castor's twin, Pollux, had packed up and carried his broken heart away when Miranda had made her choice.

Now, however, even Miranda could not keep the infamous Worthington power of deterioration at bay. Inertia, a close mate of gravity, had waited diligently in the wings for Miranda to falter in her efforts. A neat pile of things left unattended would eventually slither into a heap and remain there to gather dust. A doorjamb would stick in damp winter weather, and rather than repairing it, the family would simply leave items that belonged in that room outside the door until the entire opening was quite blocked off.

Orion couldn't remember matters ever being otherwise.

Now that Orion's eldest sister, Calliope, and his middle sister, Elektra, had left the house to marry and have homes of their own, poor weary Miranda had been tasked with the job of bringing cultivation and refinement to the pagan masses that sat around the dinner table at Worthington House.

Other than Orion's parents, Iris and Archie, there were his eldest brother, Daedalus; then his next-younger brother, Lysander; Castor and his bride, Miranda; his cousin, Bliss; and, of course, not to be excluded——

"Attie!"

Orion tilted his head to listen to his mother's call. It sounded as though thirteen-year-old Atalanta Worthington was merely missing rather than dangling dangerously from something high, or holding a flame rather too close to something explosive, or in some way endangering herself, others, or the structural integrity of the house.

Not an emergency, then.

Orion heard the pounding of heavy feet above him and made out the muffled voice of Castor, the answering monosyllabic grunt that was Lysander, and the concerned but not panicked voice lilting above them all that was most definitely gentle Miranda.

Well, then. Orion turned to the three extremely well-dressed footmen who stood awaiting his orders. In their red and black Blayne House livery, they stood out in the shabby hall of Worthington House like bright new tin soldiers would stand out in a dustbin. He nodded at them shortly and gestured to his pile of things. "If you please."

With swift efficiency that Orion found incredibly refreshing, his things were gathered and toted out to the fine carriage his new mentor had sent for him from the fine stables at Blayne House.

Orion paused just one moment longer. It was merely to straighten his waistcoat, to tug at his sleeves, and to snug his new hat down over his freshly trimmed hair. It was certainly in no way meant to delay his departure long enough for his family members to realize that they were about to miss it.

"Attie!" from upstairs.

"Attie, darling, are you under the pile of books? Knock twice for yes and once for no."

"Iris!" That was Dade. They all called their parents by their given names, and often with just the exasperated tone Dade now used. "The only answer that matters is 'yes'!"

Indeed.

Without expending another precious moment of his new life on his past one, Orion Worthington opened the door of Worthington House and left.

THE BURLY MAN raised the gleaming knife high in the air. Francesca Penrose narrowed her eyes, refusing to back away. He was a bully and an incompetent, and she was damned if she would flinch now!

Whack! The sound echoed through the kitchens of Blayne House.

The cleaver parted the pheasant's feathered head from its body easily, but because of the cook's fury, his cleaver bit far too deeply into the wooden carving block. He had to use both hands to pull it free, like a novice butcher. Francesca smirked.

She pointed at the carcass on the block. "Do you know how long that disgusting thing has been hanging in the cellar? You could have beheaded it with two fingers, it is so rotted!"

The cook sneered. "You know nothing of good English food! A bird must hang for days to get full flavor!"

She rolled her eyes. "All you need is a handful of spices and a cupful of good wine to bring out full flavor."

"Bah!" The already florid cook reddened further. "You and your outlandish spices! You and your wine!" He snatched up the neck of the pheasant and shook its limp, stinking head in her face. "Sir likes good plain English cookery, he does!"

Francesca drew back from the revolting thing with a poorly concealed snarl of defeat. Cook had brought out his largest weapon. Fuming, she stepped back from the carving block.

His employer, Sir Geoffrey Blayne, did indeed prefer his food plain—plain and bland and tasteless! Francesca could barely stomach the unseasoned meats and unsweetened puddings that her uncle favored. In the six months she had resided in this English household, she had yet to actually taste anything!

At least she could salvage her sauce. She'd been cooking it for hours, reducing the precious first *pomodori* of late spring down to a rich tomato paste, redolent of oregano and basil grown from the seeds she'd brought tied into small silk pouches, pungent with the garlic she'd packed in her trunk instead of extra shoes. The aroma sang to her of summer in Italy.

A heavy splash sounded from the scullery. With a gasp, Francesca realized that the large copper stewpot she'd been using was missing from the stove. She picked up her skirts and ran like a hoyden, but of course she was too late.

The scullery smelled divine, due to the pool of thick, red, perfect Bolognese sauce now draining from the cold stone sink.

"Oh!"

In a fury, she turned on the cook, who was wiping out the copper pot. He sneered. "Using up me good cookery pot with your foreign nonsense!"

It wasn't ladylike. It wasn't appropriate. It wasn't even particularly effective at making her point.

But sticking her hand into the steaming remnants of her

beautiful sauce and then wiping it off in a great smear across the front of Cook's proudly pristine white coat was entirely satisfying.

Of course, it was a good thing she was fast on her feet.

She hitched up her skirts again with her clean hand and bolted from the kitchens. Even the furious cook couldn't catch her when she ran!

Chapter 2

ORION Worthington stood in the foyer of Blayne House while a footman swiftly divested him of his wet hat and overcoat.

Although he was not yet accustomed to such attention to his person, neither was he disturbed by it. Although Iris and Archie never cared for abundant household help, there was no shame in keeping servants. A highly trained, highly paid position in a fine house was much sought after in these troubled times. Sir Geoffrey was exacting in his preferences, but Miss Judith Blayne, Sir Geoffrey's daughter, saw that the master's every desire was catered to.

In a way, he was also now a retainer, although laboratory assistants were more in the way of apprentices, generally there to learn and to someday progress to take their master's place.

The contrast between this serene abode and the anarchic, jumbled Worthington House was so extreme that for an instant Orion doubted his impression of his own home. While the last memory of mud was being rubbed from his gleaming boots by a kneeling footman, Orion squinted against the shimmer of pristine housekeeping perfection and brought his family home to mind.

In the foyer, one might find random deposits of books, muddy shoes, dropped gloves, books, stray machine parts collected by or for Castor, one of the inventor twins, a scowling sister, books, a vague and dreamy mother, books, a Shakespeare-quoting father—dressed, one might hope, in something more than baggy winter drawers—a dueling sword or two, a musical instrument that was meant to be sent for repair but had gathered a decade of dust to its once-polished bosom, books, a second scowling sister . . .

"Ah!"

It was his new mentor, Sir Geoffrey himself. "Mr. Worthington, at last!"

UNFORTUNATELY, IN HER flight from the cook, Francesca ran in the wrong direction. Had she headed to the right, she could have used the servant staircase to make her way to her bedchamber unseen. Instead, out of habit she headed left, and the only staircase for her to use led directly through the main living areas of the house.

She looked a terrible mess, of course. One could hardly cook, and cook well, without digging in deep. But she'd been at it since dawn, first baking the delicious crusty bread that even the cook admitted was excellent, and then beginning her sauce with all the first beautiful pickings from her little garden in honor of the new arrival! And of course, she'd had to stop to weed a little, and she'd spent a few minutes seeing to her specimens housed by the back garden . . .

No, despite her highly productive day, Sir Geoffrey would not approve of her mussed, floured, steamed, and spattered state!

She put on a burst of speed. If she was in luck, the new resident of Blayne House had not yet arrived, and she could dash up the stairs to change before—

"Ah, Mr. Worthington! At last!"

Francesca skidded to a stop just as she entered the foyer, narrowly avoiding running directly into Judith, her cousin. *Blast it!*

And of course, the occupants of Blayne House were all present and accounted for. Sir Geoffrey was stepping forward to greet the newcomer. Francesca winced when she saw that her uncle wore the Coat.

She'd lived in Blayne House long enough to recognize Sir Geoffrey's favorite surcoat, a fitted thing of dark blue wool, trimmed in gold thread, with some sort of family emblem stitched elaborately upon the back—which family she could not imagine, for she knew perfectly well that her father's lineage was not especially distinguished in history. Like her, Sir Geoffrey was descended from a long line of scholars and professors with the occasional minor explorer or military officer. Then again, she couldn't really say, for Sir Geoffrey and Papa were only half brothers.

Whatever the source, the Coat meant that Sir Geoffrey considered the arrival of Mr. Orion Worthington to be an Occasion. With horror, Francesca realized that her cousin appeared entirely prepared for an Occasion.

The statuesque, highly ornamental Judith was always perfectly attired for whatever she did, usually without a single golden hair out of place, and always with her serene expression intact upon her lovely face. Judith would look tranquil in a hurricane, her ivory brow unwrinkled even if she were pursued by dragons!

Francesca brushed furtively at her skirts and then realized that she still wore the sackcloth apron she'd donned this morning. She stripped it off quickly, hiding behind the thankfully tall Judith to do so. The stubborn strings would not untie, so she resorted to pulling it over her head.

The knotted strings caught on her hair, which took advantage of the situation to tumble down around her shoulders. Francesca had an adversarial relationship with her hair. For some time now, she had suspected that perhaps her hair was winning.

There was little she could do about it now. Sir Geoffrey would find fault no matter how she appeared, so she straightened, pasted a pleasant expression upon her face, and hoped that Mr. Orion Worthington would at least be a lively addition to this gracious but incredibly boring house.

Going up on tiptoes, Francesca peeked over Judith's shoulder for a preemptive glimpse.

Che bello!

Mr. Worthington was what Nonna Laura would call "a superior specimen." Francesca tended more toward expressive language. The words "chiseled" and "striking" and even "splendid" drifted through her mind as she stared slack-jawed in wonder.

He was tall, dark, and *magnifico*. With dark brown hair, deep blue eyes, broad shoulders, and narrow hips, he was dressed like a gentleman in somber black. A dark sapphire silk waistcoat was the only touch of color.

He didn't look like a scientist. He didn't even quite look like a gentleman! To Francesca, underneath his socially suitable clothing and demeanor, the man before her fairly vibrated with potent male power barely held in check. He looked like a wolf in a sheep meadow, holding very still in the hopes that he would go unnoticed.

Francesca had expected someone bookish, mushroom-pale, and possibly stoop-shouldered, like so many of Sir Geoffrey's colleagues, but of course, younger. Mr. Worthington looked as though he might crack a book, but only after a stimulating gallop through the woods, where he would bring down a buck with a single shot and carry it home on his shoulders.

Wipe your chin, Chessa.

She waited breathlessly for him to smile. If he smiled, or made a clever jest, or even showed the tiniest sense of the absurd, she was sure she would promptly fall in love.

Alas, Mr. Worthington remained entirely somber. His

chiseled features portrayed only the thinnest veneer of interest in the social niceties. He looked very much like a man who thought chatting about the weather was a shameful waste of valuable air.

Of course, Francesca rather agreed with that, but she decided that on Mr. Worthington, it looked ever so slightly . . . well, rude. How disappointing.

She ought not to jump to conclusions. When she'd first arrived at Blayne House, she'd thought Sir Geoffrey pompous and self-important, and Judith impossibly unemotional. And look how that had turned out!

Sir Geoffrey dripped pretensions from every word, and Judith was more like a decorative object than a person. However, that did not mean that all of Francesca's snap judgments would be so accurate. That was a gamble she was bound to lose someday.

Fine, then. Step forward to be introduced to Mr. Orion Worthington and see for yourself.

I will. Just as soon as my toes uncurl!

ORION LONGED TO see the famous Blayne House laboratory. Unfortunately, Sir Geoffrey was expounding.

Again.

"You and I, son! We shall be unstoppable in the race to isolate chlorophyll!"

Orion nodded.

Sir Geoffrey went on. "Let's teach those damned French pharmacist upstarts!"

Orion knew he was referring to Joseph Caventou and Pierre Pelletier, who were more than mere pharmacists, of course. Sir Geoffrey had a keenly developed sense of competition. While Orion saw no point in competing with anyone but himself, he had no objection to serving Sir Geoffrey's goal.

He only wished that he dared employ his usual tactic of

simply walking away from boring conversation. His sister Elektra had sat him down and delivered strict instructions on how to suffer through social niceties.

"Stand or sit for as long as necessary. Nod when someone is talking, so that they know you are listening. You don't have to talk. In fact, I think you'd best not, or you'll say something dreadfully accurate and entirely too truthful. Look at their faces." She'd poked him in the chest with a slender finger. "And pay attention."

Sir Geoffrey rocked back on his heels and narrowed his eyes at Orion. "You know, son, I'm taking a chance on you. If it were not for your sister's marriage to that Lord Aaron fellow—" Sir Geoffrey sounded mystified by precisely how such a match might have come about, but Orion wasn't about to enlighten him. Elektra would not appreciate gaining a reputation as an armed kidnapper, no matter how accurately the description might apply.

"And of course, you've made quite a name for yourself, at least in amateur circles—"

Orion did not consider himself an amateur, but he recalled Elektra's warning that accuracy made for poor conversation, and kept quiet. Should he nod again? He gave it a try. Sir Geoffrey seemed to think it appropriate.

"So I feel it is highly probable—if your reputation proves true and you are as much of an asset to my work as I hope you are—that I will indeed be sponsoring you to the Royal Fraternity of Life Sciences!"

I am more intelligent than any of the current membership, so I have no doubt of it.

Accurate, but Elektra had warned him against being accurate.

He nodded again. However, this time Sir Geoffrey seemed to expect something more. Orion held his impatience in check. This was no different from attempting an extremely particular chemical process. If one kept trying, one would determine the best sequence.

He tried again. "Thank you, Sir Geoffrey. I will work very hard."

There. Accurate, yet vague.

And incredibly boring.

Sir Geoffrey didn't seem to think Orion's gratitude boundless enough. "We shall see. You have a rather difficult reputation, you Worthingtons. Even with your sister's advantageous match, I do hope your family keeps the high jinks to a minimum from now on. Especially if you want the sort of future that association with Blayne House can give you."

Sir Geoffrey shot a significant glance toward his daughter. Orion turned his attention there as well.

Sir Geoffrey had hinted that he might approve of a match between Orion and Judith, once Orion gained acceptance with the Royal Fraternity. Indeed, Miss Judith Blayne would certainly make the perfect wife for an up-and-coming young scientist. She had served as her father's laboratory assistant, housekeeper, and hostess for several years. Although he felt in no particular hurry to wed, he felt no aversion to it, either. In this instance, it was a perfectly logical notion.

With a wife like Judith, Orion could imagine himself living just this sort of peaceful, organized life. A fine home, run to exacting standards, leaving him free to involve himself solely in his work while his bride managed the boring day-to-day details.

Blond, blue-eyed Judith was very pleasant to look upon as well, although not in a way that would at all disrupt Orion's concentration—

The woman behind Miss Judith Blayne stepped forward.

Orion felt his considerable power of concentration snap to and aim itself at the female before him, quite without his intention. She stood out in that pale, elegant hall like a flame on ice. It was more than her vivid coloring, although her shining near-black curls and dark brown eyes, contrasting with honey-tinged skin and berry-bright lips, were riveting enough. In addition, he could see that her figure was impressively curvaceous, even in the loosely fitted, dull brown gown she wore.

However, further analysis, done with lightning speed, calculated as easily as an equation, informed him that mere buxom plentitude was not the factor at play.

No, it was something more. It was the way she moved on the balls of her feet, nearly as if waltzing. It was the dance of her eyes and hands and the smile that hovered at the corners of her mouth, even as she began to speak.

"Mr. Worthington, it is a pleasure—"

His head roared. Orion stopped listening. The ever-so-slightly Italian lilt in her rich, low voice struck him with a distressing amount of force.

Without a sound or movement, Orion Worthington, stringent believer in only what he could see before him, began to fall.

Vertigo. Spinning into infinity. Some axis that he'd never realized existed had suddenly shifted. Such an odd sensation. Almost as if one of his brothers had aimed a vigorous elbow into his stomach. Breathless. Heart-stopping.

All in all, meeting Miss Francesca Penrose would linger for a long time in Orion Worthington's memory as a moment of mingled exhilaration and, well, nausea.

However, Orion abruptly became aware that the irregular thudding noise he heard was not his stuttering heart, but was instead coming from the trunk at his feet.

To be more accurate, it was coming from something inside his trunk. Or someone.

He gave a sudden awkward cough to cover the thud, aimed an answering kick to the thick oak side of the box that ought to have contained nothing but his clothing and a few precious specimens, and turned abruptly to his host. "I must put my possessions in my chamber at once."

Everyone in the hall gazed at him for a moment, obviously

taken aback by his abruptness. Orion was entirely used to this reaction, so it disturbed him not at all. He had never been one to waste time or mental energy on empty pleasantry.

It was Miss Judith Blayne who stepped forward to smooth the social strain. "Of course, Mr. Worthington. Even the shortest of journeys can be fatiguing." She clapped her hands. Two hearty footmen appeared as if by magic. "Please take Mr. Worthington's baggage to the blue room," she ordered them serenely.

Sir Geoffrey recovered next. "Champing at the bit, eh? Rightly so! It is good to see a young man who can keep his mind on the job at hand! On with it, then." He waved his hands negligently at the staff as he passed through them. "I'll meet you in the laboratory before dinner, Worthington!"

Orion took distant note of Judith's social dexterity even as he admired her efficient command of the staff. He followed the footmen as they hefted his trunk and bags and marched up the stairs in a military fashion. He did not look at Miss Francesca Penrose again. He had always had a superior level of self-control.

Ignoring the small dark beauty took every bit of his strength of will.

Chapter 3

WITH a frown, Francesca watched the handsome newcomer climb the stairs. He was as attractive going away as he was coming forward.

He had behaved as if she did not even exist. The moment she had stepped forward, his eyes had glazed over and he'd gone quite slack-jawed. Boredom? Distaste, assuredly.

She turned to her cousin. "Do I have flour on my nose?" She was admittedly a bit of a mess. Perhaps he'd supposed himself being introduced to a servant?

Judith dutifully checked the aforementioned nose. "You are entirely free of flour or flourlike debris," she said in utter seriousness. Factual as a textbook, that Judith.

Francesca sighed, her shoulders drooping dramatically for half a moment. She'd hoped Uncle Geoffrey's new assistant would provide some distraction or even some intellectual stimulation. Judith limited her conversation to stated facts, and Uncle Geoffrey did not discuss science with anyone unluckily burdened by breasts. Judith's suitors, their only visitors, were an insipid lot who preferred poetry and minuets.

Francesca's fights—er, debates—with Blayne House's vociferous cook provided her with more interesting conversation than did that spineless lot.

At least Mr. Worthington was a treat to the eye. Goodness, he was tall, dark, and toothsome! As lean as the wolf he'd brought to mind, he moved up the steps with a physical fluidity that spoke more of fencing or pugilism than a life of puttering about in a laboratory. He was, in short, absolutely, divinely delicious.

He was also cold and unbearable, despite the way he made her toes curl up in her slippers. No matter. That was merely the biological imperative at work. Well-formed, virile, highly intelligent males were bound to set off a few nerve endings.

Pity there were no other examples present on whom to test her theory.

Francesca's mood shifted swiftly—as her moods so oft tended to do—and she gazed at Judith indignantly. "Handsome is as handsome does!"

Judith blinked. "Your use of idiom does you no service in pursuit of true knowledge. Colorful speech indicates an untidy—"

Francesca threw up her hands in Gallic frustration. "An untidy mind! Yes, I believe Uncle Geoffrey has made his views most clear on that topic!"

Judith glanced up the stairs. "I must see that our newest addition is comfortable. If you will excuse me, Cousin?"

Francesca wondered, as she sometimes did, what her endlessly placid cousin would do if Francesca suddenly threw her head back and cursed loudly and fluently in Italian. Not that she was much inclined to vulgarity, really. It was only that she was so very frustrated!

All her life, she'd dreamed of traveling to her father's birthplace of England. According to her Italian mother's extended family, she was entirely too English for her own good. Francesca's lovely mother had reassured her that she was as Italian as any of them, but even as a child, Francesca had known that wasn't true. Although she knew she was loved, she did not fit in among the large Veratti clan. In the four years since Mama had passed, it had only become more apparent.

They were a very intellectual band, the Verattis. Nearly all of them were involved in scientific pursuits. Real science, they reminded her often. Physics, chemistry, botany, and biology. They did not cook, or garden, or dance, unless it was at some university function. Even then they would rather analyze the patterns in the music than simply enjoy it.

Francesca loved science, too, but mostly she loved life! No matter how fascinating the research, no matter how interesting the professor, she had found herself thinking about the first buttercups of spring, or the last mushrooms of autumn, or of dishes she had made, or longed to make.

Giocosa, they had called her. *Apatica*. Playful. Lackadaisical.

That wasn't entirely true. She studied hard and she earned her place as a biologist, but did that mean she could not have any fun?

She was too English, they told her. Just like her father.

When Francesca had suggested that she take an extended journey to England to meet her father's family at last, her aunts and uncles had been disturbingly quick to agree with the notion.

So she had written to her father's half brother, Sir Geoffrey Blayne, esteemed British biologist-inventor, to secure an invitation. One had not been immediately forthcoming. It had taken several letters, each laden with increasingly obvious hints, to prod Uncle Geoffrey into extending a grudging summons.

Francesca had been on the next coach from Bologna to the seaport of Livorno. She'd been so excited during the crossing, she could scarcely eat. It was all she could do to choke down a mere three meals a day instead of five! At last, she would be understood and accepted. She was so very English, after all. She would be allowed to pursue knowledge in her own way—nay, she would be encouraged to do so!

Sir Geoffrey's first words after "Welcome to London" had been "Women have no place in the laboratory."

As Orion climbed the stairs behind the Blayne House footmen, he mentally calculated the air volume of the trunk versus the time elapsed since it left the Worthington residence, factoring in the probable remaining contents.

No, it was no good. He lacked vital information, such as precisely when the substitution had taken place and, more important, the resting respiration rate of little sisters.

The footmen deposited Orion's belongings in an admirably careful manner, which normally he would not care one whit over, and asked if he required assistance in unpacking.

When he waved his hand at them abruptly, they bowed and left, unperturbed by his rudeness.

The latch of the shabby trunk was stuck fast. Numbers ran through Orion's head, probabilities of relative humidity, rusting rates, years—decades!—since the forging of said latch, even as he swiftly searched the chamber for a lever of some sort.

The bedchamber hearth provided a finely wrought poker, which Orion applied vigorously to the recalcitrant latch without regard to the possibility of marring either the poker or the trunk.

The latch gave, as he'd known it eventually would. The only fact that remained unknown was if it would give in time. He kicked the heavy lid up with more applied force than was probably necessary. It nearly swung shut again. He caught it and lifted it again with his hands.

Then he stood and glared down into the trunk, sick with relief. "That was poorly calculated. You nearly ran out of air."

Pale, scrawny limbs unfolded from the depths of the trunk.

A figure sat up and pushed back a mussed mop of auburn locks. Freckled, green-eyed little Atalanta Worthington looked nothing like dark-haired, blue-eyed Orion, except when it came to the intensely analytical gaze they shared.

She took a deep breath, apparently unalarmed by her brush with suffocation. "You're right. I forgot that Other People waste so much time blathering in foyers. I shall be sure to factor that in next time." She wrinkled her nose. "Or drill an air hole."

Orion shook his head. "That is not a dependable alternative. Baggage is often stacked. Your airway could easily be covered up." He stuck out his hand.

A smaller, sticky one slid into his. It shook ever so slightly in his grip as he pulled his youngest, most brilliant sibling to her feet. She'd been a little frightened after all, which of course she would admit only under penalty of death—and perhaps not even then.

She stepped from the trunk and began to peruse the chamber with her hands clasped behind her back. "Someone painted fat babies on the ceiling."

"It is a frieze. The pigment is worked right into the plaster. Those are cherubs." She knew all of that, of course. Orion knew she read widely, if erratically.

Her brows wrinkled scornfully as she gazed up. "Why?"

Orion thought for a moment. "This chamber is called the 'blue room.' Other People sometimes apply imaginative decorations. Blue is the color of sky. Sky reminds some of heaven. Heaven supposedly contains cherubim. Cherubim are traditionally portrayed as obese infants." He always answered Attie's questions as fully as he was able—at least until she walked away. He understood his little sister in ways that no one else did. Her high intelligence, like his, was accompanied by a certain lack of comprehension of the activities of Other People, as she called them. Orion, once he had realized that his scientific ambitions would be aided by a higher degree of social skills, had made a study of human facial expressions and the emotions they represented. Attie would need this information as well, someday. Both his other sisters, Calliope and Elektra, opined that Attie would grow into a Great Beauty, the likes of which Society rarely saw and subsequently placed far too much importance upon.

Since Callie and Ellie were generally considered to be very attractive themselves, one must assume that they held some expertise on this topic of relative beauty—which interested Orion not at all other than with respect to its effect upon Attie's future.

Unbidden, his thoughts slid back to the arresting features of the woman downstairs. He experienced another inexplicable jolt at the mere memory of her remarkable, vibrant presence. Her eyes . . . her lips . . . her voice . . .

"Orion? Are you . . . Are you woolgathering?"

The astonishment in Attie's tone brought Orion back to his bedchamber with a snap. He met Attie's gaze with a frown.

"I think perhaps I was."

Her eyes widened. "But we don't gather wool. Ever."

It was true. Other Worthingtons did. The family was in general a dreamy lot, prone to artistic creativity and leaps of inventiveness. They were all quite intelligent in their particular ways, even the more socially aware Elektra, now Lady Arbogast, who currently applied her considerable energy and steely determination to the ongoing restoration of the Worthington family estate in Shropshire.

However, Attie and Orion shared a capacity for intense focus that had bypassed the others. Their minds did not wander. Their attention did not fade. It might end, rather abruptly, when events became uninteresting—but it did not meander off into contemplations of shining dark hair and lustrous eyes that danced with amusement . . .

"You're doing it again!"

Orion blinked at his sister. "This is a new development."

She shook her head, her eyes wide. "Stop it. I don't like it."

"I can't say that I'm happy about it myself."

Attie shook off the very thought of his woolgathering with a visible shudder.

A tap came on the chamber door. "Mr. Worthington?"

Orion looked at Attie. "It is Miss Judith Blayne," he informed her. Orion found himself unwilling to mingle his new world with his old. As much as he loved his family, this was meant to be his time to realize his own ambitions—ambitions better achieved without the interference of his unpredictable, outrageous family. "She will wonder how you came to be here. You ought to go."

Attie shrugged, then turned toward the chamber's large, vaulted window. She scrambled onto the deep padded seat within the embrasure and opened the window. Leaning far out, she looked down.

"There's an excellent tree," she called back over her shoulder. "I'm going home now."

Orion nodded without alarm. Attie was a superior climber. He attributed it to the relative strength of her wiry arms to the scarcity of her flesh. He could toss her into the air with one hand.

He could . . . if he were feeling a tad suicidal. Attie had a tendency to bite.

He watched as Attie stuck her hem between her teeth to get her baggy skirts out of her way. Beneath them she wore a raggedly chopped-off pair of boys' trousers, probably a castoff from the twins' childhood wardrobe. She'd secured them around her waist with a bit of hemp rope.

As he watched, she leapt from the window, hands outstretched. Orion thought he probably ought to watch to be sure she made it safely to the ground, although he reasoned that there was very little he could do standing at the window to stop a fall from a tree.

Still, Callie would expect him to at least try.

Attie walked the narrow branch closest to the house like a circus performer, with her hands outstretched for balance.

When she reached the relative safety of the trunk, she turned to wiggle her fingers at him in farewell, then proceeded to swing down, from branch to branch, until she was forced to drop from the lowest one, which remained about eight feet from the ground.

It was soft, grassy ground, so she landed with a practiced roll, stood, spat out her dress hem, dusted her hands on her bottom, and sauntered around the house, out of sight.

Satisfied that he had performed his brotherly duty, Orion turned to answer the door of his new chamber. Miss Judith Blayne stood in the hall, her hands folded before her.

"Papa has asked me to show you to the laboratory. He is waiting there for us."

Yes. The laboratory. It was, after all, the reason he now found himself at Blayne House.

How odd that he'd forgotten all about it.

Chapter 4

WHEN he passed through the double carriage-house doors into the outbuilding that dominated the considerable gardens of Blayne House, Orion Worthington entered heaven.

Sir Geoffrey's laboratory was a scientist's fantasy come to life. Orion suddenly realized that all his days he had operated in a whirling chasm of chaos. Although his study in Worthington House was undoubtedly the most ordered chamber in the house, it was still a hodgepodge of salvaged equipment piled on tables he'd cobbled together from scrap, using materials he'd scrounged or bartered or, occasionally, stolen.

All in the name of science, of course.

But this . . .

He stepped forward and felt the peace of order and clarity settle into him, as if he breathed it in along with the air.

Sir Geoffrey opened his big hands expansively. "As you can see, Blayne House is equipped with all the latest in scientific invention. I have my lenses ground in Switzerland to my exact specifications. No end of trouble during wartime, I assure you. I was forced to deal with smugglers, if you can imagine."

Orion forced himself to turn his absorption from the pristine racks of gleaming beakers, in every shape and size, including some he'd never known existed. On some level he thought perhaps Sir Geoffrey wished to hear some approbation for his exquisite facility, although why the man would care what Orion Worthington thought, he could not imagine.

He opened his mouth to say something politely admiring. "I want this." He did want it, deeply, passionately, with a profound longing that he'd never known before. However, through that gut-wrenching desire, he was aware that his brief, intense statement had fallen into the room like a brick.

Sir Geoffrey's eyes bugged slightly. Then he barked a short laugh. "Give it time, son. This may all be yours . . . someday." He sent a significant glance in Judith's direction.

Judith seemed serene enough at the implied notion. Her gaze was even, her stance at ease, her golden beauty gleaming in the brightly lighted laboratory. Nevertheless, Orion found his gaze drawn to the hotly burning eyes of small, dark Francesca, who stood just behind her cousin. It seemed that this was the first that Francesca had heard of the proposed possibility of engagement.

She had the oddest expression on her face. Her widened eyes denoted surprise, her wrinkled brow expressed doubt, yet the whiteness of her knuckles as they clenched the polishing cloth seemed to signify pain of some sort.

Her lips, for once, were not curved in amusement.

Behind her, Orion saw a single corner of the laboratory that stood out from the rest of the organized perfection. A rough wooden table had been shoved into the corner opposite the door. It was piled with stacks of notes, alongside a chunk of rock and a beaker stuffed with drooping flowers. Above it, charts covered in hurriedly inked branching lines had been pinned on the two corner walls.

The scruffy little corner reminded Orion rather forcibly

of his own makeshift laboratory in Worthington House. His internal scientist flinched at the reminder. Now that he had seen the Blayne lab, how could he ever bear to go back to such a state?

Sir Geoffrey followed his gaze and sniffed. "That is Francesca's little project. I'm allowing her to dabble in a bit of crossbreeding. Of course, I was hoping that my own organizational skills would prove to be an example, but . . ." He waved a dismissive hand and turned Orion back to the rest of the lab.

Sir Geoffrey had moved on in the moment of Orion's distraction. "What do you think of this, Worthington?" He gestured toward a polished copper contraption that spouted wire and tubes at seemingly random intervals.

Orion nodded. "It is a distillation device, I believe."

Sir Geoffrey's eyes narrowed. "Not just a distillation device. One of my own invention," he stated with a touch of aggrieved arrogance in his tone.

From the side of his vision, Orion saw Judith twitch slightly. He did not know the meaning of such a movement, unless one had unexpectedly encountered a distasteful insect.

He doubted any such creature had ever entered this sterile establishment, unless it was contained in a specimen jar.

Sir Geoffrey stroked a hand over the shining copper dome of the still. "I have taken several such designs to the patent office in recent years. My mind is simply overflowing with ideas. Puts to rest any nonsense regarding my slowing down in my elder days!"

Judith folded her hands before her, her always tranquil features taking on a peculiar stillness. "Yes, Papa. The Royal Fraternity of Life Sciences needs you more than ever."

Judith must be very proud of her father, Orion decided. No doubt some of the Fraternity had grown impatient for the great man to step down from his long-held position of First Speaker. A ridiculous notion. The elegant efficiency of the device before them attested to Sir Geoffrey's continued brilliance.

Orion could not help another glance toward Francesca. She gazed down at the beaker in her hands, polishing with great ferocity. It was already perfectly shiny.

However, it seemed that Sir Geoffrey had found a flaw in his flawless equipment. "Judith."

Judith stepped forward swiftly. "Yes, Papa. I see it."

Orion didn't, not until Judith reached for a single bulbous beaker on a shelf. As it passed before the lantern, Orion thought he spotted a faint staining on the bottom of the glass, as if something had once cooked too long upon a flame. He blinked, thinking that if such a beaker were in his home laboratory, it would likely be one of the cleanest he owned.

Yet Sir Geoffrey was livid. "Judith, you know how I feel about inferior tools!"

Judith put the offending beaker behind her back. "Yes, Papa. 'Only inferior minds use inferior tools.' I shall replace it at once . . . Only, the glassblower, Papa—"

Sir Geoffrey harrumphed. "Blasted miser. The ingratitude of the man, when he secured the accounts of every member of the Royal Fraternity upon my recommendation!"

The conversation had veered to the financial, so Orion shut off his attention and turned to study the distillation apparatus. While he opened the hinged copper doors, which were adorned with a rather unnecessary amount of brass filigree in his opinion, he found himself delighted with the triple-chamber process within. The purity of the distillation would be quite unrivaled in his experience. Further, the chambers appeared to all have been blown from a single glass. He admired it enormously. So very efficient!

Somewhere in a tiny corner of his attention, he was aware that Francesca had stepped forward, claiming responsibility for both burning the beaker and for replacing it on the shelf improperly cleaned. Sir Geoffrey had some sharp words for her carelessness, accusing her of having "an untidy mind."

Orion took note of that assumption, thinking it quite likely when placed next to the undeniable facts of her irreverent expression and Sir Geoffrey's opinion that she tended toward indulgence of the senses.

Still, in a tiny recess of that tiny corner of his mind, it occurred to him to wonder why an experiment in crossbreeding would require a chemical test in a laboratory. He filed that away under "insignificant curiosity" and turned back to the other three.

"I should like to begin immediately, Sir Geoffrey."

Sir Geoffrey, who had become rather red faced in his adamancy, turned from further scolding Francesca.

"Ah! Yes, indeed. A much more profitable use of our time, to be sure. Women in the laboratory can be such a distraction." He clapped his hands. "Out, my dears!"

Judith merely granted her father and Orion a small curtsy and turned to leave without comment. Francesca glared. Orion couldn't imagine why he was the target of such indignation. She ducked a resentful curtsy and stomped out after Judith.

Outside the large double barn door of the laboratory, Judith turned to Francesca.

"You did not have to do that, Cousin."

Francesca peered into Judith's face, but if anything, her cousin appeared more distant than ever. "I did not mind. My uncle thinks little of me anyway." She sighed. "Even if I were a man, I do not think he would prize my 'untidy' mind."

Judith looked away. "There are worse things than being dismissed by Papa."

Francesca snorted. "Such as what?"

Judith gazed up at the rear facade of Blayne House, still grand even from the back. "Why, being valuable to him, of course," she said quietly.

Then she floated serenely away, her ladylike pace denoting the perfect balance between leisure and purpose. Judith never bustled, yet she accomplished so much every day.

For the first time, Francesca wondered if Judith *wanted* to spend her days on such mundane and utilitarian tasks, or if her cousin might long for something more.

*   *   *

"Why, what's the matter,
That you have such a February face,
So full of frost, of storm and cloudiness?"

A February face, in the Worthington household, was used to describe the visage of a family member deep in the throes of creative angst, or sibling-induced rage, but it was indeed most often used in current days to describe the scrunched-up dissatisfaction of the youngest Worthington, skinny, mop-haired Atalanta. At thirteen, she was snagged like a fawn in a flood by a particularly excruciating stage of growth on the way to what seemed likely to be considerable beauty.

From her perch on the second-to-lowest stair, Atalanta shot her beloved father a disgruntled look. He beamed at her expectantly, eyes bright beneath his wildly curly but thinning silver hair. Despite her unhappiness, she could never bear to disappoint Archimedes Worthington in anything. With a grudging sigh, she responded. "*Much Ado About Nothing*, act five, scene four."

Archie hiked up the legs of his trousers and settled his bony bottom on the stair next to her own skinny rear. "He'll be back, pet."

Attie wanted to lean her head on her papa's shoulder and believe that he was big and strong and would make everything better, but she'd deciphered her parents' true natures by the time she was four years of age. Archie and Iris adored each other, and every single one of their eight sons and daughters, and always had a smile and an embrace ready to hand—but they were a pair of the most naive, drifting, inconsistent dreamers ever born, refusing to acknowledge anything even vaguely resembling reality.

It had made Attie strange, that knowledge. A child should not have to raise her parents.

"Did you see much of Blayne House?" Archie asked idly.

Attie shook her head. "I shall have to reconnoiter more thoroughly another day. I heard old Sir Blowhard carrying on until I thought I might asphyxiate. There were two ladies. One was Judith Blayne, for she was very English. The other was some sort of niece. She sounded different. I think I heard that she was from Italy."

"Two young ladies in the house? Hmm." Archie smiled as he hummed. "The Italian accent is very exotic, is it not? She will be very pretty, I should think. Italian women are always so, in my experience. None to compare to Iris, of course. You should have seen your mother, lounging in a Venetian gondola, with the sunset turning her hair to fire . . ."

He sounded lost in the past again. Attie sank a little deeper into her disgruntled slump. According to all their stories, Iris and Archie had once lived a very exciting life, traveling the world and meeting all sorts of people. Now Archie strolled around the house, speaking in sonnets while Iris painted canvas after canvas, her graying locks pinned up with paintbrushes.

Attie thought both of her parents were quite brilliant, and entirely useless, especially the way that they didn't seem to see the way the family was breaking into little pieces and disappearing, but she would defend their dreams with her very life if she had to, so she only said, "Yes, Archie."

If someone was going to pluck Orion from that house of scientific temptation, it was going to have to be her and her alone.

Chapter 5

LONG after the Blayne household had gone to sleep, Orion tossed and turned in his luxurious bed. One would think that the perfection of hospitality and service in Blayne House would be peaceful, but there was a portion of Orion's mind that remained suspended in expectation.

In Worthington House, "too quiet" was usually a portent of disaster. Too quiet meant that the twins were hard at work on something that was sure to explode. Too quiet meant that Attie was silently plotting something rather interesting and likely highly destructive. Too quiet meant that Elektra was in a dangerous sulk, or that Iris had inadvertently poisoned Archie with turpentine in the teapot again and that Orion's brothers were searching through London for a physician who would not require payment anytime soon . . . or ever.

Orion considered this restlessness objectively, as he did everything. He was familiar with the concept of adaptation, where a subject could become so accustomed to even the most awful environment that the thought of safety and sanity was actually alarming in its unfamiliarity.

Surely that explained his inability to embrace sleep. It was simply that he was not yet fully adapted to his fresh surroundings. The newness would wear off, and soon he would forget about his alarming reaction to her . . . er, it. The house. Blayne House.

Francesca.

Think on something else.

He could think about the incredible laboratory, where he could pursue almost any sort of research he could conceive of. Sir Geoffrey even had a telescope, in a farmhouse located in the high country of the Yorkshire Dales, that Orion could use to peruse the stars!

First, he would maximize the opportunities offered by the marvelous equipment in the laboratory. Even the most meager items held within were of stunning quality.

His thoughts lingered on that strange moment when Sir Blayne had fixed his fury on his niece for allowing a stained bit of glassware to invade the pristine room. Now that Orion thought about it, she had looked very much like his sister Callie did when she'd sometimes taken the blame for one of Attie's bits of mayhem.

Whom had Miss Penrose been protecting? Miss Judith Blayne? It seemed unlikely that Judith would ruin a beaker. A lady of Judith's demeanor would not likely cook a chicken, much less an experiment!

She'd certainly had nothing to do with the bland fare at the table this evening. With the exception of some very fine bread, everything had been overcooked and flavorless. Not that Orion much recalled the taste of the food. His mind had been fully occupied with . . . other matters.

He sat up in bed, fueled by an unaccustomed twinge of unease as he remembered.

Orion had been seated at Sir Geoffrey's right hand, the

seat of honor. He'd felt oddly as though he were being courted, which set him on edge. Every Worthington knew to eye all free offerings with suspicion, because nothing in life came without strings attached.

What would Sir Geoffrey expect in return?

Then Orion had forgotten everything at the sight of Miss Francesca Penrose leaning forward to poke disdainfully at the pheasant on her plate. The candlelight had turned her dark sable hair to midnight and the warmly tinted skin of the tops of her full breasts to shimmering gold. Orion had been riveted by the movement of her body as she took each breath, as she turned to speak softly to her cousin a few times, as she let out a long sigh of disappointment while she listlessly pushed her food about her plate.

Every time the dining room door opened to admit another servant with another tray, the draft carried the scent of orange-blossom soap and freshly bathed woman across the table to further disrupt Orion's ability to concentrate on, well, anything.

Miss Judith Blayne must have looked very nice as well, but for the life of him, Orion could not recall what she had worn or anything she had said. Instead, imprinted on his memory were the way the dark green fabric of Francesca's gown had clung to her rounded hip when she'd twisted in her chair and the way her smoky gaze had turned to him again and again, though she'd obviously tried to keep her eyes downcast.

She'd frowned at herself, a tiny crinkle between her dark brows, when she'd caught herself glancing at him from under her thick lashes yet again, and Orion had known that she was as perplexed by him as he was by her.

He wasn't stupid. This was what physical attraction meant. He'd thought he'd understood it before, but he'd had no idea of the sheer disturbing power of it. None of his intellect could help him as he found his trousers becoming uncomfortably tight. Quite frankly, he felt rather betrayed by his body—and worse, by his own mind!

His normally finely tuned instrument of intellect would not remain fixed upon matters of serious consideration, but instead kept sliding sideways into fruitless wondering about what it would be like to dig his hands into that thick, dark hair in order to pull her down on top of him in a deep, probing kiss. Would her round breasts compress softly against his chest when he held her close? Would her body take him deep into her hot, wet center?

Sir Geoffrey spoke to him several times, and he must have answered the man, although he could not recall anything he'd said. He should thank Elektra for her annoying lessons in civil deportment, for he'd apparently managed to deliver an acceptable array of banalities at reasonable intervals.

Sir Geoffrey had dismissed them all after dinner, promising "great things, young man, great things!" on the initiation of tomorrow's research, then taken himself off to his study to "review and reflect" upon the work until that point.

Miss Judith Blayne had said something suitably hostesslike about Orion's chamber, but all Orion could clearly recall was the way Francesca had given him one last smoldering glance over her shoulder as she'd accompanied her cousin from the room.

Or maybe it was he who had smoldered. He could not be sure. He'd never felt so aflame before!

Who is she?

Orion replayed, for perhaps the fiftieth time, Sir Geoffrey's introduction.

"The daughter of my half brother, Francis Penrose. Francesca has recently joined our household from her mother's family in Bologna, Italy." Her good fortune in that family charity was implicit in Sir Geoffrey's tone.

Orion was not sure why. There was marvelous science taking place in Bologna. The university there had been a center of discovery for hundreds of years: electricity, physics, chemistry, all the topics Orion wished to explore in his lifetime. He'd learned to read Italian at the age of fourteen simply to delve into the worlds of such great minds as Professora Laura Bassi and the scientist-monk Lazzaro Spallanzani without the blur of translation getting in the way.

Francesca had seemed a bit too earthy, with her tumbled hair and flour-dusted dress, to be familiar with the goings-on at the University of Bologna. It was a pity, really. There was so much astonishing discovery happening in the world right now.

Sir Geoffrey might know more about biology and chemistry than he himself did, but Orion was beginning to suspect that his mentor had become rather too comfortable in his lush laboratory. Adversity refined one's instincts, and change kept the mind flexible. That was why he was here, after all.

Not to think about women, no matter how rich their voices, or how glowing their skin, or how lush their lips . . .

Orion abruptly tossed aside his opulent coverings and planted both bare feet on the floor. It was warm, covered by a soft carpet, nothing like the icy, mind-clearing sensation of the floor at Worthington House. Orion twitched against the comfort of his environment for a moment, longing for some bracing, near-freezing water in his washbowl, for a stimulating draft from an ill-fitting window frame, or a sudden, alertness-spiking crash from another part of the house. He felt slightly suffocated, as if the luxurious walls of Blayne House were closing in upon him, forcing him to breathe stale air. Dragging a dressing gown over his trousers and bare chest, Orion went in search of something cold to drink.

FRANCESCA PROPPED HER chin upon her fists and willed her dough to rise faster. She imagined that the many thousands of little yeast beasties could understand, for she deeply believed that they were alive, so she thought the least she could do was encourage them.

"Grow," she breathed coaxingly. "Swell. Multiply."

Nothing much seemed to be happening. She couldn't imagine why. She had proofed the yeast, which was actually descended from her own batch she'd brought from Italy in a small clay jar in her reticule. She'd thought she ought to carry it herself, or some idiot sailor or driver or innkeeper might leave it sitting in the sun, where it would grow itself to death!

But Italian yeast beasties didn't seem to care for the English chill and damp. Each generation had become less and less active. It worried her enough that she thought she ought to have another little conversation with them. She bent forward, wrapping her hands around the large pottery dough bowl to warm it.

"I want you to be strong," she crooned. "Spirited. I want you to come alive in my hands."

"GET BIGGER."

Orion hadn't expected to find the kitchen occupied at all, much less by a shapely nymph in a nightdress and wrapper, who kneeled upon a tall stool and embraced a big white bowl.

She was talking to it.

Some might find that strange, but Orion had Iris Worthington for a mother. Iris had been known to wander the house in her nightdress while conversing enthusiastically with a potted palm. She said the plant liked to tell jokes but had little sense of humor. She laughed only out of politeness.

Hence, a half-dressed girl breathing endearments into a bowl was not even spectacular enough to cause comment.

No, it wasn't that she was talking to the bowl—it was what she was saying to it.

"Grow in my hands," her low, musical voice urged. "My

hands are so warm. Can you feel them wrapped around you? I want you to swell, and enlarge. Be strong. Grow until I can feel you get—" She hesitated, then continued in murmured Italian. *"Dura come una roccia."*

Orion translated in his mind and felt his knees weaken. *As firm as a rock.*

Oh damn.

Orion felt his blood begin to pound in his ears. Then it seemed to leave his brain entirely as it pooled thickly in his loins. As his cock hardened, he leaned his forehead against the cool plaster of the wall, all the better to absorb the intensely pleasurable sound of her warm, liquid speech.

"Venire, mia cara . . ."

Come, my darling . . .

Orion suspected that he had never sported such an erection in his entire healthy male life. It strained against his trousers as if it had a mind of its own, a mind determined to fall into those small, warm, caressing hands.

That would be . . . nice. Astonishing. Quite possibly life-threatening, if his pounding heartbeat was any indication of the danger he was in.

"Lievitare per me . . ."

Rise for me . . .

He wanted her. He wanted her hands upon him, holding his cock, squeezing him. He wanted her mouth under his. He wanted those lush, deep rose lips on his mouth . . . and on his cock. He wanted to fill his hands with her, with those creamy, golden-tinged breasts, with her curving hips, with her rounded thighs while she straddled him, enveloping his cock with her sweet hot—

"I don't think this is going to work."

He heard her sigh deeply in disappointment. He could sympathize. His cock had obeyed her every throaty command and was now swollen, risen, hard as a rock and ready to come for her.

Now what do I do?

* * *

FRANCESCA SLID DOWN from her perch on her knees on the stool. Her yeast beasties were not long for this world. She patted the bowl mournfully. "That's all right. I'm sure I shall get along famously with English yeast beasties as well." With an effort, she hefted the big crockery bowl full of flaccid dough and lugged it to the scullery. Beneath the large stone sink was an enormous pail the cook called the "pig bucket."

The Blayne household did not keep a pig, but presumably the cook wasn't referring to Sir Geoffrey. The cook probably sold the scraps to some farmer and pocketed the proceeds.

She dumped the bowl and dusted her hands together. Tomorrow she would go to the baker's and beg a starter colony of English yeast. At least today she'd had that one last batch to serve the new assistant, Mr. Worthington.

Not that he'd seemed to appreciate the crusty goodness of her bread. Whenever she'd glanced his way, he'd been absently forking up the painfully bland food while staring at her. Not that she'd glanced his way often. Only three or four times.

Per minute.

She twisted a corner of her lips at the accuracy of the accusation. Yes, but that was only because he was very easy to look upon!

In truth, she'd been riveted by him. Everything about him tugged at her attention, from the way his large hands handled the cutlery with precision to the flexing of his chiseled jaw as he chewed. His dark blue eyes had seemed almost black in the candlelit dining room, and they had scorched her skin like coals when he'd looked at her.

She'd felt his gaze on her face, heating her flesh, and on her neck, making her shiver, and falling upon the exposed upper skin of her bosom, warming her like Mediterranean sunlight.

Francesca paused just before leaving the kitchens, tightening the belt of her wrapper and reminding herself that she thought Mr. Worthington to be rude and arrogant in his manner and speech.

A man that attractive? Who requires him to speak?

She shushed her biological imperative, smoothed the neckline of her nightdress, and strode from the kitchen.

"Oh!" She practically tripped over Mr. Worthington. He was leaning against the wall outside the kitchen door with his head tipped back against the whitewashed plaster and his hands folded before him. He looked rather like a guard, albeit a rather tousled and unkempt one.

Oh, I like you unkempt. Tousle me, too!

He opened his eyes and straightened slowly. "Miss—" He cleared his throat. "Miss Penrose," he said, greeting her with a distant nod, as if they had happened upon each other in the garden on an afternoon.

He was beautiful, but really rather odd.

I like odd. I am odd as well.

"Are you hungry?" She always had the impulse to feed people, and he was standing outside the kitchen in the middle of the night.

His gaze locked on hers for a single, flammable second. The force and heat that struck her made her take a step backward. Her heart began to race.

Merely biological imperative, she reminded herself.

"So that is what this is?" As he frowned, the force of his gaze increased.

Francesca froze. "Did I say that out loud?" At his nod, she swallowed. "Ah. Well. Um. Yes, I think so." She waved a hand vaguely, trying to catch her breath. "Involuntary and—"

"Unwelcome." His voice grated slightly on the word, as if it had been pulled from him.

She blinked. "I was going to say 'completely natural.'" Heavens, he was arrogant! Unwelcome, indeed! She happened to know that in Bologna, she was considered quite a catch—and not just for her cooking!

"It is this English damp." She put her hand to the thick

braid that hung over her shoulder. "It makes my hair so frizzy," she explained sorrowfully.

"Your hair . . ." He gazed down at her. If she had not just seen the flaring sexual heat in his gaze, she would have thought his expression cold. His hand lifted and his fingers twitched, stopping an inch from her plaited locks. Francesca held very still.

Then he dropped his hand, pulling back as if burned. "Your hair is of no importance," he said gruffly. "It would not matter if you had none at all, if this is simply instinct and reproductive drive."

Francesca, feeling bereft at the loss of his touch, folded her arms and lifted her chin. "I rather think my own drive would be perhaps lessened if you had no hair."

Then she had a mental image of him as an older man, still standing at her side after a loving lifetime, lean and craggy, those blue eyes sharp and piercing. Her belly quivered in response.

Or perhaps not.

They remained that way for a long, breathless moment. Francesca became aware of the lateness of the hour, and the very excitingly inappropriate nature of their attire, and the fact that she could catch his sandalwood scent and the heat of his body every time he exhaled—or was it every time she inhaled?

The moment lingered, and stretched—

A sudden creak, the sort of sound a house makes in the night, snapped the tension of the moment. They stepped away from each other simultaneously. Mr. Worthington cleared his throat.

"Good night, Miss Penrose." He bowed slightly. Francesca enjoyed that, because his dressing gown sagged open a bit and she got a marvelous glimpse of hard, rippling abdominal muscles.

She paid him back by dipping a curtsy, knowing that the neckline of her nightdress, borrowed from Judith, gaped just a bit. "Good night, Mr. Worthington." She straightened and tried not to laugh at the gob-smacked expression on his face. "I do hope the rest of your night's sleep is undisturbed."

She turned and left him there, and if she threw just a little more swing into her hips than was strictly ladylike, well, there was no one else to see, was there?

As she turned the corner and began to climb the narrow stairs into the main house, she heard him release a long, shuddering breath, and smiled. It served him right.

"Your hair is of no importance," he had said.

Ha!

Chapter 6

IF Orion normally found five minutes of small talk to be unbearable, it was because he had never before been subjected to "morning calls." For most of an hour the next morning, he was expected to sit in the Blayne House drawing room and make conversation with two ladies and three idiots—rather, suitors of Judith. Occupying the sofa opposite the chairs containing Miss Blayne and Miss Penrose were Nicholas Witherspoon, Sir Humphrey Cavendish, and Asher Langford.

Since Miss Judith Blayne was always gracious and mildly interesting in a suitably noncontroversial manner, it was no particular hardship to pass the time in her company.

On the other hand, Francesca made him most uncomfortable. Miss Penrose, he corrected himself, absently tapping his fingers lightly on the book in his hand. The cousin of the woman he was supposed to be pursuing. She might someday be his cousin, too, in a way.

The thought made him flinch slightly. Which was ridiculous. The physical attraction he felt was only the biological imperative at work. She'd said it herself last night.

Last night, in the dark and still hours, with Francesca in her nightdress, scented with orange blossoms and bread dough, which should not have been the slightest bit arousing, yet was . . .

"What is it that you have brought, Worthington? Something amusing, I hope?"

It was Nicholas Witherspoon, an incurably fashionable dandy who feigned interest in biology in order to maintain his family's three-generation membership in the Royal Fraternity of Life Sciences. The Witherspoons, according to Nicholas, were so wealthy, they practically defecated gold doubloons. Every sentence he uttered concerned himself, his wealth, or his family's reputation and wealth. Orion judged Witherspoon to be the king of the idiots, or rather "suitors," as Sir Geoffrey had named them.

"Not to worry, boy," Sir Geoffrey had murmured when he'd virtually ordered Orion to sit the calls with the ladies. "None of them have half your intellect. My daughter wouldn't have anyone less than a brilliant scientific mind to wed!"

Indeed, Miss Judith Blayne seemed entirely unperturbed either way by her gentleman callers.

Small wonder. The idiot of the second order, a Sir Humphrey Cavendish, was a stout man of middle age who had been knighted for his service in keeping the war effort well supplied with cart wheels. Orion granted that the wheel was an integral part in the forward momentum of an army, but the man himself was an unimpressive specimen. Sir Humphrey had a ridiculously long handlebar mustache that dipped itself into the tea and then dripped onto his coat. Orion could not actually judge the depth of Cavendish's conversation, for the man spoke in an entirely unintelligible whuffling mutter that reminded Orion of a discontented wolfhound.

By far the most devoted of Miss Judith Blayne's suitors was the Honorable Asher Langford, third son of the third son of a middling important lord. Asher seemed a likable enough fellow, but Orion did not feel that Sir Geoffrey's plans for his daughter were threatened, for Judith seemed not to even notice Asher's shy adoration. Furthermore, Asher, though he had no possibility of inheritance, seemed to have no purpose in life except to play the harpsichord and devote himself to Judith.

"Well, Worthington? Are you planning to share with the class?" Nicholas Witherspoon gestured languidly to the book Orion held in his hand.

Orion ignored him, but turned to present the bound volume to Judith. "My sister's work. A book of her botanical paintings that she has had published."

Miss Judith Blayne took the book, *Wildflowers of the Cotswolds*, by Calliope, Lady Porter, readily enough, thanking Orion politely, but after a brief peek into its pages, she set it aside on the sofa cushion next to her.

Orion could not avoid seeing Francesca grab it and take it away into a corner, where she delved greedily between the covers. "Oh marvelous," she breathed.

Her tone was but a whisper, but Orion heard her as clearly as any of Nicholas Witherspoon's sarcastic jests. After several minutes, Francesca lifted her head. "Judith, this is lovely! It is art and science!"

Orion thought the illustrations were quite good, himself. Then why did he hear himself dismiss them? "My sister's specimen drawings are quite correct, but there is no new knowledge represented in the volume."

Francesca simply shot him a pitying look and turned another page. "I think it is quite magical, the way one almost expects them to come to life."

"Magical?" Nicholas Witherspoon snorted. "Women love to believe in the intangible, don't they, Worthington?"

Francesca stiffened on her cushion by the window. It was the inevitable moment of Someone Belittling Her. It was a trial, spending all her time putting arrogant boors in their places. Still, she shut the book and gamely opened her mouth.

Mr. Worthington beat her to it. "Air is intangible, Witherspoon. Don't you believe in breathing?" His tone was very bored. "If not, feel free to stop anytime."

Francesca subsided on her window seat, blinking rapidly. Orion Worthington might have been a knight in gleaming armor at that moment. He had defended her . . . hadn't he? Or was he simply weary of Nicholas in general? That seemed far more likely. Francesca decided that she didn't care, and sent Mr. Worthington a grateful smile across the room.

He must have been watching her, for he drew his head back sharply at her smile. His dark blue eyes went nearly black for a moment, throwing Francesca back into the memory of the night before. The shadowy hall, the silent house, the moment stretching on and on while her heart pounded—

She tore her gaze away and turned it downward, staring blindly at the book in her hands. *Be still,* she ordered her stuttering heartbeat. After a moment, she set the volume aside and smoothed her shaking hands on her skirts. *Breathe.*

Such commands did little good to soothe her jumpy nerves. Mr. Worthington had the ability to disturb her usually cheerful disregard for the opinions of others. She cared what he thought of her.

I like him. Except that she didn't . . . or rather, she shouldn't! *I want him to like me.*

How incredibly tiresome. And disturbing. The realization made her assess herself in a way she was unaccustomed to doing.

Did he think her pretty? Did he like her hair down, as it was today, or ought she have put it up, like Judith's flawless chignon?

Francesca had never been one to worry about her appearance. She had often wondered why other ladies wanted to take so much time on their hair and gowns, when there were so many more interesting things to do. Still, sitting in the parlor next to Judith and her exquisite sky blue silk gown, Francesca felt rather like a country mouse.

She hadn't bothered to update her wardrobe once she'd arrived in England. After all, why bother with fine feathers when she had no intention of attracting a mate? She did not intend to marry, ever. Not like Judith, who assumedly had set her cap for Mr. Worthington.

Her cousin's plan would succeed, of course. Judith was beautiful, in that classic English rose way that Francesca had only heard of before moving to London. Judith was thread-of-gold and moonlight wrapped up in tasteful silk and cool serenity.

Not that Francesca envied Judith either her looks or privilege. Judith's world would make Francesca madly twitchy with restlessness. She planned to take big bites out of life. Her family's unfortunate fate had taught her that life was brief and frail. She longed to do things, to see places, to dig deep into the curiosities of life and taste heartily of its flavors.

Judith didn't even seem to notice all the magic of the world around her, not even shy Asher Langford's silent longing for her.

Well, perhaps she envied Judith just a little.

Dowdy. That was the only word Francesca could think of when she looked down at her own practical brown gabardine. Of course, her figure was quite good. She'd have to be blind not to realize that. She looked perhaps not like a mouse but more like a governess—one with rather more bosom than might be deemed appropriate in the guidance of the young.

Why should she suddenly care? In Bologna, all the women in her family dressed sensibly. They dressed for the weather and for the task at hand—and the task at hand was rarely to sit and look pretty for the admiration of men. Such a notion was shallow, and silly, and useless. Women in Italy were never useless. In Bologna, women were encouraged to pursue their talents. Art, knowledge, science, and above all, food. For her cooking alone, Francesca was an accomplished woman in Italy!

So why did she suddenly desperately long to sit prettily merely for the admiration of Orion Worthington?

He certainly wasn't looking at Judith, Francesca thought with a tiny twinge of petty satisfaction. When he'd entered, he'd cast his cool gaze at the assembled gentlemen. She could practically see him filing them away under the label "no competition."

That wasn't strictly true, she realized. While Judith certainly showed no preference for any one fellow, and that included the arrogant Orion Worthington, there was one young man whose interest in Judith ran far deeper than a mere interest in acquiring a wealthy ornament to his comfortable existence.

Poor Asher Langford. Although he was handsome, in a fair-haired, vaguely poetic fashion, and every bit as tall and well shaped as Mr. Worthington, Asher was so painfully shy that it seemed all he could do to walk into the parlor and sit in the presence of the lovely Miss Judith Blayne. Past that point, he seemed capable of no intelligent conversation, or entertaining wit, or even any words at all.

Sometimes Francesca ached for Asher Langford. What must it be like to love someone with all one's heart and never be able to say it out loud? Then again, what woman wanted a man who didn't care enough about her to risk saying the words?

Her gaze slid to Mr. Worthington again. Orion Worthington didn't seem to fear anything or anyone, not even his overbearing mentor, Sir Geoffrey. Then again, didn't one have to risk losing something to feel fear?

I don't like him. So there. I fancy him, but I don't like him.

The aforementioned passing fancy was only her normal physical drive in action. Intelligent people did not allow themselves to be ruled by their biology. She would inwardly acknowledge the attraction, and then she would forget it.

She sighed. Anytime now.

Asher Langford cleared his throat. Everyone in the room turned to gaze at him expectantly. When someone spoke rarely to never, it did tend to draw attention when they finally broke their silence.

Asher paled at their unified regard, then swallowed, then blushed furiously. "Miss B-Blayne," he began. "Will you be attending the Duke of Camberton's b-ball next week?"

"Oh how boring." Nicholas Witherspoon sent Asher an arch look, clearly meant to quell his stammering attempt to gain Judith's notice. "Another ball. I grow so weary of endless social obligations."

Judith stirred but clearly hesitated to answer. *Yes, Cousin, what possible answer would be in agreement with both men?*

Francesca felt a twist in her chest as she watched Asher sink into his shoulders, hunching and drawing back.

"Oh for pity's sake," she muttered. Shooting a hard glare at the insufferable Witherspoon, Francesca set aside the pretty book and rose to her feet. "Mr. Langford, I declare I feel quite suffocated in here." Another significant narrowing of her eyes at Witherspoon. "Would you care to take a turn around the gardens with me?"

All of this was terribly forward by British standards, of course. Judith turned to blink at her, her lovely features redistributing themselves into a faint frown.

Oh no, mustn't make a real frown, Cousin. Someone might realize you are human after all!

There was no danger of that, of course. Judith's expression soon smoothed itself into serenity once more. "Do not forget your bonnet again, Cousin. The sun is quite bright today."

Francesca cast a doubtful look out the parlor window at the English sky, which in truth was only a slightly brighter gray than usual. If Judith ever saw a vivid, blistering Italian summer day, she would wilt like a plucked daisy! With a shrug, Francesca gave in. "Very well."

Judith smiled faintly, then nodded to the servant Pennysmith, who stood at the drawing room door as if he were simply a more fully dressed version of the fig-leafed marble statuary on either side of it.

Pennysmith, in turn, nodded to one of the underbutlers, who nodded to one of the footmen, who left the room, presumably to find someone to tell someone to tell Eva, Judith's maid, to fetch Francesca a bonnet because she intended to venture twenty yards out-of-doors on a cloudy day.

I will never understand this place.

With a twinge, she suddenly recognized that there was a very great possibility that this place would never understand her, either.

Asher, in the meantime, had stood, sat, stood again, clasped his hands before him, released them, tugged at his waistcoat, clasped his hands again, and then, at long last, nodded jerkily in Francesca's general direction in acceptance of her invitation.

Shaking off her sudden bleakness, Francesca made herself send poor Asher a brilliant smile. *"Meraviglioso!"* (Marvelous!) "I could not ask for a more congenial companion."

In the corner of her vision, she thought she saw Orion Worthington twitch slightly. Was he thinking that she was common for being so forward? Or that silent, shy Asher was not anyone's notion of congenial?

She cast a superior glance at Mr. Obnoxious Worthington as she glided to Asher's side, tucking her hand into his belatedly extended arm. *I happen to like silent, shy men,* she tried to convey with her smile. In reality, it was somewhat true. Shy men were predictably good listeners, and Francesca dearly loved to talk.

To her horror, Mr. Worthington seemed to take her dismissive glance as some sort of invitation. He rose to his feet.

"I shall accompany you as well."

Francesca stared at him. "You? Now? Are you quite sure you should? Do you not have something boiling over in the laboratory?"

Orion gazed down at Miss Penrose's disbelieving expression, trying not to echo it with his own surprise. He didn't remember standing. The only thing he recalled was the wave of possessiveness that had swept him when he saw Miss Penrose smile so affectionately at Langford—and when she'd spoken to him in Italian!

The word had rolled off her tongue like cream and cinnamon and had soaked into Orion's thoughts, bringing forcefully to mind images of golden-tinged breasts and hot rose-lipped kisses. And she had given that word to another man?

They stared at each other for a long moment.

Say the same to me. Orion wanted to hear that rich, throaty language as only she could speak it. *Read the butcher's order, recite the periodic table—anything!*

"It is a fine day, isn't it? Shall we all take a turn?"

It was with surprise that Orion heard Miss Judith Blayne's very appropriately modulated English voice. He had quite forgotten Judith was in the room.

Again.

When they all set out for a stroll through the Blayne House gardens, Orion sent one glance toward the sturdy, modern barnlike edifice of the laboratory. He felt the urge to disappear within.

Then he heard Francesca talking to—or rather, at—Asher Langford about someone called Herbert as she steered him toward the kitchen gardens behind the laboratory.

"Herbert is extraordinary, really. And so intelligent. I have never seen any other subject learn more quickly."

Orion's eyes narrowed. Asher Langford was no cause for worry, but who was this Herbert fellow?

"Mr. Worthington, have you seen Papa's physic garden yet?" Miss Judith Blayne stood behind him, left there in the surge of jeal—er, curiosity he'd felt about "Herbert."

Judith is the one you plan to marry, remember?

She stood in the gentle light of the cloudy day, looking like a romantic painting of the textbook English beauty. Her perfection caught his eye, but her face and form did not disturb him. She seemed equally dispassionate about him, which was likely a good thing because, other than an academic knowledge of the female body and that single thwarted night at an exclusive brothel, he had no experience in pleasing a woman.

The notion of studying passion and pleasure with Miss Judith Blayne did not repel him, but neither did it lure him.

Judith continued to await his approach politely. "The physic garden is the culmination of fifty years' work, collecting medicinal plants from every corner of the world," she stated evenly, sounding rather like a brochure. "It has become quite renowned for the variety within."

He should be intrigued. He should be at least comfortably dutiful. It was Judith he should be trailing about the garden, fending off suitors and making himself pleasant for.

And yet even as he stood there, he felt the relentless pull to follow Francesca's scent, like a hunting dog barely leashed. The attraction was magnetic. He was iron to her polarity.

Bloody hell.

With that silent curse, he turned his back on Francesca and Asher to accompany Judith to a different portion of the grounds.

His biology was becoming ever more inconvenient. There must be a solution. Every problem had a solution.

Chapter 7

FRANCESCA chafed to put an end to the morning calls, but after the walk, there was tea to be had and then more conversation. Mr. Worthington sat silent and aloof, and Francesca tried to entice more than three words sans stammer from poor Asher, but their brief companionship in the gardens had lapsed into Asher's gazing moonstruck at Judith once more.

At least she had managed to trick Asher Langford into helping her feed her specimens and clean up after them by telling Judith stories while they worked. She didn't feel too bad for it, since physical activity clearly calmed his nerves, and the stories were even somewhat true. That was one good use of this wasted hour.

At last, the ormolu clock on the mantel chimed the hour. As if summoned by the sweet silvery ring, Pennysmith appeared with the gentlemen's hats and gloves in hand.

Francesca made a gracious farewell to Asher and the probably inoffensive Sir Humphrey (although who really knew?). She managed a stiff nod to that supercilious ass, Nicholas

Witherspoon, although he didn't really bow to her as much as slump slightly in her general direction.

Her duties as Judith's chaperone concluded, she strolled sedately away from the foyer—at least, until she was out of sight. Then she picked up her skirts and bolted for the library.

Free at last!

ATTIE WORTHINGTON HAD never worried too much about invitations as such. After all, she hadn't actually been forbidden to climb back up the tree, along the teetering branch, and into Orion's chamber window. Entering Blayne House by such a roundabout fashion might be considered unlawful entry, but Attie had long ago decided not to concern herself with semantics.

Orion was not in his room, nor had she expected him to be at this time of day. She had heard of Sir Geoffrey's astonishing laboratory. She longed to see it with her own eyes, but Sir Geoffrey sounded like one of those stuffy, unpleasant scholars who didn't understand that a superior mind could be encased in a skinny little girl's body.

Some people did not deserve to be called scientists.

Still, if everyone was occupied during the day, Attie saw no reason not to explore her brother's new home at her leisure. Orion's chamber was nothing special, in her opinion. The furniture might be unscarred and gleaming, but it was all the usual sort. The room contained a bed, a dresser, a writing desk, and a chamber pot, just like any bedchamber in her own house. And at Worthington House, such a vast room would have also contained a lively assortment of artwork, literature, cooking utensils, rusting farm implements, and other fascinating whatnots. This room was just . . . empty.

The bed, however, was marvelous for jumping.

After she exhausted her interest in that juvenile activity, Attie gently forgave herself for being a child (since it was a temporary condition and one soon cured) and set out to explore the rest of the house. She found herself in a long, boring hallway that ended in a gracefully curving set of stairs leading down, and then there was another long, boring hallway with nothing on it but doors. Attie enjoyed opening doors to places she was not supposed to enter, so that was entertaining for a while. There was a drawing room, very ladylike and posh. Her sister Elektra would've liked it very much. The next door contained a very similar drawing room, only this one had more masculine touches and a rather nice card table.

Attie approved of gambling in general, especially when people underestimated the abilities of a thirteen-year-old girl. Iris often told her that a lady had few advantages in the world, and the ones she had ought to be used wisely. Attie took that to mean that her ability to count the cards in any game should be used to her advantage.

However, no game was going on at the moment, and there was nothing of interest in any of the next rooms. There was a sort of study, but it was unexciting and anonymous. Another door led to a dining room that was too small to accommodate her fondness for skipping and running. The room after that was intriguingly locked.

Attie pondered the wisdom of picking that lock. It wasn't so much *whether* she should pick the lock as it was *when* she should pick the lock. She decided to put it off for later and felt quite virtuous for doing so, as if she had decided to eat her vegetables before eating her dessert.

The next doorway, however, led to a place that made her forget all about her tendencies toward crime.

It was the much-vaunted Blayne library. And such a library! The enormous room was two stories high, and as wide as three posh parlors put together. Attie wasn't one for neatness, tidiness, or organization of any kind, except when it came to the cataloging of books. She'd sometimes wondered what it would be like to know precisely where to find a certain book anytime she wanted, and not have to search through piles, thinking that perhaps it'd been on the steps, or perhaps it had been in the upstairs hallway, or perhaps it had been in another place altogether.

There was no such worry in this library. It was a room full of gleaming, well-dusted, neatly cataloged books. The leather-clad and gold-stamped spines glowed with all the colors of the rainbow. The shelves rose all the way to the ceiling, with a walkway along the top and an ornate spiral staircase, as well as a curlicue-adorned brass ladder that would slide on rails from one side of the door where she stood apparently all the way around the vast room and back the other side of the door. In the center of the room, arranged on the diagonal, there were more shelves, much higher than her head, polished oak shelves that one could lose oneself in, every single one filled with marvelous, wonderful books. There were more books in this library than she'd ever seen in one spot in her entire life. Which she was fairly certain made this heaven on Earth.

How could she ever bring herself to leave? Then again, with her skills, she could venture here anytime she liked.

There was enough room around the central stacks to dance, and even though Attie spent most of her time being rather surly, and uncooperative, and very little inclined to do anything that most people would consider girlish, she did love to dance. She danced around and around, whirling in a giant circle claiming the room and casting a delightful spell of ownership, albeit secret and unbeknownst to the true owners, of every single volume in the most beautiful room in the world.

"You are a lovely dancer," came a voice from above her head. Attie went still, then dropped into a feral crouch, her head whipping back and forth as her gaze searched the upper story of the library.

She heard a rustle of fabric and a step. Then, from out of the shadows of the upper tier of the library, she saw a form come to the railing. Attie recalled the slight Latin lilt from the "dancer" comment. It was that girl, the other girl, the one who wasn't Miss Judith Blayne.

Suddenly, Attie thought perhaps she knew why Orion, her dear, logical, coldhearted brother, had been so distracted yesterday.

The girl was quite pretty, with her dark hair, dark eyes, and pleasing mouth. She had a bosom that even Elektra would have envied, although Elektra wouldn't have dusted the house in that dress. However, many people were pretty. That in itself did not make them special.

The girl grinning down at her in a conspiratorial fashion had another, less definable quality. She had a clever, discerning gaze that carried amusement, disappointment, and wonder in equal portions. It was a thing that Attie had seen before only in her own family. Although she had to grudgingly admit that her married siblings, Callie, Cas, and Ellie, had found spouses with a little bit of that quality.

But this girl was something altogether different.

Attie remained where she was, but abruptly dropped her defenses and took a seat on the floor, disregarding her dress. She doubted there was a dust mote running free in this house anywhere, and she wasn't inclined to worry much about her clothing in the first place. She crossed her legs tailor-fashion and leaned back on her hands to gaze at the girl above her, her head tilted as she considered the girl like a new breed of insect.

Francesca tried not to laugh at the funny creature below her. She had not appreciated laughter when she was that age. So she leaned her hands on the finely wrought iron railing of the library and looked down upon the child beneath her very seriously.

After a moment, the girl spoke up. "How long have you lived here?"

"Nearly six months now. How long have you been here?"

"I came yesterday. My brother tied me up and packed me in his trunk. It took me all night to get out. I'm considering calling the magistrate and pressing charges."

Francesca had once been a bored, clever child. She remembered very well the urge to fabricate entertaining stories.

"I was tied up in a trunk once," she said. "Of course, I don't have a brother, so I had to depend on a giant to do the job."

The little girl sat up straight and folded her hands neatly in her lap. "You're a very good liar." Her voice held a tinge of admiration.

Francesca felt a ridiculous spurt of pride at such praise. A grown woman should not, probably, engage in a contest of creative lies with a child. However, the conversation had so far for her proved to be one of the most interesting she'd had since entering this house.

She wondered if the child would allow her to come down without running away. There was only one way to find out. "Will you allow me to come down without your running away?"

The little girl seemed to accept Francesca's olive branch of frankness.

She nodded. "I won't run away if you won't."

Francesca tried not to smile. Orion Worthington's little sister, as she must be, was proving to be nearly as interesting as her brother.

As she picked up her skirts and climbed nimbly down the spiral stairs, she continued her story. "It all started when the giant chased me from the kitchen with a wooden spoon." That was actually true. "I was trying to add herbs to a lovely Bolognese sauce when the giant caught me in the act. He picked up a spoon the size of a club that whistled through the air as he swept it over his head." Still truth. She gained the first floor and grinned at the child. "So I jumped into the trunk to hide from him. He wrapped it with the twine he uses on the goose feet and tried to bury me in the kitchen garden. I escaped, using the herbs to make myself sneeze so hard that the trunk bounced out of the hole and broke open directly."

"Not bad." The girl pursed her lips and nodded. "The bit about the sauce is good. I don't know if I believe you about the giant."

Francesca snorted. "Go down to the kitchens and have a look for yourself." She approached the seated girl and stuck out her hand. "I am—"

The child ignored her hand. "Francesca Penrose, the daughter of Sir Geoffrey's half brother, Francis Penrose." The girl finished the sentence for her. "You're nothing like Miss Judith Blayne. You are dark where she is fair, and you were born in Italy."

"My friends call me Chessa." Francesca dropped her hand and shrugged slightly. "My mother's family is Italian. You are Orion Worthington's sister. Are you a constellation as well?"

"Atalanta. Just a minor Greek half deity. We are all named for some myth. But Rion and I are both hunters."

Atalanta the Huntress, reluctant to lose her freedom to marriage, would marry only a man who could win a race against her. She outran all her suitors until one clever fellow distracted her by throwing golden apples in her path. Francesca, who sympathized greatly with the mythological woman who saw no point in marriage, nodded.

And "we all"? How many Worthington siblings were there? Unlike many people who dearly loved talking, Francesca was also an excellent listener. If she was careful, what could she learn about Blayne House's newest occupant? "I see. Your brother hunts for knowledge. What do you hunt for?"

The child narrowed her eyes at Francesca. "I hunt the people who try to ruin my family."

Francesca clapped her hands together. "Excellent!"

Atalanta stared at her. "Most people don't say that to me."

Francesca snorted. "I am not most people. I would do anything for my family." She sighed. "Even for my rather awful uncle, although I'm sure he would not say the same for me." She tilted her head. "Is someone trying to ruin your family?"

Atalanta nodded. "Your family. Sir Geoffrey lured my brother away from home with promises of fame and fortune and a boring wife. I can't believe Rion fell for it. He shouldn't care about any of that. Worthingtons generally don't, you know." Her scowl deepened. She looked so ferocious that Francesca knew she could only be fighting back tears. "I can't believe he left m—us."

It seemed the child was not in favor of the probable union of Mr. Worthington and Judith. Francesca couldn't much blame her, for she flinched at the notion herself. Probably because Judith didn't seem particularly thrilled. Francesca's instinctive objection was only a very natural concern for her cousin's happiness, of course.

Francesca put any other possibility out of her mind. Firmly. With a boot to its bottom.

Then she grinned at the adorably homicidal little Miss Atalanta Worthington. "I'm famished. The giant has gone to market to personally choose more boring, bland food for Sir Geoffrey. Shall we brave the kitchens for teacakes and biscuits? I know they are delicious, for I baked them myself!"

Atalanta eyed her warily as she rose to her feet. "Is he really a giant?"

"Oh yes," Francesca assured her airily as they headed for the kitchens for a bit of well-timed pilfering. "You can tell by the size of his spoon."

A strangled sound came from the child, and Francesca realized it was a rusty laugh, like something rarely used. Come to think of it, she had not heard Mr. Worthington laugh at all, had she?

Would his laughter be full and warm? Or low and deep?

Brushing off the shiver that went through her at the notion, Francesca led the way to baked confections and, she hoped, a few more carefully extracted details about the mysterious Mr. Orion Worthington.

Chapter 8

FRANCESCA was allowed to use the laboratory for only a few hours a day, midafternoon, while Sir Geoffrey read over his notes in his study. This, she had learned, was apparently the scientific term for "napping," for his sonorous snores could be heard through half of Blayne House.

After feeding Attie, she had spent an amusing half hour introducing her to the specimens housed in the back garden and explaining the research. Then she had shown the child a safer entry through the cellar and, after exacting a promise that Attie would not use the tree unless absolutely necessary, she'd sent the girl on her way and headed happily to the laboratory.

Now Francesca stood at the smaller wooden laboratory table that her uncle had reluctantly turned over to her for her work. Unlike the pristine, three-inch-thick sanded marble slabs that covered the other two larger tables, her bare wooden worktable was scarred by years of dissections and blackened by decades of scorching from burner stands.

However, she'd known when to accede with dignity and had fully taken over her little corner of the lab. The charts she'd drawn that tracked her research were pinned on both walls, and her notes were neatly stacked at the back of her table, held down with a chunk of Italian marble taken from her family's courtyard paving.

It was a practical way to keep her notes pinned down when someone opened the laboratory door, for her table stood directly in the draft, and she liked the way the golden warmth of Italy shimmered from the stone, even in gray, rainy England. If she kept a beaker filled with flowers on her laboratory table, it was only to test their viability as possible food for her specimens, or so she informed Sir Geoffrey when he gazed disdainfully at them.

As if an appreciation for the beauty of nature made her less of a scientist!

As she worked, she heard the door to the laboratory open behind her. Without turning, she knew it was the new assistant, Mr. Worthington. Perhaps it was intuition, or maybe she noticed something special about his step, or it could be that she could see his tall shadow fill the door reflected in the copper housing of the distillation device next to her.

He ducked slightly when he entered. It wasn't quite necessary, for the doors were nearly seven feet in height. It spoke more of a lifetime of gawky stature, which warmed her thoughts to him considerably, or at least to the gangling boy he must have been.

Then the rectangle of outside brightness disappeared as the door latch clicked shut once more. She was alone in the laboratory with him.

By some arbitrary and incomprehensible British social custom, it was likely inappropriate for them to be alone in the laboratory together—a young man and an unmarried young woman, as if in staid British minds, there might immediately ensue a riot of lascivious behavior, unleashed by the lack of proper supervision!

Francesca rolled her eyes at the oddness of English Society and turned her attention back to examining her specimen as she tried mightily to dispel the images that the thought of "lascivious behavior" had planted in her mind.

"What are you doing, Miss Penrose?"

Although his tone seemed genuinely curious, Francesca stiffened. "I am documenting traits of this specimen, in order to chart the biological repetitions through generations."

"Ah."

This time his voice came from just over her right shoulder. Now she could feel him there as well, the heat of his body warming her where she had not realized she'd been chilled. His height allowed him to look down at the top of her head, and at what her hands were doing.

He went on. "Documenting traits looks rather like petting a bunny."

Francesca looked down at her hands, which had begun to stroke the young black-and-white rabbit soothingly, although the creature itself did not seem at all alarmed.

Are you soothing the rabbit or yourself?

Fine. So Mr. Worthington managed to set off a few female-response triggers. What of it? She was a young, healthy person, at the beginning of her prime reproductive years. It was only natural that she should be physically aware of young, healthy male persons in her near vicinity!

"Affection makes them easier to handle," she pointed out coolly. "Otherwise I should have a much harder time getting my hands on the new litters." Lifting her chin, she scooped up Herbert—er, her specimen!—and turned on Mr. Worthington. "I suppose you are opposed to the theories of Jean-Baptiste Lamarck?"

He frowned down at her thoughtfully. Heavens, he was handsome! The light from the great tall windows made his cheekbones and jaw look as if they were cut from fine marble. His bone structure would be an Italian sculptor's dream. She had seen Michelangelo's *David*. It was a heart-wrenchingly beautiful sculpture of a perfect young man.

Yet, *David* would have disappeared next to Mr. Orion Worthington!

But that was simply her instinctive female response talking. Symmetry of features and intensity of the coloration of irises of the eyes—those were all just inherited traits, not earned and not worth more than any finely shaped hound or filly.

Or stallion . . .

He was talking to her now. She forced herself not to relish the way the deepness of his voice resonated through her body and to listen to his words. Of course, almost immediately she regretted giving him her attention.

"As it happens, I don't think very highly of Lamarckism." His tone was dismissive. "The entire concept that we are all just a jumbled mix of our parents' physical traits—"

"And personalities," she corrected automatically, her ire rising.

"And personalities," he allowed, though his frown deepened, "is incompatible with the ideal of the individuality of man."

"And woman," she prompted.

He tilted his head, as if puzzled by her addendum. "Yes, of course. And woman."

Francesca gazed up at Mr. Worthington while cradling the bunny Herbert—er, the Laporidae specimen—in her arms. Was the man before her handsome? Most certainly. But lest she forget, he was also so very arrogant! "You do not think studying inherited traits is worthwhile science?"

"Science is discovery. Knowledge. What you are doing is no more than counting bunny toes."

She sniffed. "Tell me, Mr. Worthington, what study are you engaged in that is so very important?"

"I—rather, Sir Geoffrey is trying to separate alkaloid compounds from plants using solvents."

She tilted her head. "Why?"

He blinked. The reason was so obvious that for a moment he didn't know what to say. "Because . . . because no biologist has ever managed to do it!"

"So, say you managed to separate the compounds. You stand in the center of the laboratory"—she pointed to a spot on the floor—"with a beaker of nice, pure compounds in your hand."

Orion frowned. "Yes," he agreed cautiously.

"What is it for? What are you going to do with it? Is it meant to be a medicine? To be a poison? To shine shoes?" She folded her arms and glared at him. "What good is knowledge without action? Pure research without higher goals amounts to selfishness. What use is a trained mind if not to better the world?"

He sputtered. "Knowledge betters the world!"

She spread her hands. "Yet, how will separating plant compounds help mankind?"

He narrowed his eyes. "How does counting bunny toes help mankind?"

Oh, the gloves were off now! Her eyes narrowed. "Your hair curls. Does your father's hair curl?"

His eyes narrowed. "By chance, yes."

"You are tall. Is your father tall?"

His jaw worked. "Many men are tall."

"Your eyes are blue." *Like twilight in deep summer . . .* She shook off the distraction. "I'll wager that your mother has blue eyes, but your father has brown."

He looked startled. "How did you know that?"

Little Attie had told her, when Francesca had grilled her about her own physical traits, but she was enjoying his discomfiture too much to admit it now. So she merely smiled archly. "Science," she pointed out, as if it were the most obvious thing in the world.

She would, of course, explain herself at some later date. Probably, anyway. She might forget.

He recovered quickly enough on his own. "There are only a limited number of eye colors in all of humanity. They are bound to repeat, even when randomized."

She shook her head. "Nothing is random, Mr. Worthington. The constellations hold their patterns as they move across the sky. All cherry blossoms have five petals. We are indeed a jumble of inherited traits—" She held up a finger to halt his protest. "Unique jumbles, I'll grant you, like a handful of dice cast again and again, coming up with different combinations every time."

He drew himself up, which made him loom over her, which in turn made her belly quiver in a most distracting way. His glower deepened. "I. Am. Nothing. Like. My. Parents."

With that pronouncement, he turned and stalked away.

Of course, he didn't get very far. The laboratory was big, but not that big.

That had been rather too easy. Francesca's lips twitched. She mustn't laugh at him. Even in Italy, her family scolded her for her frivolity. It was just so hard to keep a straight face when people were so very absurd!

Then Mr. Worthington turned back to face her with his eyes narrowed. "The reason that I believe Lamarckism is unsound is proven in your own life. You do not fit in with Sir Geoffrey and Judith at all, although you are closely related. They are serious, thoughtful individuals. You, on the other hand, are flippant and scattered. One day you are cooking; the next you are measuring bunny ears." He folded his arms and tilted his head slightly. "And I will wager that you are no more like your family in Italy!"

Francesca went very still. She felt cold all over, except for her face, which burned.

"Well, are you?"

She wasn't. Not even a little bit. Which was why she had journeyed so far . . . only to find herself a misfit yet again. "Not all of them." She lifted her chin. "But I am very much like my father."

Orion snorted. "So he is an injudicious, unfocused dabbler with too many pots on the stove and not enough spoons to stir them with?"

Francesca's embrace tightened until Herbert began to squirm a little. Her face felt hot, her belly cold. She would not cry in front of horrible, arrogant Orion Worthington. "No. Like me, and my mother, he trained as a biologist at the University of Bologna. Like me, he saw beauty and mystery in science. Unlike me, he is dead. My mother as well. So do not bother trying to blame anyone living for the way that I am."

Shocked out of his irritation, Orion finally realized he ought to shut his stupid trap. *Blast it!* Why had he let her goad him so?

Without another word, Francesca stomped out of the laboratory with the rabbit in her arms. Just outside the wide doors, the gardener had planted a flower bed around a stone bench. Orion watched as Francesca plunked her bottom down on the bench and let the rabbit slip into her lap.

She glanced back at the laboratory once, then bit her lip and turned away.

Orion couldn't see her face, but by the droop of her shoulders and even the tilt of her head, he knew she was upset.

And he could feel a chill in his gut that he finally identified as guilt.

He had committed the highest sin in science. He had jumped to conclusions. Disturbed by her appeal, upset by his own desire for her, he had made a serious mistake about Miss Francesca Penrose. She might dash about like a mad thing, with laughter perpetually lurking in her eyes, but it was clear that she took her research very seriously. She was, in fact, officially more highly educated than he was! He might have realized that sooner had he not been so distracted by the body wrapped around the mind.

Orion was not accustomed to being wrong. Even his outrageous family members listened when he spoke. They might be unpredictable and rather useless, but they believed in his genius.

Orion tried to return to his work. Although he had misbehaved, this was a professional situation, not a drawing room farce. If Francesca wanted to waste valuable laboratory time on sulking, who was he to stop her? Unfortunately, he found it very difficult to concentrate, knowing that she sat out there in distress.

Finally, he put down the beaker of saline that he'd measured four times because he kept losing track of the drops falling from the pipette. He wasn't going to get anything useful done until he fixed what he had broken.

He left the laboratory to find Francesca sitting very still on the bench. Her specimen was lazily lolloping around the perimeter of the flower bed, nibbling at primroses and alyssum. He started to point out the rabbit's inevitable jailbreak, but Francesca held up one finger without looking at him.

He went silent, curious. Advancing until he could lean over her shoulder and see into her lap, he found himself distracted by the enchanting view of her décolletage. After allowing himself only a brief—well, somewhat brief—glance down her neckline, he focused his vision a little farther afield.

"Ah." He saw that she had a sky blue butterfly resting on her sleeve near her wrist. He kept his voice low. Worthingtons knew the rules of good specimen collection. "*Polyommatus icarus*, or common blue. Very numerous in this part of England."

She looked up then, gazing at him flatly over her shoulder. "What do numbers have to do with worth?" she murmured. She looked back down at the delicate insect. "If it were the only one of its kind, it would still be precisely as beautiful as it is now."

It was a pretty thing, Orion mused. The iridescent blue of its wings shimmered in the pearly light of the cloudy day. It flexed its wings open and closed, slowly making its way across the fabric of her sleeve.

"Do you suppose it thinks the flowers on my dress are real?" Her voice was soft, which oddly only emphasized its richness.

Orion's fists clenched as her gentle voice seemed to brush across the back of his neck and give him chills. "Its cranial capacity is the size of a poppy seed," he said mechanically, his voice coming from someplace very far away. "I doubt it thinks at all."

She shook her head and released a sigh. "Do you not believe in anything you cannot measure or stir?"

Orion believed in many things. He believed in loyalty, and even honor, in an abstract, pragmatic way. He believed in his own powers of deduction and intelligence. He believed that man had only touched the edges of the science there was to learn, and the greatness of what he did not know was one of the few things in life that humbled him.

Suddenly, he wanted to tell Francesca these thoughts, and to hear what she had to say about them.

What an appalling notion. Open up his mind like a watch face and let her see his inner clockworks? If it were anyone else, he would think the notion insane.

Yet he imagined that Francesca might possibly . . . perhaps . . . understand.

Worse still, he wanted to see *her* clockworks! He suddenly found himself insatiably curious about her thoughts—even more of her odd notions about enchantment and beauty in science.

Well, not that heredity nonsense. That was utter balderdash, of course. Worse, it was elitist, for it meant that a man was no better than his beginnings, and could never rise above them.

Orion Worthington deeply wanted to rise above his beginnings. Or at least depart from them greatly. Preferably halfway across the country. And then he would build a castle and a moat to keep them away.

All, but for Attie.

Francesca obviously took his silence for the negative. She shook her head pityingly. "I prefer to think of the world as an open box of confections. Because it is, Mr. Orion Worthington. The world is a constant source of wonder and magic."

His reply was automatic, the thinking man's retort. "There is no such thing as magic. Everything has a logical explanation. We may simply not know what it is as yet."

She looked at him for a long moment. "Really? Everything? Can you explain love?"

Treacherous ground. That was a very deep hole, and Orion already felt himself teetering on the alarming, unstable edge. He took desperate refuge in logic. "Love is a chemical reaction. Attraction for the purposes of reproduction. Much the way bees are attracted to flowers, because the flowers feed them for their pollination labor."

"What if there was born a bee who did not care for flowers?"

He blinked. "What?"

She turned toward him. The blue butterfly, disturbed, fluttered drunkenly away. She did not notice, so focused was she upon her topic. "Consider it," she pleaded earnestly. "What would happen to such a bee? It would not seek flowers. It would not bring nectar and pollen back to the hive. It would not help make honey."

She seemed so serious. Orion tried to give the notion equally serious thought, unwilling to again upset this peculiar and astonishing girl.

"A hive is a carefully organized thing," he said slowly. "Its survival depends upon every member knowing its proper role. I imagine that the other bees would reject such a misfit."

Her eyes were huge and dark. "They would drive it away? Count it as useless and declare it unwelcome?"

Orion realized that he rather ached for the bee. Or for someone, at any rate. "That would be in the best interests of the hive." He spoke gently, as though he delivered terrible news. "It cannot succeed if it must feed those who do not contribute."

"So the hive remains static. It never changes, never alters? No one who does not conform is allowed to remain, or even encouraged to survive?"

Orion lifted a brow. What was her point? "I believe I already answered that."

She looked away. "It must be a very lonely thing, to be a misfit bee."

There was something in her voice that caught at Orion's attention. Sadness. Mourning.

And something else that he well understood. Isolation.

However, he was not a misfit bee. He was precisely where he was supposed to be, on his way up the scientific ladder.

So who was the misfit? Other than her recently revealed orphan state, he knew nothing of Francesca's family in Italy. Did her relatives applaud her for her gifts? Did they appreciate her ever-present laughter, devour her cooking, listen with reluctant astonishment to her opinions and then, later, secretly find themselves finding sense and value in her arguments?

If they did not, had the misfit bee left her home and flown across the water to land in a new hive—one where she was even now ill-tolerated?

Orion wasn't usually much moved by pity. By observation he'd realized that most people did enough pitying of themselves; therefore, they did not require him to exert himself on their behalf.

However, Francesca did not seem self-pitying. Rather, she seemed lost . . . or, perhaps, seeking. Orion understood seeking: seeking knowledge, seeking his purpose and place, taking unknown paths to find something he was sure existed.

He wanted to say something to help her, something true, and valuable. He wanted to aid in her search—but while he'd hesitated in silence, she'd scooped up her runaway specimen and bustled away with her head up and her shoulders set in determination.

He found himself close to smiling at the indomitable set of her chin.

Orion had no idea where the strange, unearthly Miss Francesca Penrose was going, but he was damned confident she would get there, eventually.

Chapter 9

HOURS later, Orion gazed out at the twilight of the day through the tall laboratory windows. He'd made much less progress with the methodical elimination process of solvents than he'd hoped to. Sir Geoffrey had set him the boring task for obvious reasons, for there was no point in taking up a scientist's valuable time when a competent assistant could make attempts and catalog the failures.

Unfortunately, Orion wasn't feeling terribly competent at the moment. The work was pathetically simple. Any ape with a rudimentary understanding of reading and measurement could do it—so why did he keep having to go over the same steps again and again?

Distraction. Disturbance.

Francesca.

To be more specific, his desire for Francesca.

She was everywhere. From her desk in the corner there wafted the scent of fresh flowers. His gaze was constantly arrested by her scrawled charts that contained (surely unintentionally whimsical) drawings of bunny noses, bunny ears, and, yes, bunny toes!

Worse, Orion knew that if he ventured into Blayne House, he would be further surrounded by her. She was everywhere. He would smell orange blossoms in the hallway. He would hear her laughter from the parlor. If he sat down to dinner with the family, he would taste her in every bite of food that passed his lips, even as she tempted him from across the table!

This fatal distraction had to stop.

He wanted nothing more than to win a place in the serious scientific world, a place not overshadowed by his notoriously unserious family. So why couldn't he stop thinking about the maddening Miss Francesca Penrose?

Until now, he'd had an abstract, clinical interest in women. His body felt desire, but he'd had little trouble quenching its clamor before now. Even his single visit to his brothers' favorite brothel had been more of an expedition of exploration than a sexual adventure. His rather clinical examination of his partner got him evicted before he actually—ahem, well, no sense in dwelling on the past.

Francesca, on other hand, inspired the most disquieting thoughts! He could not concentrate for thinking of her dark hair falling across his naked chest, her hot skin sliding against his own, and her sweet, slippery—ahem, well, no.

Indeed, her flashing dark eyes arrested his attention, her mind inspired his admiration, her figure inspired his obsession, but her undisciplined, insatiable approach to life reminded Orion far too much of his outrageous, erratic family.

She was lovely, though, wasn't she? Like an exotic flower, she burned so much brighter than all the pale English blooms . . .

A sudden hiss and scorched smell of burning interrupted his circular thoughts.

"Bloody hell!"

Another experiment boiled over!

* * *

"AND WORST OF all, Orion is woolgathering!"

In the parlor-cum–painting studio at Worthington House, Attie sat back after delivering that appalling bit of news and watched her family's reaction. Each face gave away something different.

The most concerned was Daedalus, of course. Dade worried about all of them, too much as far as Attie was concerned.

"I've never known Orion to do that!" Dade frowned. "Do you suppose it is the daughter, Miss Blayne, who is distracting him from his work?"

Attie considered the possibility for as long as it deserved, which was not at all. "Impossible. The girl is about as distracting as an empty seashell. It's pretty, but it doesn't do anything!"

Mama fanned herself with a folding Japanese fan dripping with faded, decaying tassels. "What of the other one?" Iris asked dreamily. "You said you got a better glimpse of her this time, didn't you?"

Attie looked down at her folded lap and plucked at a broken thread of her woolly stockings. "She's all right." She didn't want to think about Francesca, because she'd liked her, very much—and there were all those bunnies . . .

Anyway, it wasn't Chessa whom Orion was all queued up to marry, was it? It was that drip of a girl, Judith, who had about as much personality as a pinecone!

"No, Orion doesn't like her at all," Attie insisted, for if he did like Chessa, then Attie might have to do something about it. She could not allow anyone to come between her favorite brother and her beloved family—no matter how much she might like them! "I listened outside the door of the laboratory. Francesca and Orion fight about everything!"

"Ah!" Archie's expression was knowing. "'They never meet but there's a skirmish of wit between them.'"

Iris patted the gnarled hand that lay on her shoulder. "*Much*

Ado About Nothing, act one, scene one, dearest. Oh, my, yes, Archie." She smirked flirtatiously at him. "'A merry war,' indeed!"

Attie grimaced. Iris and Archie were always going off the topic at hand! The question was how were they going to get Orion out of bloody old Blayne House and back home where he belonged!

Archie seemed to drift out of his love-induced fog for a moment when he saw the disappointment on Attie's face. "Well, perhaps we ought to do something about Orion . . ."

Iris snuggled closer to her silver-haired husband and giggled. "In that house, with not one but two lovely creatures from which to choose? I can't think of a better way to crack that poor boy's shell. He's always been so terribly shy."

ORION FILLED HIS hands with twin offerings of soft, gold-tinged flesh topped with pink rosebud nipples. With a low, rich laugh, she slipped from his grasp, flowing away like warm cream. He grabbed for her, but she wasn't there.

"Rise, my darling . . ."

Her husky lilting voice swirled over his bare neck, warmed by her breath. She was behind him now.

He rose for her, his cock swelling and thickening as her hands slid over his shoulders from behind and smoothed down his sweating chest.

"Grow for me."

His body obeyed her command eagerly. Her delicate hands wandered farther down, her fingers spread wide over the twitching muscles of his belly. Lust stole his breath, choked his voice, trapped his body. He wanted to turn, to take her into his arms, to press her hard against the wall and feel her bare breasts against his chest. He could not move.

"Swell."

He swelled, his rigid cock aching with need. The ache

traveled through his entire body as he stood helplessly at her mercy.

Her roaming hands slid down between his hip bones, and at last her delicate fingers wrapped tightly around his aching, throbbing cock. She squeezed him.

The touch of her cool fingers should have sent him over the edge, so aroused was he. He had never wanted a woman more in his life. He'd never wanted anything more in his life than he wanted to thrust his swollen, aching cock into the sweet, hot, wet haven between her thighs.

He could not move. He had not the power to take matters into his own hands. He could only long to be hot aching flesh beneath her delicate touch.

It wasn't supposed to be like this. There was something he was supposed to be doing. Something important. He could not remember, and he could not bring himself to care about that lapse. There was nothing, nothing but her.

Her voice. Her hands. She ruled his senses. She commanded his every thought. He was her willing and eager supplicant, if only she would give him the release he longed for.

If only she would let him in . . .

"Come," she ordered, her lightly accented English deepening and roughening the word. Her hands enveloped him, doubled fingers entwining tightly. "Come for me."

He came.

Orion woke with a start, blinking and gasping. He looked around in confusion for a moment. The room was dark; he was alone; he was still a virgin; there was no evidence of Miss Penrose—but plenty of evidence of his desire for her.

Bloody hell!

Chapter 10

THE next morning, after sidestepping his duty to accompany the ladies into morning calls by way of breakfasting before dawn and disappearing, Orion stood in Sir Geoffrey's laboratory, lost in unaccustomed frustration.

In his own shabby, cobbled-together laboratory in Worthington House, Orion had become accustomed to using a tallow burner. He would melt a portion of smelly, yellowish, lardlike tallow on Mrs. Philpott's termperamental old woodstove and then pour it carefully into small pottery dishes he'd made ready with cotton wicks. The pots, shaped like flattened bowls, would sit beneath a flask holder, an iron tripod with a ring top, and heat whatever substance was in the flask. Orion's home-stewed tallow had smoked and blackened the exterior of the beakers. He'd had to take great pains that the mess didn't contaminate his results!

In the pristine environs of Sir Geoffrey's laboratory, no such dirt was allowed. The burning bowls were of glazed ceramic, filled with pure, white tallow. A stack of ready-made ones sat on the shelf, all set for use.

The only problem was, Orion couldn't use them.

He had tried to start the first few with a flint starter, but had given up and lighted a candle, using a splinter of wood to bring the candle flame to the virgin white wick of the burning bowl. Nothing had worked.

Orion was a patient man. He could watch a boiling beaker for hours or stir a compound together, adding one crystalline grain at a time. Reminding himself of his previously famous patience did little good as he stood filled with frustration before an array of unsuccessful attempts.

He was a learned man. He was a brilliant man. He could do elaborate sums in his head, without the need of chalk and slate. He could quote facts and figures, and yes, Shakespeare, without ever doubting his accuracy.

However, without fire, he was as powerless to do research as was the earliest cave dweller! He took a deep breath, held yet another wood splinter in the candle flame, and when it was burning, brought it to the short wick emerging from the center of the glazed bowl of fine white tallow.

The wick made a slight crackling sound, just as it had many times before, but it did not take the flame at all. Orion persisted, holding the flame on the wick, while the wooden splinter burned to black charcoal, dropping chunks and bits into the tallow-filled bowl.

"Light, damn you!"

"Having trouble with your wick?"

Orion turned to see Miss Francesca Penrose in the doorway, leaning one shoulder on the door frame with her arms folded. Her pose gave the impression she'd been lounging there for some time, watching him fail. Amusement danced in her dark eyes as she smirked at him.

"Don't worry," she consoled him mockingly. "Many people do. Inability to reach full combustion could happen to anyone."

His jaw clenched in annoyance. It was bad enough that she'd caught him in such a disadvantageous moment, but when she said things like that, perfectly innocent things that made him think decidedly not innocent thoughts, he knew she was laughing at him.

Her mockery just made his sexual frustration worse.

No, wait. I meant my performance frustration.

Oh God no. I meant my inability to combust—I mean, light my damned wick!

Bloody hell! He closed his eyes briefly. "I had no trouble with it yesterday. I will make it light." His tone came out gruff from a throat that was nearly shut tight with the sudden onslaught of lust.

She let out a small snort. "No, you truly won't." She dropped her insouciant pose and strolled toward him.

Her approach brought the scent of summer in with her, the grassy smell of the freshly cut lawn she'd just crossed mingling with her own warm orange-blossom aroma. He breathed her in despite his unwillingness, for to refrain drinking her in at every opportunity would take more self-control than he possessed.

"I can help you with your flame," she said.

Oh yes. Please, set me afire!

She came quite close, as if to oblige his questing senses. For a long, sweet moment of dream-induced fantasy, he thought she meant to press against him.

To the disappointment of a large part of him, she merely reached around him to his latest unlit burner bowl and picked it up with one hand. Holding it high where he could see it, she reached her fingers to grasp the scorched but unburned wick—and plucked it completely free of the tallow.

His jaw dropped at such rudeness. "It will never light now!"

She let the hand holding the bowl drop slightly and held the length of wick, pinched between her thumb and forefinger, insultingly close before his gaze. "It was never going to light," she said slowly, as if to a simpleton. "It's not a wick."

"What?" Orion took the two-inch white stick from her

fingers and turned toward the window, holding the thing to the light. It was stiff and hard, not at all like a flexible cotton wick. It was also somewhat translucent.

"This is made of glass!" He looked down at her, affronted. "Is this some sort of trick?"

She smiled brightly. "Wouldn't that be clever of me? But alas, I did not do this to taunt you. This is merely how Sir Geoffrey prefers it to be done. In warm weather, the tallow softens, and the wicks can slip down beneath the surface. Sir Geoffrey came up with a way to prevent it. We make the flame bowls with these glass picks in them to keep the hole free."

She turned to the shelf where the burn bowls were stored and pulled down a small tin box that Orion had overlooked. Her small hands flipped it open with the ease of long practice and held it out for his view.

He peered in to see neat lengths of wick, precut and looking waxy with tallow, ready to use.

"Go on," she urged, her laughing eyes on him. "They won't fight back."

Orion regarded her sourly but reached into the box and took a wick. The stiffened length of it slid neatly down into the hole left in the tallow, leaving just the right amount free to light and then trim as needed.

"The ones you used yesterday were set out for you in advance, with the wicks inserted." Francesca closed the tin and returned it to the shelf. "It's very clever, really. This way the bowls are always perfectly ready to use, and the wicks never take on the damp." She stepped back and gazed about the laboratory with a slight, thoughtful frown. "My uncle can be so ingenious . . . sometimes . . ."

Orion turned back to his table full of failed "combustion." With an unaccustomed embarrassment, he recalled the last three-quarters of an hour he'd spent trying to light glass sticks on fire. Now that he'd closely examined one, it was perfectly obvious that they were not cotton wicking, but cool, gleaming silicate sticks.

He'd been neatly tricked, after all, but only his own lack of observation was to blame. "'The devil has the power to assume a pleasing disguise,'" he quoted ruefully.

"*Hamlet*, Mr. Worthington?"

"Act two, scene two," Orion added without thinking.

"Oh, you are dour! Do you honestly think Shakespeare is appropriate at a time like this?"

She was laughing at him again. He knew that if he turned, he would see her bright eyes and that smile that seemed to dance ever ready at the corners of her luscious, summer-rose lips.

Then she finally seemed to notice the destruction his quest for fire had caused. The table was spattered with spilled tallow and scorch marks, while nearly a dozen bowls he had tampered with sat muddled and contaminated with ash.

With a gasp, she stepped next to him at the table. "You cad! You brute!" She had her fists plunked onto her sweetly curved hips. "Very well. When it is time to render more tallow, *you* can help Judith cook and strain the nasty stuff three times to purify it!"

"Judith makes the flame bowls?" Orion frowned. "Herself?" Judith seemed far too refined to take on such a menial task.

Francesca blinked. "Ah. Well, yes . . . but perhaps you might refrain from mentioning that to Sir Geoffrey. He is under the impression that she orders them special from the chandler. Unfortunately, Sir Geoffrey kept finding fault with the man, and then the bills—well, Judith found it simpler to refill the bowls at home and reuse the glass stems. She says that way she can be sure Sir Geoffrey will be satisfied."

Rendering tallow was a foul task. Orion felt a stab of guilt at his wastefulness. "Miss Blayne is a very caring and dutiful daughter."

"Miss Blayne is a slave," Francesca muttered, or at least, that was what Orion thought she said, but he must have been mistaken. Look at the luxurious life Judith led as the daughter of a prominent man. There was no reason to think any such thing!

But his own fault could not be denied. "I will repair the damage."

She blinked. "You will?" The doubt in her voice resolved him.

He went to work at once, patiently pulling every crumb of blackened wood from the tallow and scrubbing off all the stained, scorched glass stems. He left the purified tallow out in the sun for a while until it liquefied. Then he brought the bowls back in and reinserted the glass stems while the bowls cooled in the shade. Then he set about scrubbing all the sooty marks from the white marble tabletop.

Francesca, who pretended to work on her charts, watched him carefully. It seemed Mr. Worthington was not averse to a bit of restitution labor. She bent her head over the paper, trying not to let him see the pleased and impressed smile that insisted on taking over her lips.

She tried to think of any other man in her acquaintance who would go to such lengths to make matters right. She could not think of one who would not leave the mess to someone else, usually a woman, to clean up. At best, she might imagine a few kindly fellows like Asher Langford, who would apologize sincerely and then bring chocolates or something to "make it up" to a woman.

Her eyes would not stay away from Mr. Worthington. His efforts made her heart melt—and the ensuing warmth pooled in a location significantly lower in her body. She fought the urge to wriggle in her chair. Her gaze slid his way again. He was bent over, scrubbing at the spilled tallow on the marble. His muscled bottom flexed in time with his efforts.

Heavens! If the male population of the earth had any idea how attractive the sight of a man cleaning was to womankind, the world would be a spotless place, indeed!

Orion scrubbed at the table he'd spilled the tallow on with a little more force than he might normally have done, but his hands were on automatic while his thoughts were occupied by the beauty across the room.

God, she was enticing. When she had laughed at him, he'd wanted to laugh with her even as he'd wanted to wipe the smile off her full, pink lips with a hot, deep kiss.

As he had again and again for the last quarter hour, he watched her from beneath lowered lids as his hands went about the business of clearing up.

When she wrote in her notes, she would begin sitting up straight and scribing in a measured ladylike fashion. Then her pen would begin to fly, ink would spatter, and the sound of her rapid scribbling would be drowned out only by the murmured encouragements she bestowed upon herself. "In ancient Rome, the rabbit was revered as a symbol of lust and fertility." She paused. "Oh yes," she whispered. "Oh, that's terribly good!" Now she sat hunched over her desk, with her tongue stuck firmly in her cheek and her brows lifted in science-induced delight as her hand flew over the stack of paper, the feather of the quill twitching like a live thing in her fingers.

She was adorable. Orion wanted to watch her, observe her like a hunter in a blind observed a doe, so that he could delve deeper into the mysteries contained behind her sparkling dark eyes and laughing mouth.

He could not stop himself from wanting to know more.

He could not stop himself from *wanting*.

Why Francesca? Why this girl? Why not the other, perfectly attractive and so much more appropriate Judith?

What, in her own unique cast of the heredity die, gave Francesca Penrose this power over him?

And why must she mutter about lust in a laboratory?

Finally, he realized that he was merely scrubbing the same perfectly clean spot over and over. No more excuses. He had work to do.

Orion forced himself to focus as he began to select several types of solvent from the shelves. He lined them up neatly, and then reached absently to his right for a wooden rack of glass tubes to work with.

His hand encountered warm, soft girl instead.

"Oh!" Startled, she whirled to face him, her eyes wide.

Oh no. Had he just—

Orion took in her figure, and then referenced the height of the desired shelf with the height of her lushly rounded bottom.

Oh damn.

His fist closed on the memory of the warm, resilient handful of Francesca he'd just helped himself to.

"Ahem. I beg your pardon, Miss Penrose. I—I meant no offense."

"Ah. Well. None taken, I'm sure." She took a measuring weight off the shelf next to his desired rack of tubes and moved off slowly, walking backward away from him with her dark eyes huge in her unsmiling face. "Truly, sir, I did not mean to get in your way—"

"No, no, I ought to look where I'm— It was— I'm terribly sorry."

I am not sorry. At all.

Her flesh had felt like heaven, like the best parts of sin and temptation—like his dream.

They both busied themselves with their work, but concentration was becoming impossible for Orion. His only thought was that he wished he had reached for that rack with both hands!

Damn it. Another day with little to show for it. Sir Geoffrey was going to think him useless!

She took a step. His hearing focused instantly on the slide of her shoe on the floor and the swish of her skirts as she turned.

The draft that crossed her workbench brought her tempting scent his way, filling his senses with her. His entire being was focused on hearing her, seeing her, scenting her, oh God, *touching* her!

More than anything, more than his work, or Sir Geoffrey's

research, or even his own dreams of acclaim, Orion wanted to complete the list by *tasting* Francesca.

What would it be like to kiss her? Would her mouth be hot, flavored by the spices that she loved? Would she part her lips to let him in her wet, open mouth?

Across the room, she let out a soft, barely audible sigh of frustration. Orion's eyes nearly crossed at the sound. What sort of noises would she make during lovemaking? Would she be quiet, all soft, warm sighs? Would she cry out? Moan?

Would she wail helplessly in ecstasy?

You will never know because you are going to marry Judith someday, and then you must treat Francesca as a dear, companionable cousin in whom you have no interest in giving shrieking orgasms!

The quill she had been using suddenly snapped in two, no doubt from Francesca's feverish pace of notation. *"Cacchio!"* (Bother!) She muttered wrathfully beneath her breath as she examined it. Orion's tattered nerves jumped as if she'd burned him.

"God!" He turned on her. "It is like trying to concentrate in a chimpanzee cage! Can you not work somewhere else?"

With her eyes narrowed, she glared at him. Then she set down the broken quill, bent one arm, and pawed at her armpit. "Ooh-ooh-ooh," she grunted.

If his blood had not been heated to a boiling point, he might have laughed. As it was, her bold irreverence only brought his desire up a few more degrees.

Never taking her gaze from his, she said, "I have as much right to be here as you do. Sir Geoffrey gave me this space to do my research." She folded her arms, and her face took on a disgruntled aspect. "I had to force his hand by threatening to set the rest of my family on him. He gave in, but only because Nonna Laura wrote him a very firm letter."

She said the name Laura in the Italian manner. Low-ra. *Nonna* meant "grandmother."

Part of Orion's mind sailed far into the future, wondering

what Francesca would be like as a grandmother. Her sable hair would fade, and her smooth golden skin would crease, but he rather thought that even in their old age, those luminous dark eyes would flash sparks at him just as they did now.

He fought back the notion with difficulty. "Just—just try to be less"—*succulent, desirable*—"distracting, if you please."

One of her dark eyebrows rose in question as her head tilted.

"Just take this, then!" Orion snatched his own quill from the tabletop, jumped from his stool, and thrust it in her direction. The sight of the long, vivid royal blue feather made her smile.

"Well, thank you. Indeed, it appears you have unexplored depths of lavishness, Mr. Worthington."

"What?" He would tolerate no more of this distraction. He had to get back to work. "If you must know, it is a tail feather from my own bird, an *Anodorhynchus hyacinthinus*, a hyacinth macaw."

"You have a pet bird?"

"Attie is caring for it at the moment, and it is a specimen, not a pet. Now, might you please minimize the noise?"

Francesca curtsied with the utmost politeness, sweeping high the large blue feather in her fingertips. "As you command, Your Lordship."

Chapter 11

THEY both turned back to their work. Orion busied himself stacking his notes neatly on the opposite table. Francesca sat quietly upon her stool, reading through her pages of observations, making corrections and additions every so often.

Orion's own notes were kept tidily within the leather folio that he'd found in his bedchamber, provided for his use by Sir Geoffrey, he assumed, although there seemed to be no economy of paper practiced in this house, certainly not by Francesca. He wrote down every step of every experiment and each result. It was important that all the pertinent facts be orderly and easy to follow, for one never knew when some untoward result would propel one forward—or backward!—in one's research. He could hardly re-create or prevent the re-creation if he didn't know precisely how it had come about!

Now that he had managed to quell Miss Penrose's distracting presence somewhat, he continued his elimination of solvents. Two showed some promise in parting the green coloration from the plant fibers, so Orion set them aside on a shelf he'd clearly marked as "Substances with Potential."

"Do you know what has potential?" mused Francesca from across the laboratory. "The study of heredity. Do you know what has potential? The study of medicine."

Orion twitched. The hell of it was, he wanted to hear her voice, even when she was provoking him. "Where do you think medicines come from? The study of chemistry."

Even she had no retort for that. Instead, she fell back upon the weaker tactic of changing the subject. "Are you planning to join Judith and me when we go to the Duke of Camberton's ball?"

Orion had not intended to waste his time doing any such thing—until that moment. "I suppose I shall be expected to, if Sir Geoffrey wishes me to."

Francesca snorted. "Yes, by all means, we should all follow Sir Geoffrey's wishes."

Orion didn't even glance at her. "There is no shame in being polite to my mentor. He does me a great service by allowing access to his laboratory."

"Access? Is that what you call it when you run courses of boring experiments that any junior technician could do for a result that you do not even personally care about?"

Although he'd had a few of those thoughts himself over the last few days, Orion looked up at last. "I do not consider myself above building a foundation of solid science for my research." Except that it wasn't his research, was it?

"Except that it isn't *your* research, is it?"

Orion turned to face her fully then. "If you please, I am trying to concentrate on my notes—" He gestured toward the stack of neat papers lying within the unfolded folio, but the leather-bound volume wasn't there. "Wait—"

As his gaze scanned the room, he spotted Judith outside the window, walking away from the laboratory toward the main house, with his folded and tied folio in her hands.

He blinked in surprise. "Miss Blayne was here?"

Francesca stared at him. "Of course she was, for several minutes. Why do you think I was asking you about the ball?"

How could he not have realized Judith's presence—especially when he seemed to be so finely tuned to every movement and exhalation to emanate from Francesca?

"Are all men dolts?" She scowled at him. "Judith is not some well-trained servant you are supposed to ignore. I don't know how you cannot see that, but I suppose you are just like Sir Geoffrey—you don't care as long as your beakers are washed and your shirts are pressed!" She slapped her palms down upon the chart she was drawing, then spread them wide. "*Dio*, you men are frustrating! How can you be so *impermeabile*?" (Impervious.)

Orion could not deny that he had done precisely that, ignoring Judith just as he would take no notice of Pennysmith's silent efficiency.

Damn it! He was supposed to be *courting* Judith! Judith, and Sir Geoffrey, held the keys to the kingdom of scientific respect and acclaim!

With a muttered curse, Orion plunked a stifle over his final burn bowl and hurried from the lab. He caught up to Judith near the fountain that centered the grounds behind the house.

"Miss Blayne!"

She did not stop. Orion increased his pace. "Miss Blayne, if you please—"

She hesitated, slowing, then finally stopped entirely and turned toward him. She looked very lovely, posed there with her even features lifted to the light and her hands behind her back, showing her figure to advantage in the bright afternoon.

"You wished to speak to me, Mr. Worthington?"

Orion, drawing upon the training his sister Elektra had drummed into him, dropped a slight bow. "Miss Blayne, I must apologize for my inattention in the laboratory. I meant no offense."

She gazed at him evenly. "I am the daughter of a scientist,

Mr. Worthington. I am well accustomed to that particular state of inattention."

That fact alone should make her all the more attractive to him—imagine, a woman who didn't mind being ignored!—but all the realization did was to make him feel worse. If he spent the rest of his life in the laboratory, as he fully intended to, what would that mean for the woman he would marry? "You shouldn't," he blurted.

She drew back. "I should not what, Mr. Worthington?"

"You shouldn't have to become accustomed to inattention," he said. He wasn't sure what he had meant to say. It was only that he'd had the sudden thought that he would not wish any of his sisters to endure a marriage composed of nothing but drought and duty.

For the first time in their acquaintance, Judith's calm gaze warmed slightly as she looked at him. "Why, Mr. Worthington, that is the nicest thing you have ever said to me."

He bobbed his head again. "Then I must apologize again for such spare conversation, that such a meager thing should be the best I have done."

Her gaze shifted slightly, resting upon the rear facade of Blayne House. "Oh, not so meager, sir. Not at all." Then she turned back to him and offered him the closest thing to a smile he'd yet seen from her, a graceful upturning of the corners of her lips. "I think perhaps Francesca is mistaken about you, Mr. Worthington."

He blinked. "I—but—what did she say?"

She leaned slightly closer. "She said, 'Handsome is as handsome does,'" she confided. "But that was on first acquaintance. I'm sure she has revised her opinion by now." With that, she began to turn away. Orion caught sight of his folio clasped behind her back.

"Ah, Miss Blayne, why do you need my notes?"

She turned to him again. Her face had resumed its usual perfect marble stillness. "Papa prefers for me to transcribe all the progress for him at the end of the day. He dislikes having to decipher other people's script. He will review it during his hour of contemplation."

Orion frowned slightly. "But my notes are most well organized. I'm sure there is no need for you to go to all that trouble."

"No trouble at all," she said distantly. Orion was seized by the feeling that he was keeping her from something terribly urgent but that she was too polite to say so.

"Oh. Yes. I am quite busy myself." He stepped back slightly and bowed again. "I hope we shall have more time to talk during the Duke of Camberton's ball in three nights' time."

"Yes, Mr. Worthington. I shall look forward to it." Her expression was serene as always, yet Orion had the impression that she could not care less about the ball.

Something else they had in common.

He watched her as she turned away and floated gracefully across the lawn, in no visible hurry, yet managing to reach the house in very little time. It was a good match for the both of them. She was so very appropriate.

So why did his steps quicken as he turned back to the laboratory—and Francesca?

"Handsome is as handsome does," she had said.

Francesca thought him handsome?

BEHIND THE CENTRAL spire of the fountain, a pair of skinny legs in boys' trousers held very still in the knee-deep water as Attie listened. That Judith girl wasn't so bad, perhaps—just a bit of a bore. Fortunately, Orion didn't seem to be too terribly interested in her after all.

Still, Attie had never known her calm, logical brother to chase a single step after a woman, much less halfway across a vast lawn. Her eyes narrowed as she watched Orion duck back into the laboratory; then her gaze slid sideways to contemplate the house.

Further research was in order. Fortunately, thanks to Chessa, Attie knew just how to get into Blayne House undetected. She even thought she knew where that dreary girl was going to do her transcription.

It took only a few moments for Attie to work her skinny form through the small cellar window, which was actually more of a ventilation slit than a true window. As she passed the entrance to the main kitchen, she heard Judith's calm voice talking about stewed goose. A deep rumble answered her, resentful and sour in tone, though Attie could not make out the words.

Chessa's silly story ran through her head as she listened.

As tempting as it was to spy on the kitchen and see if the cook really was a giant, Attie realized that she might be able to beat Judith to the girl's destination. If Attie recalled correctly—and she always recalled correctly—the plain, featureless study she'd seen on her first visit was on the main floor, the fourth door on the left. She would wager the compass she'd stolen from her eldest brother Dade's dressing table that dull Judith used that boring room.

Evasion was second nature for Attie, given that she'd been evading Dade for a week now as he looked for his compass. Stealth was actually less difficult in Worthington House because it was packed to the rafters with marvelous, interesting things.

Hiding in Blayne House was like attempting to hide in an empty meadow. It was all about holding still in the shadows while all the busy, busy servants went about their busy, busy business. As the gaunt butler in all his brass buttons strode past without noticing her, intent on his aforementioned business, she rolled her eyes. This place housed an army of help! What did they find to do all day?

By ducking into this room and slipping past that doorway, she secretly made her way to the lackluster study.

In truth, it was a perfectly acceptable room. It simply held nothing of interest to her inquisitive mind. There were no foreign curiosities crowding the mantel, nor battered and mysterious books on the desk.

The dainty but unadorned desk itself held only an inkstand, a blotter, and, in the perfect center of the blotter, a stack of paper. Attie bet an even number of pages were stacked there, lined up perfectly perpendicular to the long inkstand that rested down the center of the desk.

Aside from the desk and simple wooden chair, there stood a graceful wingback chair by the fire, with a small tea table beside it. All very feminine, in a plain sort of way. Attie supposed it could be worse. The place could be dripping in embroidery and tatted lace. At least Judith didn't seem to waste her time stitching footstools and runners and such.

Yes, the room was sensible, if dull. Just like Attie's impression of Judith.

The latch jiggled. Attie took two unhurried steps and slipped out of sight behind the drapery panel on one side of the far window. She liked hiding in draperies because she was skinny enough not to cause a noticeable bulge. Also, it was much easier to duck out the window than to run toward a door. People always went to block the door first.

Even as Judith settled herself behind the desk, Attie reached out a slow hand to check the window latch. She smiled as the latch gave way with well-oiled silence. Perhaps there was something to be said for an army of servants after all.

She watched through the weave of the cloth as Judith set down her cup of tea and pulled Orion's folio of notes closer. Attie's eyes narrowed as she saw Judith stroke a hesitant finger over the leather cover, her expression deep in thought. Did that action seem . . . romantic? Or only pensive?

Attie had heard the girl tell Orion that something he'd said was nice. Orion didn't say *nice* things. He said *true* things. To imagine Orion saying something gallant or—ew!—*amorous* seemed like an expedient way to lose one's lunch.

Judith inked a quill and began to copy. At one juncture, she leaned back to regard her page with a frown. Then she picked it up and ripped it in half.

The sudden angry gesture made Attie jump slightly. The drapery waved in response. Attie held her breath, but Judith only let out a long breath and began to copy once more. Attie couldn't think what might make Judith angry about Orion's notes, but she had to admit she was relieved to see some sign of emotion coming from the girl. Attie was used to loud people, who laughed, or sang, or recited Shakespeare in booming stage voices, or shouted—mostly at her!—or called—mostly for her!—so Judith's eerie decorum made Attie feel as though she were inspecting an entirely different species of human.

However, her current safari to study the native habitat of Other People aside, Attie soon began to feel bored.

That was, until Judith stood up with the stack of Orion's original notes in her hands—and flung them into the fireplace!

It was all Attie could do not to hurl herself onto the hearth to grab her brother's notes back. That was when she realized that there was no fire. The hearth, although piled with fresh tinder, was not lit. Attie waited.

Judith took a twisted paper spill from a container on the mantel and held it to the lighted candle at her desk. Attie tensed her body, ready to spring out at the horrible, wicked girl who meant to destroy all of Orion's hard work!

As Attie waited with balled-up fists, she watched Judith gaze expressionlessly at the burning spill. At the last moment before it might have burned her fingers, Judith lifted it up and blew it most decisively out. Attie drew back, unsure.

Judith kneeled before the cold hearth and began to carefully retrieve Orion's notes. She stacked them neatly, even reordering them. For the first time, she moved quickly, glancing over her shoulder occasionally. Attie knew that feeling well—it was the sensation one had when one was doing something one wasn't supposed to be doing. Attie found it hard to go through an entire day without feeling just that way at least twice.

So . . . burning Orion's notes did not make Judith feel apprehensive, but salvaging them did? Who was it that the girl thought might come through her study door?

Since Attie generally approved of sneaking about, she remained where she was while Judith cast a worried glance about the room. *Looking for a hiding place, are you?*

For a moment, Attie wondered if she was going to need to climb down another tree to escape, but Judith turned away from the window, and, after taking something from a desk drawer, she made for the upholstered chair by the fireplace. The girl sank to her knees and did something behind the chair. There was a ripping sound and a rustle of paper. Then Judith rose to her feet and serenely brushed out her skirts before floating from the room on silent, slipper-clad feet.

It was mere seconds before Attie was down on her knees behind the chair. *Ah.* Attie grimaced in reluctant approval. Not a bad hiding place for a beginner!

The sheaf of notes had been tucked under the chair, then slipped through a slit in the heavy canvas that covered the woven leather strapping that held up the seat cushion. The hole was small and neat. Judith must have taken her quill knife to it.

Leave the notes there, or take them away for safekeeping?

Attie decided that far from being an enemy, Judith was actually someone who wished to preserve Orion's work. Attie itched to understand. When Other People did odd things, she liked to know *why*.

After all, she thought as she swung out onto the tree limb outside the study window, she was supposed to be the only one who did odd things!

Chapter 12

ORION stood at his marble table in the laboratory while Francesca sat on a stool at her workbench, a small brown rabbit in her lap. She was ostensibly measuring the length of its velvety ears. However, just like him, she seemed distracted.

The late-afternoon light slanted in through the high windows, glinting from lazily floating dust motes. Its summery warmth seemed to calm them both momentarily from their constant squabbling.

However, Orion could not help glancing over at Francesca's hands as they rubbed and soothed the downy little creature, who seemed, to Orion, to be gazing smugly back at him as if to say, "You wish it were you!"

After a brief spurt of concentration that enabled him to eliminate two entire solvents from the process, Orion glanced back.

Now the rabbit seemed to be looking at the doorway.

Orion followed its glassy dark gaze to see his sister Attie standing quietly there. With a start, he realized that she'd

made her way through the entire Blayne household undetected. He shot a wary look at Francesca, wondering what she
thought about such an untoward intruder, but she only lifted
her attention for a moment to smile a welcome to Attie.

His posture eased. They had already met, it seemed. Trust
Francesca to keep that fact to herself. At least she seemed to
like Attie. Few people understood his brilliant little sister. If
anyone could, it would be Francesca!

Then his gaze narrowed on Attie. Something was odd. Her
lanky form leaned ever so casually against the door frame,
as if she'd merely decided to stop by to quietly check on their
progress.

Attie didn't do anything quietly—ever!—unless she was
in full covert mode.

Like all the Worthington clan, Orion knew perfectly
well that prolonged silence—or worse, astonishingly good
behavior!—from Attie was a danger signal of the highest
order. *Blast it.* He'd been too long in the peaceful confines of
Blayne House. His instincts had deteriorated from his former
state of high alert.

He put down his beaker. "Attie? What have you done?"

She lifted her chin. "It wasn't my fault."

He gazed at her evenly. "Attie."

Heat flushed her freckled cheeks. "I didn't mean to!"

Guilt? From Attie? *Oh hell.* He kept his gaze cool. "And?"

Her green gaze slid from his in shame. "I just wanted to
give the rabbits a little time in the grass. It's such a nice sunny
day—"

Francesca looked up. "Rabbits?" She stood and shifted her
current subject from her lap into the lidded basket she used
to convey them.

Attie glanced down to where her bony fingers laced together before her. "It isn't as though they can leave the
grounds, not with that wall all around."

"Oh my heavens!" Francesca hurried to the door. "You
didn't mix the genders, did you?"

Attie scowled. "Of course not!"

Orion stepped forward, but Francesca waved a hand as she dashed from the lab. "No, don't let us interrupt you! We can handle this, can't we, Attie?"

Attie nodded in sharp agreement and ran out after Francesca, looking like a skinny puppet on badly tied strings compared to Francesca with her light, dancing grace. However, the young girl was fast.

Orion kept working but also kept one eye on the window, just in case he was needed. Not that he would be. Chasing rabbits was clearly a pastime meant for people somewhat lower to the ground than he was!

Francesca, of course, found the entire matter hilarious. Orion could hear her bubbling giggle—a constant disturbance—through the window, although he noticed that laughter did not slow her down, nor deter her from serious rabbit-gathering technique.

Francesca's hair fell down at once, of course, and thereafter followed her like a sable flag. Her cheeks became pink, her dark eyes sparkled, and her even white teeth flashed in the afternoon light as she urged Attie onward. Orion found himself riveted by the charming amount of jiggle produced by rabbit chasing. She looked so alive. So vibrant. So alluring.

So damned frustrating!

He wanted her so badly that he could barely breathe when the lust struck him like a white-hot spike through his gut. Yet she was aggravating, and contentious, and never, ever simply agreed with him, or had any faith that he knew what he was doing, like most people did, and worst of all, she was so damned *open*! She employed no reserve, no boundary, no dam to the brook of her soul. Every emotion she felt appeared on her lovely face with foolhardy clarity, forcing him to listen, to look, to pay attention—to care.

She was everything he never wanted—but he could not stop thinking about her in his bed, over him, under him, wrapped hot and wet around him.

Or far, far worse—holding him, listening to him, laughing at him . . .

A strange smell caught at his attention. He looked down to see that his solvent had boiled over and was running off the tabletop to drip steaming onto his boots. The blacking had already begun to leach from the leather!

Bloody hell!

With superhuman effort, Orion managed to bring his simmering obsession under control enough to concentrate. Time began to alter in the manner of deep focus, as if his mind were ticking to a different clock than the rest of the world. What seemed like only minutes later, Orion looked out the window to see a disheveled and weary Francesca walking back from the rear of the grounds. Francesca said something to the lagging Attie over her shoulder.

Attie threw back her head—

And laughed out loud.

Orion caught his breath. He had seen angry Attie, vengeful Attie, even cold, logical Attie. Had he ever seen happy Attie?

He loved his little sister and understood her very well. Yet in all her thirteen years, no matter how he might have wished to, he'd never been able to bring that sort of innocent joy to her pointed little face.

Within days, Francesca had.

With absent care, Orion stopped to remove his solvent from the burner stand. Then he opened the door to the laboratory and walked out into the beautiful day to meet happy Attie and miraculous Francesca in the garden.

"Of course, they are all named for poets," Francesca was saying to Attie as Orion approached them. "My father dearly loved rhyme. And he was fond of rabbits as well."

Another precious clue to the mystery of Francesca, dropped easily to Attie but not to him. "So," he said, thinking over his classics, "Herbert is named after George Herbert?"

Both girls turned to him with surprised expressions. Attie rolled her eyes. "Of course not!"

Francesca's smile danced. "Herbert is named after Mary Herbert, of course."

Orion blinked. "Herbert is female?"

Attie gave him her standard "Could you be any more obtuse?" look, but the laughter still lingered at the corners of her mouth. It warmed him to see her usual bleakness eased.

Orion smiled indulgently. "So *Miss* Herbert is safely back home with the others, then?"

Attie looked at Francesca, as if expecting her to answer. Francesca looked at Attie in the same way. Attie frowned.

"I thought you had Herbert in the lab."

Francesca shook her head. "No, I was measuring Dante. I thought I saw you catching Herbert in the hedgerow."

Attie's eyes grew wide. "No, that was Voltaire."

It seemed the rabbit hunt was not over yet. Orion thought he might rather enjoy joining in on a leisurely tramp through the garden in search of the elusive Herbert.

A deep roar of rage sounded from another part of the grounds. "Bloody little *thief*!"

Attie blinked. "Is that the giant?"

Francesca paled. "The cook's garden, Attie!"

Orion could see that Attie hadn't thought of that. In a whirl of faded skirts and lanky ankles, she was gone, running for the kitchen garden. It was mere seconds before they followed Attie, but she far outpaced them both.

Unfortunately, five seconds was more than enough time for Atalanta Worthington to get herself and others into dire straits.

Orion's legs were longer, but Francesca was perhaps slightly more motivated, since it was her rabbit, after all. She whisked by him, her skirts held shamelessly high and her body bent in the pose of a serious runner. She was fast—and Orion was not immune to the bolt of sudden lust inspired by her golden, rounded thighs and the flash of underthings. The startling power of it snagged his attention so thoroughly that his pace almost slowed in sheer surprise.

So he was a few seconds behind both females. A Worthington man ought to know better than to allow any Worthington female—or one similar to a Worthington female!—to outrun him into trouble!

When Orion finished his mad dash for the kitchen garden perimeter, he could see nothing past the flourishing height of the plants within—but he could hear someone yelling in anger. The cook? He was angry about the rabbit invasion, no doubt. Orion wasn't much good at placation, since he rarely cared what anyone else cared about, but he knew that Francesca could not be in the same vicinity as the coarse fellow without a great display of Italian cursing and a high probability of flying food. He hurried.

The deep voice changed from anger to a hoarse yelp of alarm. *Oh damn.* Only Attie on a rampage could bring out that sort of fear in a grown man.

When he rounded the asparagus bed and took a sharp left past the carrot patch, he found Francesca dancing between the two opponents, obviously trying to negotiate some sort of peace. Which should inform one as to the degree of animosity present, if temperamental Francesca was playing peacekeeper.

Then Orion realized that the cook was holding a rabbit up by the scruff of its neck. Orion could see the black-and-white patchwork coat clearly. *Damn. Herbert.*

Then he realized that Attie was waving something as well. As he neared the fray, he saw his baby sister was attempting to wreak permanent damage to Blayne House's head cook with one of the man's own meat cleavers.

Blast it! Attie with no more resources than her own imagination was bad enough. Armed, she was prone to outrageous acts of reprisal, although Orion had to admit that using a cleaver was new. Usually she resorted to firearms, or sometimes poison. She was also fond of blackmail, although Iris claimed that it had only been a prepubescent phase.

"Get her off me!" the cook cried, his voice becoming rather shrill for a man of his weight class. "She's a maniac, that one!"

The maniac was undeterred by their arrival. "Put Herbert down, you murdering blackguard! I'll carve *you* up, you brute, and see how you like it!" Attie whirled the cleaver by the handle in an intricate and alarmingly assassin-like maneuver. Orion blinked at her skill with the blade. Obviously they had not been imaginative enough when clearing all weapons from Worthington House. It was clear that Attie had been practicing on the sly.

A note to himself: Strip the kitchen down to the spoons. He hated to think what his little sister could do with a spatula!

However, she was not the only one with fighting skills. Orion stepped forward, ducked, grabbed—and snatched the blade from his baby sister's hand in midtwirl. She turned on him, eyes narrowed. Although she scarcely came up to his breastbone, Orion fought the urge to step back out of range of her burning green gaze.

"He"—Attie pointed an indignant finger of accusation at the cook like the pocket version of Lady Justice declaring her verdict—"wants to feed you Herbert for dinner!" She turned to blast her mighty ginger rage at the cowering man. "Cannibal!"

Orion put the butcher knife behind his back. "Attie, you have eaten rabbit many times yourself."

"Oh!" Attie stamped her foot. This ought to have made her seem more like a little girl, and perhaps it would have if one hadn't half expected the earth to shake fearfully in response. "You are becoming one of *them*, Orion Worthington!"

Attie didn't rage. She certainly didn't cry. Attie, on the whole, simply walked away in the moment, seemingly sanguine about her defeat—and then took long-lasting, delayed revenge at some other time—usually the worst possible time, to tell the truth.

Orion had never seen the tears that flowed freely down Attie's freckled cheeks. It surprised him so that his hands dropped to his sides and the butcher knife came back into his little sister's range. She took a step toward him, her arms held out as if for a consoling hug. This was so unexpected that Orion nearly stepped back in suspicion. For a fraction of a second, he hesitated, concerned what the watching Francesca would think of him if he did.

Which was how Attie got her hands on the knife again.

Chapter 13

ORION looked down at his empty hands in shock, then glanced at Francesca. She shook her head pityingly, as if to say, "I cannot believe you fell for that." Then she hiked up her skirts and dashed after Attie as she ran for the pitiable cook. Come to think of it, he ought not to feel bad. After all, Attie had managed to nick the cleaver from the giant cook in the first place.

The big man was on his knees in a flash, holding Herbert out in a shaking fist. The black-and-white bundle of fuzz twitched its downy nose at Attie, by all evidence unalarmed by the flying tempers and flashing blades. Full white whiskers fluffed and relaxed. Rabbits didn't smile. They didn't, and Orion refused to give in to imagination.

Attie dropped the blade in the grass and gathered Herbert into her skinny arms. With her cause won and her righteous wrath eased, she gazed down at the abject chef with disdain. "And I'll bet you're a terrible cook, too."

Orion heard a muffled snort from beside him. He looked down to see Francesca with both hands pressed to her mouth.

She could suppress her laughter, but nothing could hide the dancing light of glee in her large brown eyes.

"He's not that bad," Orion stated, obscurely motivated to defend Sir Geoffrey's taste in staff. "And everything's always piping hot. You should try eating at my house after Mrs. P. has been at her arthritis tea." Or when Iris whimsically took a turn in the kitchen, where one might find one's gravy flavored with a hint of linseed oil.

So it was all resolved. Attie was disarmed, the cook was contrite—or at least cowed—and young Herbert had a fine adventure to relate to all the admiring males back in the hutches, a fact guaranteed to result in a whole new generation of fuzzy, vegetable-patch enthusiasts.

Orion let out a slow breath, relieved that disaster had been averted. Now, if they could just convince the cook to refrain from mentioning anything to—

"What is the meaning of this?" Sir Geoffrey's bellow made even Herbert's whiskers droop. "Worthington? Francesca? Ha! I should expect to find *you* at the center of any uproar! And who is this—this—this young *person*?"

Sir Geoffrey's tone implied much doubt as to the truth of that description. Orion tried not to twitch. He was never good at diplomacy. "Sir Geoffrey, may I present my youngest sister, Miss Atalanta Worthington?"

Sir Geoffrey stared at Attie. Attie, being Attie, pushed back her tangled fiery locks and glared right back, freckles still aglow with her pale-skinned ire. Judith stepped from behind Sir Geoffrey, but one glance at the impatience and irritation on her father's face moved her to stand off to one side.

Judith's behavior should have served as a warning for them all.

Sir Geoffrey turned to sneer at Francesca. "It *would* have something to do with your creatures!" he shouted. "I've been tolerant of your playing at science, and I've allowed you to house those vermin on my property long enough! You have until the presentation to get your 'research'"—he spat the word with enough venom to make Francesca visibly flinch—"off my grounds before I have the lot skinned for their fur!"

Orion felt Francesca's icy fear like a lance through his own body. He stepped forward, moving in front of her as if he could protect her with his larger form.

"Sir Geoffrey, it is not necessary—"

The scientist turned on Orion. His lined face and bloodshot eyes seemed very nearly demonic in his red-faced rage.

"You'll shut up and get back to the lab, you lollygagging whelp! You're here to serve me, not *her*!"

Orion heard Francesca gasp, and even Attie let out a strangled sound of surprise. He let his placating hands drop to his sides. "Sir Geoffrey, you are overwrought, so I will not demand an apology for your tone." He let a bit of ice frost his voice. "However, nor will I allow you to threaten your daughter and your niece. If you wish to continue our association, I believe I can look past this afternoon's display—if you can."

Sir Geoffrey was not accustomed to being calmly confronted. Orion could see the man's mind, as if he had a lens through the older man's skull, trying to decide whether to back down or to blast them all from his sight.

Orion was coming to the conclusion that the great and brilliant Sir Geoffrey was something of a bully. Normally, Orion would have cared nothing about another man's personality flaws—but this particular man had power over the women in Orion's life, power that Sir Geoffrey seemed inclined to abuse.

Orion delivered his one true weapon—or peace offering. It depended on how Sir Geoffrey chose to take it. "If we are to have something definitive to put forward in your presentation to the Royal Fraternity of Life Sciences this week, I think it best if we waste no more time on this afternoon's . . . events."

Sir Geoffrey could not do it without him. Orion had seen enough of the man over the past few days to know that the king was teetering on his throne. Sir Geoffrey's temper had become far too uncertain, and his energies were too sapped to do it on his own. He seemed to avoid the laboratory at all costs, apparently more inclined to rest upon his past accomplishments. Orion was not sure what illness the older man fought, but in a moment of insight, he suspected that Sir Geoffrey's finely bladed mind had lost its edge. He had very little evidence to support that theory, but he knew it was true all the same.

And as Sir Geoffrey stared at him with narrowed eyes, Orion realized that Sir Geoffrey knew what Orion had deduced. The only question was, would that chink in the older scientist's armor prompt him toward reconciliation—or revenge?

Orion waited. His future hung in the balance as well. Did Sir Geoffrey realize that?

Perhaps he ought to have placated the man somehow. However this situation resolved itself, his first concern was getting Attie out of the thick of things.

They all waited—Orion, Francesca, Attie, and even Judith, whose tension might not show in her serene expression, but Orion saw that her hands were so tightly clasped that her knuckles had gone white.

Orion was fairly certain the only one not hanging on Sir Geoffrey's next words was Herbert, who had the end of Attie's ratty braid in her mouth and was nibbling it in a leisurely, unconcerned fashion.

At last, Sir Geoffrey exhaled and jerked his hardened jaw a few times. "This is a waste of time," he announced. "Judith, see to the cook. Worthington—"

"I shall make sure the rabbits are secure," Orion put in, nodding as if he'd foreseen his mentor's request. "And if you don't mind, Sir Geoffrey, I'd like to request that Miss Penrose escort my sister back to Worthington House."

"God yes!" Sir Geoffrey very nearly snarled the words.

Orion hustled Attie and Francesca into the house as

quickly as he could. He didn't want Attie walking back to
Worthington House this late—or worse, jumping on the back
of a hackney cab!—but he dared not venture home just now.
Nor did he want to. Home meant crowding and theatrics and
clutter, and he found he simply couldn't stand the notion.

When they got to the front door, Pennysmith had already
summoned Eva to the front hall. The maid stood ready with
Francesca's bonnet and spencer.

Attie thrust Herbert into Orion's arms after a last, sniffling
embrace. "If that man hurts Herbert . . ."

Orion went down on one knee to look his little sister in the
eye. "I will protect Herbert with my life," he promised sol-
emnly, folding the creature into his elbow. "Now, go on home.
And . . . you had best keep away from Blayne House for a few
days, until Sir Geoffrey has made his presentation. He is
bound to be a bit—"

"Sir Geoffrey," Francesca put in, from where Eva was
stuffing her into her short jacket, "will be an absolute bear.
Bears are fierce and difficult to clean up after. Hmm. I'll come
and live at Worthington House for the interim, shall I? Judith,
let's move to Worthington House together, right now, before
supper. I shall pack us a trunk full of lemon tarts—"

"And rabbits!" Attie joined in Francesca's silliness.

"And rabbits, and perhaps some books—"

"No books!" Orion and Attie protested simultaneously.

Francesca looked at the both of them with her head tilted
quizzically, one arm behind her as Eva worked her snug spencer up over her shoulder. "You *are* related, aren't you? That
sounded like a single voice!"

She turned to her cousin, towing Eva with her. "Will you
be all right, Judith? Truly?" Her teasing tone was gone, and
real concern tinged her voice.

"Oh my, yes, Cousin," Judith stated serenely. "Papa needs
a good supper and a brandy, that's all. Eva, that will never fit
her, for it is mine. Fetch the brown one. Papa takes his work
most seriously, you know," she continued seamlessly. "He'll

be right as rain once he has impressed the Fraternity with his presentation."

Francesca slid a glance in Orion's direction as Eva jerked the ill-fitting spencer from her, and Orion knew what she was thinking. *Will there be anything worth presenting?*

Not if he did not get back to the laboratory and find it!

Chapter 14

FRANCESCA, clad in the brown spencer, which was ugly but much more comfortable in the bodice, leaned back in the Blayne carriage and regarded the young girl sitting across from her. Atalanta Worthington took up most of the opposite bench, one arm and her head lolling out of the carriage window like a dog.

She might as well enjoy her last few months of childhood. Francesca wished she could tell the girl to be in no hurry for adulthood—although perhaps Attie already knew that. It might account for some of the ferocious protection of her family from outsiders.

Orion had been quite protective as well. Francesca had enjoyed watching her uncle sputter helplessly when Orion had threatened to withdraw his assistance if Sir Geoffrey did not discontinue his ill behavior. It had not all been for Attie's benefit, either, Francesca was sure. Orion had stood between Sir Geoffrey and her, Judith, and Attie.

Then he'd further charmed her when he'd gone down on one knee to reassure Attie and had sworn to protect Herbert.

Francesca smiled fondly at the memory. She might tease him about that later—or she might not.

"You are thinking about my brother, aren't you?"

Francesca met Attie's narrowed green gaze. "Yes," she replied simply, then turned to gaze from her own window. Orion had smiled when he'd strolled out to meet them on the lawn.

Had she ever seen him smile before?

It had been an easy thing, that smile, as if he had smiled at her a thousand times before and would a thousand times more. Simply thinking of it warmed her again, just as it had in the moment.

Well, this is a pickle. Her father used to say that to her when she'd flung herself about in one youthful agony or another. She'd wondered what "a pickle" meant.

Now she knew.

She liked Orion Worthington. She liked him a great deal. She hadn't wanted to, but she did.

Papa, this is a pickle, indeed.

"WE CAN'T GO home yet." Attie clambered up onto her seat and banged her fist on the trapdoor. The driver flipped it open, and Attie gave him an address.

The driver leaned down to exchange glances with Chessa, who simply shrugged and waved a hand for him to carry on. Not a single silly question.

Attie liked that about Chessa. It wasn't until she dropped back down to her tufted-velvet bench that Chessa raised a questioning brow at her.

"I need to see my friend," Attie told her. "And you need a dress for the Duke of Camberton's ball."

Chessa just blinked at her. "I do not. I have a silk gown that I brought from Italy."

Attie grimaced. "I'll wager that it is brown."

Chessa frowned. "As a matter of fact, it is. How did you know?"

Attie rolled her eyes. "Brown is just so—so brown!" She shook her head in frustration. "My friend will explain it better. At least, he always makes it sound sensible when he's trying to get me to wear a new dress."

Chessa looked stubborn but curious. "And who is this friend? Why does he make you dresses?"

Attie smiled slyly. "Oh, he's just a dressmaker I know. Perhaps you might have heard of Lementeur? That is his stage name, so to speak. We call him Button."

Chessa shrugged. "I don't follow fashion. Is he very good?"

"Well, at any rate, be very nice to him. He's sad." She leaned forward in her seat. Chessa automatically did as well.

Attie was becoming very fond of Chessa!

"He has been *disappointed* in *Love*," Attie whispered with dramatic flair. She leaned back and went on in a more matter-of-fact tone. "Making you a gown will be a very cheering project for him, I think. He does enjoy a blank slate."

Chessa blinked mildly at that. "Happy to oblige, I suppose."

Attie did not approve of Button's pain. His love for Cabot, his rather much younger assistant, was not more powerful than his ethics against taking advantage of someone over whom he might be said to have undue influence—which Attie thought was balderdash.

Because of the age difference between him and his talented assistant, Button had spent a decade pretending not to see Cabot's pining for more than a mentor/protégé relationship. Several months ago, when Cabot was offered a position as personal dresser to the Prince Regent, Button had sent him on his way, kindly but firmly rejecting Cabot's final plea. The Worthingtons all suspected that Button had broken his own heart that day, as well as Cabot's.

Button loved Cabot. Cabot loved Button right back. Attie didn't see what age had to do with anything.

Within her own household, Attie often felt conflicted as her siblings had begun to fall in love and marry—and sometimes leave! Her own family might be spreading out and growing, and she wasn't sure how she felt about it—but she entertained no such reservations when it came to Button and Cabot!

Attie had thought Chessa would go into spasms of delight at the very notion of meeting Lementeur. At first, she found Chessa's underwhelm disappointing—but then she thought that it might be rather interesting to see what happened when her dearest Button finally met someone who wasn't his instant slave.

If that didn't shake him from his melancholy, Attie didn't know what would!

THE FAMOUS LEMENTEUR, dressmaker supreme and the very last word in fashion, sat in his crowded, chaotic, cluttered, littered workroom . . . and stared blankly at the sheet of paper on which he had meant to sketch out a new gown for Lady Fogarty's masquerade ball—six hours ago.

He realized that he was waiting.

Waiting for Cabot.

There came no tap on his door. There came no tall, painfully attractive assistant with tea and cakes on a tray, with questions about his mentor's plans, with pointed dry commentary upon the client's manners or habits that would make his mentor chuckle, make his mentor's eyes begin to gleam, make his mentor's fingers set to pencil in a first dynamic burst of inspiration . . .

Cabot had work of his own now, as the primary designer of His Royal Highness's wardrobes, both court finery and personal! He was far too busy and important to fetch tea and cakes! He had people to fetch and carry for him—and perhaps people to fetch and carry for them as well!

Button applauded Cabot's decision to take that leap. His assistant was more than qualified, both in talent and in the discretion necessary to waiting upon the notoriously fickle Prince Regent.

"He's incomparable, that's what he is! Brilliant!"

Button heard his own emphatic tones echoing in the tiny chamber and frowned. "Talking to yourself is a swift and certain way to find yourself twiddling your thumbs in Bedlam, you old fool!"

He was an old fool! Too old to dream of love, too foolish to evade it! Love had found him—and when he had flinched from it, love had lost him again!

Button sighed and used his fingertips to set his pencil spinning like a dial on his large, intimidating white sheet of paper. He let out a noisy, self-pitying sigh . . .

And waited.

Button looked up hopefully as something rather catlike scratched at his office door. However, he knew that noise, and it wasn't Cabot.

"Is that you, Miss Atalanta?"

The door opened to reveal poor darling Attie Worthington, looking rather worse than usual. Button blinked back his own melancholy as concern for his strange little friend took precedence. "Heavens, pet! Have you been wrestling a bear?"

She shrugged as she wandered in. "Rabbits, butcher knives, and a giant cook."

"No, really, what happened?"

Attie looked at him. "I told you."

Button smiled, but his attempt to be reassured did not come to fruition. Attie's face was grimy and rather suspiciously clean about the eyes. Still, her mood seemed nearly cheerful.

Attie turned to look behind her. "Come on in, Chessa."

Button looked up to see a very lovely girl with an astonishing bosom and dark Latin eyes enter hesitantly. She wore a shockingly ugly frock. At once, Button's listless fingers began to twitch.

Attie gave him a knowing look. "Chessa, Button. Button, Chessa needs clothes."

The girl's need was dire, indeed. However, Button drew back on the reins of his creative mount. Without Cabot at his side, he found himself constantly behind in his work— although whether through mournful woolgathering or simple disorganization, he could not seem to pinpoint the cause.

"Attie, I don't know, my dear. I have so much to do." He waved helplessly at the stacks of chaos around him.

Attie looked as well, and seemed to grasp that there was a distinct difference between the chaos of "creativity" and the chaos of "overwhelm." Still, her pointy little chin firmed relentlessly.

"I'm sorry, Button, but Chessa *must* have clothes."

The girl behind Attie waved her hands. "Oh no. I'm fine. Please, Attie, leave the poor fellow alone. Any old gown will do for me."

Both Button and Attie turned to gape at the dark-haired beauty. She was turning down one of his gowns? The fact that he hadn't offered her one didn't signify. He was Lementeur! The princess herself was on a waiting list!

Attie folded her arms and shook her head pityingly. "Button, it isn't her fault. She's from Italy. And she's a scientist. Hardly a normal girl at all."

Button shared a humorous glance with the strange girl at Attie's remark—Attie, who was the furthest creature from a normal girl he had ever known. Suddenly reassured that he dealt with a benevolent sort of person, he stood up and bowed at last.

"My dear Chessa—may I call you Chessa?"

The girl held out her hand and gave a lovely curtsy. "Francesca Penrose, and yes, Chessa will do."

Button noticed the lyrical voice and seductive accents, along with perfect diction, and the softness of her hands. A lady, surely. And Penrose . . . Wasn't Orion staying with some family with a Penrose connection? Hmm. Yes, that stuffy Sir Geoffrey, with his perpetual series of laboratory assistants— one of whom was now Orion himself.

Two young ladies in that house, if he recalled correctly. There were the Blayne girl and a cousin, Miss Penrose. Button made it his business to keep track of all the ladies of Society—both as potential clients and because some time ago he'd quite caught the matchmaking habit.

Ah. So the exotic buxom beauty in the awful dress and tumbled hair was more than she seemed.

Button leaned toward Attie with a questioning peak to his brows.

Attie quickly whispered that she had been spying on both Judith and Francesca—and that she was not sure which one Orion preferred, but if forced to it, *she* would choose Chessa.

"And you mean to stack the deck on her side?" Button pursed his lips. "This is a break from your usual forms of sabotage."

Attie sniffed. "I'm expanding my horizons. Besides, I've outgrown bullets and laxatives."

Button coughed. "Glad to hear it, pet," he said mildly. Then he turned back to the attractive newcomer, whose eyes were greedily devouring the sketches pinned upon his walls. *Not interested in fashion, eh?* "What science, pray tell?"

Chessa turned and smiled at him with delight. *Oh yes. Stunning.*

"Most people in England want to know who my father was, not who I am." She straightened proudly. "I am a biologist, trained at the University of Bologna. I am half-English, half-Italian. And although I am delighted to meet a friend of Attie's, I did not come here to trouble you for a gown. There is no need. I have four."

Button passed a hand over his lips. It would not do to laugh at the beautiful, intelligent, and kindly Miss Penrose—for she must be kindly to have befriended Attie, who was more adroit at making enemies than friends, poor duckling—but most ladies in London Society would not tolerate a mere four handkerchiefs, much less a measly four gowns! And if the present one was any example, very bad gowns, indeed.

"Er . . . if I may ask"—Button waved a hand at her shapeless brown gabardine covered by a deeply offensive brown spencer that sagged in the bodice—"who made this—this *creation* for you?" Who would have dreamed that two brown colors could actually clash so?

Chessa blinked and looked down at herself. "Oh . . . this was made by my aunt's dressmaker, but it came back too snug in the sleeves, so my aunt gave it to me. The spencer belonged to another aunt. She gave it to me when I realized I needed a few more warm things for England."

Button had to clasp his fingers together to hide his horror. The high, pious neckline . . . the restricting sleeves . . . the horse-apple brown color? "Your aunt, you say? How—if I may be so bold . . . Is your aunt perhaps a lady of advanced years?"

Chessa nodded. "Yes. She is actually my great-aunt. How did you guess?"

"He's a genius," Attie put in. "And your dress and spencer are very hideous. I wouldn't bury the cook in them."

Button blinked. "So . . . there really was a cook? A giant cook?"

Chessa smiled ruefully. "And a butcher knife. And many, many rabbits."

Button encouraged her with a smile, and the whole story came out. And while Chessa talked and Attie embellished with some very entertaining mime, if Button noted down a few mental measurements and doodled a charming décolletage and fiddled with a number of swatches, no one commented upon his distraction.

And if, when the presently pretty Miss Penrose and the someday stunning Miss Worthington left the establishment of the foremost mantua-maker of London Society, a certain fellow began to rifle through his fabrics with renewed inspiration and energy—well, there was no one to see.

Chapter 15

DUSK found Orion in the laboratory, hard at work appeasing Sir Geoffrey's quest for everlasting fame and scientific accolade.

The lanterns were lighted, casting bright, efficient glow. Silence reigned. His concentration was absolute.

Yet Orion found the laboratory far too quiet. Oddly, the very silence was distracting to him now. He missed the rare but peaceful moments of working side by side with Francesca, his thoughts keeping time with the even sound of her breathing and the rustling of her gown.

However, he did manage to get a great portion of his work done and had at last eliminated the final solvents from the experiment. On the shelf of potentials now stood nine bottles, arranged neatly in a line.

He was ready to begin the next stage of the experiment.

Unfortunately, he had no notion of what ought to be done next. He was fairly certain Sir Geoffrey didn't, either—hence the man's avoidance of his own lab!

Orion leaned his hips back against the marble-topped laboratory table and regarded the single shelf of bottles with weary indecision.

I wish Francesca were here.

Which was ridiculous. She could offer him no new knowledge of chemistry, no insights into botanical compounds, no fact he did not already know.

I want to talk to her about it.

I want to listen to her voice and have her laugh at me and say radical things that make me see the world differently.

Blinking, he rubbed his hands over his face. Where was she?

He lifted his head sharply. *Oh no.*

He'd matched up the subversive with the barmy, the rebellious with the cracked. He'd unthinkingly sent the most outrageously imaginative woman he'd ever met into the center of all things mad, into the seething den of chaos itself.

Worthington House.

What have I done?

FRANCESCA STIRRED THE giant pot of tomato sauce, talking all the while.

"But I found Ophelia to be more of a place marker of a character," she said to charming Archie Worthington, who was nodding in agreement. "She was the object of desire, instead of a real woman."

"Yes, thank you. That onion is perfectly chopped," she said to lovely Mrs. Philpott. She turned and waved a saucy spoon at Castor Worthington. "Have you considered the elastic properties of the boiled sap of the rubber tree, which was my uncle's previous field of study? I think it would help reduce the noise of the turning gears, don't you?"

With that, she plunked the spoon down upon the stove and

went to hover over where silent Lysander sat peeling potatoes with intense concentration. Without speaking, she scooped up his work so far and left him to his efforts with a simple pat on the shoulder.

Attie sat on a high stool at the end of the scarred kitchen worktable, industriously chopping basil. Actually, she was obliterating it with enthusiasm, so Francesca mentally changed her menu to include a nice pesto.

Stately Iris drifted through the kitchen like a lacy wisp of smoke, bestowing beatific smiles upon her children and husband. "Oh, how wonderful. Goodness, aren't you gifted?" And for Francesca's sauce? "Heavens, darling, that's simply divine!"

Francesca smiled to herself and went back to stirring. Iris's uncomplicated support might not be very discerning, but a mother's love was pure and unconditional, was it not?

For the first time since she had left Bologna, Francesca felt surrounded by family. For the first time in an even longer time, she felt surrounded by acceptance.

My journey is done. I have found my people.

Except that they weren't, not really. But they were Orion's people, and Attie's people, and from what she could gather, they were also Mr. Button's people.

If a person could be judged by the people he surrounded himself with, then Orion must be an amazing human being, even aside from his formidable mind.

Then again, he'd left this warm and wonderful place for the cold, efficient environs of Blayne House—and worse, he actually seemed to prefer it!

Attie brought Francesca the cutting board with the basil, which had been reduced to a pulpy smear. Francesca smiled at her. "That's marvelous! And so consistently cut!" She set the younger girl to planing the hard cheese. Note to her future self: Attie's help should be saved for when she needed her ingredients disintegrated.

"Rion, dearest, you've come home at last!" Iris trilled over the chaos.

Francesca looked up from her pot to see Orion's lean form filling the doorway of the main kitchen. His dark gaze was fixed upon her like a hunter who had at last spotted his prey. She smiled at him broadly and without repentance. It was his own fault that she'd stayed for dinner. He ought to have suspected what would happen when she finally found people who liked to eat!

"Rion!" Attie popped up and ran to her newly arrived brother. "Mrs. Philpott gave over the kitchen to Francesca, and we are having pasta Bolognese!" She grabbed Orion's hand and began to drag him toward the stove. "I chopped basil. And Chessa helped Cas solve his noise-reduction problem! Didn't she, Cas?"

Castor nodded to his brother. "It's a very good idea." He turned his sketch sideways. "See? If I add a disc of the boiled rubber here, and another here, it should absorb the worst of the vibration."

Orion's dark gaze left Francesca's long enough to scan the drawing. "Yes, I see." He looked back at Francesca, his blue eyes like windows of night sky. "Francesca has a way of seeing right to the center of a problem."

Francesca's heart pounded. He so rarely paid compliments. That was one thing that differed from the rest of the Worthington clan. Orion held approval back like a miser—yet when he gave it, it seemed to mean so much more.

She looked away from his intense scrutiny. *Mind your spoon, Chessa. You're splashing!*

"I came to take Miss Penrose back to Blayne House," Orion stated calmly into the din. Silence fell at once.

Francesca lifted her chin and kept stirring. "You and what platoon, may I ask?"

He came closer. "You have to go home."

I am home. But if she said that out loud, it would sound

silly, and then he would say something sensible and painfully accurate and truthful. So she swallowed hard and put the spoon down carefully, then turned to him as she wiped her hands on her apron.

"Give me one good reason why I should." She waved a hand at the people filling the kitchen, people who crowded around the worktable just to be together, and to get to know her. It could not be more dismally different at Blayne House.

He advanced two more steps until he stood over her, close enough to touch. He gazed down at her as if they were the only two people in the room. "I would like for you to return to Blayne House," he said, his voice deepening, "because if you do not, I will miss you."

Oh. My. Heavens. She could not tear her gaze from his. Were her knees actually going weak? Over the pounding in her ears, Francesca heard Iris sigh and Archie chuckle. Even Lysander paused in his dutiful peeling to wait for her reply.

A deep breath restored the starch to her knees. She smiled merrily at Orion. "Well, then, all the more reason to sit down to supper sooner. There is celery that needs chopping, and I believe you are just the man for the job."

FOR MOST OF his life, Orion had eaten at the long table in the cluttered dining room at Worthington House.

So why was this night so different?

His father sat at the head of the table, as Archie always did if he could be pulled from his lifelong study of the works of Shakespeare. At the other end, Iris sat—unless she was perched on Archie's lap, being fed tidbits of the meal as if the two of them were alone.

Perhaps they were, alone together in a dreamworld of their own making.

However, tonight they were both present and fully engaged with the rest of the party. Iris was perched on Archie's knee to free a chair for Francesca, but her eyes were bright and sparkling, instead of vague and dreamy.

Archie seemed enraptured with Francesca, and he laughed aloud at a story she told about the time she tried to spice up Sir Geoffrey's stewed prunes with a bit of cinnamon—except that in her hurry to be stealthy, she mistakenly loaded the dish with ground red pepper!

The Worthingtons did not know how vicious Sir Geoffrey's temper could be, so they only laughed at Francesca as she acted out Sir Geoffrey fanning his mouth, trying to call for water. Orion found himself wondering what form his mentor's vengeance had taken. He would wager that it was not at all amusing.

Francesca did not belong at Blayne House. If anything, she belonged here, where all eyes were brightened by her laughter, and every speck of her cooking had been heartily eaten—yes, Orion had helped himself to thirds, beating his brother Castor out with a two-second lead.

Then he had shared his spoils with Attie, who grew so quickly that she remained too thin. It had hurt to lose even a spoonful of noodles in thick, spicy red sauce and the balls of spiced beef that had been stewed in it.

Archie had dusted off an ancient bottle of red wine, and even Attie had enjoyed a taste. Francesca had pronounced it to be absolutely terrible. She drank two glasses.

It seemed everyone had a story they wanted to share with Francesca as well, and Orion heard some of them for the first time. He could not help but wonder, when had these things happened to his family? Where had he been at the time?

"You were in your study."

"You had your nose in a book."

"You told me to go away before I contaminated your samples."

Francesca defended him against his family's all-too-prompt responses, laughing all the while. "Orion is a genius—

you should see him in the laboratory. He was born to do research!"

Then his family wanted to hear all about his work. Orion looked at Francesca, but she only smiled and waved him onward. Slowly, keeping his explanations simple, he told his family about the competition to discover a method to extract compounds from plants. He waited for them to become confused or bored, but they truly listened to him.

Francesca helped, directing his story with anecdotes of her own and recounting how she'd had to teach him how to use the flame bowls. Attie chimed in, giving a blow-by-blow account of the Great Rabbit Dispute.

Orion realized, somewhere between glass wicks that wouldn't burn and rabbits named after poets, that he'd never enjoyed a dinner with his family more. And, from the looks of engaged wonder in their eyes, neither had they.

Had it been his doing, that distance? Had he become so withdrawn from his fellow Worthingtons that they no longer bothered trying to reach him?

Deep down, Orion loved them. He knew they loved him in return.

But tonight, for the first time in memory, he felt understood by them. And bright-eyed, laughing Francesca was the reason why.

Like a song, or a perfect passage in a book, or the first words one understood in learning a new language, Francesca opened doors with her lively interest and her engaging nature.

She was disheveled from her long day of chasing rabbits, fending off knife-wielding cooks, and rolling meatballs—but Orion found himself mesmerized by her effortless beauty. She had a nicely shaped face and her figure was certainly marvelous, but it was the spice and flame within her that brought out the best—and worst!—in everyone she encountered. She was a human barometer of character.

In the company of the Worthingtons, she brought out their laughter and their loving natures. But with the occupants of

Blayne House, Francesca seemed to bring out only anger and impatience. Perhaps that did not reflect badly on her at all. Perhaps it meant precisely what Orion had been avoiding acknowledging for the past several days—that Sir Geoffrey was not a good man.

Castor elbowed Orion out of his reverie. "She's marvelous, Rion! Look, I think Lysander is almost smiling!"

Orion looked around the table at his mad, odd, irritating, chaotic family with the lively, shimmering, annoying Francesca at the very center and found that he was almost smiling as well.

Chapter 16

THE next day of Orion's stay in Blayne House began with all the usual swift efficiency. Orion found his breakfast on the side table in his room, eggs and kippers, this time along with some breathtakingly light crumpets that tasted of basil and honey. If Orion closed his eyes in silent ecstasy as he chewed them, there was no one to know.

His clothing had been brushed and laid out for him by the stealthy staff of Blayne House, and the pitcher on his dressing table held steaming water for his washing. It was astonishing how quickly one became accustomed to such luxury. Orion approved of comfort, if it allowed him more time for science.

He ate and bathed quickly, except for some secret momentary savoring of Francesca's baking, for he had an appointment with Sir Geoffrey downstairs.

Once again, Orion was made to wait upon guests. However, this time he did not mind so much being kept from the laboratory, for Sir Geoffrey had invited a fellow scientist to call. Orion, after guessing that Sir Geoffrey would don the Coat, as Francesca called it, brushed off his best deep blue surcoat and turned up dutifully in the foyer a few minutes early.

"Ah, Worthington! Your timing is, as always, impeccable."

Orion turned to greet his mentor. Sir Geoffrey was descending the stairs with a stately lack of speed. As Orion was used to a much more gravitational rumble of his brothers' and sisters' feet, Orion admired the older man's thoughtful pace. In the midst of musing that it might add a little something to his own stateliness, Orion caught sight of Sir Geoffrey's white-knuckle grip upon the railing.

Orion looked more sharply at Sir Geoffrey's face for signs of strain. A line of perspiration droplets, no larger than grains of millet, had popped out upon the marble pallor of the man's brow and upper lip.

Concerned, Orion hesitated. If Sir Geoffrey wished for assistance, he possessed an entire household of people simply panting to open his door or sweep a pebble from his path. Ergo, Sir Geoffrey did not wish such a fuss to be made over his possible ailment.

Ordinarily, Orion felt entirely comfortable ignoring the needs of others—especially when the heat of the experimental process bloomed in the laboratory. However, he could not help but hear a voice in his mind telling him to give the man a blasted hand! The voice had an Italian lilt.

Sir Geoffrey simply waved him off and made his way shakily to the parlor. Pennysmith appeared within seconds with a steaming pot of tea and a fine china cup. Just one. It seemed that Orion had already had all the tea he was going to receive from the staff today!

The tea seemed to do the job, for a few moments later Sir Geoffrey was his old self as Pennysmith announced the arrivals.

"Dr. Darwin, sir, with his grandson."

Sir Geoffrey bounced to his feet.

"Ah! Erasmus!" He stepped forward and clasped hands with a florid, jowly septuagenarian who sported an outmoded

brown coat and a powdered wig from a previous decade. Then
he glanced down at the small boy at Dr. Darwin's side. "And
this must be young Charlie." This was uttered with somewhat
less enthusiasm. "He's grown a bit since I last saw him."

"Young Charlie" looked to be six or seven years of age,
an appealing, brown-haired cherub, but he was old enough to
narrow his eyes in obvious annoyance at being spoken above.
Orion mused upon what Attie would do if subjected to such
a slight. Then he fought back a shudder.

Sir Geoffrey turned to beckon at Orion, clicking his fingers, rather like summoning the dog. Perhaps it was having
Attie on his mind, but Orion had to fight back a twitch of
annoyance as well. However, he managed to step forward and
bow politely to Dr. Darwin. He knew the man's reputation as
a physician and philosopher. Although Orion found questions
of the meaning of life uninteresting, he did find medicine
fascinating.

However, once introduced, Orion was dismissed, as was
Young Charlie. Sadly, Orion was not ordered to go where he
wished to go, the laboratory. Instead, Sir Geoffrey went to
the door and spoke a word to the hovering Pennysmith.

In seconds, Judith appeared—and she was dressed to go
out in a walking gown and spencer, her bonnet strings already
tied.

"Ah, my dear!" Sir Geoffrey greeted her expansively, as
if he'd not ignored her during the previous hours of the day.
"You look lovely. Are you here to steal Mr. Worthington
away?"

Judith gazed evenly at Orion, though she spoke to her
father. "I thought he might enjoy the walk to the tobacconist's
shop. I want to get you some more of that African blend you
like so much, Papa."

"Lovely! What a thoughtful girl you are!"

Judith seemed entirely unperturbed by Sir Geoffrey's obvious, to Orion, falsification of extreme affection. Orion had
the feeling that it happened to her often. His own family was

highly affectionate, sometimes annoyingly so—but it was always entirely sincere. What must it be like for a daughter to experience such a thing only when her father found it socially useful?

For the first time, Orion found himself wondering what was truly going on behind Miss Judith Blayne's impassive beauty.

He bowed. "Thank you, Miss Blayne. I should enjoy a walk." There, even Elektra could not find fault with that! As he made his way from the room, he took a moment to bend down to whisper in Young Charlie's ear.

"There are rabbits in the back garden. Take the path all the way, then follow the wall to your right."

Then he took his hat from Pennysmith's ready hand, although he'd not yet asked for it, and offered Judith his arm. Miss Penrose was nowhere in sight, so it seemed this was meant to be an exclusive stroll.

It hardly seemed necessary. The amount of time he would spend away from the laboratory itched at him, but Sir Geoffrey wished him to walk, so he would walk.

As they left, Pennysmith moved to close the door on the conversation between Sir Geoffrey and Dr. Darwin.

"Erasmus, you must take a look at my notes! The development of my process is going very well, indeed—"

The door clicked shut on further words, so Orion did not get to hear Sir Geoffrey tell Dr. Darwin about Orion's own contribution to the progress. Which Sir Geoffrey would doubtless do.

Eventually.

CHARLIE SLID A glance toward the two older men, then ducked out through the glass garden doors of the drawing room and into the sunlight. Rabbits were more interesting than stuffy old men talking about Plato and such. Charlie already knew more about the Greek philosophers than anyone needed to. Dusty dead thoughts weren't nearly as much fun as living, breathing animals!

He wandered happily down the path, passing the rose beds and the croquet lawn, though he did linger at the large circular fountain. He dabbled his fingers into the stream of water pouring from stone jars that were balanced in the hands of marble ladies who ought to put on more clothes.

The formal gardens began to turn a bit more workaday. First, the sculpted beds gave way to a cutting garden where the flowers for the house were grown. In the center of the practical rows of gladiolas and poppies, there stood a woven grass basket on a stump—a bee skep. Charlie spent a happy ten minutes watching the honeybees. The fuzzy things were so occupied with the business of gathering pollen that he could bend to watch from inches away, the tip of his nose almost touching the petals.

"Pollen basket," he whispered to himself, naming the parts of the bee. "Mandible. Antennae. Pro . . . prob . . . *proboscis.*" It was all most absorbing.

Bees, however, could not be cuddled. Rabbits could.

Back on the path, Charlie stuck his hands deep in his pockets and dreamed of having his own rabbits—and goats, and horses, and maybe even an elephant. His current ambition was to be a keeper at the Royal Menagerie, but Grandpapa scoffed at the idea of working with one's hands.

Charlie didn't know why, since physicians used their hands all the time, poking and prodding at people.

People, Charlie had decided, long ago when he was five years old, were boring.

He reached the end of the path and turned right, because he knew all about left and right, then followed the wall. As the tall man had promised, there were rabbits there! Hutches full of them, row upon row, soft and fluffy, hopping with long ears and tufted tails, and all different kinds, too! Charlie had never known rabbits to come in so many colors!

They came to him readily, pressing tender noses into the

holes in the wire to sniff at his fingertips. Charlie looked around, but he was all alone with a wealth of bunnies to cuddle. Surely no one would mind if he took out just one?

He opened a cage and reached within. The gentle fuzzy creatures did not flee his hand but in fact approached him. He could not resist lifting one into his arms, although he did remember to push the cage door closed again.

Rabbits were delightful. Rabbits were lovely. He promptly decided that they were his new best animal, for he'd been favoring cats for two whole weeks in a row and it was time to move on. The rabbit settled comfortably into the curve of one arm. Charlie thought then that two rabbits would be far better than just one. He reached for the door to the hutch again.

"I wouldn't if I were you."

Charlie stopped short and clutched "his" bunny close. Standing on the path along the wall was a girl, a big girl, the kind of girl who was almost a lady but not yet.

Except she didn't look like a lady. Charlie gawked. She was wearing a faded, too-short dress over pegged knee breeches, topped with a boys' coat. She even had a boys' cap on her head, like his, but it looked oddly stuffed and rounded, as if it were very full of hair.

Amber red fringe poked out from the sides of the cap. She was skinny and freckled, and stood with her bony arms folded as she scowled at him.

Charlie decided that her oddness negated her authority somewhat. He lifted his chin and stiffened his knees. "Why should I do as you say?"

She unfolded her arms and put her hands on her narrow hips. "Go ahead, then. Don't let me stop you. But it's a downward spiral, ending in chaos and mayhem. I should know. I let them all out yesterday." She went to the side of one of the hutches and stuck her fingers through the wire to caress a very nice black-and-white bunny. "Herbert was almost killed."

Charlie gulped. He didn't want any of the bunnies to get

hurt. He clutched the one in his arms a little more tightly. "Very well, then. I shall learn from your mistake. Only one bun—rabbit at a time."

Satisfied, she nodded. "I'm Attie, by the way. I am Francesca Penrose's laboratory assistant, and we are studying Lamarckism. Who are you?"

Charlie was fully occupied with petting his new friend. "I am Charles Erasmus Darwin. I'm a genius."

"Me, too." Attie snorted. "So what? You can't throw a rock without hitting a genius around here."

Charlie smiled to himself. She was funny. He'd never met a funny genius before. Most of them were terribly stuffy and boring.

"They look hungry," she said. "I'll be right back."

She ran like a boy, too, with long skinny legs whisking rapidly through the overgrown lawn by the wall.

Charlie couldn't wait until he got tall and skinny and could run that fast, instead of plump and short and always out of breath.

The girl flew back to the rabbit yard. In one fist she clutched a handful of fresh radishes with their greens still attached. Clumps of black soil dropped from them as she shook them out.

"Here." She gave him one for the rabbit that he held. Then she distributed the rest among the hutches, although he noticed that she gave most to the cage that held Herbert.

Charlie peered at the very fresh radish that his bunny was crunching. Its bright leafy greens looked familiar. "Did you *steal* these from the vegetable garden?" he asked in horror.

She looked at him for a long moment while the black-and-white rabbit nibbled at her fingertips. "You are not the usual genius. All the ones I know are very curious and rebellious, and nothing gets in their way."

Charlie felt obscurely ashamed of his own law-abiding disposition, although at home it brought much praise.

"I am not always so obedient," he protested. "I took an

extra sweet bun yesterday, when the governess wasn't watching." It sounded silly when he said it out loud, but his heart had pounded and he'd felt rather guilty afterward.

But the wondrous red-haired girl did not laugh. She nodded. "Extra pastries are a perfectly acceptable beginning," she stated seriously. "Still, perhaps something with a bit more scope next time."

Charlie looked down at his bunny, astounded by the casual hint of incipient crime in her words.

However, he had recently come to the conclusion that he was more intelligent than most of the people he encountered, even his grandfather's cronies. With this realization, the seeds of rebellion, if not actually planted, had already been scattered upon the ground.

This Attie person's casually revolutionary nature was merely a bit of strategically applied fertilizer.

So it was not very difficult at all for Charlie to follow her into the forbidden delights of Sir Geoffrey Blayne's famous lab when she scooped up his rabbit to tuck it back into its hutch and said, "Everyone is busy. Let's go look at the laboratory!"

She was wonderful! And he thought her gangling limbs and glowing freckles were the most beautiful things he'd ever seen!

As he followed her long strides with his own short, pattering steps, it occurred to him that he liked her a lot more than he liked most people. Maybe it was because she seemed kind of like an animal to him. Or another genius.

Or maybe both.

Chapter 17

BLAYNE House and its grounds stood in the midst of other fine homes in the neighborhood of Mayfair. Orion and Judith stopped at the tobacconist's shop and then continued on. A pleasant turn around the block led strollers to a picturesque park that, while not as large as some, allowed for looping walkways through flowering beds and an appealing green lawn where stripe-gowned nurses and brown-clad governesses chased the children of their wealthy employers.

A slender governess in a typical brown gabardine dress found Orion worthy of a second glance. Or perhaps she was merely admiring Judith's fetching walking ensemble. What did he know of women? He couldn't think of a thing to say to his companion. Was he supposed to say pretty words? Make promises? Woo?

What an incredible waste of time.

Also, he hadn't the faintest notion of how to go about it.

You would if you were with Francesca.

Still, Judith seemed like a sensible person, entirely unlike the women of his family. A day out with them would be maddening, irritating, and possibly lethal. Iris would drift about, seeing mythic theater in something as mundane as the blowing of the breeze through the trees. Callie would sprawl on the grass with a sketchbook, pencils jutting from her falling hair. Elektra would be engaged in some sort of management of minions, making them march in time to the beat of drums or some such. Attie—well, Attie would likely be plotting chaos, causing chaos, or running from chaos.

Judith, however, simply walked. In a straight line, gazing straight ahead, her gloved hands clasped appropriately before her. Orion could not see her expression for her bonnet, but he imagined that it was, as always, unflappable and serene.

It occurred to Orion for the first time that whatever else his mother and sisters might be, they were never ever boring.

No. Judith wasn't boring. He mustn't think that. She was . . . soothing. Unlike certain other young ladies who rumpled a fellow's attention and ruined his concentration, Judith never rumpled, never ruined.

Never stirred. Never stimulated.

Never aroused.

Stop that.

Orion firmly decided to be soothed by the complete lack of small talk and pretty niceties. What a pleasure it was to simply walk without resenting the need to fill the perfectly acceptable silence with meaningless chatter!

It was such a pleasure that Orion caught himself in a yawn. He turned his head down as if to admire a profusion of asters along the path and clenched his jaw against the urge. *I am not bored. I am soothed, blast it!*

Judith paused the instant he slowed his pace. "They take good care of the plantings here," she commented. "They are nearly as good as those at Blayne House." This was no boast, for her tone was that of a teacher reciting facts. Moreover, it was a true statement.

"Blayne House has a very good gardener," Orion contributed.

Judith shifted slightly, as if keeping herself from turning toward him. "Papa takes very good care of his staff. They are all most loyal to him."

That last statement of fact rang oddly in Orion's ears. "And to you as well, of course."

Judith nodded without hesitation. "Of course." But her gaze was down, still focused on the asters nodding pink and spiky in the breeze. "Does your sister's book contain a botanical drawing of asters like these?"

"No. Although comprehensive in its way, it includes only wildflowers."

"Ah." Another long moment stretched. "Her work is very skilled. She must have had access to an excellent drawing master."

Orion blinked. Worthington children did not take lessons from masters of anything. Archie had taught them fencing and horsemanship, in a random fashion. Iris did not so much teach them as allow them unfettered access to all manner of paints and pencils. In all other things, they had mainly been spurred by their own interests, along with good-natured sibling rivalry, to teach themselves and surpass one another.

And books. Worthington House might be shabby and cluttered, but it had more books than any place he'd ever seen except for the palace itself. The extensive library looked more like a heavy snowfall of bound pages, piled in drifts against walls and pouring down the stairs, but Orion doubted that even Blayne House had more.

"Ah . . . my sister most likely learned from my mother, who is an avid painter."

"Her mother taught her? How . . . nice for her."

Only because he was watching, he saw Judith's gloved hands tighten around each other for a long moment. In the near silence of the open park, he could have sworn he heard threads pop.

Belatedly he remembered Sir Geoffrey's brief, offhand explanation that his wife had passed many years before. How old had Judith been when her mother went away?

After a moment, Judith eased her grip on herself, turned on her heel, and continued her measured pace without further commentary.

Orion frowned as he followed her half a step behind. Perhaps he was merely giving in to some Worthington-like imagination, but he had just had the startling impression that Miss Judith Blayne was not boring at all.

In fact, she had seemed, for a strange jarring second, decidedly mysterious.

IN THE FAMOUS Blayne laboratory, Attie and Charlie were faced with the unique problem of too many options to choose from.

"I could mix a combination of aluminum oxide and ammonia," Charlie was saying. "It makes a lovely purple smoke."

If little Charlie thought he was going to out-scientist her, he had no notion of with whom he dealt! Attie wasn't about to be one-upped by a genius half her age, or half her size, for that matter.

Attie folded her arms. "Smoke? Why make smoke when you can make fire?"

"Or I can silver-plate a copper penny . . . if there is any silver nitrate." Charlie squinted up at the high shelves of neatly labeled chemicals. "It isn't as though we need to actually make anything . . ."

Attie seized upon that idea. "Exactly. We should invent something of our own." She narrowed her eyes in speculation. "Something entirely new."

Charlie blinked at her admiringly. "Really? You can do that?"

Attie was well aware that pride was a dangerous element to add to any experiment, but the shine of admiration in little

Charlie Darwin's eyes was quite inspiring, especially as the rest of the world seemed inclined to see her as something between an oddity and a criminal.

"I don't see why not," she said airily. "After all, many great inventions were discovered when someone added the wrong thing by mistake. Why not simply make a mistake . . . on purpose?"

Charlie's pale blue eyes widened. "But . . . my grandpapa said that playing in the laboratory is dangerous. He said that no one should try anything unless they know what they are doing."

Attie could not let the idea go now. To do something new, to make even Orion widen his eyes in surprise or, dare she hope, wonder . . .

"I will select three items," she decided, calm now that her resolve was set. "One from each shelf. To ensure that my selections are random, I shall close my eyes."

The top shelves were very high. Attie would bet even Orion had to go on tiptoe to reach the glass containers, tightly lidded, some sealed to keep air from entering. The shelves were little more than a foot apart in height. They would make an admirable ladder.

Swiftly, before her own common sense managed to stop her—poor, weary common sense; she hardly knew why it bothered anymore—she clambered up the shelves to the topmost. Just as she'd promised, she closed her eyes before reaching for the farthest jar she could manage.

Clutching it tightly against her chest, Attie climbed nimbly back down to the floor. She handed the jar to Charlie without looking at it. He juggled the large jar to see the label.

"It is—"

Attie interrupted him with a single imperiously raised finger. "No, don't tell me."

She returned to the ladder of shelves and grabbed another random jar from the second-highest shelf. After repeating the procedure once more from the next-lowest shelf, she watched as little Charlie hefted the third jar onto the marble-topped laboratory table.

Attie hopped down the last few shelves and landed in a crouch. Charlie hadn't seen that adept maneuver, as he was peering at the neatly written labels and sounding out the contents aloud.

"Gyp-sum."

Hmm. Attie frowned in disappointment. Gypsum was rather inert, as chemicals went. Really just ground chalk, in fact.

The next jar Charlie read was better.

"A-qua For-tis."

Attie didn't recognize the name, but she knew her Latin. *Strong water.*

Ooh. She might be able to work with that.

The third made Charlie pause. He shook the jar, disturbing the white powder within. "Spir-its of Salt." He looked over his shoulder at her. "Does that mean it is just ordinary salt?"

He seemed disappointed. Attie took action. With a grand gesture, she fetched a large beaker from the shelf of glass receptacles. "I shall begin with the gypsum," she pronounced gravely.

Charlie rested his arms on the edge of the table and stood on tiptoe to rest his chin on them while he watched her measure out a small pile of gypsum powder on the scale. Attie wasn't sure why she should measure, but measuring was fun, and it gave her something to do while she hid her hesitation from Charlie.

Her common sense was barking like a guard dog at a band of sneak-thieves, and the loudness of it in her head made her strongly consider stopping before matters got entirely out of hand.

Then she made the scale balance perfectly with a casual

pinch of extra gypsum, and Charlie pursed his lips. "Ooh," he whispered. "You're very good."

His admiration was a balm to her self-respect. Attie shut the guard dog in the cellar and latched the door.

She slid the small pile of gypsum into the beaker and reached for the next jar, "Spirits of Salt," its contents powdered as well. She decided to measure out twice as much of it, purely for the sake of effect. That went well, and she felt that Charlie was suitably impressed. Thus distracted, she absentmindedly dumped the spirits of salt into the beaker all at once. The impact of the pile of powder sent a small cloud of dust into the air.

They both backed up, coughing and wiping their eyes.

"That seems strong," Charlie said hesitantly. "Are you sure we ought to do this?"

The guard dog was digging furiously at the locked cellar door, but Attie had come too far to back out now. Charlie wouldn't find her so impressive or clever if she did.

"Just wait," she told him with a sniff. "We are about to set modern science back on its heels."

She turned to the "Aqua Fortis" jar and tugged at its waxed cap.

AFTER LEAVING THE park, Orion and Judith turned the corner onto the square where Blayne House stood. As they approached it, Orion regarded the pristine white marble facade with a new eye.

If Judith was a model of exemplary English womanhood, then Blayne House was a matching paragon of neoclassical British architecture. Both were flawless, stylish, elegant—and housed more mysteries within than an observer might first detect.

The only difference being that Judith was—despite occasional evidence to the contrary—an entirely human woman.

She should not feel forced to be so cold, so perfect, so impenetrable. She should be laughing, or arguing, or even crying. A Worthington woman would have likely done all three in the past hour alone. Judith had done no more than clasp her hands, yet somehow she had managed to project emotion powerful enough to undo the stitches in her gloves.

Orion was beginning to wonder if in their own way, the occupants of Blayne House were not every bit as mad as those of Worthington House!

The door opened magically before them, in that otherworldly way Pennysmith had about him. In the front hall they encountered Francesca and a footman.

Francesca greeted them both with a grin, even though Judith's maid, Eva, was helping her into her outerwear.

Orion recalled that he had never seen Eva flutter about Judith, waving a dropped glove while trying to tie the dangling strings of her bonnet beneath her chin.

Orion stood with Judith and watched the beleaguered Eva attempt to dress Francesca, who was far too busy chattering on about her proposed adventure to Portobello Road.

Judith turned her measured gaze upon Orion. "She means to purchase books." Her tone merely reported a fact.

Orion supposed that from Judith's perspective, bringing anything home from a dusty London shop to join the superbly selected Blayne collection seemed rather unnecessary and wasteful of her time. However, he could not help but feel his gaze drawn to Francesca's bright eyes and flashing grin.

Her excitement was contagious. Thinking of the sight of leather bindings, full of new worlds and ancient discoveries, Orion felt an acquisitive tingle in his own fingertips. His home might split wide down the center if he tried to bring any more books into it, but that had yet to stop any Worthington from trying to wedge a few more volumes onto the bowing bookshelves within.

The temptation arose within him to offer his company on

the excursion. He pictured a madly ecstatic Francesca, armed with her canny Italian bargaining skills, turned loose upon the booksellers of Portobello Road. The result might be akin to a trip with Attie to buy sweets. Or books. Even Attie herself would be hard-pressed to choose between the two things that made life worth living.

However, it was obvious that Judith felt such a day out was a poor use of one's time. It was certain that Sir Geoffrey would hold the same view. Orion must remember that he had much to prove to the Royal Fraternity. Whiling a day away poring through jumbled shelves of shabby volumes would do nothing to further that goal.

With a tinge of regret, Orion held his tongue. When Eva breathlessly threw up her hands and backed away, Francesca appeared to be a slightly off-kilter version of Judith.

Except from the front, of course. And the rear, Orion observed as the ladies turned away. Eva turned to assist Judith in removing the outerwear she had just shoved Francesca into.

Judith's slender grace gave her twill overcoat a statuesque trace of style, while Francesca's shorter, rounder form did its best to remind the male of the species of his duty to find a mate and procreate!

Orion blinked back a sudden urge to chase after Francesca to guard her—claim her!—from any other fellow with a functioning cardiac system and at least one working eye!

That was when Erasmus Darwin hurried into the foyer. His wig was askew and his eyes worried. "Has anyone seen my little grandson, Charles? He went to play in the garden, but he isn't there any longer."

Francesca's eyes grew wide. She shot him a glance of alarm. Orion stepped quietly to her side.

"What is it?" he asked her in a low voice.

She leaned close enough for him to catch her orange-blossom scent. "I saw Attie earlier. She came in the back way to feed the rabbits for me."

Chaos followed Attie like a faithful pup. Chaos was loud and furious and easily detected.

Chaos, although disruptive, was vastly to be preferred over quiet.

They listened for a long moment.

"Damn," Orion cursed softly. "It's too quiet."

Chapter 18

ORION put one hand on the latch of the laboratory door, but instead of resisting, it swung open at once. A tingle of warning went through him. Then he heard his sister's voice. The alarm transformed into full-blown panic.

"And now I'm going to add the aqua fortis to the spirits of salt mixture—"

The two main ingredients of hydrochloric acid.

"No!" Orion flung himself into the laboratory. He saw Attie pause in shock and half turn toward the door. The little boy, Charlie, turned his head to gaze pale and openmouthed, the picture-perfect image of a child caught in the act.

Even as Orion's long legs ate up the distance between them, he could see the clear liquid trembling on the lip of the jar in Attie's hand. With her attention on his mad dash forward, she had frozen as commanded. However, that was the funny thing about gravity. It was always there when one least wished it to be.

The moment stretched, but Orion could see that he was too late, even as he flung himself at the two children. The momentum from Attie's startled turn had sent the liquid in the jar sloshing to the back. Now it sloshed forward again, forward . . . and out.

"Get down!" Even as he shouted the warning, he was there. Stretching both long arms, he caught a child in each, eliciting a yelp from Attie and a high, feminine scream from little Charlie. Spinning his body, he clutched the two genius brats close and bent his back to shield them from the—

Crack!

The crystalline shatter filled the room as the glass beaker disintegrated from the explosive heat of the sudden chemical reaction. Orion felt boiling liquid spatter over the back of his coat and upper sleeves. The heat was intense—but that was only the beginning, he knew.

He hefted both youngsters into his arms and ran from the laboratory. As he flashed through the doorway, he glimpsed a pale Francesca just outside, her back still pressed to the outer wall of the building. Her eyes widened even further when she saw him. He thrust Charlie at her, sending the boy through the air without allowing his little booted feet to touch the grass. "Check him!"

His back muscles twitched from the heat. It wouldn't be long now—but first he had to make sure Attie was all right.

With shaking hands, he ran long fingers up her bare arms and over her face and neck, tugging her hair roughly aside to search her skin. It was clear and unmarked by heat or worse.

"Orion, look!"

Orion looked down to where Attie pointed at his sleeve where the acid had splashed. The corrosive had already eaten away at the wool of his jacket. Tiny dots widened before their eyes, first showing the dark lining of the sleeve, then, as it was eaten away, the white of his shirtsleeve.

Already he could feel the heat from the chemical reaction through his next layer of clothing.

Small quick hands pulled at the back of his collar. "Quickly!"

Orion dropped his shoulders to allow the much-shorter Francesca to pull his jacket off him. Already he could feel the sting of a hundred tiny droplets on the skin of his arms.

"Attie, get help! You, too, Charlie! Run!"

Attie took off, her long skinny legs flying across the lawn. Young Charlie scooted after her, although he threw one wide-eyed glance back at Orion as he ran.

"Bloody hell!" The heat began to spread. Dimly, Orion realized that Francesca's fingers were tugging madly at his cravat. She'd already half pulled his waistcoat off.

The stinging turned to fire. The caustic had worked its way through everything he wore and now meant to eat its way through his very skin! Francesca yanked on his arm. He pulled away from her. "Don't get it on you!"

She ran around to the other side of him and began to push. "The fountain! Get in the water! It will—"

"Dilution! Yes!" He ran for the circular fountain in the center of the lawn behind the house. As he pelted the last few yards, he tugged off his cravat and pulled his shirt over his head, sending his shirt studs flying unlamented into the grass.

The flames were lancing deeper now, the tiny stings becoming red-hot welts. Soon they would be wounds!

Orion flung himself into the knee-high water of the fountain, boots and all. A second after he fell backward into the sweet, cold relief of the fountain, he heard another splash beside him.

Small cold hands began to scoop water over him, sluicing the acid from his shoulders and upper chest and neck. Orion dropped his face into the greenish water without a thought to the likely impurities and scrubbed more water into his hair.

Together, their hands colliding and entwining, scooping and sluicing, Orion and Francesca washed every inch of his upper body with the blessedly cold water of the fountain.

Francesca pushed his head back under the surface to scrub at his left earlobe, easing a burn he'd not even realized was there. He came up gasping, his heart pumping madly with the adrenaline of fear and relief.

Her hands fell away, and she stared at him.

Orion wiped water from his eyes. "What?" He twisted his neck to glance around himself. "Am I badly burned?" He didn't think so. Already the flaming pain had retreated to a throbbing sting that would be gone in a few hours.

He looked at Francesca again. Her gaze was wide and dark—and hungry. As he watched her, the tip of her tongue slipped along the seam of her lips.

"You—"

Francesca swallowed back the tightness in her throat. "You are *magnifico*!" Her voice was a strained whisper. She hardly recognized it as her own.

Dio, he was gorgeous!

The pearly sunlight gleamed on his wet skin, highlighting the corded muscles wrapping his broad shoulders and winding down his bare arms. The sprinkling of dark hair on his chest sparkled with diamond droplets. She followed the path of the water as it ran down between his thick pectorals, joining other drops to stream between the ridges of his abdominal muscles, following the trail of dark hair down to the soaked, sagging waist of his trousers that hung on his narrow hips.

"Come delicioso . . ." She heard her voice again. Had she said that aloud? She certainly hadn't meant to, and she had no doubt that she would blush heartily later, but at that moment she could hardly bring herself to care.

He stepped toward her through the knee-high water. "Chessa—"

At hearing her family nickname, she jerked her gaze upward in surprise. His blue eyes had gone black with desire as he stalked intently toward her.

His skin would be cool and damp to her touch, she knew. Her fingers flexed at the memory of touching him just moments ago. In her hurry to help him, she'd only thought to cleanse the caustic away. However, now she remembered the sensation of running her bare hands over his naked skin, stroking her palms down his hot flesh . . .

I want him.

He wanted her as well. By the set of his shoulders and the hunting intensity of his lowered head, she knew the wolf was on her trail. Like trapped prey, she could not look away from the desire in his gaze. She didn't want to look away. She didn't want to flee her fate at his hands.

All thought of what might be considered wise or prudent or even simply harmless had been washed away by the water running down his astonishing body.

He came so close that droplets falling from his damp curls fell upon her bosom, shockingly cold on her desperately heated flesh.

"Chessa," he murmured. "Your hands."

Dazed by his nearness, she lifted her hands and gazed down at the tiny white blisters forming on her fingers and palms. They matched the spots on his skin.

His deep voice took on a tenderness she'd never heard before. "Look what you did to yourself . . . for me." He lifted his hands as if to take her by the shoulders and pull her close.

Her eyelids drifted closed in surrender as his intensity overwhelmed her. Her own hunger throbbed between her thighs, the drumbeat of her pulse like running feet. Was she fleeing—or was she the hunter? She wanted him to take her. She wanted to take him.

She ached.

O Dio, how I want him! She leaned forward, pulled as if by a force larger than herself. *Touch me. Take me.*

Love m—

"Mr. Worthington! Are you all right?"

A simultaneous reflex pulled them apart, first one step, then two, just as Judith came around the hedge with Pennysmith and two footmen carrying blankets.

Orion turned his shoulder to Francesca and faced Judith. "Yes, Miss Blayne. I believe Miss Penrose and I have removed the worst of the acid."

Francesca turned away and busied herself by gathering up her soaked skirts. She lifted them enough to step across the bowl of the fountain to the lip, where she allowed one of the footmen to aid her escape—er, ladylike exit.

"Oh, Cousin, you must be chilled to the bone! You're shaking!" Judith rounded the fountain and wrapped one of the blankets around Francesca. "And that water is none too clean. Pennysmith, have baths drawn for both Miss Penrose and Mr. Worthington. Cool, not hot! And bring a bit of ice from the cellar."

Alas, though bathing with Mr. Worthington sounded like a fine idea, that was not Judith's intention for her cousin.

Moments later, Francesca found herself in her chamber before the fire, at the mercy of Eva, who stripped her in a businesslike fashion and thrust her into the deep copper tub, carefully scrubbing her down with cold, soapy water and a fluffy washing cloth.

Unfortunately, nothing could cool the heat still simmering in her blood.

When she had decided to never marry, Francesca had disdained any thought of missing out on physical intimacy with a husband. If one did not plan on having children, then what was the point of such laborious activity? She'd been smug in her secure knowledge that she would have much more time to pursue her own interests without a man and his progeny to look after!

She'd thought herself immune to flirting and sighs and, most of all, to thrilled girlish discussions of boys and men and what was to come when she was a wife.

She still didn't wish to marry. She didn't. This mad, animal yearning for Orion Worthington was nothing more than—than a single mating season!

Mating season. Secured in a thick wrapper and forced into a chair by the fire, although she still burned from within, Francesca pondered the notion of the mating season.

Every spring, all over the world, animals and birds and even reptiles sought out a member of the opposite gender. It was the biological imperative at work, pulling all creatures away from hunting and eating and sleeping just to roll around with a mate for a little while.

There were several creatures that mated for life. Swans. Wolves. Even some classes of fish.

Humans were not considered to be one of them, biologically speaking.

So . . . what if she was merely interested in one such season?

Or, to be more specific, one such night?

Chapter 19

THOUGH the day had offered much in terms of dramatic excitement, by evening Orion hadn't spent a single moment focused on his only responsibility at Blayne House—Sir Geoffrey's research. Determined that the day should not be utterly devoid of serious inquiry, Orion decided to review his notes from the previous day and put his thoughts in order so that he might start fresh in the morning. Unfortunately, Sir Geoffrey was in possession of Orion's most recent notations, and it was too late to disturb an elderly man, especially one of such unpredictable temper. Orion decided to retrieve the notes for himself.

As much as he tended to distance himself from his family's eccentricities, Orion had to admit there were benefits to growing up a Worthington, including the development of certain skills outside the norms of gentle Society. So it was that he set the candle near his feet, slipped a pick and lever from his trouser pocket, and began to carefully open the lock to Sir Geoffrey's study. The latch gave way, and he let himself in, sure that it was a quick and harmless errand. Besides, with all the chaos of the day, no one in the Blayne household would notice or even care if he had fetched his own notes in the middle of the night.

One story above, Francesca was on a mission of her own. She moved with stealth through the pitch-black house, holding her skirts so they would not brush against the floor as she rushed breathlessly toward Mr. Worthington's bedroom, and toward her own sensual liberation. Oh, it was scandalous indeed to succumb to desire! But after wrestling with her own mind for several hours, she realized she had no choice—social standards were arbitrary creations of civilization, but biological imperative was the force of creation itself. Who was she to deny nature? Why would she even want to?

Of course, there would be consequences. She would betray Judith the moment she offered herself to Orion Worthington, and for that she felt a twinge of guilt. But only a twinge. She did not want to hurt Judith, who had always been kind, if a bit distant. But Francesca had observed with interest how passively her cousin accepted Mr. Worthington as a suitor. There was no passion in the dance of their courtship. In fact, Judith seemed to have simply surrendered to her fate, caught in the matrimonial net and pinned onto Orion Worthington's future like a butterfly in a collection, powerless to extract herself.

That was how Francesca knew that pursuing her own desires would not hurt Judith, because Judith's true yearnings, though cloaked, must surely reside elsewhere. Perhaps one day Judith would reveal the true yearnings of her heart—or the truth about anything at all.

Just as she passed the top of the stairs, Francesca's ears pricked and her eyes darted toward movement. In the dimness, she caught sight of a tall and broad male figure opening the door to her uncle's study. She pressed a hand to her mouth to suppress a gasp—it was Orion himself! What in the world was he up to? Sir Geoffrey's study was off-limits. Curious indeed!

Silently she slipped down the staircase and through the hall, reaching the study just as Orion eased himself inside. Francesca pushed against the door when Orion tried to close it.

"Hello," she said.

Orion jumped, his spine stiffening as his eyes narrowed in the dark. "What in heaven's name are you doing here?" he hissed.

Francesca smiled at his face shadowed in candlelight. "One might ask you the very same question, Mr. Worthington."

"Shh. Come. Hurry." Orion grabbed her by the elbow, glanced quickly up and down the hallway, and drew her into the confines of the dark study.

Now what? Francesca froze, her back to the wall. The two stood awkwardly close, their rapid breathing the only detectable sound in the room. They were truly alone. In a room lit only by a single candle and a shaft of moonlight. And in close proximity. The intimacy of it was overwhelming to Francesca, and she felt her heart bang away under her ribs.

But wasn't this what she came looking for?

"I was merely retrieving my research notes," Orion said, his voice overly formal. "In all the bedlam today, I forgot to ask Sir Geoffrey to return them to me."

Francesca let the back of her head touch the wall behind her, trying to slow her pulse and breath.

Orion tilted his handsome head, his frown deepening and his eyes straying from Francesca's face, down to her bosom, and up again. He seemed agitated. Could it be that he had struggled with his desires the same as she had today?

"Orion—"

"I only wanted to review my work so that I could be prepared to start again in the morning. I—"

"I don't give a fig about your notes, Mr. Worthington!" Francesca straightened, calling forth every bit of courage she possessed. Oh, how she hoped this was not pure folly! "I sought you out this evening to . . . to offer you a proposition."

His confused scowl and the way he absently passed a hand through his mussed-up hair caused her to smile. Still, icy butterflies fluttered madly in her belly at the thought of what she was about to say. She clasped her hands tightly before her.

"I propose that we see it through, sir."

He seemed fascinated by the pulse pounding in her throat. "See what through, Miss Penrose?"

She lifted her hand and allowed it to do something it had longed to do. Her fingers trembled as she trailed them through his disheveled hair, then let them drift to caress the point of his chiseled cheekbone. "This," she said simply.

His eyes widened. His fisted hands opened. For an instant, she thought he might step closer and reach for her. *Oh yes. Please.*

Then he seemed to shake off his first inclination. He drew back. "We should not even be having this conversation. We should not be in this room, in the dark, alone. You know perfectly well that I am expected to court Judith. She is an excellent match."

Francesca laughed at him. "Oh, Mr. Worthington! I don't want to marry you." She shook her head, still laughing. "Can you imagine it? We'd kill each other within a year!"

He frowned again, seemingly miffed at the notion that she might not want to marry him. She'd been too frank. Goodness, men were sensitive!

"I mean to say," she began again more carefully, "that I do not ever intend to marry. That sort of imprisonment does not interest me. I wish to spend my life on my work, not on my husband!"

His brow eased. "I don't see what husbands have to do with it. My mother wants to paint, so she paints. All day long if she likes."

Francesca nodded. "That is how it was in my family as well. Many of my female relatives pursue their own careers— but those who do rarely marry." She sighed. "And marriage seems like such a bother, don't you think? Always asking, 'What do you think, dear?' and 'Won't you take me dancing, dear?'" She nodded. "If I wish to dance, I shall dance." *And if I wish to take a lover, I shall take a lover.*

Orion eased forward to better examine this strange specimen of a female more closely. He could not disagree with her reasoning. He himself would not be interested in marriage if it were not beneficial to his scientific career. And if it could cost him that career? Then hell no!

So, she meant to become one of those bluestocking women who never wed. Orion was well acquainted with the sort. His own aunts, Clemmie and Poppy, had never wed. The two old birds tramped freely about England, accountable to no one, looking at the gardens of great houses and raising obnoxious little dogs that Clemmie was prone to carrying about in her loose, drooping bodice.

In his imagination, he pictured lovely Francesca out on safari, studying the biology of Africa and counting lion toes. It made him smile inwardly. And why shouldn't she? If he were a lion and such a bossy, dark-eyed vixen of a biologist wanted to count his toes, he would allow it!

She was watching him carefully. "That doesn't shock you?" she asked.

He shrugged. "I can't think why it would. You have a very fine mind. It would be a shame to waste it on running a house if you don't care to."

She blinked. "Oh. Thank you. I thought I was 'frivolous and scattered.'"

"You are. You are all of the above, Miss Penrose. Intelligent, talented, scattered, and occasionally frivolous." *And much more. Beautiful. Fascinating. Extraordinary.*

She thought about that for a long moment. Then she grinned at him. "I believe I find that appraisal acceptable."

Orion did smile then. She was so endearing—in the way that hedgehogs were endearing, yet also difficult to handle and prone to jabbing a fellow when he least expected it.

"Now," he said, attempting to steer the conversation back to a more linear path. "Explain 'see it through.'"

Her grin faded as she swallowed hard. "I—" She cleared her throat.

Orion considered her with some surprise. Was the brash, indomitable Francesca Penrose *nervous*?

She took a breath. "We do not like each other, but you must admit that our attraction is undeniable. What is needed is full combustion—the opportunity to burn through our sexual attraction and be done with it." She lifted her chin. "I think we should become lovers."

Oh yes. God yes.

She inhaled again, then hurried on. "I propose a single night. We are spending far too much of our valuable time wondering about each other. It is much more efficient to light the flame than simply let it smolder." She held up a single finger. "One night to explore and eradicate this unwanted distraction, to do whatever is necessary to turn our burning desires into ash."

Yes, please.

He didn't say it out loud, thank goodness. Instead, he managed to simply stare at her. His jaw dropped, but he was fairly certain he did not drool.

He hoped.

Then he found himself clearing his own throat nervously. "I—" *Oh, shut up, man, and take her up on it!* "I do not think that would be appropriate."

She looked down at her hands. "Because you mean to wed someone else? Are you saving yourself for marriage, then? What a lovely bride you will make some lucky fellow."

He couldn't read her expression, but he could hear it in her voice. She was laughing at him again!

He wasn't about to tell her that she wasn't far from the truth. His virginity had never been much of a problem for him before, but now the idea that he might actually need to confess such a thing to her—

Ah. Just the argument. "I cannot in good conscience take your virtue, Miss Penrose. While you do not wish to wed at this time, you may change your mind—"

She looked up then. "No, I won't. I really, truly won't."

He continued virtuously. "And I would not wish to be the cause of costing you that option."

"That is no one's affair but mine."

He held up a hand. "Your lack of virtue would become my affair, if we—" *Affair.* Oh God, he really, truly wanted to be her lover! "If we took a step down that road."

She looked at him then, with her head tilted and her eyes narrowed. "Hmm. Define virtue, if you please."

Chapter 20

DEFINE virtue? This was not a question that life had ever posed to Orion. He floundered somewhat. "What?"

Francesca blinked at him innocently. "It is you who are setting the rules. I am simply asking for clarification of the parameters."

He blinked. "Well . . . ah . . ." Warning bells began to go off in the dim recesses of his mind—bells he suspected had been ringing in male minds since the dawn of time.

She stepped forward and took his hand in hers, lacing her small fingers into his. "Some people consider the touching of bare palms between a man and a maiden to impinge upon her virtue. Am I now compromised, because we took off our gloves? If so, then we might as well take off our clothes."

Take your hand back. Take it back and step away and—

Her small cool hand felt remarkably good in his. He could not help but tighten his fingers around her softer ones. Her gaze rose to meet his.

"I do not think you irrevocably compromised because we hold hands." Was that his voice, gone husky and low?

The ancient male warning system threw up its hands and turned its back on him, leaving him to fight this battle on his own.

Good.

Francesca's eyes were wide and dark, so deep brown that he thought he might fall into her soul and never want to escape. She lifted their joined hands and moved in close, as if they were dancing. With another single step, she pressed her bosom to his chest.

"Some might say that waltzing so close as this would besmirch a young lady's reputation." She inhaled deeply, and Orion could not help but match her breath for breath. The sweet orange-blossom scent of her surrounded him, invaded him, fogging his mind further.

She went on. "Am I no longer marriageable, Mr. Worthington, because we danced?"

He cleared his throat against the tightness in it. "I will not tell if you do not tell."

Her smile flirted with the corners of her mouth, but her gaze remained deeply serious as she pressed her other palm to the front of his waistcoat, over his heart. After a breath, she began to slide her hand up his chest until he felt her warm palm pass his high collar and rest upon the back of his neck as her fingertips slipped into his hair. Shivers of hot and cold emanated from that small contact.

Then she went up on her tiptoes and slowly, carefully pressed her lips to his. The kiss was warm and soft and really quite chaste—but her lips lingered just a second too long. That tiny increment of time was long enough to tempt, to tease, to promise so much more.

When she went back down on her heels, his mouth tried to follow hers, just to cling for a little longer to the tender sweetness of her lips. She drew back. "There," she said calmly, although her voice squeaked slightly and rosy color flushed her cheeks, so he knew she was not completely unaffected. "I have kissed a man on the mouth. Am I not done for, in Society's eyes?"

He wanted to kiss her again.

He wanted to kiss her forever. And when forever was done, he wanted the rest of her, too.

She was still gazing at him. "Well?" she prompted. "Am I not most thoroughly sullied?"

"I . . . It isn't what I think that matters. It is what Society thinks."

Her brows drew together in disbelief. "Pish and tosh. You don't care one fig what Society thinks, and you know it!"

That was true. He really didn't care—except for the opinion of the scientific community. He didn't think the upright members of the Royal Fraternity of Life Sciences would think highly of a member who went about despoiling virgins.

"I will not tell if you do not tell," he had told her.

He wanted to brush her hair back from her face. What was the name for this compulsion? The cause?

The effect?

Without conscious command, his hand rose. He watched his fingers catch the wayward strand and gently stroke it behind her ear.

The effect was immediate. Her dark gaze snapped to capture his, and her breath caught. He felt the jolt that coursed through her as if an electrical current had bolted through him as well.

"Your eyes . . ." Was that his voice? "I go to sleep at night thinking about your eyes." *God, you sound like a fool!*

Amusement flashed in the sable brown of those eyes. "I fear it is some other part of your anatomy that I go to sleep thinking about."

She was laughing at him again. He found he did not mind. She laughed as others breathed. Joy was her air.

I am such an idiot.

"You make me feel like a fool," he admitted out loud. "You would not credit the nonsense that erupts in my mind when I think about you."

Her eyes narrowed playfully. "If you tell me that I smell of alpine air, or that my skin feels like silk woven through ivory, I shall laugh in your face. That is simply a warning."

Her skin. His hand still lingered at her ear. He let the side of his thumb graze her cheek from her temple to her jaw. "Your skin feels like . . . you. Warm and full of life, delicate and vulnerable."

She blinked. He saw her brow crease. "I don't think 'delicate' applies," she corrected him. "Have you not noted my figure? I am anything but insubstantial. My uncle thinks I am too fond of second helpings."

God, how he wanted second helpings of her! "I stand corrected. My error, I fear, for I have never, not for one moment, taken note of the substantial nature of your figure."

Her eyes widened. "Mr. Worthington, I hesitate to inform you—for I know you shall be as shocked as I—but I believe you just made a jest!"

Orion did not protest the ridiculous accusation. He was too busy tilting his head to watch his fingertips trace down behind her ear, following the exquisite skin of her neck to the hollow of her collarbone. "From the underlying skeletal structure, I believe that you are indeed quite delicately formed, Miss Penrose."

She swallowed hard. "Er—"

He followed the shape of her clavicle out to her shoulder, his fingertips slipping the impractical little cap sleeve of her gown out of his way without hesitation. "You see here, the distance is long, compared to the diameter of the bone, which implies that your skeletal frame is indeed delicate. I daresay even on the fragile side."

Her breath had quickened. "Oh . . . my."

A sudden rattle at the door sent a wash of cold alarm through Orion. Fortunately, Francesca's reaction time was even faster than his own. In a swish of skirts and a yank on his hand, she pulled them both behind the draperies that had been drawn over the moonlit windows. Orion blew out the candle in his hand on the way.

With her back pressed to his front, Orion could see easily over her head. Through the slight parting of the draperies, probably due to their hasty entry into the window embrasure, he could see the study clearly as Sir Geoffrey entered with a candlestick of his own in hand. The wavering light of his single flame cast unflattering shadows over the man's face.

When had Sir Geoffrey begun to look so old? Orion thought back to that morning, when his mentor had seemed suddenly frail on the stairs. It had not taken long for him to liven up again, so Orion had put it out of his mind.

Now, however, Orion could see the deep lines of age and something else—illness?—in Sir Geoffrey's noble features. The hand that held the candlestick shook with a constant tremor.

Sir Geoffrey seemed not to see the disarray on his desk. He moved directly to the cupboard standing behind it. With his free hand, he pulled his watch fob from his pocket. On the end, along with the medal of the Royal Fraternity of Life Sciences, dangled a tiny key.

The key fit into the lock on the cupboard after several tries. Sir Geoffrey's tremor seemed to be worsening by the minute.

When the cabinet doors were opened, Orion saw a tiny laboratory within. There was a beaker stand, along with several of the flame bowls, stacked and ready to use. A number of bottles and flasks filled the highest shelf, but their neatly printed labels were too small for Orion to read from this distance.

Francesca tugged on his coat sleeve. When their eyes met, he saw his own questions reflected in her gaze. A small divot appeared on her forehead. What was Sir Geoffrey doing? Why did he have a private laboratory? And what was in those jars?

Orion shook his head at Francesca. He had no answers.

Neither of them could see what Sir Geoffrey did with the contents of the cupboard. The man's imposing figure hid his activity.

Francesca tilted her head to see better through the slit in the draperies, and Orion suddenly became entirely aware of Francesca's body pressed to his. He ducked his head slightly until her untamed curls tickled his chin and cheek. Inhaling her deeply, he allowed the spicy, citrusy scent of her to take over his mind.

His thoughts slowed. The carefully defended machine of his concentration ceased the constant turning of its mental gears. All went quiet within him as he felt the heat of her curvaceous body melt into his skin. He rubbed his cheek slowly against the warm silk of her hair, and breathed, and wanted.

Chapter 21

ORION opened his palm over her shoulder even as he slid his other hand around her waist in order to turn her body slightly perpendicular to his own. Her warm skin filled his hand so enjoyably that he continued down her arm until the sleeve would push no farther without drawing down her bodice as well.

Ah.

Yes. Indeed.

His other hand tightened involuntarily upon her waist as he wrapped his fingers around the little sleeve and pulled quite relentlessly. The bodice of her gown peeled away in a very satisfactory fashion, revealing a low-cut chemise of supremely fine lawn. Her golden-tinged skin glowed through the tissue-thin fabric. Her erect nipple might as well have been entirely revealed, for the chemise was defeated entirely by the fullness of her breast and the excited rigidity of that delightful point.

Fully aware that he was being entirely improper, Orion chanced a look at Francesca's expression. He wanted her, but he would never distress her with his desire if it was unwelcome.

Her eyes were closed, her full, insanely long lashes at rest upon her creamy cheeks. Her full pink lips were parted softly, as if she'd been interrupted before she could speak. As he gazed down at something rarely seen—a still Francesca!—she allowed her head to fall back slowly in capitulation.

He might not be terribly experienced, but no man had yet been born who did not recognize sexual surrender when he saw it!

Yet he did not immediately rejoin his quest after her breast. For a single long moment, he merely drank in the new and different beauty of her quiescence. How lovely she was, in every way. From the rich luster of her wild dark curls to the rather unexpected sprinkle of freckles upon her nose, she answered every notion he held of desirable femininity—even those he'd never known he had. How could he predict the effect of a teasing grin upon his attention? Or the way her slightly lilted accents would musically please his ear? Or that her scampering energy would lift and regenerate his spirits?

And this. This breathless surrender in his arms? He felt as though something new shone in the world, something that cast brighter lights and darker shadows. New definition sharpened his vision; new heat entered his blood. The way she felt against him—so pliant, so giving, so . . . trusting.

A chill spiral wound through him. She trusted him.

She ought not to. He was not at all convinced that he was a terribly honorable sort of person. He tended more toward the pragmatic approach, and to hell with rules or expectations.

That was as it should be. A scientist who would not sacrifice whatever necessary in the pursuit of knowledge was a poseur and a dilettante.

Yet he found himself sliding that ineffective little sleeve back up her arm, covering that enticing breast, hiding that unbearably delicious nipple behind the sturdy weave of propriety and honor after all.

When he turned her toward him, supporting her relaxed neck with his hand, she blinked her eyes open in confusion. Her dark gaze was confused.

"Why did you stop?" she whispered. "Did you not like what you saw? I happen to know that I have superior breasts. All the women in my family do."

Orion found himself oddly without words. What should he say? Don't trust me? Don't want me the way that I want you?

Stay away?

He didn't want to say those things. So instead, he slid his hand from where it wrapped about the warm skin of her neck, regretfully enjoying the silk of her hair against his skin, and dropped it to his side.

"Is it my unruly hair?"

Orion opened his mouth to respond to her absurd insecurity just as they heard Sir Geoffrey exit the small laboratory and lock its doors. They went still and silent, watching from behind the draperies as the elderly man shuffled across the room. Orion noticed how, though his mentor's hands no longer shook, his face had gone slack and his posture had loosened, almost as if he were inebriated.

Once the study door was shut and locked, Orion and Francesca found themselves pressed together, faces inches apart, with a new awkwardness between them. Her lovely brown eyes searched his face, but Orion had no answer to give. He gently separated himself from her and opened the drapes.

"I don't understand," Francesca said, her voice unsteady.

God, how he wanted her. He wanted her so badly, he ached. But the heat of the moment had passed, and there he was, making the honorable choice. It was for Francesca's benefit, was it not?

"Francesca, you are lovely. But this is not proper behavior for a lady. I feel it is my duty to protect you from a poor decision."

She laughed at him. "You care nothing of propriety and you know it! You kneel at the altar of science, not Society!"

It sounded silly even to his own ears. It wasn't that he was especially defiant of convention—he simply didn't see that it should apply to him. Rules were for people who could not or would not think for themselves.

He slid the tip of his tongue over his bottom lip, tasting her there. This beautiful, exotic creature was throwing herself at him, begging him to deliver a good and proper despoiling . . . and he was going to refuse her.

I can't believe I'm going to refuse her.

He could tell himself it was the honorable choice, but he knew better. The cost was too high. His future career aside, the logical man he had so carefully cultivated could not allow himself to be swayed by anything so irrational, so impetuous. He was *not* one of those impulsive, unrestrained Worthingtons!

This woman was everything he'd fought so hard to escape. She drew him like a force of nature, but he panicked at the whirling chaos of his desire for her.

It had nothing to do with honor. He was motivated by bald-faced fear, and he wasn't strong enough to battle it back.

He eased away from Francesca one step, then two. It was by far the hardest thing he'd ever done. When safely out of reach of her warm hands and sweet lips and full, inviting body, he bobbed an awkward bow. "As flattering as I find your offer, Miss Penrose, I fear I—I require time to ponder your proposal."

Francesca couldn't believe it. He truly meant to walk away? From her place behind the draperies, she watched the handsome Orion Worthington turn his back on her and disappear into the dark hallway.

She raised her hand to her hair. *It is this damned English damp. I know it is! I must look like Medusa!*

* * *

"No, I'll take care of any little mess," Judith informed Pennysmith smoothly. "You know how particular Sir Geoffrey is about his laboratory."

Pennysmith nodded with his usual minimal respect and turned away. Judith knew that the man was thinking he'd be delighted to point at Judith, were there any later protests of disorder.

Pennysmith was a bit of an ass.

Just to prove that there was nothing in the laboratory worth worrying about, Judith made sure she was seen walking to the outbuilding in the morning sunlight with nothing but a handful of cleaning cloths. *Yes, that's right. I'm simply heading out for a little meditative dusting and sorting.*

Once inside the lab, she locked the door behind her.

She'd taken a deep breath before entering. Now, holding it, she picked up her skirts and ran to open every window in the lab. By the time she'd finished, the acrid air was clearing enough that she felt able to face the chaos.

It was as if an ape and an elephant had fought for their lives in the middle of the laboratory. Shattered glass crunched beneath her feet. The acid had sprayed over a large area. Luckily, most of what it had struck had been the stone floor and the marble tabletops. The acid would have eaten through wood with no problem. The stone was merely scarred and pitted, although in some areas quite deeply.

It looked to be a very long night of sanding and scraping the tables and floor.

For the merest moment, Judith allowed her shoulders to sag in weary defeat. There was no one to see her eyes close upon incipient tears. There was no one to hear the long sigh she let slip through her lips.

After approximately thirty seconds of such self-indulgence, Judith straightened her spine and lifted her chin. "No time to sit in a corner and cry," she murmured to herself.

She could have enlisted the help of the staff, but none of them would dare keep a secret from their master. Life in Blayne House would become even more unbearable if Sir Geoffrey ever realized the full truth of what the children had done to his laboratory.

Sweeping up the millions of tiny shards of glass was the easy part.

In a cupboard tucked back behind the shelves of chemicals, Judith kept her true cleaning things. This was hardly the first time she'd had to erase a disaster. Thankfully, Papa rarely worked in the laboratory himself anymore. He'd never said a word to her, but she knew he no longer felt truly able.

Usually, his laboratory assistants were more tidy—but nothing had truly been tidy since Cousin Francesca had arrived.

As Judith tied a voluminous canvas apron over her gown and gathered up the scrubbing sand and brushes for the stone surfaces, she allowed herself a moment of uncharitable resentment toward Francesca. Before her lively cousin had arrived, Judith had managed to firmly lock away the spirited girl she had once been. There had been no time for frivolity since Mama passed.

Judith had once loved to draw and paint and read silly novels, like most girls. That seemed a hundred years ago. Now her life was lived for Papa, who was an exacting taskmaster. Her duties as his housekeeper and hostess and laboratory assistant and general minion required Judith's fullest attention.

And now the pitted tabletop did as well. Judith put on a pair of leather gloves and set about restoring the high polish with sand and a sanding stone. The gritty work took strength and stamina. There was no point in wasting another moment on what might have been.

WHENEVER ORION REACHED an impasse in his scientific pursuits and was torn as to which way to turn, it simply meant he did not have enough information to make a decision. Additional research was required. So it was with the Francesca dilemma. After spending the entire day in silent debate with himself—while he was supposed to be moving on to the next stage of the experiment—he had decided enough was enough.

Dithering was foreign to his nature, and he had had his fill. Besides, if he stepped back and informed himself further, he would not be acting impulsively, would he? He had clearly reached the limit of his knowledge of the science of coitus and needed additional information before he proceeded. And where did one go to research romantic liaisons? Why, to an expert, of course!

His restlessness compelled him to walk, rather than call forth Sir Geoffrey's driver. There was no reason for his mentor to know of this business.

It was an uninviting evening. A chill rose from the direction of the Thames, and the London streets already grew dusky, in spite of the long days of early summer.

Not that there was anything particularly outré about his destination. Just a visit to an old friend.

In deciding upon the best course of action regarding the distracting Miss Francesca Penrose, Orion didn't want to involve his family, but there was someone who would not judge such an unconventional solution—family friend and gown designer Lementeur, fondly known as Mr. Button. Button had a long history of putting lovers together. Iris said it was because he favored making wedding gowns over any other sort.

There was no sign above Lementeur's establishment, no address or advertising needed. If one didn't know where he was, one couldn't afford him, anyway.

Once he was past the ornately carved door, Lementeur's boutique seemed far too quiet. Not that the unearthly Cabot had been a noisy sort—he had always just been there, as Button's guardian, companion, and creative sounding board.

Orion found Button holed up in his tiny cluttered office.

He looked rather small, sitting tailor-fashion in the center of the floor, surrounded by more mess than seemed usual.

By the look of things, a golden bomb had exploded. Shimmering gold silk fabric was heaped here and there, ethereal gold chiffon ribbon unspooled across Button's lap, while over one shoulder dangled strings of pearls with a secretive golden flush.

The mess reminded Orion rather startlingly of Francesca, of the shimmer of summer sunlight in her brown eyes and the kiss of Mediterranean glow upon her skin.

"What ho, Button?"

Button looked up and blinked at Orion. For a moment his shadowed gaze looked confused, as if he had been a hundred miles away. Then his weary face crinkled in a welcoming smile.

Just as quickly, he frowned, squinting at Orion's brown coat. "Why are you wearing that old thing? What happened to the marvelous blue one I made up for your new position at Blayne House?"

It had been a very nice surcoat, but then, Button always saw to it that the Worthingtons made a dashing sight despite their impoverishment. He called it advertising. Archie and Iris seemed to consider it a perfectly fair arrangement, although their children did not know precisely why.

Orion made a slight face. "Two words. 'Acid' and 'Attie.'" He turned his head to one side and tugged his loosely tied cravat down a bit to show the minor burns on his neck. "We made it out alive. Your coat saved me, as you can see."

Button blinked. "Then it died an honorable death." He let out a sigh. "You Worthingtons do run through your garments." However, the twinkle in his eyes belied his criticism. "Lives lived livelier, I suppose."

Orion didn't bother denying that he was anything like the rest of his clan. Not when he was here to beg advice on something decidedly against the grain of Society. "I have a problem." He took a deep breath. "I want a woman."

Button listened to Orion's case, both for and against an affair with Miss Penrose. His pale blue eyes were wide but entirely without condemnation.

When Orion realized that he was nattering on about Francesca's astonishing voice, he forced himself to silence. He waited for a long moment, but Button made no commentary whatsoever.

"Well, what do you think I should do?"

Button raised a kindly brow. "Do you want me to tell you if I think you should be wise, or unwise?"

"Well . . . yes."

Button smiled sadly. "But which is which?"

Orion opened his mouth, then realized that he himself wasn't sure. Society would surely call the proposed night of sexual gratification unwise—but Orion didn't care what Society said. In another interpretation, continuing to let their work suffer while they physically pined for each other might be the unwise choice.

Orion's head began to spin. He shook it to clear his spiraling thoughts. "What would you do? What decision would you make, if you wanted someone so badly that you couldn't think of anything else?"

Button blinked. "I—" He went rather unaccountably pale, but Orion rushed on, his thoughts coming almost too fast to speak them.

"What if there is no such thing as right or wrong here? *Is* something actually wrong, if there are no consequences due? If two sane, adult people want something that harms no one, that serves them and them alone, then . . ." He spread his hands, suddenly out of words.

Button sat very still, staring at some point just over Orion's left shoulder. "Then why not?" The words were the merest whisper, a breath of speech that would not have been audible had the shop not been so silent.

Yes.

Orion nodded sharply. Then he turned on his heel and

strode down the hall, out of the shop, and back down the damp cobbled street—

To Francesca.

So focused was he on his destination that he did not hear Button's breathless protest. "No, Orion! Wait—"

Chapter 22

ORION left Lementeur's, intent upon his new purpose. He would fulfill his distracting desire for the sumptuous Francesca, and by doing so, would reorient his attention to his work, and his future career. It was an excellent plan, and *not* an impulsive decision.

Francesca.

His pulse rate increased even as his pace lengthened. His long-legged stride made good time, but not fast enough to avoid the equally long legs of the young man who chased him down on the street outside the shop. Orion blinked at the sound of his name. "Oh, Cabot." Then he made to brush past him. "I haven't time to talk—"

"Wait." Cabot stepped in front of Orion again. Orion drew back. Cabot was never so tasteless. Ever.

He looked more closely at the younger man. Not that Cabot was all that much younger. Probably twenty-seven or thereabouts. From what Orion had learned of Cabot's background as an orphan and street thief, he wondered if Cabot himself knew his age. He was certainly no child, no matter what Button might think.

No child ever had eyes like Cabot's, cool, distant gray eyes that sometimes betrayed the pain of his early years.

Like now. After looking more closely, Orion saw the same signs of tension he'd seen on Button's face.

Belatedly, it occurred to Orion that some people might have larger problems than his own unconsummated lust for Miss Francesca Penrose.

"Er, Cabot . . . I say," he finished lamely. Emotions had never been his territory. Give him a good old chemical reaction any day. Like aqua fortis and spirits of salt. Simple, clear, and easily explained.

Button and Cabot were the stuff of plays, or opera. They were something taut and fraught and truly out of Orion's purview . . .

Still, he could not help but put a sympathetic hand on the other man's shoulder. "How can I help?"

Cabot's shoulder felt like an overwound spring. He'd always been a distant, cool sort of person—although ever ready to help when needed. He'd saved Orion's sister Callie when Attie had accidentally put a bullet hole in her. The family owed Cabot a great deal.

Cabot shot a glance back at Lementeur's shop. "He hasn't been out of there in days."

Orion blinked. "Have you been waiting out here?"

Cabot shook his head. "No. The Prince Regent keeps me far too busy for that. I—I have my sources. But you just saw him. Tell me—"

Orion frowned. "Tell you what?"

Cabot shrugged helplessly. "Anything. Everything. Is he eating? Is he sleeping? He'll stay up all night, working, if no one is there to mind him. And I doubt that his housekeeper even knows what kind of tea he likes . . . It is hard to get him to eat. He's like a child sometimes . . ."

Orion tried not to take a step back from Cabot's outpouring of worry. They had all known that Cabot looked after Button, but this did rather explain the messy state of things, and Button's weariness, and the circles beneath his eyes. The ones that matched Cabot's own set.

"He's all right," Orion said carefully. "Working away in there. I suppose things could be a bit neater, but I don't think he's going to starve himself." Then, because Cabot looked so desperate, he said, "I think he misses you." And because it was true, he added, "We all miss you. Attie especially."

Cabot shook his head. "Oh, I see Attie all the time. She visits me at work."

Orion blinked. "Attie just strolls into the *palace*?"

Cabot's lips quirked. "Attie goes where Attie goes. It's rather like trying to keep a cat out . . . or in."

Orion shuddered. "Just . . . don't let anyone behead her."

But Cabot had forgotten Attie already. His gaze had been drawn magnetically back to the fancifully carved door. "Do you really think he's all right in there?"

Orion shook his head and left him there, hurrying back to Blayne House through the spreading darkness. Cabot and Button might find themselves torn, but Orion knew precisely what he wanted!

FRANCESCA DABBED HER forearm across her heat-dampened brow. The kitchen had become quite stuffy after she spent the entire evening baking a dozen poppy-seed cakes, and she felt sticky, but she could not use her hands quite yet.

With fingers well smeared with icing, she picked up the pastry bag and began to ice the last cake. She cooked when she was sad, but she baked when she was frustrated. She always had done so, but never so often as she did now at Blayne House!

It was all very well to retreat to the kitchen when she found the world too difficult or disturbing, but if Orion kept refusing her perfectly straightforward advances, Francesca feared that she would end up as wide in the arse as her great-aunt Rosaria!

Her mind spun back a few hours, as it had over and over again—which went a long way to explaining the full dozen cakes!—to relive his large, warm hands on her skin.

Her body still vibrated with need. She already longed for him. That breathless taste of his touch as they stood hidden behind the draperies in Sir Geoffrey's study had only made matters worse! Francesca bit her bottom lip as she squeezed a perfect swirling design of creamy icing onto the top of the final cake.

She promised herself that she would not eat them all alone. Sir Geoffrey might complain about her "overstimulating" spices, but she had long ago noticed that no one seemed to mind a pantry full of sweets!

Then again, what did it matter if she gained a bit more arse? The only man she'd ever desired wanted her to save herself for marriage!

She wished that she didn't find that rather charming, and admirable, and, damn it, honorable that he didn't want to despoil her wretched, worthless virginity! It was a silly, useless thing to hang on to when she would never wed anyway . . . and she so wanted to let go of it in Orion Worthington's arms.

Letting out another gusting sigh, because she was all alone and could wax as melodramatic as she pleased, Francesca concentrated in the dim lamplight and produced the final, delicate touches to the icing. There. All done.

She gazed across the cake-studded table in a state of complete desolation. Twelve cakes and no one to feed. She did so love to feed people.

But she didn't really have any people, did she?

With an expression of crumpling resolution, she reached out to pick off a chunk of iced cake with her fingers. So she would put eleven cakes into the pantry. No one would care.

She was about to pop the guilty pleasure into her mouth when she heard ringing bootheels striding down the hallway outside the kitchens. Orion? No one else in Blayne House moved with such long paces—but heavens, he must be nearly running!

Turning with the sticky chunk of yellow, black-seeded cake forgotten in her fingers, she felt her jaw drop as Orion Worthington, tall and daunting, with his mussed hair still misted from the fog outside, came striding into the kitchen.

Francesca blinked. "Ah . . ." Her gaze slid guiltily to the wad of cake and icing in her hand. "Want some?" She impulsively held it out to him.

It was then that she saw the flare of untamed lust in his midnight eyes.

Someone let the wolf out.

With a thrill, Francesca realized that it was she.

Without a word, he came forward to gaze down at her with those eyes filled with dark need. Francesca swallowed hard.

You called the wolf. Don't be a sheep!

His large hand wrapped around her wrist and raised the bit of cake up high. Without altering his riveting gaze, he opened his mouth and consumed the morsel with zeal. Then he carefully licked every crumb from her fingertips.

Oh heavens. Francesca felt her heartbeat speed so suddenly to a gallop that faintness threatened.

Don't you dare, her inner seductress admonished. *We don't want to miss a minute of this!*

No, she most certainly did not.

He enveloped her other wrist with his other hand and lifted it to his mouth to suck the remaining icing from those fingers as well.

Then, releasing one hand, he turned to tow her from the kitchen like a naughty child in need of a spanking.

The very thought nearly made her stumble. Luckily, her inner seductress was a nimble wench and kept her feet. With her free hand, Francesca whipped her apron over her head and left it on the kitchen floor behind her.

Her hair tumbled free of its pins. Since she rather thought Orion wouldn't mind, she let it fall.

His long legs were moving so fast that she had to scamper behind him, nearly dancing to keep up. This was all very mysterious and exciting, but she was already overly warm, and if he didn't land somewhere soon, she feared her face would become red as a beet!

He dragged her up the stairs into the front hall. As they sped through, she noticed his greatcoat left damp and crumpled on the marble floor of the foyer.

All the servants were abed. It must be later than she'd realized.

Excellent.

Orion pulled her into Sir Geoffrey's study and shut the door behind them. Then he whirled on her, put both his big hands on her shoulders, and pressed her firmly against the closed door.

Francesca felt a strange, cold thrill in her belly. She wasn't afraid, not really. Still, this black intensity was something she'd only sensed in him. She'd deliberately called forth the wolf.

How would the wolf behave?

Slowly, as if he could not bear to let a single inch of her skin go untouched, he slid each of his hands from her shoulders, then across her bare collarbone until his long fingers wrapped loosely about her throat. Francesca's own wolf began to scratch at the door to get out.

With his large hands cupping her jaw, she allowed him to lift her mouth to his. In fact, she went up on her tiptoes and clutched his lapels to get there, but it was well worth the trip.

Orion kissed the way he did everything—with deadly focus. Francesca practically purred as he took possession of her mouth with his. Had any kiss ever been so hot, so demanding, yet so coaxing at the same time?

He wanted her to join him in his lust.

She wrapped her arms about his neck and did her best to convince him that she was already there.

A groan sounded deep in his throat. His arms wrapped about her waist, and he lifted her off her feet, pressing her to the door with his body.

Francesca found herself standing on nothing at all. *I have always wanted to fly,* she thought, just as any coherence of thought shredded away, torn to bits by the whirling storm of her desire for him.

Her lips parted on a sigh, and he took it as an invitation. His tongue delved within and stroked hungrily against hers. As innocent as she was, she recognized the rhythm of his invasion. She moaned into his mouth. Dimly, she realized that her hands were fisted in his thick hair, clinging to him as if she were drowning and his kiss, the only succor.

It was wild and raw and unbelievably wonderful to release her longing at last—but it still wasn't enough.

"I want to touch you."

Those were the first words he'd spoken to her. They were hot and urgent words, and the need in them echoed her own.

She laughed against his lips. "Sir, I assure you that the desire is mutual. I suggest you remove your clothing."

She wanted to see him naked, and to run her fingers over his bare skin again—this time without the acid bath! She wanted him hot and hard, not cold and wet, although she would take him any way she could get him. It was a fine idea, this one.

She was so pleased that she'd had it.

Surely if they kissed and touched and fondled each other all night, they could have their fill! She'd been so hungry for him, and it seemed as if she'd been hungry forever. How else could she drink her fill of him in one night if she did not leap right in?

He didn't seem to object, nor wish to judge her for being forward. Instead, he seemed more than willing now that he'd come to his decision. His hands tightened on her waist as she reached behind her head to undo the top buttons of her gown. As the neckline of the plain gown drooped, his gaze fell down to watch her breasts being revealed.

But first, there was the lace-edged chemise that she wore beneath the plain gabardine. It was quite low-cut, for it was borrowed from Judith and therefore rather too long in all. All of Francesca's things had been too lightweight for England, but for a few practical winter gowns. Judith had the idea to add more layers of underthings just to keep from shivering at the dinner table.

Now, in high British summer, she was down to a single, thin chemise.

Orion had never seen a woman's underthings. It seemed exotic, and erotic, to solve that puzzle and know that secret. Orion had always loved to solve puzzles . . .

All thought of clothing fell from his mind as she pulled at the strings tying the neckline of her chemise closed. He held his breath, waiting—

The thin batiste fell away, and her beautiful breasts fell into his ready hands. They were round and full and soft and tipped with sweet, tender coral nipples that he could not live one more minute without sucking into his mouth—

Francesca gasped as his large hot hands closed over her bare breasts. He took ownership of her flesh as if it had always belonged to him and only him. With all the focus she had ever seen in his dark blue eyes, he bent his head to watch her soft flesh give beneath his avid touch.

Yet, he was gentle. Uncompromising and firm, but he never hurt her, even when he pressed her breasts high to take each nipple into his mouth in turn. The low moan that escaped her at the sweet, nearly painful sucking sensation brought out a growl from his throat.

The wolf was there, lurking behind the mild-mannered exterior. No suit or pair of spectacles could hide him from her. She saw the beast within the man, unleashed at last.

The beast had been set free, and it was hunting her.

His hands were urgent and hard, but his mouth was achingly tender as he tasted her. The sweet, gentle pull of his mouth seemed to tingle through her. It reached up and made her eyes fall shut. It reached out and made her fingers tighten in his hair. It reached down and melted her from within as the place between her thighs throbbed and softened with every roll of his tongue and tug of suction from his mouth.

Francesca rather thought that now would be a good time to release her own beast.

Freed at last, she moaned his name aloud as she buried her hands in his hair, fisting her fingers in the silk curls without fear. What she did, anything she did, would be matched and outmatched by his own fervor. She knew it as certainly as she knew that when she tugged at his hair, he would bring his head up to kiss her again, to devour her mouth even as he had just devoured her nipples, and that she would consume him in return.

The knowledge frightened and exhilarated her at the same time. The man she knew, the cool and severe creature of exacting control, had slipped from the beast as easily as an ill-fitting suit, leaving the naked soul of the hungry animal before her.

She was barely aware that he continued to pull her clothing away. Her gown and chemise pooled about her naked hips, slipping farther downward as he slid his large hard hands around her back to squeeze large handfuls of her bottom. He pulled her closer, away from the door, and carried her across the room.

The fireplace still held coals glowing from earlier in the evening. The large wingback chair was the perfect size to hold them both. He fell back into the chair, and she straddled his lap.

Yes. She could feel his hardness pressing to her softness. He tilted his hips slowly, rolling himself against her bare vulva. She hissed and rolled with him, pressing herself against the growing hard length of him.

Her nipples grew hard and pink in his mouth, and gleamed wetly when she pulled away at last. "You, too," she gasped as she tugged at his shirt studs.

"Yes." Orion wanted to feel her rigid nipples against the skin of his chest. He reluctantly slid his hands away from the lush handfuls of sweet bottom that he held and reached to fumble at his clothing.

She leaned back to help him, and his heart thudded at the sight of her half-naked on his lap, her beautiful skin gleaming like a golden idol in the firelight, her rigid nipples shining like tender rubies set in the full, rounded sculpture of her breasts. Even the dainty ripple of her abdominal muscles as she balanced herself on his lap entranced him. He could watch her for hours, for every move she made danced with grace and light.

But he did not have hours. He had only this one night to devour her freely—only this one chance to take her to the very edge of reason, and he meant to do it over and over again before the sun rose upon them!

He rolled suddenly, taking them both from the chair to the carpet before the fire. He lifted her with him until she lay upon him, her body stretched along his. The thickness of his erection pressed to her belly as she squirmed, making him moan aloud. Now he had her right where she wanted him! She took his hands and slid them from her bottom, wrapping her fingers around his and urging him to gather up her gown. He took to the task adroitly, and soon her gown lay in a pool of gabardine on the floor. Now, naked but for her stockings and garters, she straddled her bare thighs over his trouser-shielded groin. It was his turn.

Francesca had been undoing buttons all her life, and men's buttons were ludicrously large compared to the tiny ones applied to women's gowns. She didn't even have to look at her hands, which allowed her to kiss him hard, battling tongues with him as she undid his trouser fastenings.

She wanted him entirely naked, so once she tugged the buttons free from his trousers, she turned her attention to the upper garments. The waistcoat was simple. No need to look at what her hands were doing, no need to tear her lips from his, no need to deprive herself of the wild, hot taste of him.

His waistcoat and jacket got a bit stuck near the shoulders when she tried to push them off him. He obliged her attempts by sitting up and meeting her mouth in matching hunger while he wrenched himself free of the snug clothing. His shirt was looser but was complicated by the cravat at his throat.

Orion, clever fellow that he was, solved the dilemma for her by wrapping one large hand around the back of her head to keep her mouth on his as he tugged the knot of his cravat free with the other hand. Francesca busied herself with the studs of his shirt, pulling them through the holes with rough abandon until the placket was entirely open. Her hungry hands explored the portion of his chest that was left exposed as they kissed, until she wanted more.

Moving her hands to his hips, she began to tug his shirt free from his trousers. This time, Orion was no help at all, for he was now far more interested in caressing her naked body. That was extremely distracting and entirely unfair! She moaned at his possessive touch.

Orion slid his hands over the warm silk of Francesca's naked back, then filled his hands with soft, resilient bottom. Yes. He'd wanted that bottom in his hands ever since that accidental groping he'd given it in the laboratory. And the bottom in question was everything he'd dreamed, rich full curves covered in the finest, sweetest, softest skin—far more lovely than he could have imagined in his limited range of knowledge! Pulling her luscious bottom closer had the happy result of pressing the heat of her vulva against his hardness.

The damp warmth of her sank through his loosened trousers, calling to his cock like a siren luring a sailor.

Although he had every intention of resisting the actual act of diving into that sweet, dangerous sea between her thighs, there was no doubt that he wanted to. In fact, he was quite certain that he'd never wanted anything more!

Chapter 23

EVENTUALLY, Orion realized that Francesca's sweet moans of arousal sounded rather more like miffed grunts of frustration, and that the rhythmic tugging he'd been ignoring was her attempt to pull his shirt up over his head.

Yes. Yes, he wanted that, too—to press his chest against her soft naked breasts, to feel her hardened nipples against his skin, to roll naked with her before the fire.

Although it pained him that he did not have enough hands to enjoy every part of her at once, he released her sweet buttocks to aid her in her quest for mutual nudity.

After that, and a rather amusing bit of gymnastics that freed him of his boots and trousers as well, he rolled her, bare and giggling, beneath him. He pressed her softness down, pinning her safely to the rug where he could get at all of her at once.

Francesca naked was a revelation. The dips and swells of sweet, golden-tinged skin, the full, round generosity of her breasts and thighs and bottom—how could he have waited so long to touch her? If he had only known, he would have carried her off to his room the first night he'd encountered her in the hall outside the kitchen.

When he told her as much, between long deep kisses that made them both pant with need, she, of course, only laughed. "You might have tried," she warned. "But Worthingtons aren't the only ones who know how to use a butcher knife!"

She was fierce and independent, yet warm and welcoming and so, so sweet. Now that he had her naked beneath him, skin to skin, mouth to mouth, Orion allowed himself to slow down, to savor every taste, every kiss, every slide of his hand over her satin surfaces.

She eased beneath him, responding to his soothing strokes. Stretching like a cat, she pressed herself to him with slow sensuality, allowing the heat of him to cover her, to sink into her and warm the corners of her soul that had been so empty for so long. The world was cold for one without close family. Aunts and uncles and cousins were all very fine, but they did not hold one, or stroke one, or comfort one in the same way. To be touched, to be held, to be soothed eased her loneliness in a way she'd never imagined possible.

Francesca had thought herself simply in need of sexual gratification. How could she have realized that her needs went so much deeper? Frightened by the strength of her need, she hid her face against his neck and allowed him to soothe that fear as well, though he might think it simple arousal.

As her sudden fear abated, she found herself in a state of languorous awakening. Touching each other, kissing each other, satisfying each other until that overwhelming desire was quenched at last—that was purpose enough.

He rolled to one side of her, his long body still pressed close. She limply felt him lift her head with one large hand while he slid his other arm about her shoulders. As he pulled her in close for a long kiss, she allowed her body to ooze into his as she slid her free hand down his lean, muscled flank. *Oh my . . .*

His other hand, large and gentle, slid down her body, sweeping slowly down over her curves, touching and exploring, delighting them both as he filled his hands with soft, pliable woman. Down the outside of one rounded thigh, and then up the inside.

Francesca let her thighs part in unspoken permission and pleading. She'd craved his touch. Now was not the time to turn shy, although to be caressed where no one else had ever seen turned a lifetime of halfhearted propriety on its head. She'd always been a good girl, not out of devotion to her purity, but out of lack of interest in being otherwise.

Now, it seemed, she had never been a good girl at all—merely a seductress in waiting.

Waiting for the warm, firm, gentle touch of this particular man.

He cupped his big hot palm over the vee of her pubis. Francesca found the urge to rise up to meet him irresistible. His kiss deepened as he moaned at her eagerness. Why should she pretend otherwise? She wanted him. He wanted her. All was as it should be—or at least, it would be if he meant to get on with things! She rose again, rolling her hips high to press herself to his hand.

Orion hesitated. If he touched her, aroused her, satisfied her with his hand, would he not be crossing over into some territory he might find it hard to someday leave?

Then she rolled again, and his fingertips slipped into the wet heat of her. They both shuddered at the contact. She released a mewl of need into his mouth.

Francesca had never ached for anything so much in her life. As he gently parted her to slide his fingertips up and down along her slit, she found herself grasping his muscled biceps, clinging as if she might shatter and fly away at the pleasure that rolled through her.

His touch became firmer and more sure, but the perfectly erotic pressure never became too much. He seemed to understand precisely what she needed. In some corner of her thoughts, she was astonished at her shamelessness as she panted and moaned into his mouth while he slid his fingers up and down, rolling and pinching and tugging at her clitoris with each pass. She wanted more. She wanted him to become part of her, inside her.

She slid one hand down his rocklike muscled arm to his hand. Covering it with her own smaller one, she pressed him into her until one long finger slid within. The penetration felt so good, so right, that she cried out in pleasure.

He took her cries into his mouth as he stroked that long finger deeply into her, then withdrew, sliding up along her slit, still teasing at her clitoris with every stroke. The pleasure rose as he increased his pace, until she hung helpless at the precipice of such pleasure as she could never have imagined. She left her hand over his as he stroked her, until their wet fingers tangled and clasped as she panted and cried out her first release into his hungry mouth.

Orion held her shuddering body close, letting his kiss soften and become tender. The wonder of her stunned him. Everything, from the scent of exotic spice in her hair to the texture of her delicate gold-tinted skin, to the color of her coral-tipped nipples in the firelight as she arched into him with abandon as he covered her mound with his mouth.

This beautiful creature had given herself to him. Why? What had he done to deserve such a gift? Not that he meant to refuse it again, no matter his unworthiness! He might have been momentarily misguided when he walked away from her the night before, but Worthingtons were not fools! With such a banquet before him, he would be mad to pass up a single bite of delicious, fragrant Francesca.

All but that one—all but the last forbidden morsel. As much as his body urged him to roll onto her, to thrust into her wet willingness, to drive them both higher than they had ever been. Ah, but he wanted to. His body trembled with the effort to resist.

Why, when something was forbidden, did it become so much more desirable?

He had to fight the powerful urge to plunge his cock into her soft, hot, wet opening, and switching position, he moved down her body kiss by kiss, concentrating on pleasuring her with his lips, tongue, and teeth instead. With the last rational shred of his mind, he found her small hand with his. It took very little silent instruction for her to understand what he needed. His mouth never left her sweet center, but a low, rough moan escaped him when he felt her warm fingers wrap tightly around his cock. She slid slowly up and down, just as he'd demonstrated, but in her inexperience, her grip was delicate and torturous instead of firm and steady.

If anything, it aroused him further. Her unintentionally teasing touch would not bring him to fulfillment, but instead kept him hard and aching for her. Driven nearly insane with the ache, he redoubled his attentions to her labia and clitoris.

Francesca gasped and writhed, rolling her head upon his muscular thigh, but there was no escaping the relentless pleasure of his mouth on her. His tongue stroked and circled and dipped and tasted, and she had no choice but to pant her pleasure into the stillness of the room. In her wild state, she tried to hang on to something solid as her pleasure soared. His hard cock filled her hand. She twisted toward it, reaching with her other hand to wrap it more thoroughly in her grip. When she did so, his tongue increased its actions, flipping wetly across her clitoris faster and faster, driving her higher.

Then his rigid cock was in both her hands. With her lids barely parted, she realized how close it was to her mouth. She wanted him inside her, deep inside her . . .

When Orion felt warm, wet lips wrap around the blunt tip of his cock, he let out a harsh groan of need. She answered it by licking and sucking him farther between her lips, until his cock probed over her panting tongue. He could not help flexing his hips, pushing deeper into her, as the wondrous heat of her tentative mouth enveloped most of his length.

It was not deep enough, but he could not force her—

She sucked him deeper. The sweet heat of her mouth, the slow stroke of her tongue, the inadvertent suction as he tried to pull back so as not to choke her . . . then the reflexive thrust that he could not help. God, he wanted her. He wanted—

With his cock in her mouth and his tongue upon her clitoris, Francesca felt the rising orgasm flood her entire being. He drove her onward, higher and higher, as lost in her as she was lost in him, neither knowing where they ended or began.

Francesca tumbled and then she flew. Hot, harsh gasps of pleasure sounded in the room, and she dimly realized that some of them were hers as she exploded with varicolored lights shimmering outward from his wonderful, talented tongue.

The vibration of her moans around his cock in her mouth sent Orion over his own precipice. He buried his face in her thigh as he groaned deeply, the harsh, animal sound escaping him into her silken flesh as he jerked and spasmed into her sweet, hot mouth.

She did not stop sucking, as a more experienced woman might. Even as he filled her mouth, she continued to roll her tongue over him, continued to pull at him with soft suction. When she swallowed around him, he closed his eyes and turned to kiss the damp, salty skin of her inner thigh in thanks.

They lay like that for several long moments as their pounding hearts eased their frantic pulses and their gasping lungs settled into deep, peaceful breaths. Francesca allowed his cock to slip from her lips and let her cheek rest on his hip as she collected her shattered awareness back into herself. With her eyes still closed, she listened to the hiss and crack of the fire, felt the heat along one side of her body from the hearth, and along the other side of her where she pressed against the naked man she had just possessed.

It had been wonderful. How had she lived so long without the feel of him? It seemed mad that it had been only a few weeks since she'd been bored and lonely in Blayne House, wishing something—anything!—would happen to break the tedium of perfect order and organization.

She fought back a laugh. Goodness! No wonder people wrote entire plays about love!

Except, of course, that this wasn't love. This was merely the physical expression of desire. The biological imperative.

Lust.

Replete with pleasure, she lazily ran her fingertips up his muscled stomach and over the hard plates of his chest. The sprinkling of hair there teased at her fingers. He was so different from her. Even his skin felt dissimilar, not as fine, yet sleeker somehow as it wrapped taut around his muscular form.

She'd been right about him from the first moment she had seen him in the foyer of Blayne House. He was a sleek and beautiful beast in gentlemen's clothing. His demeanor seemed so cool, yet he burned so very hot beneath the isolating facade of logic.

And he was all hers.

For one night.

HUNGER DROVE THEM back to the kitchen. He wore only his trousers. She wore only his shirt. They had stuffed her gown into a large Chinese vase that stood in the foyer, promising each other in whispers that they would resist the urge to allow the servants to discover it in the morning.

Orion frowned slightly as he took in the long kitchen worktable covered in iced seed cakes. They stood in rows. "A regiment of pastry soldiers," he muttered. "How did I miss this earlier?"

"What did you say?" Francesca was elbow deep into a shelf in the larder. She emerged with a heel of ham on a wooden board and a chunk of hard cheese.

Orion thought she looked like a meal for a king. He pointed at the cakes. "Did you bake all these?"

She grinned at him and blew a curl away from her laughing eyes. "I bake when I can't have what I want."

Orion let his gaze roam over the signs of her frustration. "You must have wanted me very much." He liked being wanted, he realized.

"Still want you," she said, around a muffling bit of ham. She was carving the meat and cheese with an enormous knife that Orion recognized from the now-infamous Rabbit Wrangle.

She was smiling, but the look in her eyes pinned him with a question.

Orion let his smile slide away to gaze somberly back at her. "I want you more than I have ever wanted anything," he told her plainly. "But I won't endanger your future."

Her eyes narrowed slightly. "You are very noble, Mr. Worthington, but as it is my future we speak of, perhaps I ought to decide that?"

He shook his head. "That is my only rule for this night. Virgins to the end."

She blinked. "You were serious, then? You haven't—"

He rubbed the back of his neck. "Of course I know what to do . . . intellectually."

She blinked at him. "Really . . . never?"

Orion wasn't sure why he should feel embarrassed about it. Still, his face heated. "Once. Almost. But I became distracted."

Francesca tilted her head. If he wasn't careful, he was going to make her laugh at him again, and she didn't think now was quite the moment. "I think I'd like to know more . . . but not if you don't want to tell me." *Oh, but I must know.*

He shrugged. "It isn't of any great importance. My twin brothers insisted that I should accompany them to their favorite brothel, Mrs. Blythe's House of Pleasure. I chose a young lady to spend the evening with—and I certainly had every intention of—well—but then I realized that I had a singular opportunity to thoroughly understand the female anatomy."

Francesca pressed her fingers to her lips, hard. Oh, he was such a dear! The look on his face! As if he still didn't understand the subject matter. For a moment, Francesca found herself feeling a bit sorry for the anonymous prostitute. Then it occurred to her that the woman might have had the opportunity to take Orion into her arms first, to kiss him, to touch him, to push her fingers through that thick dark hair—and the trickle of sympathy shut off instantly.

"But you didn't—in the end?"

Orion let out a breath. "No. The young lady complained, and Mrs. Blythe showed me the door. She told me to come back when my desire for pleasure outweighed my desire for knowledge."

Francesca finally allowed herself to smile at him. "And now? Shall I be examined? Or given pleasure?"

His expression became very serious as his awareness fixed intensely upon her. "Miss Penrose, pleasuring you is all I think about."

Her smile widening, she tossed her hair over her shoulder and stood very straight, which she knew would set her bosom up high for his attention. Just to be sure she prevented further distraction, she inhaled deeply.

His concentration was everything she could ask for. His blue eyes darkened to midnight, and his jaw tightened as his gaze ran over her. She saw his hands tighten to fists at his sides. Wonder and hot, spiced need flowed through her. To be wanted so much was a heady brew. She would gulp herself drunk upon it—see if she wouldn't!

Opposite her, Orion rode his lust like an unruly horse. It bucked rebelliously within him, fighting the shredding rope of his control. It was all he could do to keep from flinging this delectable creature to the stone kitchen floor and turning loose his inner steed of need upon her. The very thought nearly made his eyes cross as his cock hardened impossibly more.

I want to—everything. I want it all.

Now.

Francesca, apparently also wearied of waiting, took one step forward and reached out her hand. Another step, and her cool fingers stroked hesitantly over his jaw. "Don't you want to kiss m—?"

Orion let his mouth fall down upon hers like a hawk diving on a dove. She let out a single muffled squeak of surprise, but then her lips parted and her mouth melted into his. He kept going, pressing into her, his hands on her shoulders, until two steps backward pushed her spine against the wall. Francesca sighed as his body pressed into her and his hands slid up to wrap around her throat and jaw, tilting her head back to invade her mouth.

Yes. Yes, invade me.

She opened her mouth to let him in, even as her thighs longed to part for him, even as her arms opened to climb up and tangle around the back of his neck.

It was hot, and wet and sweet—so sweet!—inside Francesca. Orion ached to consume her, to drink her and eat her and fuck her until he lost himself in that sweet, soft land inside her.

Every moan from her throat sent him deeper into her. Every roll of her body as it writhed enthusiastically against him drew him in, pulling him further away from himself and into her. Soon there was no Orion, no man of science, no voice of logic and reason.

There was only her. His own being was reduced to the parts of him that wanted to be within her.

She braced her palms against his chest and pushed him, hard. Startled, thinking that she objected, he fought to recall himself. He began to draw away, though it made him ache painfully to do so.

However, it seemed she had no intention of objecting, for her mouth followed as her lips clung to his. She kept pushing, and he kept backing away, until he felt something hit the backs of his knees. One last imperious shove and he fell into the hard wooden chair before the fire. There was no point in objecting to this new position, because his lap was immediately filled with sweet, soft girl as she lifted his shirt above her knees and clambered astride him. Not once had her mouth left his. A tiny fragment of rational thought admired her creativity, for at last they were face-to-face, eye-to-eye—and most important, lips and tongue and mouth-to-mouth.

Oh yes. He sank his fingers into her tumbled hair and drew her mouth more firmly to his, pressing his tongue past her lips in a rhythm as old as time.

The food remained uneaten. The dozen cakes stood guard as the only two souls awake in the house moaned and sighed and fed upon each other, instead.

Full combustion, indeed.

Chapter 24

ORION took Francesca's desperate moans into his mouth, kissing her deeply. She shuddered in his grasp as he slid his fingers up and around her clitoris.

He'd meant to walk her to her room and see that she got a bit of rest before the new day began. With the very best of intentions, he'd helped her clean the kitchen and tidy the study and retrieve her gown from the large vase in the front hall.

They'd walked in companionable silence until they had reached the door to her bedchamber. The house remained dark and silent around them. Soon, however, the staff would begin to stir. If they wished their night of full combustion to remain a secret piece of the past, it was time to part.

Then Francesca turned to him, smiled wickedly, and held out her hand with false primness. "Thank you for a lovely evening," she said.

He stifled a laugh. Clearly, he had no choice but to kiss that sweet, saucy smile directly from her lips, daring to do so even as they stood in the upstairs hallway. And when she'd arched against him, pressing her breasts into his chest—he simply could not keep his hands to himself.

Just once more, he had told himself. *Just one more taste, just one more touch . . .*

Now he held one hand high, pinning her wrists over her head and against the exterior of her bedroom door. His other hand moved with growing urgency as she bucked and undulated against his touch with a last, helpless orgasm.

Yes, he thought. *Mine. One last time.*

Releasing her hands left her unsteady on trembling legs, so he gladly kept one arm about her tiny waist as he brushed her wildly tossed hair from her face. "Shh." He dropped tender kisses onto her closed eyelids.

Still quivering, she clung to his arm for a long moment.

Then she took her weight on her own two feet. She dropped her hands. And she stepped away from him.

I don't want to let her go.

Which was ridiculous. They had played out their plan most thoroughly. Lust had been appeased. Attraction had been snuffed. Distraction had been removed. Alas, Orion had a sneaking suspicion that rather than burning out their passion, they had only inflamed it further.

He straightened his spine.

She tucked a strand of hair behind one ear and bestowed a polite smile on him. "I think we've managed quite well. Thank goodness we didn't pass the point of no return!"

He nodded sharply. "Indeed. I look forward to the lack of distraction in the laboratory."

She bobbed her head slightly in agreement, then reached for the door latch. "Well, good night, then. And . . . good-bye."

He cleared his throat. "Yes."

She slipped through the door to her bedchamber. It closed, shutting him out with a firm click of the latch.

It was over.

Orion turned away to make his way to his own bedchamber. He ought to feel satisfied. They had pleasured each other in every way they could think of, aside from the one way they could not dare. And yet, all he could think was that he wished he could kiss her.

Just one more time.

He passed a drowsy footman walking the opposite direction down the hall. The new day had begun. Last night would forever be only a memory.

As it should be.

Forever.

Damn it.

HAD THERE EVER been a time in his life when he had not spun in an orbit of desire around Francesca like a planet of ice thawing helplessly before the heat of a golden sun?

There must have been. He had met her only a few short weeks before!

But I was waiting for her.

Nonsense. Rubbish. Fanciful daydreaming nonsense!

Except that it seems to be true.

Well, there was that. To be sure, since their wild night of unfulfilled pleasure had ended, Orion's moment-to-moment vision had tunneled down to the fine points of Francesca's voice, Francesca's scent, Francesca's miraculous, magical skin . . .

If he'd had the presence of mind of a pumpkin, he would have been alarmed and offended by the betrayal of his intellect. However, he could not reason his way free of his obsession. He could not extrapolate a way to erase the memory of her hot mouth on his cock. He could not think his way out of the maze of her soft, luscious body naked in his greedily exploring hands!

His attention was not his own. At the mere possibility that he might hear her voice, or her laugh, or the rustle of her skirts, he could think of nothing but her.

Damn it, I'm doing it again right now!

Carefully not glancing at the woman who sat at her work-table across the laboratory—near enough to obsess him, but so very far away!—Orion gazed at the two glass tubes he held in his raised hands. He'd been pouring from one to the other . . . but he couldn't remember which. Bloody hell, he couldn't even remember why!

With great care, he placed both tubes back in their stand, then spread his palms on the cool steel surface of the table.

Francesca.

He wanted her again. He wanted her *more*.

He wanted it all.

Francesca.

With a sound that ranged somewhere between a growl of frustration and a moan of pure longing, he dropped his head down between his hands as if the chilled metal of the table could cool his volcanic lust.

Please, make this go away. I liked being cold. I liked being a man of the mind, not the body. I liked being alone.

No, you didn't. You really, truly didn't. You just thought you had no choice.

He jerked upright. That wasn't true. That couldn't be true. If it was, then he would lose everything he'd ever wanted.

Having Francesca meant losing the engagement to Judith, which meant losing the support of Sir Geoffrey, which meant that he would go back to being one of *those* Worthingtons— and would never be taken seriously in scientific circles again, not when Sir Geoffrey carried the tale of his fickleness to the Royal Fraternity!

With the full power of his focused concentration, he could will his lust away. He would lock down every memory, every fantasy, every urge—killing them one by one and dragging their limp carcasses into the cellar of his mind and throwing away the key!

He was Orion Worthington, a man of science!

A deep breath, then another, helped to settle his pounding pulse and quiet his constant near erection. With slow, deliberate movements, he drew out two more glass tubes and began his test again from the beginning.

Cold, clear concentration.

Dark hair, warm from the heat of the fire, sweeping over the bare skin of his chest as she kissed her way down . . .

Francesca.

Orion blinked and glared at the two glass tubes he held in his hands. Which one?

Bloody hell!

That was the moment he gave in. He raised his eyes to Francesca, who sat just a few yards away from the marble-topped laboratory table at which he unsuccessfully toiled. He looked up just in time to see her catch herself as she began to doze. Remaining quite still, Orion watched as she lifted her head and blinked quickly several times.

She must be very tired. He was as well, except that he was also revitalized. His entire body hummed with satisfaction. For the first time in his life, he knew what it meant to spend the night with a woman.

There was so much more to it than simple orgasms. Those could be had cheaply and privately, if one were so inclined. No, those seven hours with Francesca—with Chessa!—had shown him another world entirely. Her softness, her sweetness, her eagerness had driven him mad even while they had soothed something deep inside him. To be *wanted*—that was a thing he'd never known.

As he thought about her eager, seeking hands on him, he watched her full lashes slip lower over her eyes. The morning sun must be dazzling her vision—but she dazzled him. She shimmered in that beam of light. Her sun-sweetened skin glowed, and the lights within her hair burned with reds and bronzes that he'd never seen before. Her stillness shifted only with her deep breaths—inhalations that swelled that marvelous bosom and pressed it higher into the sunlight, just for him. There she sat, as if nothing had happened the previous night—as if the world had not shifted on its axis, as if north had not suddenly twisted south and left him stranded on some strange, rocky shore!

Her head began to droop. Her pencil slipped from her fingers and fell to the chart she had been marking. Still Orion simply sat watching. He could hear the depth of her breathing. He saw the moment when her lips parted slightly in relaxation.

However, the instant she began to droop on her stool, he was at her side.

"Chessa," he whispered. Putting his arm around her shoulders seemed like the friendly, supportive thing to do, so that she would not lose her balance. "Chessa."

"Rion," she murmured softly. He'd thought she would jerk awake, perhaps be surprised and slightly embarrassed and thoroughly adorable. Instead, she turned her face into his neck and kissed the place where his pulse throbbed.

The touch of her lips was sweet and familiar, and shocking. They were finished. They'd both proclaimed themselves so, and had parted with cool smiles and distant fondness.

So why did her lips burn with soft and terrifying heat on his skin? Why did his hand slide up into her hair and tilt her head back? Why did her eyes open, dark and bottomless and sultry as she lifted her gaze to his?

Orion bent, because to not bend would have snapped his soul in half, and brushed his mouth over her soft, parted lips. It was less than a kiss, but yet far more than he ought to bestow upon a simple colleague—a friend.

She sighed, and he breathed in the sweetness of her. There was no one near. He could kiss her hard and deeply, as he longed to do. She would allow it—and likely give as good as she got—but it would not be enough.

It will never be enough.

She flinched in his embrace. "What did you say?" She drew back, pressing her palms to his chest to look him in the eye.

"I—" Orion shook his head and straightened abruptly. "I didn't—"

Francesca pulled away. In doing so, she overbalanced on the stool. Orion grabbed her upper arm to steady her. She recoiled so powerfully that they had to scramble to keep their footing. The stool clattered to the marble floor and tried valiantly to trip them both.

"O Dio!" Francesca aimed an injudicious kick at the stool, and it spun away, clattering woodenly across the floor. "Ow!"

Orion reached for her. She ducked away from him as if his hands were aflame. "Don't touch me!" Her hip rebounded against her worktable. A chunk of stone rocked sideways, nearly rolling from the table.

Orion withdrew sharply. "Oh for pity's sake, Chessa! You'll hurt yourself!"

She sidestepped into clear floor, holding her hands up before her. "You kissed me! Why did you kiss me?"

Orion opened his mouth, but he had no answer. *You kissed me first.* "I—you—I haven't the faintest idea," he muttered finally.

Francesca frowned and folded her arms before her. It was a slight improvement over actively fending him off as if he were a bandit after her reticule, but not much.

She glared at him. "You shouldn't have done that. We said we wouldn't do that. We said—"

"I know!" Orion ran his hands through his hair. "I know what we said. I meant it—I still mean it! I don't want"—I *want* you—"some sort of torrid entanglement! I want"—I want *you*—"to work, just as you want to work!" He spread his hands. "I—I just—" He sighed. "This is going to take some getting used to."

She scowled but dropped her defensive posture somewhat. "I suppose that's understandable." She rubbed her hands together pensively. "After all, we crossed a great many boundaries last night."

Orion could not help a self-conscious grin at those particular words. She pursed her lips to keep from smiling back, but her cheeks pinked even as her eyes danced. "It might take a bit longer to rebuild those walls than we originally theorized," she said primly.

She was delectable.

Am I truly going to go the rest of my life without taking her into my arms again?

Yes. Absolutely. He would never, ever hold her again.

She must have been thinking along similar lines, for she pressed her open hands down, smoothing her skirts. "It is a good thing we are going to the ball tonight. The laboratory is too—"

Secluded. Secret. Theirs and theirs alone.

"Private," he finished for her.

She nodded. "Yes. Exactly what I meant." She checked the dainty watch she wore pinned to her bodice. "Speaking of the ball, I must get some rest if I'm going to last the night." She gathered up her notes into a neat stack and replaced the paperweight stone upon them. Then she stepped back and yawned widely. "Oh, pardon me!" She pressed her hands to her cheeks. "I feel as though I could sleep for a week! And I don't know how I shall be able to dance, when my body is so sore—"

Her eyes widened, and she clapped a hand over her mouth. Orion wished he could capture the expression on her lovely face forever—mingled mortification and mischief—for it perfectly summed up his unique and marvelous Francesca.

He looked down at her fondly. "If you expect me to apologize, I have no intention of doing so. I feel as if I were run over by an ale cart!"

She smiled freely up at him for the first time since they'd risen that morning. "You'll get no remorse from me, Mr. Worthington!"

With that, she slipped past him with a laugh and a breath of orange blossoms and scampered from the laboratory.

Orion's smile faded slowly.

"No remorse from me, Mr. Worthington," she had said.

He hoped she would never regret last night. He just wasn't sure that either of them could be sure of such a thing. When something changed one's life, one was bound to suffer from those changes, somehow.

Chapter 25

As she dressed and arranged her hair, Francesca tried her best to avoid becoming excited about the evening's ball. After all, the point of a London Society event such as this was making matches, wasn't it? She had no interest in matching with anyone!

Unless that anyone is Orion Worthington?

No, despite her enjoyment of his company—and his touch, and his kiss!—she still had no intention of losing her independence in something as restrictive as holy wedlock. That was not for her. It was true that she had seen a few good matches in her life. Her mother had fallen in love, and had married a fine man and had a child, herself. Her grandmother had fallen in love and married another fine man, and had twelve children, to boot!

Francesca knew that marriage was a perfectly workable solution—but only some of the time. Marriage also could be a trap into which a woman disappeared, losing herself in her husband's needs and losing her life within the context of his.

So it wasn't the matchmaking she was looking forward to, certainly not!

However, she did love to dance.

Francesca stood before the large oval mirror, studying a most unusual vision, indeed—herself, poured into golden silk and adorned with seed pearls and lace, a pair of large pearl drops dangling from her earlobes. She gave her new gown an experimental twirl, noting the dramatic sweep of the lightweight silk as it brushed over the tops of her matching dancing slippers. And look! She had somehow managed to braid and coil her recalcitrant dark curls just as dear Mr. Button had instructed, with ribbon and pearls in the style he'd used to create a garden-vine pattern of her bodice. It was perfection! Upon closer inspection, Francesca decided she looked rather like an exceptionally decorated and gilded cake—curls at the top and slippers at the bottom—with her own admittedly excellent bosom making up the middle tier!

Mr. Button was a genius, indeed. And an extremely fast worker. Francesca hadn't truly expected to receive the dress for weeks, despite Attie's numerous assurances that it would be ready in time for the Duke of Camberton's ball.

It was not until Francesca made her way skipping down the stairs to meet the others in the front hall, twirling the matching reticule from her wrist all the while, that she realized just how much of a genius was the renowned Lementeur, known to her as Button!

Judith actually gasped. Out loud. Francesca greatly enjoyed the look of obvious, albeit brief, astonished consternation on her cousin's lovely face. And, for once, Francesca did not feel outshone by the serene Judith, even as she wore a perfectly lovely silk gown of palest cornflower blue. Perfectly lovely and perfectly appropriate.

"Is—" Judith shook her head in wonder. "Is that a Lementeur gown?"

"Yes!" Francesca gave another spin, this time for her audience's benefit. "I think it's quite pretty."

"Pretty?" Judith pressed her lips together. "Women wait months—years!—to get on Lementeur's client list. And the gowns cost nearly a hundred pounds!"

Francesca blinked and looked down at herself in disbelief. "Oops. Perhaps I ought to have insisted upon paying for it, after all."

Judith seemed to be having trouble breathing. "But—are you saying it was a *gift*? From Lementeur *himself*? *H-how?*"

Francesca smiled benignly at Judith. What a marvelous moment. "Would you like one, too? I shall ask him for you." In all truth, Francesca had never wished to be in competition with her cousin. She was above all that sort of thing, after all. Or she would be, very soon, perhaps tomorrow, after Society had seen her in this gilded confection of a dress!

Her gaze fell upon her uncle, who also seemed a little taken aback by her appearance. He was looking her up and down. "You look acceptable . . ."

Francesca widened her eyes in surprise.

Then a surly expression formed on his lined face. "For once."

Ah, that was better. Francesca felt much more comfortable with her uncle scowling at her—familiar and sure of her place in the world.

Finally, at long last, she dared to look at Mr. Worthington. He stood quite still, his appearance lean and dark next to Sir Geoffrey's ostentatious frilled shirt and embroidered waist-coat.

It was the picture of a lone wolf standing next to a sheep-herder. Was she the only one to see Orion Worthington for what he truly was?

Perhaps not. Though he looked much like he usually did, save for the finely cut evening attire, Francesca had seen past his understated clothing and studious expression to the naked magnificence beneath. In fact, according to Mr. Worthington, she was the only woman who had ever had the privilege.

Francesca's gaze locked with Orion's, his eyes a deep blue

deepened by the black fire of his desire. It was a desire she knew was reflected in her own gaze.

He wants me.

I want him right back.

A few too many seconds had passed for propriety, and Orion knew he should have already commented on Miss Penrose's gown. But how could he be expected to speak when he could barely draw breath? His chest tightened and his fingers twitched. His mouth had gone dry. And all he could think was, *That stunning woman is mine.*

She had been lovely in her plain and frumpy gowns. He'd thought she was astonishing naked on the rug. However, he'd not properly prepared himself for the sight of Francesca draped in shimmering, golden silk and twined with ribbon and pearls. It was almost too much richness to comprehend.

He vaguely remembered seeing Button sitting on the floor of his office in a pool of golden cloth, a strand of pearls tossed over his shoulder. Now, as if by magic, that scattered mess had become a shimmering setting for the jewel of Francesca, one that set off her summery skin, complemented the golden gleam in her dark brown hair, and presented her generous bosom for the world to enjoy.

She was nothing less than a goddess in gold. And not some out-of-reach perfect goddess, but an earthy, voluptuous goddess of laughter, and cake, and Bolognese sauce, a bit of divine female with a sweet, hot liquid center and the capacity for loud, enthusiastic orgasms.

Eventually he managed to make his mouth work. "You look very nice, Miss Penrose," he said simply.

Francesca knew that he had likely said the very same thing to Judith when he saw her, but she also knew that he had not looked at Judith as if he wanted to strip every stitch of silk from her body and lay her down on the carpet for seven hours.

Oh heavens. Yes, please. Let us turn back the clock a day so that you can be all mine again.

She bobbed a little curtsy. "Why, thank you, sir," she said

airily, turning back to Judith. "Are we quite ready to leave? I am greatly looking forward to dancing!"

Sir Geoffrey harrumphed. "This is the Duke of Camberton's ball. He is a major patron of the Royal Fraternity of Life Sciences. We are not going there to dance!"

"Of course not, Papa," Judith said soothingly. "Francesca fully realizes her responsibility to represent the family well before the Fraternity, I'm sure."

Francesca smiled at her very frustrating uncle. "Francesca fully realizes her responsibility to dance until her slippers fall to pieces!" And she said it out loud. Or rather, muttered it. Whispered really, after her uncle had turned his back on her.

You lump of cold porridge!

But no matter. She was on her way to a real London Society ball. In a wonderful dress in a carriage with her family and a magnificent man.

A man who is going to marry your cousin.

Pish and tosh. I shall not allow that to spoil my first English ball!

However, when she was seated next to her uncle, across from Judith, she had to admit that her cousin and Mr. Worthington made a handsome couple. The biologist in her could not help but calculate the high probability of tall, blue-eyed, extremely attractive offspring.

By the time the carriage had crossed the three-quarters of a mile to the grand Mayfair home of the Duke of Camberton, Francesca had lost a certain amount of her gaiety to the sobering understanding that perhaps he was not her Mr. Worthington after all.

ORION ASCENDED THE ornate staircase and stepped into the Duke of Camberton's shimmering ballroom. Judith was at his side, and Sir Geoffrey and Francesca were directly behind. He had been dragged to a number of the Duke of Camberton's events during the past months as escort for his cousin, Bliss.

Until he heard Judith catch her breath and tighten her gloved hand on his forearm, he never even considered that first-time guests might be surprised at the extravagant ballroom.

Judith raised her eyes to the four monstrous crystal chandeliers overhead, her lips parting in awe. "Impressive," she said.

"Quite," Orion concurred.

Francesca, never one to favor restraint, gasped loudly and released a mellifluous string of Italian superlatives. *"Bellisimo! Molto bello! Favoloso!"*

Orion stifled a smile, secretly amused at the unleashed exuberance that was Miss Francesca Penrose.

In truth, Francesca had not exaggerated. The Duke of Camberton's ballroom was as lavish as anything Orion had seen in St. James's Palace, the home of the Prince Regent himself. It was a shining testament to Neville's—er, the duke's—unlimited resources and exquisite taste.

Beneath their feet, an iridescent marble floor stretched out, inlaid with a subtle basket-weave pattern of cream and rose. The pale mint green walls towered at least three stories high and were offset by moldings painted with gold leaf. There were immense palladium windows, stately doors opened to the fragrant outside terraces, and a dozen marble columns draped in rich fabric. Along the walls, every manner of manicured greenery and exotic potted palm was displayed, each set in an individual golden planter.

Amid the overwhelming splendor, there were two main focal points in the room. A grand marble staircase swooped down from a mezzanine above, hinting of many a grand entrance. Orion thought that in Francesca's magically inclined mind it might be the chandeliers that ruled the ballroom. Hundreds of candles blazed in four huge, multitiered fixtures, their flames refracted endlessly in the glass. The effect was that a magical luminosity shimmered down upon those below, accenting every jewel, every bit of silk, satin, and brocade. Beneath such grand lighting, it seemed that every woman might appear beautiful and every gentleman tall. The notion made him smile.

Within moments, the party of four had been swallowed in the ebb and flow of finery, and Orion noted that Sir Geoffrey gravitated toward a small gathering of Society members. Francesca wandered off by herself toward the sweets table. He could not help but watch her walk away. Her decadent bare shoulders and golden curves looked as if they belonged here. Indeed, the entire ballroom appeared as if it had been designed around Francesca, for she was just as luscious, just as unrestrained, as the Duke of Camberton's decorating tastes.

The voice of the duke himself jarred Orion from his dreamy reverie.

"Miss Blayne," Orion heard him say. "You look lovely tonight. Welcome." Neville bowed graciously before Judith, and she answered with the daintiest of curtsies and her sincere gratitude for being invited to such a fine event.

"On the contrary," he said, his boyish face set off by a friendly smile. "I am honored that you and Sir Geoffrey could join us this evening." He turned to Orion. "Mr. Worthington! I am well pleased to see you."

"And I you, Your Grace." Orion bowed courteously.

The duke waved off the social niceties. He and Orion had been friendly acquaintances nearly a year, as Neville was a school chum of Orion's brother-in-law, Elektra's husband, Lord Aaron Arbogast. Neville was a bookish man, with dark hair and pale skin, slight in build but kind of heart. Orion had always enjoyed his company. In fact, he thought Neville a rarity in the aristocracy, presenting himself as a gentleman of science first and a duke as an afterthought.

"It has been too long," Neville said, grinning at Orion. "And no more of this 'Your Grace' nonsense."

"Indeed, Your . . . er . . . Neville. It's been months, I'm afraid."

"Is your apprenticeship with Sir Geoffrey progressing

nicely?" The duke smiled again at Judith, sure to include her in the conversation.

Suddenly, Orion found himself in a pickle. The truth was, he had no grasp of the state of his apprenticeship. Orion couldn't say he had much by way of affection for his mentor, or even a working familiarity.

He answered as judiciously as possible. "I may need more time to answer that question correctly, Your Grace." He glanced at Judith, who remained pleasantly impassive, her hands clasped to her waist, her lips set in that smile-yet-not-a-smile she so often displayed. She showed no interest whatsoever in the conversation.

The duke raised an eyebrow. "Oh? How so?"

Orion had no desire to be disrespectful of Sir Geoffrey. Not only did he rely on that alliance to further his career as a scientist; he had never been one to gossip behind another's back. "It has been quite an education working with such an accomplished member of the Royal Fraternity of Life Sciences," Orion said diplomatically. "It is my hope that I shall join your ranks sometime soon."

"Splendid!" Neville leaned closer to Orion, clearly ready to move on to the next topic, one that must have interested him a great deal more than Sir Geoffrey and the Fraternity, if the twinkle in his eye was any indication. "Might you have accompanied your cousin, Bliss, here this evening? I made a point of sending her an invitation, along with the rest of your family, of course."

"Ah." Orion scanned the huge ballroom for the telltale signs of a cluster of Worthingtons—formal dress a little too colorful, smiles a little too open. It took him mere seconds to locate Archie and Iris, his brother Dade, and yes, his cousin, Bliss.

At past engagements the duke had not bothered to hide his fondness for Orion's pretty young cousin. He suspected it had more to do with her straightforward manner and stunning figure than her industrious nature. Bliss was as hardworking and practical as a farmwife, qualities not typically found in a duchess.

Before Orion could inform the Duke of Camberton that he had, in fact, located Bliss, he heard Neville exhale quickly.

"Who, pray tell, is that vision in gold?"

Orion and Judith turned in unison to follow the duke's blatant stare. And there came Francesca, returning from the sweets table with a dainty cake balanced in her fingers. She was weaving in and out of the ballroom crowd, her eyes sparkling with delight.

Orion was suddenly awash in an emotion he had never before experienced. It was thoroughly unpleasant, a hot and sharp dread laced with protective anger. It was *jealousy*, of all things. The thought that another man might admire Francesca's beauty—even the kindly Neville—was unacceptable to him. To make matters even more unpleasant, a generous sprinkling of guilt had just added itself to the emotional mix. Orion was supposed to be courting Judith, was he not? Yet they stood next to each other as stiff and cold as the marble floor beneath their feet as all his heat and desire were directed toward the girl with the cake!

What a tangled mess!

"I see Bliss, Your Grace." That was how Orion decided to redirect Neville's attention. "She is standing there, toward the bottom of the staircase." Orion placed a gentle hand on the duke's shoulder and turned his body until it faced away from Francesca. "Do you see? In the blue?"

"Ah, yes! Of course." Neville promised to visit with them later in the evening. "Enjoy yourselves. Now, if you would please excuse me."

The moment Neville stepped away, a chill crept over Orion. Judith stood at his side, her perfectly shaped head perched upon her elegant neck, her pretty eyes gazing out a window. He could not help but stare at her, his scientific mind searching for an answer that had thus far eluded him. How could it be that Judith was everything he assumed he would one day desire in a female companion, yet she left him unaffected, unchanged? He considered the fine shape of her cheek, her intelligence, the pink of her lips, her decorum, the delicate earlobe, her soothing voice . . . She possessed all the desired elements, yet she did not stir him.

Francesca stirred him.

Astounding. Judith Blayne was a lovely and perfect English rose, yet she had no effect on him.

Francesca, the Italian wildflower, affected every part of him—mind, body, and heart.

Orion was stabbed by a sudden pang of shame. It was so clear to him now. Courting a lady for whom he had no feelings was a lie. It was wrong to seek a lady's hand as a way to advance his career. And it would be nothing less than a sin to marry a woman he did not wish to spend his life with.

Suddenly, the silence between them became deafening. Judith daintily cleared her throat.

"Shall I get you a lemonade, Miss Blayne?" Despite the turmoil in his soul, Orion found himself behaving like a trained monkey. He promised himself he would find a way to rectify the situation to everyone's betterment, and soon.

Judith turned to him. Her mouth had curled up into a smile, but her eyes remained a pale and placid blue. "Yes, that would be lovely, Mr. Worthington. Thank you."

"And may I be promised the first quadrille of the evening?"

"Of course." She nodded, then glanced down and away. That was his cue to take his leave.

Was it wrong that once he excused himself from Judith's company, relief rushed over him like a cool breeze? Good God! How had this happened? He had arrived at Blayne House, intending to immerse himself in the study of botanical compounds. Anything and everything else had been inconsequential. Yet here he was, trapped in a romantic quagmire! Such a messy, disorganized state of affairs re-minded him far too much of his own family's modus ope-randi, and he could not believe he had put himself in such a situation.

"Well, what do we have here?" a voice said from behind him. "If it isn't Sir Geoffrey's fresh meat!"

Chapter 26

THE tiny hairs on the nape of Orion's neck had already begun to rise as he turned around. Who had spoken those odd words? He should not have been shocked by the visage that greeted him—Nicholas Witherspoon, the utmost of the idiotic suitors who called on Blayne House far too regularly.

"Witherspoon." Orion scowled as the fop's words echoed in his mind. *Fresh meat?* What could he possibly have been implying? "Good evening to you."

Moments like these were precisely why Orion preferred science over Society. The rules of science were straightforward and observable. Hydrogen was always hydrogen. It did not frolic through ballrooms masquerading as oxygen, nor could it pretend to be magnesium even in the darkest of lighting. By comparison, London Society could be a twisted maze of artifice and politics, and Witherspoon was one of its finest creations. It was common knowledge that the man's claims of serious scientific inquiry into the field of biology were suspect. But his family's wealth and connections had paved the way for his membership in the Fraternity, and his lack of serious technical accomplishment was ignored by his army of rich and powerful cronies. Should Orion wish to join the ranks of the Fraternity, Witherspoon, though a pompous ass, was not someone he could afford to offend.

Witherspoon's sneer lingered like the odor of whiskey on his breath. "So, how are things with Sir Pilfery?"

Sir Pilfery? Although Orion felt no deep affection for his mentor, he did feel obligated to defend against such cowardly slander from the likes of this reptile.

"What exactly are you implying, Witherspoon?" Too late, Orion realized he had pressed close enough to enter the thick of Witherspoon's ethanol vapor. He leaned away.

Witherspoon chuckled. "Oh, you'll find out soon enough, Worthington. All of his assistants find out eventually." The sneer widened. "And say, don't forget to visit the card room this evening—Camberton never skimps on the quality of his whiskey."

With that, the idiot, whiskey fumes trailing behind him, paraded off into the crowd of guests, leaving Orion's mind in a state of mayhem. What next? Masked highwaymen? Flood? He felt his jaw clench and his stomach roil. What had promised to be just another tedious Society ball was developing into a drama worthy of a staging in the Worthington family parlor!

Orion continued with his errand to fetch lemonade for Judith, but he was so distracted, he accidentally jostled several guests and found himself apologizing again and again.

"Please excuse me. So sorry . . ."

What had Witherspoon meant? Orion racked his brain for the memory of any rumor, anything he had ever heard about Sir Geoffrey or his previous assistants, and that was when it occurred to him that he had never heard anything about the ongoing careers of Sir Geoffrey's research assistants. Might that in itself be a concern? Had Orion ever heard the names of any previous assistants? Were any of them now pursuing their own scientific studies? And why was the position with Sir Geoffrey available in the first place?

It all funneled into another question, one that plagued Orion more than anything else: Why him? Why had Sir Geoffrey summoned Orion as his assistant and suggested that Judith and he were a good match? Orion had always conducted his research somewhat outside the established scientific circles, and though his work was acknowledged, he had never promoted himself or implied he was available to work as an assistant to a well-established London scientist.

Orion procured the lemonade and returned to Judith, aware that his distracted behavior bordered on rude. He stood by her as she took delicate sips of her drink, yet he was unable to engage in small talk. When the quadrille began, he held her gloved hand in his and absently led her around the dance floor, weaving in and out of other dancers, pulling away, then returning, passing by other couples, switching partners, then returning once more. Orion only snapped out of his private fog when the unmistakable scent of Francesca tantalized his senses and he found himself touching hands with the shimmering dark-haired beauty.

She smiled up at him. "Are you enjoying yourself, Mr. Worthington?"

He felt his lips part, but no words escaped.

"I'll take that as a 'yes,'" she said, suddenly swept away by her dancing partner, none other than the duke himself.

Orion returned to Judith in proper turn, and though he tried very hard to keep his focus on his dance partner, he could not keep his eyes from scanning the ballroom in search of a flash of gold silk and dark curls. His blood began to heat. Orion suddenly felt a completely inappropriate and illogical distaste for the affable Duke of Camberton!

Never in his life had Orion felt so without tether. Francesca. Judith. Sir Geoffrey. Neville . . . All was disjointed and unsettled, out of order.

"You are a skilled dancer."

Orion's gaze snapped to Judith's, and he attempted to summon his manners. "Thank you. As are you, Miss Blayne."

"Thank you."

The quadrille was coming to a close. Orion realized with alarm that he was losing his opportunity to gain the information he needed. "Has your father had many assistants before me?" he asked abruptly.

Judith raised her eyebrows and shrugged as if the conversation already bored her. "I'm afraid I can't remember the exact count."

"Exact count?" He heard his voice sharpen. "Then there have been many? Have any of them moved on to do their own research? Might any of them be here tonight?"

Orion had been so consumed by his own circling thoughts that he hadn't noticed the music had ceased and that he and Judith now stood unmoving in the center of the marble dance floor. He noticed the smallest patch of pink spread over her flawless cheeks.

"Oh what a shame!" Judith placed her gloved hand on Orion's forearm and urged him to walk. "Look! Francesca is sitting all alone. It would be most kind if you asked her to dance."

JUDITH NUDGED MR. Worthington toward Francesca and, with great relief, made her escape. She was happy to let Francesca dance with the fellow. She seemed to find him more interesting than Judith ever had.

At the edge of the dance floor, she hesitated. Judith was so rarely left alone, but she decided she quite enjoyed it compared to the alternative: to go off looking for Papa. Surely, he would be orating to a group of his cronies, and if she were in their company, he would only succumb to his usual performance. Papa would shower her with artificial affection and parade her before his crowd like a prized Pomeranian. *No, thank you.*

Someone familiar caught her eye. Across the room, Mr. Nicholas Witherspoon seemed to be making his way to her general location, although his obvious drunken state caused his progress to veer to and fro. Judith turned her back to his approach, closing her eyes for strength. *Again, no. Really, so very unwanted.*

"H-hello, Miss Blayne!"

That's better. Judith opened her eyes and let out her breath, turning to Asher Langford with relief. "Good evening, Mr. Langford!" She allowed him a small smile. Dear Asher. It was quite reassuring to see a friendly face—at least, a face that did not wish to buy her, sell her, or otherwise utilize her.

It was restful, being with someone who made so few demands. Of course, she had known Asher forever. They had always been comfortable in each other's company. Their mothers had been close friends, and she had played at his house when she was a child.

Was I ever a child? The idea was shocking to her, since she felt a hundred years old at that moment.

Asher seemed to sense her weariness. "Er . . . may I . . . lemonade?"

Judith shuddered. She had no taste for sugary things, after a lifetime of Papa's bland preferences. It was only since Francesca's arrival that sweets had been part of her life—and she had had enough of bubbly, liberated Francesca and her culinary offerings. "No, thank you, sir. Let us sit for a moment, here by the garden doors."

Asher bobbed a nod. "Yes . . . it's cooler . . ."

Sitting would hide them behind the dancers, out of sight of all those she wished to avoid. The drunken, sarcastic Witherspoon. The dutiful, distracted Worthington. And especially Papa.

Asher pulled out two chairs from the line set aside for wallflowers and elder dames of Society. They sat in companionable silence. Judith felt the ever-present tightness of her spine relax somewhat in Asher's nonjudgmental company.

She let out a breath and tipped her head back slightly to gaze at the elegant ceiling medallions from which the grand crystal chandeliers dangled. "It is a lovely hall, is it not?"

Asher looked around the exquisite ballroom. "It is . . . er . . . very grand. I . . . I'd rather not dance, though . . . if . . . if you don't mind . . ."

Judith blinked. "Heavens no. I dislike such public displays. I should like to dance with someone only if we could be by ourselves on a rooftop, with no one else watching, or judging, or looking for fault—" Suddenly aware that her facade was slipping, she straightened in her chair. "It is a very successful event," she stated. "The Duke of Camberton must be quite pleased with the turnout."

When she dared a glance at Asher, she saw with surprise that he had a slight smile on his sweet, familiar face. With surprise she realized that he was quite handsome when he smiled. "Don't worry," he said to her quietly. "I won't tell anyone."

Judith breathed a small sigh of relief. Dear Asher. He was such a good friend. So handsome when he smiled.

With the utmost gentleness, Asher leaned closer and brushed the back of his gloved knuckles against hers. It was such a gentle gesture and ended as soon as it began. But somewhere deep inside, Judith felt a knot release. Lightness expanded inside her chest. It was a most extraordinary sensation.

THE NEXT DANCE was a waltz, but Francesca knew it was a bit late for the two of them to fret over tiny improprieties. So of course she said yes when Orion stood before her—much like a wolf cornering its prey—and asked her to dance.

Perhaps she agreed a little too enthusiastically. She blamed the champagne.

As Orion led her to the center of the ballroom, she mar-

veled at his lack of concern for the rules of Society. She found
it most refreshing. But perhaps he didn't even realize what he
was walking into, that an unattached couple locked in a waltz
would surely inspire comment.

It did not matter. Either way would suffice for Francesca,
since the end result was a forbidden waltz with the dark and
desirable Orion Worthington.

Francesca was abruptly swept into Orion's arms, carried
away in a swell of stringed instrumentation. His hand expertly
pressed against the small of her back, holding their bodies a
hairbreadth apart. When he pulled her into a turn, she lost
her footing. Suddenly, her breasts were crushed against the
front of Orion's lean body.

"Hiccup!"

He promptly set her to rights, then gazed down with a flash
of curious amusement in his eyes. "Would you care for a glass
of champagne after our dance?"

"No, thank you," she said primly, keeping up with the
steps. "I have already had a taste or two."

"And was the quality up to your standards, Miss Penrose?"

"Hmm," she answered, pondering her response as she
swayed in his confident hold. "It was not Prosecco, certainly,
but I did find both glasses quite refreshing."

"I see." Orion quirked his lips with the barest hint of a
smile. "And the cakes?"

"The three I had were quite sumptuous."

They continued waltzing, Orion more cautious with his
turns, careful to steady Francesca with each change of direction.

She gazed up at him with an unrestrained grin. "You are
a fine dancer, Mr. Worthington."

"You are a fine partner, Miss Penrose."

"Then let it be said that we dance well together." She nodded, quite satisfied with the accuracy of the statement. Francesca pondered whether Orion was even aware of how

effortlessly they moved together. "Indeed, the bonds of some partnerships are stronger than others. In some cases they add up to more than the sum of their parts."

"A sound conclusion."

"Indeed! For example, on their own, basil and oregano are perfectly useful spices, yet together they form the foundation for an entire cuisine!"

Orion pulled back a bit to get a better look at Francesca, the ballroom philosopher. A segment of errant curls had loosened from its ribbon and now brushed against the side of her creamy neck. Her cheeks were flushed from the champagne . . . or the cakes . . . or the waltz. Or all three.

What was it about Francesca that captured him so, kicked down his hard exterior, and melted the cold core he'd always believed to be at the center of him? Was it her good-hearted innocence? Her disregard for the trivial "should-and-should-nots" of London Society? Perhaps it was merely the Italian in her, an upbringing that gave her a zest for living, an appetite for only the most delicious of life's morsels.

Whatever contributed to it, the overall effect was that Orion found Francesca indescribably sweet and open, and she intrigued him more than any single person ever had, man or woman.

"You are quite the original thinker, Miss Penrose."

Francesca rolled her eyes at him. "I'll take that as a compliment."

"As you should." Orion heard something in his own voice. If he didn't know better, he would think it was happiness. Maybe even joy.

DANCING WITH ORION was a pleasant surprise. In Francesca's experience, male scientists thought their time too important to learn to dance well. Orion moved smoothly, leading her in a whirling path through the other dancing couples, as if they all stood still while she and Orion flowed freely like a stream through rocks.

The strength with which he led quite took her breath away, if truth were told. His firm hand on her back guided her across the floor, and his hand around hers made it easier to follow, as easy as a walk through a park. Even if she had never danced before and knew none of the steps, she could have danced with Orion.

It was more than simple skill on the ballroom floor, more than following the music and avoiding stepping on each other's toes. Their dancing contained a unique quality, an effortlessness not shared by the other couples at the ball. Francesca wondered if he even noticed. Orion so often seemed to be above normal, everyday concerns—oblivious in the way that only true genius could be. Did Mr. Orion Worthington realize how rare their partnership was? And if he did, could he feel the bond growing between them with every touch, every look? If he did, then how could he continue the pretense that he meant to marry Judith?

Perhaps because he still had every intention of doing so.

Was she being a fool? Was she building castles of fog in her imagination, believing that just because she loved him, he must love her in return?

If it were not for Orion's mastery of his dance partner, Francesca surely would have stumbled.

I love him.

Oh no.

Chapter 27

L OVE?
Oh yes. Francesca had never been more sure of anything.

For a long moment, careful to keep her eyes from meeting his, she allowed herself to absorb the wonder of it. She'd assumed her heart was immune, for she had never felt more than a passing interest in any man before. One might have had a nice smile, but his candle burned too dimly. Another provided good conversation, but she felt nothing stir at the sound of his voice.

So when it struck her that she was in love—how could she be so very sure?

Because if he turned and walked away from me at this very moment, I am quite sure that my heart would tear itself from my chest to follow him!

It was horrible. It was marvelous. It was dizzying, and tragic—and the worst mistake she could have possibly made.

Oh heavens, how did I let this happen?

The musicians brought the waltz to a close, and her feet

slowed at Orion's unspoken cue. Numbly, as if her hands and feet were frozen in a killing winter frost, Francesca allowed him to guide her back to where Judith waited. To Orion's credit, it was obvious that he knew something was wrong. He did not bother with inane questions regarding her health. Instead, he barked a single command to Judith as he walked past. "Water!"

Judith gasped at the expression on Francesca's face. "Of course!" She turned to move quickly toward the refreshment table, her blue silk skirts flaring.

With his arm still around Francesca, Orion guided her to the graceful double doors leading to the balcony outside the ballroom.

Once she was on the terrace, the chill, damp air stole some of Francesca's numbness away. Unfortunately, that only made more room for the pain.

Orion bent to look her in the eye as he tilted her chin up with one finger. "What happened to you in there? Was it the heat of the crush, the crowd? No, no, that wouldn't bother you, would it, being from warmer climes? What was it, then? Tell me!"

Francesca blinked back the dampness in her eyes and met the concern in his gaze. How could she tell him that in a single second of mind-twisting clarity, she had at long last found love—found him!—and just as quickly had lost him again? For their one night was over, and he intended to wed her cousin.

He still held her hand in his. Taking refuge in the warmth of his fingers wrapped around hers, she closed her eyes and simply ached. The bittersweet pain that flooded her might pass in time. She was not a fool. She knew that disappointment in love did not kill.

It only felt as though she might die from it.

I want to tell him.

But she must not tell him.

What good it is to love someone if they do not know?

But why tell him something that he most certainly did not wish to hear?

And what good would it do, other than expose her silly heart? What purpose would be gained with that? If Orion loved her, surely she would know it. He liked her body, and obviously enjoyed her touch. He had said he admired her mind. He certainly enjoyed her cooking!

That was not love. That was friendship, or perhaps some more amorous version of friendship. Most of the time they argued like fishwives over nothing at all. Unless they were kissing . . . or more. But that was only lust, and it was over with.

I do not want it to be done!

"Kiss me," she whispered.

Orion did not hesitate. All he heard was that she needed him. All he knew was that he could no longer fight the power she had over him. Whatever she asked of him would be done in an instant.

To deny Francesca would be to deny himself.

The moment the words left her lips, Orion tugged the hand that he held, pulled her two steps closer, and pressed her open palm to his chest. He slid the fingers of his other hand up into her hair and tilted her head back. He cradled her there before him. Possessiveness swept him as he lowered his mouth to hers.

Mine.

The first touch of Orion's lips upon hers was warm and gentle, even questioning. She could feel his concern for her—he sought to understand what caused her mood to shift in the ballroom. But Francesca ignored his gentle questioning, his tender concern, and instead made it clear that she wanted something more. She wanted to ride the wild tide of love and need within her. Francesca rose up on her tiptoes, pressed her mouth to his, and parted her lips. She began to dart her tongue across his. She nibbled at his lips. She opened for him and welcomed him in.

With a low, surprised moan, Orion responded instantly. Warm hands became hot and demanding as he pulled her hard against him. His tongue tangled with hers. She felt his erection rise against her lower belly, and her own body yielded in response. Within seconds the core of her had gone hot and wet, ready for all he had to give and all he wanted to take—all from just one taste of him!

Somewhere, dimly, in the recesses of his mind, Orion was aware that they were on the balcony outside of the Duke of Camberton's elaborate ballroom, in plain sight of anyone who happened to glance out the double doors or step out for a breath of air. The odd thing was that the concern seemed trivial. What was important was that Orion had not touched Francesca for an eternity. A day? A decade? These were details that belonged in the realm of logic and reason, which he had clearly left behind. All he understood was that he had missed her, and he would be making up for lost time.

At that moment, Orion was lost in a wonderland of lust. His heart beat with the truth of his desire for her. His lungs burned with her heady female scent. He knew he had no choice but to claw at the golden silk of her gown like an animal, tear away her bodice, sweep his hands up the naked flesh of her back as she writhed in his grasp . . .

Out of nowhere, something—or someone—flicked at his ear.

"*Cacchio!* Drat! Someone was here!"

As if emerging from a black pool of confusion, Orion opened his eyes and reared his head back. Francesca stood before him, wild-eyed and frowning. But how had this come to be? Just a moment ago there was the ripping of her gown, the writhing of her naked flesh.

Or perhaps not.

The fully clothed Francesca smacked him in the arm. "Look! There!"

Orion followed Francesca's trembling finger to see a single, lonely crystal goblet filled with water. It had been placed close to where they stood, balanced on the flat surface of a stone balustrade. A fascinating pattern of condensation had begun to form on the outside of the cut glass . . .

Orion suddenly snapped to awareness. *"Merda!"* He quickly glanced toward Francesca. "I do apologize for my language."

"Your language? I don't give a fig about your language!" She gestured wildly. "Someone has seen us—and I think it may have been Judith!"

ONCE ORION HAD straightened his waistcoat and realigned the buttons of his dress coat—and sought one last visual confirmation that Francesca's ball gown was indeed still intact—he escorted Miss Penrose back into the festivities. He did not wish to know if any of the gentlemen stared. He did not notice if any of the ladies whispered, or giggled, or hid their comments behind a gloved hand as he and Francesca strolled by. Orion simply put one foot ahead of the other, his head held high, with Francesca's delicate hand balanced on his forearm.

But he did see Sir Geoffrey cutting a path through the dance floor and heading their way. His benefactor resembled a frothing horse after a long journey. Clearly the evening had been too much for the elderly gentleman, as Orion noticed how his hands shook and beads of sweat formed on his pasty brow.

The instant Sir Geoffrey opened his mouth to speak— something unkind, in all likelihood—Judith swept in, placing herself in front of Orion and Francesca.

"Papa! You look ever so tired!" She supported his elbow and turned him toward the front staircase and the exit that lay beyond. "Let me call for our carriage," she said, supporting her father as they walked.

Orion exchanged a brief glance with Francesca, and he saw his own question reflected in her eyes: Had Judith just intervened on their behalf? Had she just spared them embarrassment of some kind? After they had betrayed her so?

Moments later, Orion sat rigid upon the carriage seat, his mind harkening back to his childhood. As a Worthington, he had been forced to endure many a strange carriage ride. There was the time Iris staged an entire production of Shakespeare's *Much Ado About Nothing* inside the carriage while traveling from London to Shropshire. And the time Elektra and Callie had been forced to strap the twins to the luggage rack because the reeking boys had wrestled each other into a pit of sheep dung. But that night in Sir Geoffrey's stately carriage was by far the most excruciating three-quarters of a mile of his life.

Indeed, Orion was surprised the horses could pull the weight of all the misery contained within that one small carriage compartment.

He was positioned next to Judith and across from Sir Geoffrey and Francesca. No one made eye contact or attempted small talk. It was as if each person had been depleted from the events of the evening and was now walled off from the others, each lost in his own particular brand of wretchedness.

It was no longer sheer speculation that Sir Geoffrey suffered from some manner of illness. His skin appeared gray in the dim carriage light, and he was sweating profusely. Judith had taken measures to ensure his comfort, but he refused any assistance offered from Orion or Francesca. Her father was slumped against the seat directly across from Judith, his gaze averted.

To Orion's right, Miss Blayne alternated her absent stares between the open carriage window and her father, her face remaining a blank page all the while. Judith's posture was as regal as always, and she held her clasped hands in her lap as if she were on a leisurely day trip in the country. But there was a tightness around her eyes and mouth that Orion had never before noticed. She reminded him of a violin string wound too tightly, about to spring loose from its tuning peg.

And then there was Francesca. She bit her lip and wrung her hands, her curls now surrendering to gravity and tumbling with abandon from their pins and pearls. The golden skin of her chest was flushed, and she stared down at her dancing slippers as if they were the most fascinating footwear in London. Orion's chest tightened with guilt. It was his fault she was distraught. He was responsible for her fear that they had been seen on the balcony, and by Judith no less. He was to blame for it all. He had lost his mind, abandoning the reason and logic that had always separated him from typical Worthington madness.

However, Orion had to admit that the entire evening could have been a page from the *Worthington Family Chronicles*, complete with unrestrained emotion, mayhem, subterfuge, and avoidance of reality. The night had been a mess, pure and simple, and this carriage compartment had become a stewpot of human foibles.

All the while, Francesca's scent surrounded him, squeezed his heart, and intoxicated his blood. There was no escape.

Orion closed his eyes and forced himself to return to the world in which he belonged. The world of science—chemistry, botany, beakers, and laboratories. He needed to immerse himself in the clean and precise rules of science, where everything made sense.

The carriage wheel caught on an uneven cobblestone, and the little group was jostled about inside the compartment. Judith was thrown close to his right leg.

"Pardon me," Orion said. She turned away.

And that was when it occurred to Orion that he could never marry Judith. That meant he would not be able to marry himself into the Royal Fraternity of Life Sciences—and why would he need to? He was Orion Worthington, and he was perfectly capable of earning admission on his own merit. The Fraternity would eventually welcome him because it would be unable to ignore the importance of his contribution to science. It might take him a bit longer with his limited resources, but Orion had never lacked faith in his own abilities.

It was settled. The instant Orion returned to Blayne House, he would pack his thankfully scanty belongings and leave. He would focus anew on his own experiments and make his own way into scientific history.

Chapter 28

SIR Geoffrey and Mr. Worthington had said their good nights. Francesca and Judith stood side by side in the foyer of Blayne House while Eva, the lady's maid, took their wraps. Francesca was jittery. A queasy ball of unease had taken up residence in her belly. She knew what had to be done and prayed she was brave enough to do it.

The truth would have to be brought out into the open.

Francesca watched Judith pass her reticule to Eva and begin the long process of unbuttoning her evening gloves. Her cousin was so lovely and calm, always so kind to Francesca. Judith had certainly never caused her harm. In fact, Francesca liked Judith and never even imagined keeping a secret from her. Yet as of that evening, Francesca had betrayed her. A lie was now wedged between them, like a splinter in a fingertip, and it had to be removed for relief to be found.

"Judith, may I speak with you a moment?"

Her cousin's cool blue gaze settled on Francesca. "Of course."

Eva extended her hand for Francesca's reticule, and she nearly dropped it in her nervousness.

Oh! Where was she to begin? There was so much she wished to say to Judith—and learn from her—and yet she was afraid that her cousin might shrink away from a serving of honesty in its more direct form. In addition, she worried any confession could damage Orion's chances at membership in the Fraternity.

To complicate matters further, Francesca wasn't even certain she should feel guilty. Were Orion and Judith truly involved? Was there any kind of formal understanding at all?

Judith stood before her, impenetrable as always, obviously waiting for Francesca to speak. How ridiculous she would seem if she asked for a conversation she was unable to start!

"Er . . . thank you for the water."

One of Judith's fair eyebrows arched slightly in question.

"The water you brought out to the terrace when I was feeling unwell."

Judith's mouth produced a tight smile. "Of course. I instructed a servant to bring it to you."

A servant? Highly unlikely. Francesca knew what she had heard and seen—a brief flash of cornflower blue out of the corner of her eye, a small gasp of surprise, the rustle of silk followed by the sound of quickly retreating footsteps. Granted, Francesca had been in the throes of being thoroughly and enthusiastically kissed at that moment. Perhaps there was an infinitesimally small possibility she was mistaken.

Had the quick footsteps she had heard been the fleeing of a shocked lady, or merely the sound of a busy servant with better things to do?

She studied her cousin. On the surface, Judith seemed her usual composed self, yet Francesca could see the tendons in her neck tighten. It broke her heart to think she had caused her cousin pain.

"I do not wish to hurt you."

Judith handed her gloves to Eva without a trace of reaction. "There is no danger of that, Cousin. I assure you."

Francesca was puzzled. Had Judith just implied she did not care for Orion? Or had she hinted that there was no feeling between them? "I don't under—"

"Perhaps I shall take a page from your book and never wed at all!"

Francesca swore she saw Judith's lip twitch involuntarily. Could it be that Francesca was seeing the first crack in her cousin's facade of porcelain perfection?

"Judith?"

"I am off to bed. Papa will expect me to be useful in the morning. Good night, Francesca."

Judith made an elegant turn and glided off toward the staircase. Francesca felt her jaw unhinge as she watched her cousin ascend the stairs.

That night she tossed in bed for hours, unable to sleep despite her deep exhaustion. If Judith was not fond of Orion, she needed to tell him so. If the courtship was some kind of ruse, he needed to know the truth.

Yet it was not Francesca's place to right these wrongs. The matter was between Judith and Orion.

So then, what could she do?

Francesca punched her pillow and let out a giant sigh of frustration, flopping onto her back. She stared up at the dark ceiling, thinking . . .

She wanted Orion Worthington. Her epiphany on the ballroom floor was not the product of champagne. She loved him. It was a fact. It was permanent. It was undeniable.

She had thought she'd known who she was and what she wanted. Marriage had seemed like a restraint that would stunt her dreams and prevent her from seeing and experiencing and taking large bites out of the world!

For the first time, it occurred to her that it might depend on *whom* one married. Perhaps an ordinary man would try to tame Francesca's ambitions—but Orion Worthington was no ordinary man! Orion felt that his mother should paint and that his sister should publish more botanicals and that ferocious little Attie's mind was even better than his own!

I want it all.

Oh yes. She wanted liberty *and* understanding. She wanted to see the world *and* to share it with someone. The very possibility that she could indeed have everything a woman could desire, personal fulfillment *and* marital happiness, sent a wild thrill of delight through her.

I could have freedom . . . and I could have a family of my own, at last.

Perhaps her duty was to persuade Orion to break off any understanding he might have with Judith. And the best way to do that would be to tell him she loved him and make it impossible for him to deny that he loved her.

Chapter 29

THE laboratory was blissfully silent and, better yet, entirely lacking in emotional turmoil. Orion preferred to pack his few things here before stepping back into the fraught environment of Blayne House.

Orion pulled his formal cravat loose and tossed the choking thing onto Francesca's worktable as he undid his collar studs. His fine coat followed the cravat. Now in his shirtsleeves, he stretched the tightness from his shoulders.

The presentation to the Fraternity was to be the following night—and Orion would not be there. The Fraternity had loomed so large in his hopes for so long. He'd thought he would do anything to win its acclaim, but it seemed even his most fiery ambition halted at pledging his life to someone he did not care for. He would have to get there another way. He faced the shelf of solvents, leaned his rear against the marble worktable, and willed himself to think of some alternative to returning to Worthington House.

He tried, he truly did, but he became distracted by the lingering scent of orange blossoms. Where was it coming from? The laboratory had been thoroughly cleaned of all traces of the explosive chemical reaction the day before. Surely Francesca's perfume had not survived the scrubbing?

Then Orion realized that Francesca was on him, all over his hands and, yes, perfuming his waistcoat. With a growl, he pulled it off and tossed it away. It was just as well, because despite the night chill pervading the laboratory, his blood seemed to still be running rather hot.

He closed his eyes and ran his hands through his hair. *Think about the future, damn it.*

When he opened his eyes, he could still see Francesca looking sweetly mussed in the moonlight, gazing at him with wonder and alarm in her beautiful eyes . . .

He blinked her away. He was in the laboratory, alone. He focused on the marble floor at his feet. *Clear. Your. Mind.*

Marble was perhaps not the best notion for the flooring of a laboratory. Orion could see where someone, probably a footman, had sanded valiantly at the lesions in the stone left by the splashes of hydrochloric acid.

His heart began to pound in remembered fear. If he'd been even a second later through the door . . .

Stop dwelling on a tragedy that never happened. Attie and her little friend were fine. The damage had been limited to an insignificant coat and the laboratory floor.

The marble might have a grand flair and present a nice, sterile appearance, but in truth the stone was very vulnerable. The calcite in the marble had reacted with the acid. The floor would never be the same.

The materials in a laboratory ought to be durable, more resistant to solvents and acids, and, as he thought about his own afternoon of scrubbing under Francesca's watchful eyes, easier to clean.

His mind threatened to veer off to lose itself in the hills and valleys of Francesca's sumptuous body. No. He flexed his neck and shook his head. The future. Not about Francesca. Not about the almost-tragic acid spill.

He gazed at the shelves of chemicals before him. How had Attie even happened upon the precise mixture for hydrochloric acid?

"Indeed, the bonds of some partnerships are stronger than others," Francesca had said.

They had been talking about dancing—or perhaps cooking. With Francesca's clever but outrageous mind, the words could have applied to either. Or both.

Bonds. Partnerships.

Orion's gaze focused suddenly and fiercely on the single shelf of viable solvents he'd classified. None of them were quite right, in themselves. Perhaps he should have tried stronger concentrations—

Or a combination.

Like basil and oregano.

Two thousand years before, Archimedes discovered immersion measurement and declared, "Eureka!"

In a British laboratory two millennia later, Orion Worthington widened his eyes, inhaled the scent of orange blossoms, and whispered, *"Favoloso!"*

IN HIS CHILDHOOD at Worthington Manor, far away in the Shropshire countryside, Orion would often be awakened by a cock's crow.

In London, the trundling of the night-soil cart wheels on cobbles had the same result.

He blinked and lifted his head from his folded arms to realize that he was seated on a stool at the laboratory table. *Yes, that's right.* He'd processed another combination of solvents with the freshly crushed leaves of salad greens from the cook's garden.

The plant matter itself wasn't particularly important. Any fresh, dark green plant would do. The frustration was that although the solvents had dissolved the plant matter, none of them had managed to separate the cellular bonds to release the compounds within.

Orion blinked wearily at the line of test tubes resting in the wooden rack before him. The first four were filled with even green fluid. These were his controls. Two of them contained greens dissolved in acetone, and two of them contained greens dissolved in an alkane solution.

The next five tubes were of varying combinations of the alkane and acetone solvents. Twenty-five percent to seventy-five percent, fifty percent to fifty percent, and so on.

There, sitting in the precise center of the rack, like a queen on her throne, was a single, beautiful test tube unlike all the others.

Layers of color, clearly distinct, ranged from nearly clear to deep green to a strange and mysterious orange.

Complete separation.

At last.

Orion bolted upright. The stool fell to the floor behind him as he leaned closer to the rack of test tubes. He had done it. He had actually done something that no scientist before him had ever managed to do. He had opened the door to an entirely new branch of scientific discovery.

I must tell Francesca!

No, it was Sir Geoffrey he must tell first. Although Orion meant to leave Blayne House behind, it had been his mentor's facility and his interest in this investigation that had prompted Orion's breakthrough in the first place. Sir Geoffrey should hear of this as soon as possible. Then Orion would leave.

In triumph!

Orion glanced through the high windows at the first tinge of dawn light. Sir Geoffrey would not wake for hours yet, and if he held true to form, Orion knew his benefactor would need to take his morning tea before he would be ready for any type of conversation. Orion checked the sky again. He could run the panel once more, just to be sure.

And this time he would stay awake. He smiled to himself. He could not wait to see the chemical reaction with his own eyes!

ORION WAS WAITING for Sir Geoffrey when the man descended the stairs to take his morning tea, this time in the private breakfast room in the back of the house instead of the front parlor. Pennysmith brought the tea tray, with only one teacup, as usual. Orion waited tensely for Sir Geoffrey to imbibe enough of his special tea to regain a bit of color in his cheeks and a glint in his eyes.

Finally, Sir Geoffrey set aside his empty cup—after his third serving!—and bestowed a disgruntled glare upon Orion.

"Out with it, Worthington."

Orion drew in a breath. Part of him wanted to savor the moment. However, Sir Geoffrey was an impatient fellow.

"I've done it. I have found the combination of solvents that will separate the compounds."

Sir Geoffrey blinked. "Theory or practice?"

Orion allowed himself a slight smile. "Practice. I have done it effectively three times in succession."

"When?" Sir Geoffrey's voice was a commanding bark. "In my laboratory? Whom have you told?"

Orion drew back slightly. "Early this morning. Yes, here in your facility. I worked all night. You are the first I have told, out of courtesy for your support."

Sir Geoffrey leapt to his feet and began to stride between the fireplace and the door, his step bouncing and energetic. "Excellent! I knew it!" He thrust out a finger, pointing at the ceiling. "Ha! Those mewling bastards in the Fraternity will have no standing now! Imagine, spreading the notion that I am past my prime! Wait until they hear what I have done!"

Orion blinked. "You mean, what *we* have done." He had

no issue with sharing the credit, for Sir Geoffrey had provided the facility.

Sir Geoffrey turned on Orion viciously. "I wouldn't spread that about if I were you," he snarled. "It is *my* laboratory. *My* supplies. *My* discovery."

Orion drew back from Sir Geoffrey in distaste. "You cannot be serious. How can you expect me to remain silent about this?"

"You'll shut up and be grateful for it." Sir Geoffrey narrowed his eyes to rabid slits. "I can ruin you with a single word, just as I did those other ungrateful assistants I hired. I am renowned the world over, and you are just one of *those* Worthingtons!" His chuckle was a feral growl.

Orion's gut turned to ice. It was all clear now. The wide range of Sir Geoffrey's "contributions" to science, from engineering to chemistry, made much more sense.

The well-timed opening for a new assistant, when such placements were so rare, that came just before Sir Geoffrey's annual presentation to the Royal Fraternity of Life Sciences.

Fresh meat. Sir Pilfery.

His mentor was volatile and unstable—and a thief of the worst kind, stealing a man's very mind from him. He stole his assistants' ideas.

Sir Geoffrey was not done. "If you show proper gratitude, then I think there's no reason to delay the announcement of your engagement to my daughter." He smiled sweetly, his mood turning on a dime.

Orion lifted his chin, sure of his stance now. That particular bait no longer held sway. "No, thank you, sir. I withdraw my suit. I intend to leave Blayne House forthwith."

Sir Geoffrey shook his head, chuckling. "Nonsense. You'll wed my dear Judith. You'll continue doing research for me. A mind like yours comes along rarely. I intend to keep that brilliance on tap, so to speak." He leaned back in his chair, his fingertips steepled over his stout middle, and beamed at

Orion with malignant delight. "Just think of what I can do, my boy! Oh yes, the future is bright, indeed!"

Orion set his teeth. "My future is bright. Yours is finished when I report this malfeasance to the Fraternity."

Sir Geoffrey merely shook his head pleasantly. "Worthington, you have no credibility whatsoever. Your family is well-known for its illicit tomfoolery."

Orion tilted his head, as if examining a new specimen of creature now revealed to him. "My family is not without friends . . . some of them quite powerful."

"And will your powerful friends stand with you when I reveal your crimes committed in my household?"

Crimes? Orion thought quickly back over the length of his stay at Blayne House. Other than a bit of playful breaking and entering by Attie, he hadn't been there long enough to commit any criminal acts.

What about Francesca?

That would look ill upon him, indeed, when viewed from the outside. Interfering with a respectable girl while under his mentor's roof? He had done just that. For the first time, Orion felt a sharp twinge of shame.

However, Francesca would never betray their night together to this man. Furthermore, Orion was certain they had concealed their activities completely from the busybody staff at Blayne House.

"I have nothing to defend. You are bluffing."

Sir Geoffrey simply gazed at him pityingly. He did not seem to be bluffing. And a Worthington could read a man's tells before he could read a news sheet.

Orion felt alarm begin to ring within him.

"Blood will tell, Worthington," Sir Geoffrey said with a sad sigh. "Not your fault, I suppose."

Orion shook his head. "You cannot believe that I will continue to do your research!"

Sir Geoffrey laughed lightly, his eyes sparkling. "Silly boy. Of course you will! If you leave my service, who will take you on? No one, after I tell them that you assaulted my daughter."

"I did no such thing!" Yet—

Francesca. Orion could not help his visible flinch of guilt.

Sir Geoffrey's smile widened. "On the contrary, Penny-smith would be happy to testify to just such an event. And dear Judith will not gainsay me."

Stunned, Orion could only stare at the man. He used to think *his* family was mad. Now, faced with true insanity, he finally saw the difference.

Sir Geoffrey went on in the face of Orion's continued silence. He leaned forward with a vicious glint in his eyes. "Oh yes. You'll be fortunate to avoid a prison sentence—but I wouldn't want to be too public. That would reflect badly on my judgment, of course. Just a few words in the right ears, that sort of thing."

Orion's gut turned to ice. A smear of such magnitude from such a reputable source would indeed bring an end to Orion's future in the world of scientific research—and in Society in general. Such whisper campaigns were impossible to fight, or deny, or defend.

Worse yet, no one would even bother to doubt it. After all, he was one of *those* Worthingtons.

Sir Geoffrey settled into his chair once more and picked up the bell to ring for Pennysmith. "Now go. You look like hell, Worthington. You should get some rest before the presentation. Tonight is going to be very exciting, indeed!"

Chapter 30

REELING inwardly, Orion turned and walked stiffly from the breakfast room and away from the man he'd believed to be his mentor.

What had just happened? How had his triumph so quickly turned to catastrophe?

Numb, he made his way to his room. After all, where else could he go? His choices were painfully clear: He could remain in servitude to Geoffrey Blayne, or he could return to Worthington House and spread his ruin to his family.

Indeed, it was not only his own future that was jeopardized. If Sir Geoffrey held fast to his threat to disgrace Orion—and Orion had no reason to believe the man would weaken!—then the Worthington family honor, already a little tattered at the edges with the scandalous exploits of the twins, the hurried marriages of his sisters, and the general lack of genteel aplomb—would crumble into dust forever. He could not do that to his parents. Archie and Iris had already been shaken nearly out of their minds by illness, the loss of the family fortune and the manor house in Shropshire, and more lately Lysander's rumored death and still-broken state. They might never recover from the addition of Orion's failure.

It was all his fault. His arrogance had led him to accept without question his good fortune in securing such a plum position. He'd not bothered to thoroughly investigate Sir Geoffrey or speak to any of his previous apprentices. He'd ignored his own instincts when Sir Geoffrey never appeared in the laboratory and when his own notes went missing. The unpredictable temper and swings from weakness to manic energy should have made him realize that his supposed mentor was not entirely sane.

Yet if he left Blayne House now, and tried to brave the accusations, it would not matter if he was convicted of anything. The gossips would do more damage than prison ever could. Attie would never make a decent match, for who would want a rapist at the table during family holidays?

Stay away from Uncle Orion, children. He's a very bad man, indeed!

Orion walked across his bedchamber to stare out at the early-morning street in front of the house. He lifted his hand, pressing his palm to the window as he considered the view from his luxurious new prison.

SIR GEOFFREY COULD not be more satisfied with how perfectly his plan was progressing. Everything was falling into place. Fate had surely smiled on him the day Orion Worthington wandered into Blayne House.

"Pennysmith!"

Where was the man? What kind of butler was nowhere to be found when his master required his immediate assistance?

Sir Geoffrey slammed his fist down upon the fragile inlay of the side table, rattling the silver tea service. "Pennysmith!"

There was much to do today and no time to waste. He must prepare his presentation to the Fraternity. "Penny—!"

"Yes, Sir Geoffrey?"

Sir Geoffrey narrowed his eyes at the lean, narrow-faced man suddenly lurking in the doorway. Sometimes, he was certain he saw a smirk on his servant's face, a particularly ill-tempered and disrespectful smirk, at that. Indeed, it was entirely plausible that Pennysmith had been up to no good just a moment before. It would not shock him to discover that his allegedly loyal butler had already organized the entire household staff in an effort to vex the master of the house— just for sport!

"How can I help you, sir?"

"What?" Sir Geoffrey had lost his train of thought.

"Did you require my service, sir?"

"Yes!" He felt his hands begin to shake and glanced at the tea service. He remembered now. "I should like another pot of tea. I should like you to use the number six special blend."

"Yes, sir. Of course, sir." Pennysmith slithered his way into the breakfast room to fetch the tea tray. "But, if I may point out to you, sir, you have stated on many occasions that you do not wish to drink more than three cups of any of the special blends per day. Are you certain—"

Sir Geoffrey attempted to stand but thought better of it. "Tea! Now."

"Yes, Sir Geoffrey."

"And this time be certain the poppy pods are crushed to the finest powder. I felt grit in my teeth this morning. Do you have any idea what an unpleasant sensation that is?"

"Of course, sir."

"Pennysmith!"

The butler turned back before he exited the breakfast room. "Yes, sir?"

Sir Geoffrey snapped his fingers. "Fetch Judith."

"Of course, sir."

IT WAS A new day. And despite the arrival of yet another dreary English morning, the difficulties of the prior evening

seemed far less dire. The rain could not dampen Francesca's
renewed hope. She knew that all things were possible because
she had a plan.

A plan that involved food, *naturalmente*.

Francesca hummed, retied the canvas apron around her
waist, and scanned the larder. As luck would have it, it was
market day for the cook, which meant his giant presence and
poor hygiene would be absent from the kitchen for hours on
end! It was all hers—the worktable, the wine cellar, the ovens,
the stove, the pots and ladles! And thus far, everything was
on schedule.

Two loaves of crusty bread were baking. With pride she
noted the sweet and creamy *panna cotta* cooling on a larder
shelf.

She had just returned from the rain-sprinkled garden,
where she gathered the fresh ingredients needed for the
sauce—tomatoes and herbs. All she needed now was the garlic and onion. "There you are," she said, and skipped back to
the worktable.

Francesca blew a strand of hair from her cheek as she
worked, the sharp knife mincing the garlic, chopping the herbs,
sliding through the ripe and fleshy *pomodori*. By the time she
had finished dicing, her hands and forearms ran wet with tomato juices.

Today she would compose a sonnet with food. She would
profess her love for Orion with her very best dish, her *lasagne
al forno*. He would surrender before the magnificent layers
of richly browned beef, the sensuous *ragù*, the al dente give
of the *lasagne* noodles in his teeth. She would touch his heart
and soul when the bread melted on his tongue. She would
ease his worries with Chianti, coax the truth from hiding with
the sweet and creamy *panna cotta*.

And she felt no shame about any of it. Yes, she was setting
a trap for Orion, but she did it out of love. Today she would
do more than tell him she loved him; she would show him.

Nonna Laura used to tell her to never hide her brains and

talent for the comfort of others. She used to say, *"Chessa, mia cara, a tutto spiano"*—at full blast.

Francesca saw the table spread with ingredients and laughed out loud, the joyful sound filling the kitchen. She knew Nonna Laura would have been proud—no one would dare call the meal she was preparing insipid or bland! It would be a feast. A celebration. It would be the sum of who she was.

"You called for me, Papa?"

Sir Geoffrey tried to focus his vision on the form of his daughter, standing in the center of the breakfast room. She was seemly, tidy, and punctual, and fate had now ensured she would always be there to serve him.

There was no need to explain the details to her. Judith obeyed him. She had long acknowledged that he knew what was best for her. And now, due to the morning's fortuitous turn of events, Sir Geoffrey could continue to rely on Judith. As a bonus, he could drain Worthington like a maple tree.

"I shall be announcing your engagement at tonight's Fraternity presentation."

She didn't flinch. Sir Geoffrey was not entirely sure she was breathing.

"Did you hear what I said, birdbrain? I shall be announcing your engagement to Worthington tonight."

"I thought we had an agreement." Her voice was soft and flat. Her eyes remained expressionless. "You promised I would never have to marry any of them. You said it was just a way to bribe them, make them stay on as your assistants. You told me I would always stay here."

"And you will!" Sir Geoffrey clapped his hands together in merriment. "Worthington will retain his position as my assistant, and you will continue with your duties, as always."

She said nothing.

"Indeed! Two birds in the hand!" He began to guffaw.

Her father was once a decent man, Judith remembered, but

over the years, he had become less honorable and more un-feeling.

As a child, Judith had adopted her mother's belief that beneath his arrogance and self-centeredness, her father truly cared about their well-being. When her mother had passed suddenly from a bout of influenza, Sir Geoffrey had been pale and silent in the face of Judith's heartbroken grief.

He had spent all his days in his laboratory then, leaving her to her governess. When she was old enough to restrain her curious hands, he had sometimes allowed her within. She recalled with a strange painful joy the first time he had per-mitted her to clean the beakers.

She had been proud to be the daughter of the great scien-tist. When he had been knighted, she had worn her first court gown to his ceremony and had been awed when he had kneeled before the Prince Regent himself.

But it seemed her father had only one moment of greatness in him. The next year, he had presented a wonderful new concept in the cross-pollination of fruit—and a clever, broken young man had fled the country.

Year after year, Sir Geoffrey had cozened, copied, and robbed his assistants of their genius. They were all poor but gifted, all ready to do whatever was asked of them in order to gain fame and fortune equal to that of their mentor. Some lasted one year. Some lasted longer, especially after Judith's hand in marriage had begun to be offered in roundabout brib-ery.

She had loathed some of these "suitors," liked a rare few, but loved none of them. They had opened her eyes to the fact that she was nothing but nicely wrapped currency to men. Her worth was measured in her usefulness to them all, in-cluding her own father.

But Judith was not the only one to pay the price.

Sir Geoffrey's fears of inadequacy in the face of all that youthful zeal and talent had driven him to drink. Then, when overindulgence had threatened his public image, he'd turned to the more subtle effects of the poppy. It gave him the godlike feeling of power that he craved and the manic energy that made him feel young and able again.

Judith had tried to limit his consumption for a while, but he had become more and more dependent upon the tea he made from the ground poppy pods, thanks to Pennysmith's loyal support.

It was only in the last six months, however, that he had tumbled into insanity. The man who sprawled in the breakfast room wing chair, clapping his hands in glee, was nothing more than an addict and a bully. His "special blends" had destroyed his humanity.

Though painful to admit, the only reason Judith remained at Blayne House was because she had nowhere else to go. Though her father saw her as just another piece of laboratory equipment, he was the only family she had.

Her father chortled. Then cackled. And in between, he spoke of manna from heaven and luck and the resurrection of his reputation. He had forgotten she was there.

Judith turned and walked out.

Chapter 31

"I love you," Francesca said beseechingly. Then, more firmly, with command. "I love you."

With a huff of frustration, she tried again. *Simply say it!* "I love you, Orion Worthington."

Yes, that was it. It was best to speak to him in a plain, straightforward manner. She and Orion had never been about beseeching or commanding. They were equals, after all.

But what if the moment to speak arrived just before Orion kissed her? If their faces were drawn close, she would require a more delicate approach, a whisper perhaps. Francesca brought her face to within an inch of the oval mirror. "Orion Worthington," she breathed. "I love—"

She heard a rap on her door. The scullery boy, right on time! She snatched the pennies from the table and raced to the door of her bedchamber.

"Carefully. Put it here." She ushered him in, shut the door, and instructed him to set the huge picnic basket on her dressing table. "Did you remove anything?"

"No, miss."

"Did anyone see you?"

"No, miss."

She handed him one penny, which he pocketed immediately. "That is for your assistance," she said. She handed him the second penny, which he shoved into the same pocket. "And that is for your silence."

"Yes, miss."

The boy ran out. Francesca immediately began checking the contents of the basket. Indeed, the luncheon she had prepared was a veritable menu of sensuality. There were hearty *lasagne al forno*, still hot in its well-wrapped crockery baking dish, and smooth, custardy *panna cotta*. There were the first berries of summer from the garden, bread, olives, and not one but two bottles of the best Chianti that Sir Geoffrey's meager cellar had to offer. Tucked into the side of the basket were the pretty picnic cloth, two place settings of the figured china she had stolen from the butler's pantry, two crystal goblets, and silverware.

Perfetto.

It was time.

When Francesca turned to smooth out her gown, her gaze fell on the bed. It occurred to her that for all the adventurous things she and Orion had done to each other on that marvelous occasion of two nights before, they had avoided doing any of them in an actual bed. There had been a mutual, silent agreement, born of some inner knowing, that to take each other to bed would be too much like making love.

Love, however, was exactly what Francesca was after this time. She loved him, and she meant to prove to him that he loved her. He needed to understand that they were meant for each other—and only each other!—and that marriage was meant to be a melding of hearts, not a pathway to career advancement.

Banishing the last twinge of guilt she felt for this attempt to steal away Judith's possible but obviously unwanted suitor, she picked up the large basket.

Enough stalling, she told herself. *Pull up your bootstraps and make your move. Now is the time. The meal is prepared. Your hair is done. You've even counted the days of your cycle to ensure pleasure will be the only consequence!* She glanced down at the basket. *And your* lasagne al forno *will soon be cold.*

ORION'S BEDCHAMBER WAS only a few doors down from Francesca's own. She knew he was still in there, because she could hear his pacing stride from outside the door. She knew he should be resting instead of pacing. She had seen him disappear wearily into the room shortly after dawn as she headed to the kitchens to start her preparations. Apparently, he had spent the entire night in the laboratory, because he had still worn his evening dress coat!

That meant that the poor man had gone two consecutive nights without sleep. As she adjusted the heavy basket in her hands, Francesca hoped he was rested enough to, well, eat, and . . .

Oh for pity's sake, just knock!

Francesca noted that her inner voice was beginning to sound very English. However, it was also quite right. She licked her lips, lifted her hand, and rapped gently on Orion Worthington's bedchamber door.

For a long moment, she heard nothing come from the room. Had he slipped out when she wasn't aware? Then, at last, she heard a thump, as if someone were getting out of bed.

He answered the door in his dress shirt and trousers. The sleeves were rolled up, exposing the muscles and twining tendons of his forearm. The shirt studs were gone, leaving the front placket open halfway down his chest. She could see the springy dark curls there. Her fingertips itched to run through them as she lifted her gaze upward.

"You look awful," she said bluntly. In fact, she thought he

looked rather appealing, half-dressed and mussed and un-
shaven, with his curling dark hair falling over his brow. He
looked dangerous and brooding.

She had always had a weakness for romantic tales of highwaymen.

"I made you something." She began to fidget with the
weight of the basket.

He'd not said a word but stood gazing at her with those
dark, midnight eyes, then considered the contents of the basket. He raised an eyebrow.

"A bit of refreshment. I—I know you worked all night."

Orion flinched a bit at that. What was the matter? Was the
experiment not going well?

"I'm not hungry," he said at last. His voice was raw and
harsh.

Francesca transferred the basket from one hand to the
other and adjusted her stance. "That isn't true. I feed people.
That's what I do best. And I happen to know that you haven't
had a bite to eat since before the ball!"

"Give me that." He reached down and lifted the basket
from her hands, and she had to admit she was grateful. But
he said nothing.

She peered at him. Clearly, he was in no mood for inconsequential chatter. She would have to keep the conversation
going in order to keep his door open. "I spoke to Judith last
night. She didn't admit to seeing us, but I believe she would
not have been too heartbroken if she had."

He flinched again. "Chessa, please go away."

"No," she replied, sure of her ground now. After all, he
still held the picnic basket! "I am going to stand right here
and pester you until you are fed. You haven't experienced my
vast repertoire of pestering yet, but I assure you, I did not
wrest a worktable in Sir Geoffrey's laboratory by doing cart-
wheels!"

A short bark of laughter escaped him at that. His shadowed

eyes crinkled just a bit at the corners. Francesca decided to press him a bit more.

"I know you are tired," she said gently. "That's why I brought the picnic to you." She reached out and placed her hand on his bare forearm. "Come, now, Rion. Let me feed you."

He stepped to the side enough to let her into his bedchamber.

"Thank you, kind sir."

He closed the door behind her.

Francesca scanned the tidy room, noticing immediately that his bed was perfectly made, indicating he had not rested. "You must be exhausted, Orion." When she received no response, she turned, smiling, only to find him standing with the basket, staring absentmindedly out the rain-covered window.

Something was wrong with him, other than exhaustion. She could see it. No matter. She would soon know what plagued him—pasta and wine did wonders to loosen one's secrets.

The *panna cotta* was just for insurance.

Francesca plopped herself down on the carpet before the fire, spread out her skirts, and patted her hand on the floor. "Right here. Let's have our picnic!"

Moments later, Orion found himself seated tailor-fashion on a cloth on the floor of his bedchamber, a plateful of food balanced on his knee. Although bereft of his freedom, of the life he'd planned for himself, of the man he'd wanted to be, still he had found himself agreeing that it was a fine time for a picnic.

Clearly, Francesca had taken advantage of him during a vulnerable, bleary moment, for there was a great deal wrong in his life, yet he managed to fork in the first mouthful of savory, layered noodles despite his woes.

He nearly groaned aloud at the flavor. The braised beef

saturated with herbs and sauce stimulated his battered senses and nourished his famished soul. The crisp, cool greens woke up his thoughts. The heady, fragrant red wine unwound his tension.

The next thing he knew, his plate was clean and his body was suffused with a hint of well-being. Francesca sat across from him, clad in a rose pink muslin gown that was a bit too large so that it tended to slide off one shoulder, with her long hair down in the back. She looked glowing and luscious. He watched her pop a last olive into her mouth to savor with half-closed eyes. Her plate was clean as well. She was no frail flower, no pale English ninny toying with a piece of toast and complaining of indigestion. Francesca ate as if food were as necessary as air.

A sensible viewpoint, for it was. Especially when it was like this—hearty, honest food cooked with passion. *I can taste her in her food.*

The wine allowed him to smile crookedly at her through the desolation that bound him. "Attie was right. I was wrong. Blayne House's cook is abominable. We should have let her carve him to pieces for keeping you out of the kitchen."

Francesca grinned at him. "You say the sweetest things. But we are not quite finished." She rose to her knees and leaned across the spread cloth that was now a display of empty dishes and wanton consumption.

She came near enough to Orion that he caught a teasing glimpse down her neckline and the tantalizing scent of orange blossoms. His heart—which had seemed to slow almost to stopping in the last several hours—began to beat faster in his chest.

Perhaps I am hungry, after all.

She leaned close to him, reaching for a last covered saucer. Her long hair slipped over her shoulder to tickle the back of his wrist and slide cool and enticing over his bare forearm. He inhaled deeply, feeling his pulse begin to thrum in earnest.

While he'd been distracted by his own pounding heart,

she'd uncovered a dish and spooned out a mouthful of something creamy and white. When she held it to his lips, still
kneeling before him, he gazed into her deep brown eyes and
opened his mouth.

The sweet, velvety stuff melted on his tongue, filling his
head with vanilla and cream. When she leaned forward and
licked a tiny smear from his bottom lip, he ought to have
frozen, or withdrawn from her, or otherwise shown a modi-
cum of sense, for he was a trapped fool with no future and no
way out.

Leaning forward even half an inch would lead to a kiss.
A kiss would lead to a touch. A touch would lead to so much
more. He could not risk it again. They'd almost been caught
at the ball the night before. He could not allow himself to be
driven by the biological imperative any longer.

Especially now.

"There is no point to this," he said softly, almost to her
lips. "I have an understanding with Judith."

He felt the jolt that ran through her. She drew back slightly
so she could meet his gaze. Orion forced himself not to shy
away from her hurt brown eyes.

"You don't love Judith," she whispered. "And Judith most
assuredly does not love you."

Orion did not waver. He dared not waver.

"Yet *I* love you," she said softly.

Oh God. The most wonderful knowledge in the world,
given at the worst possible moment.

"It makes no difference," he said flatly.

She moved closer, crawling right through the dishes and
smearing custard on her gown. "I love you, Orion Worthington."

"You cannot. We have only just met. You do not know me."

On her knees, she was positioned just a little taller than he
was seated. She gazed down at him with a small smile on her
rose pink lips. "I love that you can't go to sleep at night, just
like me."

He swallowed hard, remembering the sight of Francesca, deliciously bundled in her wrapper, in the dark hallway on the first night he spent in Blayne House.

She knee-walked closer, until her thighs touched his knees. "I love that you put that awful Witherspoon in his place. I love that you argue theories with me without ever implying that having breasts precludes having a considered opinion."

Orion's head began to swim. Such heavenly, marvelous breasts . . .

"I love that you cleaned the laboratory after getting tallow everywhere," she said into his ear. When had she managed to straddle his lap? "I love that you risked everything to save the children the day of the acid spill." She framed his face in small warm hands and gazed down at him fondly. The certainty in her deep, dark gaze was balm to his aching spirit. "I love that you can't help moaning when you eat my food, that you keep the feathers of your pet bird, and, oh! How I love the way you dance!"

Francesca settled into his lap and curled up to his chest. She reached up to stroke tender fingertips over his lips. "I love that you kiss me like we are the only two people in the entire world."

When he drove his lips down over hers, no one was more surprised than he.

Chapter 32

LIKE a sunflower bending to catch the last rays of warmth, he had bent to her without thinking, without even knowing what he did.

Her lips were soft. He'd never known anything so sweet and soft as her tremulous mouth under his. She let out a small sigh, and he found the inner sweetness of her mouth. Exploring further, he wrapped both large hands around her head and slid his tongue between her lips.

Would it be so wrong for them to pleasure each other one last time?

Please, just once more!

He felt her hands grab fistfuls of his shirt to pull him down into her. The difference in their height seemed to call for a change in position.

Orion was in favor of it. Without losing a second of her kiss, he wrapped both arms about her small, rounded form and lifted them both from the floor. His bed was only steps away. His mouth still bound to hers, he laid her down on the coverlet.

Now his hands were free to slide down her sweet-smelling neck and spread across her delicate collarbone until his fingers pressed her silly little sleeves right down her arms. He bent his knees to kiss the soft, incredibly feminine place where her neck met her shoulders.

She gasped and her hands clutched at his biceps. Stepping back, he reluctantly pulled his lips away from her skin long enough to strip the damned borrowed gown off her and fling it away. His shirt followed, but his mouth could not bear to be separated from hers even for an instant. He dove at her again, pressing into her with his hands buried in her hair, devouring her like a man starved for the simple unique flavor of her.

He couldn't get enough. The taste of her, the scent of her, the heat coming off her skin—

More skin. He needed more skin! He felt a tugging at his waist. She must feel it, too, for she was yanking at the buttons of his trousers with blind, crazed fingers. He shucked his boots and his trousers. She sat up to tear her chemise over her head.

She was beautifully naked underneath it. Orion crawled onto the mattress over her, pressing her down again as he advanced. Locking his mouth to hers, he ran his hands up her rounded thighs, over her tender belly, and filled his palms with her breasts.

Francesca moaned aloud. The heat of his palms sank into her skin. When he pressed her breasts high to take a nipple into his mouth, she cried out. How could they have thought one night was enough? A thousand nights would not be enough!

She wound her fingers into his hair. "I love you," she whispered.

He had not said it back to her yet. He did not need to. She could taste how he loved her in his hot, devouring kiss. She could hear his passion in the thudding of his heart. And his touch, both tender and commanding, made her feel beautiful and womanly and wanted as no other woman had ever been wanted.

Her hands wandered down his neck to his muscled shoulders. So beautiful, so sculpted and perfect and strong. He could break down a door, and he could rescue a child. He could roughly rip her gown from her body, and he could tenderly tease her nipples into tingling points.

She tugged gently on his hair, pulling his mouth to hers for a deep, mutually ravenous kiss. Every part of her felt alive with him. He abandoned her mouth to kiss his way down her trembling belly.

"Oh yes. Please," she begged him. "Oh, please put your mouth on me."

He growled into her skin. Her words had excited him, which in turn drove her higher!

"Kiss me there," she moaned for him. "Use your tongue on me—"

He ran his tongue down, into her slit, and swirled it around her clitoris. Her body gave an involuntary jerk as pleasure jolted through her. "Yes," she whispered. "Lick me, please! I need you to lick me!"

He crouched between her widely spread thighs and spread her labia aside with his thumbs. She had never felt so vulnerable and open in her life. She tossed her head restlessly on the bed, shyly allowing her hair to cover her face.

The coverlet rustled as he lifted his head. A second later, she felt his warm fingers brushing aside her concealing locks. He pulled the pillow down from the top of the bed to raise her head.

"I'm going to watch you come for me," he told her, his voice deep and sure. "Again and again."

Her breath left her in a rush. She swallowed, then nodded. He kissed his way down her body again, and this time, he used his hands to press her wrists into the mattress at her sides, holding her still for his consumption. He devoured her as he had devoured her cooking. His mastery made her shiver.

At some point, the tables had turned on her, and he was now in control.

She had always been adaptable. Being this man's plaything was no punishment, truly.

As he commanded with his lips and tongue and, *Dio*, even teeth!—she came for him. Again and again.

At last, panting and quivering and dripping with perspiration, she begged him to stop. She'd tried to before, but every time she uttered the words "mouth" or "lick," he pinned her down and went back for second and third and fourth helpings.

"Please," she whispered through a throat hoarse with restrained cries, "please, I must breathe!"

At that, he crawled up her body until he could kiss that breath right out of her. She felt his knee wedge itself between her thighs, pressing firmly to her labia. It felt so good, she could not help but squirm against it, rocking her body, rubbing her highly aroused clitoris against the muscled hardness of his thigh.

Then she felt his other knee press between her legs. *Oh yes*.

She wrapped her arms about his neck and kissed him with all the love she bore in her heart. Still he hesitated. He pulled away from her kiss, turning his face into her neck. She could feel him shaking with his need for her. She wanted him just as much. Why did he hesitate?

Without another thought, Francesca wrapped her supple arms around his shoulders and her sturdy thighs over Orion's hips and drew the man she loved down into her body.

Orion gasped into her neck as his rigid hardness pressed to her slick and giving softness. He jerked in protest. She did not let him go.

"I love you," she whispered into her ear. "I want you inside me. It is where you belong."

His breath left him in a hot rush over her throat. She felt his resistance melt as he lowered his body over hers. The thick bluntness of him began to press inward.

It felt so wonderful. She was slippery and ready and—

Ow. Perhaps he was a bit large—

Ow. She might not be as prepared for this as she thought—

She flinched as he continued to pierce her. That was when she felt him stop. His body stiffened, and she felt him lifting his weight from her.

He was leaving? Now?

Passare sul mio cadavere! Over my dead body!

With all the strength in her supple form, Francesca brought him back where he belonged, gritting her teeth against the burning pressure.

Why did she have to love such a *big* man?

Then he seated himself deeply into her with a groan of pleasure. She was happy that he was happy, but she could not help the two tears leaking from the corners of her eyes.

"Shh," he whispered against her lips as he brushed her hair back from her face. He dropped soft kisses on her damp eyelids. "Relax, Chessa. Be still. I have heard the pain will pass."

His tender care soothed her tension. She willed her body to stop fighting the fullness and strain within her. When his lips moved to lightly kiss hers, she kissed him back, focusing on the taste of his mouth, the smooth texture of his tongue sliding against hers, the way his hands buried themselves in her hair . . .

Suddenly she realized that her sex no longer ached. She felt much more at ease.

"I'm going to move my cock slowly," he told her gently. "You must tell me if you wish me to stop."

He began to withdraw. At first, she felt a slight sting at the movement, but he kissed her again, more deeply and more passionately. Soon she was kissing him wildly as he moved in and out of her body, into her, out of her, *with* her—together as they had never been before.

Together as they were always meant to be.

Chapter 33

ORION would put off the inevitable for one more moment. He would allow himself to luxuriate in the entirety of that instant in time: Francesca's wild curls across his chest, the sound of her slow breath, the gentle brush of her fingertip traveling down the center of his chest.

Such intense pleasure. Such sweet release. And now, the bone-deep calm that blanketed their bodies, their minds, their hearts.

The wonder of it. Orion had just made love to a woman, and the event went far beyond mere bodily gratification. He knew why. Francesca was the woman who had accompanied him on the journey. She had given herself freely to him, body and soul, and the gates to heaven were flung wide.

He should not have given in to her, but he had. Now he could not bring himself to regret it . . . yet. He wanted to savor this moment, in the hopes that the memory might ease the pain of all the moments still to come.

Francesca stirred. He pressed his palm to her warm, bare

back, attempting to hold her still. He was not ready for words. He was not ready for what must come next.

She kissed his cheek. Orion closed his eyes and let her go. Francesca popped up on her elbows, a knowing smile on her lips. "See?" She brushed a finger through his hair and giggled. "I told you! You do not love Judith—you love me!"

Orion felt his face go hard and cold. It had to be done. There was no other way. No, he had not intended to make love with Francesca when he accepted her invitation. Yes, she had seduced him with food and wine and her own magnificence. But he made the choice. He fell into her arms, her body, her love. He was the man who took her chastity. And only he would be culpable for all the tragedy now to come.

He had compromised her but could not marry her. If he did, Sir Geoffrey would make good on his plan to ruin him, which would in turn ruin his wife. In Society's eyes, she would be the wife of a rapist, a criminal. Francesca would serve a life sentence for a crime no one committed. He could not do that to her. The pain of his rejection would fade, but social ruin was forever.

And though he wished to tell Francesca the truth, he could not. Again, it was for her own protection. Orion had gone over the possibilities again and again while pacing his bedchamber, but there was only one outcome. If Francesca knew of Sir Geoffrey's repeated theft, she would vow to seek justice. If she learned of how he used engagement to his daughter as bait to attract assistants, she would become Judith's champion, damn the consequences. If she knew how Sir Geoffrey threatened Orion with ruin if he did not marry Judith and would take credit for all his scientific work, she would declare an all-out war.

He knew Francesca. He knew she was too impassioned to hold these facts close, to say and do nothing. The instant she spoke her mind, Sir Geoffrey would go in for the kill. With a word he would destroy Francesca, ruin her reputation, and leave her no choice but to return to Italy, carrying the shame of the false accusations back home to her family.

And then there was the scientific breakthrough . . . Francesca was the first and only person with whom Orion had longed to share his moment of triumph, Now, with all that had happened, he would never be able to tell her about the discovery, because Francesca would confront Sir Geoffrey the moment he took credit.

Orion studied her beautiful face, sure this would be the last time he saw her eyes filled with joy. His next words would surely break Francesca's heart.

"Did you not hear me?" She leaned down and kissed his lips playfully, her hair tickling his cheeks. "I said you love me. Admit it!"

"I am to marry Judith. Our engagement will be announced at tonight's Fraternity presentation."

Her first inclination was to laugh, but when she saw no mirth in his expression, she quickly corrected herself and frowned. "What?"

"I cannot love you. I'm sorry, Chessa. I will marry Judith as planned. It is decided."

It was torturous for Orion to watch as Francesca allowed his words to find purchase in her mind. Her eyes widened. Her lips parted. It pained him when she pushed herself up and balanced on her knees on the bed, staring down at him. "You are not jesting, then. You and Judith are to marry."

"It is no jest." Orion sat up and leaned against the headboard. He felt as if he were submitting himself for a flogging—one that he deserved.

"You . . ." Francesca waved her hands about her head, clearly nonplussed. "You are *that* determined to marry your way to success? Is that it?"

He let out a sigh of resignation. "I would be mad not to."

"How can you. . . ? *Dio aiutami!* God help me!" She flung herself off the bed and stood, snatching the coverlet to hide her exquisite body. He could see she was shaking with emotion . . . anger, shock, sadness. He knew that one day soon she would hate him.

Orion wished there was something—anything—he could do to spare her this suffering.

"Francesca—"

"I fell in love with a man who did not exist, a mere product of my imagination." Orion watched the life drain from Francesca's face. "They are right about me—I am a silly dreamer."

He sat straight. He longed to go to her, but he could not. Frozen with grief, he heard the cold words come from his lips: "Far too much of a dreamer for this world, I'm afraid."

She gasped as if burned. Francesca turned away and bent to retrieve the ill-fitting gown he'd slipped from her curves only hours before. With her back to him, she let the coverlet drop. She stood in the firelight, her supple thighs, rounded hips, and flawless, golden back on display. For the last time, he gazed at the perfection of her luscious bottom.

Orion choked. Her splendor would be forever lost to him.

"Where are you going, Francesca?" She looked a tousled mess. In fact, she looked exactly what she was—fresh out of bed with her lover.

"Anywhere but here!" She spun around, her dark hair falling wildly about her shoulders, her bosom rising and falling. Francesca's eyes were as hard as dark glass. "I find I have had enough of this house, and this climate—you English are all so cold. Perhaps I should return to Italy." She glared at him, but he knew she was begging him to tell her not to leave.

He ached at the abruptness of her decision but nodded gravely. "Perhaps you should."

With the release of a single agonized sob, Francesca ran to the door and slammed it behind her. She was gone.

His heart pounded fruitlessly against his prison walls.

IT WAS NOT enough to leave Orion's bedchamber. Francesca kept going, down the stairs, through the main floor, and out the back door of the house.

The walls of the rain-soaked garden threatened to close in upon her. It was not enough to leave the house.

I cannot bear to stay here and watch him marry Judith. I cannot force myself to sit at the dinner table across from Mr. and Mrs. Worthington.

Orion was quite correct, as usual.

I must go.

Go? Leaving Orion would mean tearing her heart from her body and leaving it behind.

Yet staying would be worse. She paused her pacing near the fountain to press her palms over her burning eyes. Wouldn't it be better for her poor heart to die quickly than endure a long and tortured demise?

Her spirit threatened to leap from her body if she did not keep moving. She circled the fountain, walking fast with her arms wrapped about her midriff and her head bowed. She paid no notice to the grass soaking the hem of her gown. If she could, she would walk away now. She would keep putting one foot in front of the other until she walked across the sea, back to Bologna.

Yet nothing awaited her there. Her sensible Italian family, although perhaps having sympathy for being disappointed by love, would expect her to resume her place in the family structure—that of a loved but disappointing child, fondly snubbed as a dreamer, one who was far too English. Her efforts to pursue her own branch of science would still be overshadowed by the shining achievements of the others before her.

In truth, she loved them all, but she had enjoyed the freedom of expectation that she had found here. It had allowed her to find her own way. She knew what direction her research should take. As a scientist, she believed in herself at last.

As a woman, she considered herself a miserable failure. She had given her heart and her body to a man who did not want her.

Her rapid path led her by habit to the door of the laboratory.

She stared at the latch with hot eyes. How she'd dreamed of coming to this place. How she'd hoped to find what had eluded her in Italy.

She had learned so much since then.

Falling in love with Orion had taught her a great deal. His discipline coupled with his creative thought processes had shown her how to dream in a way that made it seem possible for those dreams to bear fruit in reality. And he had accepted her in his sphere—

No, he hadn't.

Far too much a dreamer for this world.

The pain twisted deeper. Her broken heart fought with her shattered pride to win the prize for greater injury. She heard voices in the garden, the servants passing by.

The instinct to hide her reddened eyes and nose drove her inside the lab. The large barn door closed behind her with a dull thud. She blinked to banish the dazzle of daylight—and her threatening tears. She pressed her palms to her heated forehead.

"Are you ill, Cousin?" asked a voice.

UNABLE TO REMAIN within the confines of his nicely appointed cell, Orion dressed and left Blayne House. His prison was one of blackmail and dread, but he could leave it, for Sir Geoffrey knew he would always come back.

Orion found himself walking slowly through the soaked streets of London. The rain had abated. He'd not noticed when, for he'd been far too busy pleasuring his lovely Francesca.

And then losing her.

His long strides ate away at the distance, and it was not long before he found himself at a familiar door.

Worthington House.

With a sound like a dog that had been kicked, he flung himself up the steps and into the welcoming chaos of home.

"Rion!" Archie was seated on the floor of the foyer, sorting through a stack of moldy books. Orion's father blinked up at him with vague happiness. "I cannot find Beatrice and Benedick," Archie complained cheerfully.

Orion gazed down at his father with desperate fondness. The house probably contained a dozen copies of *Much Ado About Nothing*. "Have you looked on the stairs? Shakespeare's comedies always seem to gravitate to the landing."

"Ah!" Archie smiled sweetly at Orion. "I knew you could help."

Help? Orion felt ill. He'd wedged himself into a vile situation with his arrogance and his eagerness to walk out on his kin. The consequences of his error threatened everything his beleaguered family had left.

His long-shielded heart, cracked open by Francesca's generosity and warmth, shattered by her loss, now melted completely beneath the fierce and sudden vehemence of his love for his family.

How could I ever believe I could leave them all behind me? I would wed a hundred Judiths to protect them. I would enslave myself for several lifetimes to keep any more heartbreak from them.

Attie wandered into the front hallway, eating an apple. For once, her wild auburn hair was tamed into two relatively tidy braids. If anything, it only made her seem more alarming, at least to someone who knew her well.

Orion half expected a joyous greeting, but she only glared. "What are you doing here? I thought Sir Pompous was having his grand to-do tonight."

Attie's disrespect grated. "How about, 'Thank you for making sure I wasn't doused with acid'?"

Attie just looked sour. "You survived just fine. I'm still pondering my revenge on that cook. And I hate the rain." Then she proceeded to stomp her way up the stairs, still munching.

Miranda appeared just where Attie had emerged. She held a hairbrush in her hand. She looked very pregnant and very weary. "I'm afraid she's just realized that the damp makes her hair frizz." She smiled at Orion and tucked the brush into the pocket of the vast pinafore stretched over her future blessed event. "It is nice to see you again so soon. Shall I tell your mother that you have arrived?"

Orion shook his head. "Formalities are wasted in this house. You know that. Go, sit and rest. I can find Iris on my own." He nudged his distracted father with his knee. "Archie, Miranda needs a cushion for her back and a pot of tea."

Archie looked up, blinking vaguely. "She does? Oh, hello, dear! My, you do look fatigued. I mean, blooming and lovely—but fatigued." He rose to his feet, still spry, if a bit creaky in the knees. He held out his arm to Miranda. "Let's get you in a chair by the stove. I shall make you the most wonderful tea."

"Check the teapot for turpentine, Archie!" Orion called after them.

Since he had no real purpose in his unplanned visit, Orion wandered into the front parlor where Iris was usually to be found. Sure enough, she stood at her easel with a paintbrush in one hand and a cup of tea in the other.

Orion's cousin, Bliss, sat in a purple-draped chair, holding a purple ball of knitting yarn and wearing a quilted purple doublet with round hose. Her fair locks, blonder even than Elektra's, were stuffed haphazardly into a bulbous padded cap. Bliss's buxom country beauty looked rather odd crammed into an Elizabethan men's costume.

I am most assuredly home.

"Hello, Bliss."

"Good afternoon, Orion." Bliss remained entirely still. Patient and even-tempered by nature, she was a far better artistic subject than Orion had ever been.

He moved to stand behind Iris. "*Shakespeare with Yarn?*"

Iris chuckled warmly. "Don't be silly, dear. It is titled *Shakespeare with Purple Yarn.*" She lifted her cheek for a kiss without a pause in her work. "Welcome home, sweet boy."

They were all "dear" or "sweet boy" when Iris was hard at work. Apparently, Iris's thoughts could not hold art and her children's names in the same space.

In her defense, she did have rather a lot of children.

An aching regret stole over Orion. He was no child. This was no longer his home. It might never be again. At least he could keep it safe for all of them.

Attie wandered into the room. Orion recalled that it was always like that, just as Cabot had said. She was rather like a cat, never happy to stay still.

This time Attie gnawed on a carrot. The greens still hung from one end.

Bliss perked up slightly. "Attie, may I have a bite? I've been sitting for hours."

Attie narrowed her eyes. Someone in the mad household had slacked when given the responsibility of making sure Attie knew how to share. "I am open to negotiations," she told Bliss.

Bliss's benign smile never wavered. "I know where you go on Thursday mornings."

Attie handed over the carrot at once and scuttled away. The whole thing, minus the bite she now chewed as she gazed innocently over her mother's shoulder at the painting.

Orion rather thought he knew, too. "Attie visits me at my work," Cabot had told him. He said nothing.

How could he admonish his little sister, when he'd abandoned her and all of them so easily just a week before?

As if sensing his restraint, Attie turned her head to stare curiously at Orion. "You're sad. You don't get sad." She peered at him more closely. "Did you muck things up with Francesca?" Her vivid green eyes widened until she looked like a startled elf. "You did muck it up! I can tell! What happened? Did you let the male rabbits mix with the females?"

Something like that. Orion bit back the words, but he must have let his turmoil show, for suddenly Bliss and even Iris stared at him with dismay.

Chapter 34

ORION flinched from the combined power of the blue and green feminine gazes.

Oh, little sister, I have done so much worse than that. Orion gazed regretfully at Attie, knowing there was no point in trying to hide his pain from one as watchful as his youngest sibling. "I am to wed Judith. Sir Geoffrey is announcing the engagement tonight." With one hand, he reached out and rescued Iris's tea from her hand just as she was about to absently clean her brush in it.

"That's all wrong." Attie scowled. "Francesca is the one I picked. Judith isn't what you think she is."

From the hallway outside the parlor, Orion could hear his father intoning lines to poor, harassed Miranda.

"And the watchman says, 'If we know him to be a thief, shall we not lay hands on him?'"

A quote from *Much Ado About Nothing*, act three, scene three. Orion could not help himself. He and his siblings had been quizzed cheerfully but relentlessly.

Archie had been a stage actor in his youth. Even after so

many years, Orion found himself arrested by the intensity in his father's voice as he played the rough-voiced watchman.

Archie went on in the fruity, assuming tones of Dogberry as the constable answered the watchman. "'The most peaceable way for you, if you do take a thief, is to let him show himself what he is.'"

Orion went very still.

Sir Pilfery.

Let him show himself what he is.

A heated wash of anger and knife-edged clarity swept over him. What the hell was he thinking on?

He was a Worthington. Worthingtons didn't get duped. Worthingtons committed the duping!

Apparently, Attie still had her observant eye on him, for she smiled, an evil twist of her childish lips. "Orion's not sad anymore," she told her mother.

"That's nice, dear," Iris said vaguely.

Although there was nothing amusing about his situation, Orion wanted to laugh out loud. It was true. He was a mad Worthington after all!

And there was nothing madder in the world than a Worthington bent on vengeance!

Orion returned Attie's evil little smile. "Gather up the clan, will you, Attie? I have a little revenge to plot."

And where did one go to research mayhem and chaos? Why, to the experts, of course!

WITH HER BACK pressed to the large double doors of the laboratory, Francesca gazed with surprise at the image before her. Judith stood in the laboratory, wrapped in a vast canvas apron that entirely concealed her perfect figure, with even her slender wrists disappearing into rugged work gloves.

Truly, Judith was the last person Francesca wanted to see. Well, perhaps the second-to-last . . .

With effort, Francesca repressed her anguish when all she

really wished to do was to sob uncontrollably. "I'm fine," she choked out past the pain wedged in her throat. Except that she knew she looked anything but fine. She amended the lie. "Perhaps I am feeling a—a bit under the weather."

Judith did not seem inclined to pry further. She simply nodded and continued scrubbing at the marble-topped laboratory table with a heavy brush. Francesca watched for a moment, still awash in the agony of Orion's betrayal.

Then awareness pierced the fog around her swirling thoughts. Her eyes narrowed as she peered at her cousin.

Judith had reddened eyes, and her lips were pressed together in flat lines of distress.

Francesca, who had never been able to shut her mouth when it was most called for, leaned forward suddenly. "You are upset about the engagement?"

Judith reared her head back like a startled horse. Francesca caught a glimpse of pallid cheeks with twin red splotches of anger before her cousin quickly turned away. "I don't know what you mean."

Francesca walked slowly around the table before she approached Judith. Her cousin ignored her. Judith ripped off the work gloves and tossed them aside. Still refusing to acknowledge Francesca, she pulled a polishing cloth from where it hung from her apron, snapped it out, and began polishing an empty beaker from the shelf before her.

With wonder, Francesca saw that cool, serene Judith's hands were shaking.

"Why?" Francesca whispered. "Why would you want to be betrothed to a man you don't love?"

Judith flinched. Then she went on polishing with great industry. "I have no idea what you speak of. Mr. Worthington is an acceptable match. His family is a bit . . . eccentric, but surprisingly well connected."

"You don't love him." Francesca's own pain swirled with pity, even though she really wished to resent Judith. "He doesn't love you."

"Emotional illusions are of no importance." Judith obviously sought to sound serene, and she almost managed to attain her usual distant tone, until her voice cracked on the last word.

"I love him," Francesca said softly. Unlike Judith, she saw no point in hiding the pain in her voice.

Judith went still. Her fingers tightened on the neck of the glass beaker she had polished to a pristine clarity. "I know." She gazed straight ahead, not looking at Francesca at all. "I saw the two of you kissing on the duke's terrace."

The glass in the moonlight, water beading on the sides of the cut crystal . . . "I thought it might have been you," Francesca said.

Judith never took her gaze from the shelf of glass before her. "I hate you sometimes, you know." Her voice was flat and as brittle as the glass in her hands.

It was Francesca's turn to flinch. "Because I kissed the man you are supposed to wed?" *Kissed and touched and so much more.*

Judith made a small cracked noise that Francesca belatedly realized was a laugh. "No." She put the flask back on the shelf and selected another to polish. "You don't appreciate the freedom you have. You traipse from one continent to another as if you are simply crossing the street. I have to beg permission to visit the milliner—and only if I have first completed a lengthy catalog of chores."

Francesca opened her mouth to say something—she had no idea what—but Judith continued. "I am a servant in my own house! Worse than that, as servants are paid!" Her words came faster and faster as she went on. "I am twenty-six years old. I have been my father's servant since I was a schoolgirl. For nearly a decade I have labored for him, assisted his work, run his household—" Her voice began to rise as she continued. "Chosen his cigars, cleaned his laboratory, prepared his tea, covered for him, lied for him, stole—no."

She halted her tirade abruptly, and her chest rose and fell

rapidly. Francesca waited, almost afraid to move or say anything, for Judith seemed strangely fragile in this state, as if she might shatter. It was painful to see. She looked away.

Crash!

Francesca started, thinking Judith had dropped a beaker.

Crash!

Judith was methodically flinging beakers at the wall. Francesca, who approved of emotional release on a regular basis, stepped out of the line of fire.

Judith inhaled deeply. *Crash!* "I am a serf about to be sold to a new master." *Crash!* "I don't even *like* science!" *Crash!* "And no one will ever—*ever!*—kiss me the way that Orion Worthington kissed you last night!"

Francesca had been waiting for this opening for months. "What about Asher Langford?"

Judith ran the back of her wrist over her damp eyes and blinked at Francesca. "Asher? But . . . *Asher*?"

Francesca raised a brow. "If ever a man would be happy to assist you in your quest to be kissed brainless, it is Asher Langford. That poor man adores you. As far as I can tell, he always has."

Judith suddenly became aware that her hair was awry. Her fingers fussed with it, pinning it back up with shaky imprecision. "Asher? But he is merely a friend. After all, we've played together since we were children." Judith glanced at the angle of the watery afternoon sunlight through the window. "Oh, I have so much to do before the Royal Fraternity presentation tonight!" She began to tug at the ties of the voluminous apron. "And Asher will be there!"

Then, with growing wonder, she said, "Do you truly think Asher . . . loves me?"

Love. Francesca's heart sank and her mood with it. What did she know about love? "I couldn't say. Why don't you ask him?" It occurred to her that she had just told Orion's imminent fiancée to go kiss another man.

Serves him right.

"And what will you do, Chessa? Will you join us tonight at the presentation?"

She stared at her cousin a moment, noting the sincere concern in Judith's voice. "I will meet everyone there later. First, I need to pack my things. Tomorrow, I'm going home."

MR. BUTTON'S SHIMMERING ball gown was spread across Francesca's bed, yards of golden silk neatly arranged in gentle folds. Surrounding the dress were all the matching accessories from the night she enjoyed her first—and last—dance with Orion Worthington. The dancing slippers were placed just below the lacy hem, the hair ribbons and pearls above the bodice, and the reticule adjacent to the skirts. Francesca sat on the mattress, caressing the garment with the fingers of one hand, as if offering comfort to an ill friend.

Or, perhaps she was attempting to comfort herself.

The ball gown had been worn by a dreamy young girl, a fool who preferred fantasy and magical thinking to reality. And though the dress might still adhere perfectly to Francesca's shape, she knew it no longer fit her.

"I will have no need for you in Italy," she whispered to the dress. Francesca laced a string of pearls through her fingers. "Yet Judith will appreciate you. Of that I am certain."

Francesca stood from the bed, glancing down once more to make sure the dress was angled to the best advantage. She imagined how Judith would go searching for her late that night after the announcement of her and Orion's engagement. Judith would knock on the door to Francesca's bedchamber, only to find her gone. The dress would be spread out, an offering of affection from one cousin to another.

It saddened her that Judith was only now revealing her true nature, too late to have an impact on their friendship. Francesca suspected they would have become quite close, perhaps like sisters.

The book!

She turned to her dressing table and retrieved the bound volume of botanical paintings by Calliope, Lady Porter, Orion's sister. As much as Francesca had adored the lifelike illustrations, *Wildflowers of the Cotswolds* was a gift from Orion to Judith, and the volume was not Francesca's to keep. She placed the book at an angle on top of the silken skirts, thinking that she would prefer to leave a note, but what would she say? Francesca had fallen deeply in love with Orion and had done her best to derail Judith's engagement to him. She did not have the words to smooth such an offense.

Francesca tidied her hair with a sigh and turned to the half-completed task at hand. She was packing her iron-bound sea chest with everything she had brought to England. Francesca would leave just two things: her notes on the rabbits of Blayne House—if Attie wished to continue Francesca's research—and the garden seeds she brought from Bologna to populate the Blaynes' kitchen garden. She realized that her Lamarckism research might never be brought to fruition, but her San Marzano *pomodori* could live on year after year. She supposed if anything symbolized her contribution to England, her tomatoes would.

A brisk knock on the door startled her. She closed the trunk lid. "Yes?"

"The carriage has arrived, miss." It was Eva. "It's nearly time to leave for the presentation. Do you need help dressing, miss?"

Reaching for the latch, Francesca made sure the door was locked, then slowly lowered her forehead to the polished interior of its wood. It felt cool on her hot skin. "No, Eva. I fell asleep and I'm not ready. I know Sir Geoffrey will not want to wait, so please tell him I shall come along later."

"Yes, miss."

As Francesca listened for Eva's footsteps to disappear down the hallway, she suddenly had to clutch at her abdomen and stifle the sob that threatened to emerge.

How *could* he? How could Orion feel such passion for her

one minute, then turn his back on her to pursue marriage to someone else, someone he did not love? What kind of man had so little honor?

She hurt. She hurt so terribly. And the only person she wished to ask for counsel, the only person with whom she wished to share her agonies, was the one who hurt her.

As a scientist, Francesca knew the pain of lost love would not kill her, but her heart was not convinced.

It was all her own doing, of course, and she took responsibility for it. She had laid a trap for Orion, a trap of food and breasts and wine, and he had tried to turn her away. She would not let him. She marched in with her picnic basket and her *panna cotta* and crawled into his lap and told him she loved him. Orion was not a liar. Francesca would never accuse him thus. He told her he planned to marry Judith, yet what did she do? She pressed on! She attempted to change his mind!

The truth was as simple as it was painful—Orion Worthington cared for his career more than love, more than Francesca. It was something she would never understand, now that she'd felt true love for herself. Could she possibly stay at Blayne House and sit across from Mr. and Mrs. Worthington at the dining table? Of course not!

Her only choice was to return to Bologna and carve out a life and a field of study for herself. She would manage. She always managed. But it was sure to be a colorless future compared to the one she had created in her imagination just last night—a life of love and passion, ideas, food, waltzing, and kisses on terraces.

Francesca heard a clatter outside the window. She hurried across the room to peer from behind the drawn draperies. The well-dressed threesome was heading off to a celebratory evening, Sir Geoffrey in the Coat, Judith in her signature pale blue silk, and Orion stiff and proper in his formal attire.

Sir Geoffrey was the only one who looked happy.

Francesca resumed her work on the trunk. She carefully folded the dark brown gabardine gown, followed by the too-large rose gown. Next went an olive green gown. She would wear the light brown gown and brown spencer for her journey. She had packed all her other belongings earlier—her shifts, aprons, hair ribbons, books, and cotton stockings. Rising, she made one last glance around the room for anything she might have overlooked.

The large and vividly blue quill was exactly where she had left it, on the writing desk on the far wall. She would not take it. She was leaving England without anything to remind her of Orion Worthington or of the girl who had arrived with a head full of fantasies.

That girl was gone forever.

Chapter 35

JUDITH lingered outside the door to the presentation room of the Royal Fraternity of Life Sciences. The hallway of Somerset House was filled with milling members, all wearing their sashes of rank. General membership, known as the Brothers, wore a white silk band slanting across the chest, while the ranking members, the Speakers and the Keepers, wore the blood red of the Cross of Saint George.

There were a few wives present and even a few thick-skinned women of science, defiantly displaying their honorary membership sashes of garish green silk, so Judith's solitary presence did not cause comment.

From the snippets of conversation she heard, the Brothers were very interested in hearing the annual presentation of the First Speaker, Sir Geoffrey Blayne. Judith kept her distaste to herself, projecting only the serene acceptance of the honor of being the daughter of the Great Man.

Papa had already disappeared into the presentation hall. He likely thought she had entered just behind him, but she had slipped away at an opportune moment. She had not come here tonight to see her father steal yet another discovery.

She had come to see Asher Langford.

Asher was not a member, but his father was, and entry was never denied to promising scions of accomplished members. Now, as she fidgeted nervously with her reticule, Judith wondered if Asher would even come.

He hadn't actually said he planned to attend—but then, he always came when he knew she was going to accompany her father!

"If ever a man would be happy to assist you in your quest to be kissed brainless, it is Asher Langford."

How strange knowledge was. Once something was known, it could not be unknown, no matter how one might wish. Ever since Francesca had told Judith that Asher had feelings for her, Judith had been able to think on nothing else. She'd realized in that moment that she *wanted* to be kissed by Asher Langford. How had she not seen it all this time?

Suddenly, the Asher of the past stood in an entirely new light. In this hope-tinged glow, Asher's constant attendance on her was tinted with affection. His chronic inability to speak was shadowed with fear and highlighted with longing.

His dear face suddenly seemed handsome to her, and his tall, broad-shouldered form most pleasing to her mind's eye.

But Asher was not here. It was only minutes from the time to seat the assembled Brothers, and she could not see Asher's fair hair and manly shoulders anywhere.

Her eyes began to sting with disappointment, although she would never dream of letting on in public. What was she doing? In an hour, her engagement to Orion Worthington would be publicly announced, and there would be no getting out of it without hideous damage to her reputation.

Mr. Worthington seemed to have no such reservations. Despite Francesca's claims that he did not love Judith, he had seemed quite unruffled during the carriage ride down the Strand. When Papa had informed them that he meant to announce the engagement immediately on taking the podium, Orion had mildly opined that Sir Geoffrey's opponents might take such a seemingly random announcement as a sign of mental confusion. He ought to make his presentation first, then segue into the announcement.

Judith didn't care if the announcement was made sooner rather than later. What did it matter? She had this one moment, before she was betrothed, before she would need to keep to a promise of fidelity, to steal a single moment of passion to sustain her for a lifetime!

But Asher had missed it.

With her shoulders sagging, she turned to follow the queue of members lining up to enter the presentation hall. When she left that hall again, she would be formally engaged. She was no wanton. She would cleave to the man she made oath to until the day death parted them.

The man who was not Asher.

"M-Miss Blayne!"

Joy swept her. By the time she swiveled on her toes to spy his dear face coming through the crowd, her heart had risen from the floor to the sky.

A smile broke through her usual reserve. Asher blinked and his jaw dropped. He came to a standstill as he gazed at her in shock.

Judith's floating heart gave wings to her feet. She darted forward and took Asher's hand in hers. Without hesitation, she drew him aside from the teeming members into a side chamber off the main room.

Only a heavy velvet curtain separated the chamber from the hall. She knew from her father's boasting that sometimes the Prince Regent came to listen to the Speakers. A chamber like this would be lavishly but temporarily decorated as a retiring room, stocked with wine and tidbits, on the off chance that the fickle Prinny would actually arrive.

Tonight the room was bereft of anything but privacy, which made it perfect for Judith's purpose.

Asher stood very still. His hand was lax in hers. He did not pull away, but neither did he hold on to her.

"M-Miss Blayne?"

Judith found herself suddenly inhibited. What if Francesca was wrong? Her cousin did tend toward the fanciful. Oh goodness, she was making a terrible fool of herself, wasn't she?

I don't care. I'd rather be a fool for a moment than a stranger to passion for the rest of my life.

"Mr. Langford—Asher—" Judith took a breath. Leaping before one looked was harder than it seemed. "Do you care for me, Asher?"

Asher paled. His hand slipped from hers. He swallowed hard.

And said nothing.

Judith felt bitter disappointment rise within her. He was gazing at her as if he'd never seen her before. Her entire being screamed at her to step back, to dissemble, to cover her error before it was too late, before she embarrassed herself beyond redemption.

What would Francesca do?

The thought had barely crossed the border of her mind before she took a single step forward, went up on her tiptoes, and pressed her lips to Asher's.

He went shock-still for a second. Then his strong arms wrapped about her and pulled her tight to his big body. When Judith gasped at the power of his embrace, he delved between her parted lips with potent need and longing.

Asher had always been a man of few words. For the first time, Judith realized that it was because Asher's lips were meant for finer things.

So this is what it means to be kissed brainless . . .

ORION WATCHED CALMLY as his former mentor expounded upon his own greatness.

"I'll take the Royal Fraternity by storm, see if I won't!

Ha!" Sir Geoffrey threw out his hands as he paced his retiring room, the one reserved for the First Speaker alone. "I can't wait to see the expression on that sniveling Witherspoon's face when I announce that I have triumphed with the greatest scientific achievement since Robert Hooke discovered cellular construction!"

Orion simply nodded as the man he had hoped to learn from paced erratic loops around the luxurious but small chamber. He had gained a great deal of understanding—that was true. Unfortunately, it had been a tutelage in how not to behave!

Sir Geoffrey would be called to the presentation soon. Orion did not have much time to make the switch. He ran a casual hand down his own snug formal coat. Nothing as grand as the Coat that Sir Geoffrey sported, but it had a singular advantage. While Orion had helped Attie forge new speaking notes for Sir Geoffrey, using Orion's acceptance letter from Blayne House to copy from, Bliss had matter-of-factly slit and resewn a secret opening in the side of Orion's coat.

Just as every Worthington sibling had a fair grasp of fighting and lock picking, each was also an accomplished pickpocket. Practicing nicking items from Archie's coat pockets was just a typical rainy-day activity in a Worthington childhood.

"Oh!" Orion exclaimed. "Sir Geoffrey, what is that on your lapel?"

Orion kept it simple, for he was by far the worst actor in the family. He stepped forward as Sir Geoffrey stopped to gaze frantically down at the Coat. "Here, sir. Let me."

As he brushed assiduously with one hand at the imaginary speck on the royal blue velvet, it was incredibly easy to reach into Sir Geoffrey's breast pocket with the other. In a single smooth action, Orion extracted the stack of notes and exchanged them for the ones he carried in his coat's secret compartment.

The swap had better be undetectable, for he'd practiced it

on Castor this afternoon until his exacting brother had pronounced himself satisfied.

Orion gave the velvet a final pat. "That did the job, sir. All set."

Sir Geoffrey stepped back and peered at his lapel intently. "Hmph." He shot Orion a glare, then turned away without so much as a nod of thanks.

No need to thank me, you lying sod. I shall be quite satisfied with your complete and eternal ruin.

No one betrayed a Worthington and got away with it.

Sir Geoffrey was called to the podium. Orion calmly made his way to the back of the room, where he sat among the other nobodies.

The presentation hall of the Royal Fraternity of Life Sciences exuded grand intellectual pursuit. The high ceiling was frothy with ornate moldings from which the chandeliers hung. The lifeless gray plastered walls—surely a color designed to instruct the mind to remain upon serious matters!—were hung with full-sized portraits of past luminaries, bewigged and besashed, wearing haughty expressions of analytical superiority.

"If you come hither," they seemed to say, "you had better know what you're talking about!"

Orion permitted himself a small smile at such fancy.

At the front of the room were three chairs. The central seat, upholstered in plush gold velvet, was the largest and highest. This chair, very nearly a throne, was the seat of the First Speaker.

The other two chairs were very luxurious, but of more ordinary dimensions. They sat before a long bench, and would hold the illustrious bottoms of the Second Speaker and the Head Keeper, who was in charge of the Fraternity's extensive collections of records, artifacts, and specimens.

Before this stood the podium.

Facing the chairs and podium were the pews of the Fraternity. The first few rows of benches had cushions and carved backs. These were reserved for the highest-ranking members, those with colored sashes. The next several rows, which seated the white-sashed members, bore no cushions but did come equipped with backs.

The rest, like Orion's utilitarian bench, were naught but bare polished wood. No sash equaled no privilege.

Orion passed a hand over his own breast pocket, which contained his own notes about the process of separating compounds from green plants. When the right moment struck for him to reveal his discovery, these sash-wearing dignitaries would be begging him to join their ranks.

His thoughts lost in future acclaim, he did not at first register the disgruntled noises coming from the other end of his bench. Then Attie finished pushing her way through the barricade of male legs to plunk her bottom down on the bench next to Orion.

He tilted his head as he gazed down at her. She had braided her hair again and was actually wearing a dress. An old one of Elektra's, the garment was too large on Attie's skinny frame, but it was something of a surprise to see his little sister looking almost normal.

However, something was still amiss. He leaned down. "How did you get in here? You have to have an invitation if you are not a member."

Attie blinked at him slowly. Orion remembered where Attie disappeared to on Thursday mornings. Illegally entering Somerset House was child's play after sneaking into St. James's Palace!

The man next to Orion elbowed him. "Shh! He's starting!"

It was true. The tedious reading of minutes and nominations of new members had ended, and the crowd stirred expectantly. Every one of the past years, on First Speaker's night, Sir Geoffrey Blayne had brought forth a dynamic and compelling discovery into the world—and had ruined another assistant's life.

Sir Geoffrey left his cushioned throne and strode stiffly to the podium. Once there, he postured for a few seconds—tugging his waistcoat straight, staring down a few remaining whisperers, and flamboyantly pulling his stack of notes from the breast pocket of his grand velvet surcoat.

Orion and Attie exchanged small diabolical smiles.

"Yes, miss?"

"I wish to call a carriage, please, Pennysmith." Francesca, dressed for her travels, stood in the front hall of Blayne House, her small valise in her gloved grasp.

Pennysmith peered at her from beneath half-closed eyelids, as if a full opening were more than he could manage. "With the family out this evening, Sir Geoffrey's finest carriage is not available for your use, I'm afraid."

She didn't bother to point out to the insufferable manservant that she was, in fact, a member of "the family." After all, what was the point when tomorrow she would be leaving England forever? Indeed, Francesca had never been an admirer of the butler of Blayne House, yet she had always attempted to be as charitable as possible. But since this evening was her last in residence, she decided she would allow herself the freedom to see him as he was. She would classify him as a ferret, but she did not wish to insult ferrets, which were rather cuddly. Pennysmith was nothing but a weasel in household livery.

"I realize Sir Geoffrey is out this evening," she said. "I simply need a vehicle to take me and my things to the docklands, and I do not care if it is a farm cart pulled by a giant *ass.*"

That got his eyelids to open. "Of course, Miss Penrose." The butler then called for a footman, who would call for an underfootman, who would call for a secondary driver, who would then order the stable boy to prepare the horses. That was how Blayne House operated. Francesca couldn't say that she would miss it.

Pennysmith cleared his throat. "Will the young miss be going home for a brief visit? How long will we be deprived of your company?"

"Forever, Pennysmith. Congratulations."

The butler nearly skipped with joy. "Oy, move it along!" He clapped his hands and shouted out instructions for the livery boys to fetch the trunk from her bedchamber. Francesca took a seat in a small rosewood armchair near the door, and Pennysmith resumed his rigid stance, nose up, looking anywhere but at her. After a long moment, he suddenly turned her way and smiled.

"With the young miss soon to be absent, I take it that rabbit shall be back on the menu?"

A hot jolt of alarm sent her to her feet. *Dio!* How foolish she'd been to think she could simply leave the rabbits here for Attie to study! The cook would have them stewed and served before Francesca's ship left the dock! She certainly could not take one hundred rabbits on an ocean voyage, so what would she do?

The Worthingtons. She would send them to Worthington House with a note of explanation, sure in the knowledge that Attie would keep them safe.

"Pennysmith, I shall need several footmen to assist with the rabbit hutches," she said perfunctorily. "I should like all the rabbits driven to Worthington House immediately."

His eyelids drooped again. He looked down his long weasel-like nose at her. "Would miss like this accomplished before or after her trunk is taken to the docklands?"

"Oh, dear Pennysmith!" She looked at him with false concern. "Is the prospect of coordinating two things at once distressing for you? Do you fear you may actually have to *do* something?"

He said nothing. His upper lip spasmed.

"I want the rabbits delivered first, then the trunk." She retrieved her valise. "And I shall be in the laboratory for a little while before I assist with packing the rabbits."

"Yes, miss."

Just as she turned to leave, a loud clamor emanated from the street. Francesca peered out a front window to see a roofless, rickety wooden freight cart pulled by a single dray horse.

"Your chariot awaits," said Pennysmith.

She leveled her gaze at the self-satisfied butler. "Then I suggest you send it 'round back before it turns into a pumpkin."

Chapter 36

"... **A**ND investigating this process took years of folderol and balderdash."

Folderol?

Sir Geoffrey stared at the cards. Alarm jolted through him. What he had just uttered aloud was nothing but nonsense. Was his vision impaired? Had he selected the wrong notes?

And then slow, desperate fear crept over him—he had used too much! Pennysmith had not been here to prepare his tea for him, so Sir Geoffrey had ground some dried pods to bring to Somerset House. He'd dosed his tea on the sly because that damned Worthington wouldn't give him a second to himself!

He took a sip of water from the goblet provided for him and tried to focus his racing thoughts. Then he tried reading again.

"The immediate result of using the two solvents"—*ah, that sounded acceptable!*—"was to separate the multicolored feces of the unicorn"—*what the hell?* But his lips were already forming the next words—"from the previously collected flatulence of the hedgehog—"

He heard the first snickers begin in the gallery. He felt his face reddening as he gazed in horror at the cards. A drop of sour sweat fell from his brow to the ink. In a panic, he scrabbled through the notes, but it just got worse.

"High concentrates of doltish perambulators . . . while mixing equal parts acids and piglets . . . through repeated applications of Cornish pasties."

With dismay he heard his own voice ringing through the hall. Indeed, he had dosed himself incorrectly, and now his mouth was running away on him. But that was not all—he realized he'd been the victim of a prank, and most likely by the ingrate Worthington himself. And yet he could not stop . . . Everything that went into his mind through his hypersharpened vision spewed from his mouth, unfiltered by any shred of self-control. With horror, he heard his volume increase as the laughter in the hall grew louder and more mocking, sounding like church bells ringing his death knell!

Sir Geoffrey looked frantically through the audience until he located Worthington at the back of the hall. The backstabber appeared calm, a slightly mocking smile on his lips.

Judith. I need Judith. She will help me, come to my aid, ensure I recover from this sabotage! But . . . where is she?

She was not present!

As if to guarantee that Sir Geoffrey's ruin was irreversible, the snide Nicholas Witherspoon stood and gestured grandly toward the podium. "Remarkable! Our much-admired First Speaker has just expounded on the biochemical properties of unicorn dung, piglets, and pasties!"

Sir Geoffrey threw his notes in a rage, and they fluttered to the floor. He hurried from the presentation hall, only to be halted when the rear doorway would not open. Sir Geoffrey jiggled and jostled the latch, and finally, with the roaring laughter echoing through the presentation hall at his back, he threw his considerable bulk at the door. It gave with a splintering of fine wood, and Sir Geoffrey, innovator, forward thinker, Renaissance man, and all-around paragon of science,

fled the raucous mockery of his erstwhile peers, running away
into the night.

FRANCESCA UNPINNED THE last chart and laid it flat upon
the steel laboratory table. She took the single thick roll she'd
fashioned from the other charts and began to carefully incor-
porate the last one into the roll.

The laboratory was so silent that the faint rasp of the thick
paper against itself seemed loud in comparison. With the task
complete, she stood quietly in the room for one last moment,
the charts clutched tight in her arms.

She had had such hopes in this place. Hopes that her research would be taken seriously, hopes that she would find
her place in the world among family . . . and then, upon finding Orion Worthington, sweet, impossible hopes that she had
perhaps found the heart that beat at the same pace as hers.

Her arms tightened around the roll of paper for a moment,
until the crackle made her realize she was crushing it. She
eased her grasp. A memory had just flashed before her, the
memory of something real and true: Orion's eyes, softened
and laughing as they lay together on the carpet before the fire.
His touch, once somewhat clinical, was now tender. Orion's
kiss was now as gentle and solemn as a vow. Orion's body
melded with hers, thrumming to a shared heartbeat.

But his words, wounding and indifferent, came from a man
apparently cold to the core. When he pushed her away, it was
harsh. And final. But almost as if spoken by another man
entirely.

In the hours since, Francesca had developed a theory as
to why his actions did not match his words. She believed that
Orion chose to marry Judith to advance his career and that
he placed more importance on his academic reputation than
on Francesca. But a thought had been niggling at the corner
of her mind, a thought that told her it might not be that simple,
that other forces were at work. The First Law of Proof: If the

evidence does not support the theory, one needs a new theory. Did she need a new theory about why Orion Worthington had rejected her? Was there something here that she had not fully analyzed?

Francesca kept her feet planted on the same spot on the laboratory floor, afraid that if she moved, she would lose her train of thought. She needed to ponder this matter carefully and thoroughly.

First, she was certain that Orion was already deeply disturbed by something before she arrived with the picnic basket. She heard him pacing in his bedchamber. She saw the slope of his shoulders and the desolation in his eyes. It was almost as if he were dogged by something outside of himself that he had no power to shake off, as if he were being manipulated, forced.

Francesca was ashamed—she'd seen his pain and then forgotten it. She had been too busy seducing him, and then wallowing in righteous self-pity after he had scorned her.

It hurt Francesca so to hear his words—but what if it hurt Orion just as much to say them?

Second, it was clear Judith did not wish to marry Orion; therefore, the pressure would not be coming from her.

Which pointed to Sir Geoffrey. Could he be forcing Orion along a particular path, one that included marriage to his daughter? If so, what were his leverage and his motivation? How had he bent Orion, a strong-willed and determined man, to his will? And why?

She could ignore it no longer—Francesca admitted to herself that something was amiss with her uncle. He treated his daughter like a scullery maid and spoke kindly to her only in public. His moods and health seemed unpredictable, running the gamut from sunny and spry to dark and diseased, sometimes within the span of minutes. And there was the surprising litany of offenses that had slipped from Judith's mouth in a moment of weakness—"covered for him, lied for him, stol—"

Had Judith nearly accused her father of theft?

But theft of what? What would he need to steal that he could not easily procure for himself?

Francesca tilted her head and felt herself scowl under the weight of her suspicions. She had always been puzzled by the fact that Sir Geoffrey, a man acclaimed for his scientific acumen, barely set foot in his own laboratory. And if he were presenting new findings at tonight's meeting, what might these new findings be?

Whose findings?

"Orion!" Francesca lifted her chin, the knowledge prickling down the length of her spine. Sir Geoffrey was behind all of this. He had to have found a way to corner Orion, to threaten him where it would hurt him the most.

She felt her lip curl in disgust. *"Feccia sporca!* Filthy scum!"

Francesca spun around in a rage, the roll of charts knocking into a mortar and pestle sitting near the end of a table.

Out of reflex, Francesca grabbed the stone mortar by the neck before it could tip from its perch. Then she frowned down at it. "That's odd," she said aloud. When she had swept up the remains of Judith's emotional breakage that morning, everything had been neatly put away, including the mortar and pestle. She knew Orion had not returned to work, nor had she.

Sir Geoffrey must have come in that afternoon, before he'd begun preparing for his important night. Goodness, the scientist had done some actual science?

Curiosity, considered a fault in a young lady, but a virtue in a scientist, brought the mortar closer to her nose for a careful sniff. There was a familiarity to the sweet, slightly rotten scent.

Francesca's eyes widened. She thrust her pinkie into the mortar bowl and dabbed at the inner surface. Then she touched it to her tongue with a frown.

Ground poppy? It was unmistakable, and quite intense.

She recalled the poppy flowers blooming in the garden. Every household kept some form of poppy pain medication about, usually in the form of laudanum syrup, but this?

"Oh, Uncle." Her shocked whisper rasped through the empty laboratory. "What have you *done* to yourself?"

It was a raw powder of pure poppy pods. A few grains of this concentration would act simultaneously as a soother and a stimulant, although there would be a great possibility of addiction. Just then she remembered the night she and Orion hid behind the draperies in Sir Geoffrey's study. Her uncle entered, shaking and unsteady, and unlocked a cupboard fitted with laboratory supplies. They had not been able to see what Sir Geoffrey did, but when he left many moments later, his pace was brisk and steady.

Francesca's breath left her in a gasp. The absentminded air. The occasional stagger. The smiling geniality that abruptly turned to rage. And the inability to focus a formerly sharp mind to new and innovative experimentation—an inability that might drive a man to do terrible, unscrupulous things to maintain his position!

Chapter 37

HE took the carriage—to hell with that conniving, backstabbing Worthington! He could rot in the gutter for all Sir Geoffrey cared! And Judith—abandoning him at his time of need. Ingrates everywhere he looked! Turncoats! Frauds!

Oh, the horror of this night.

He raised his clenched fists and smashed them down into the tufted velvet seat at either side of his body. *Pound. Pound. Pound.* His head reeled. "How could this—? How did this—? What would become—?"

Sir Geoffrey began smacking his palms against his forehead over and over and over.

Worthington.

Worthington!

He snatched his walking stick and began violently poking its silver end piece, a lion's head, into the ceiling. Soon he began a wild swinging to and fro inside the carriage, finding some solace in the sound of ripping and tearing velvet. Shred, rip, slice, tear.

Of course Worthington was responsible for the vicious prank! And to think . . . he had the gall to turn on him after all he had done for the man! Sir Geoffrey rescued that rat from the disgrace of his notorious name! Promised him the hand of his truest treasure, his darling Judith!

The carriage rolled to a stop in front of Blayne House. He shoved his way out of the carriage, noting how the two footmen tried to evade his keen eye. "What are you looking at, you two layabouts?" He smashed his walking stick against the side of the carriage, for emphasis, and both men turned and busied themselves with the horses.

The difficulty in finding good help!

He staggered up the steps and waited for the door to open. "Pennysmith!" Sir Geoffrey beat at the door with his walking stick.

Many seconds passed. The door remained closed in his face. Sir Geoffrey was forced to open *his own door* and, as additional insult, *no one* was there to greet him in his front hall! Where the bloody hell was everyone?

The world was crumbling before his eyes!

THE PRESENTATION ROOM at Somerset House was in an uproar with laughter and outrage and chaos. Worthington vengeance, indeed! The crowd seemed to have particularly relished Iris's contribution concerning unicorn dung.

Orion sauntered toward the podium with Attie scampering in a circle of glee around him.

"Attie," he cautioned her, not able to stop smiling. "Show some decorum, please."

With his smile lingering, Orion passed his hand over his own neat stack of notes. In a moment, when the uproar died down, he meant to take the podium himself—and present his own research. He rather thought his own measured and logical manner would provide a charming contrast to Sir Geoffrey's breakdown.

He frowned slightly through his triumph, thinking of Sir Geoffrey's behavior. He'd meant the man to be flustered, to make him fumble, and then, since the research and knowledge weren't truly his, to be unable to recover publicly. Orion had even prepared a few pithy questions to throw at the man while he dithered, to make the audience realize that at the very least, Sir Geoffrey didn't fully understand his topic. He'd hoped they would see that the ideas Sir Geoffrey claimed as his own were, in fact, those of one Orion Worthington.

However, the simple prank had gone even more horribly awry than it was meant to. Sir Geoffrey had truly fallen apart! He'd babbled like a madman, his words coming faster and faster, as if he'd lost all control. Orion pictured the man's face—dripping perspiration and flushing so deeply that Orion had almost feared for his heart!

Orion meant to understand the meaning of that behavior, but further investigation would have to wait until after his own triumphant turn at the podium.

Then a slender hand touched his arm. "Mr. Worthington?"

Orion saw Attie scowl. He turned to see Judith there, with that Asher Langford bloke hovering behind. Judith looked very odd to Orion, quite unlike her usual cool, remote self. She was rosy cheeked. Her golden hair was mussed, with wispy strands coming down from the pins. Moreover, her lips were very pink, and a bit swollen.

Orion's recent experience with Francesca led him to the inescapable conclusion that Judith had been recently kissed, and very thoroughly at that!

He cast a glance at Langford, who also showed signs of romantic pawing. The big fellow blushed at Orion's knowing look, but he also thrust out his chin, as if daring Orion to comment.

Heaven forbid. Judith could go kiss a regiment for all he cared. If Asher Langford had turned poor, brittle Miss Judith Blayne from a porcelain statue to a real girl, then bully for him!

"Mr. Worthington, what has happened? Where is Papa?"

Orion frowned down at Judith. He'd forgotten to consider the consequences for Sir Geoffrey's daughter when he'd plotted his revenge.

Orion tried to tell himself that Sir Geoffrey hadn't cared if his actions caused problems for his only child, but guilt still pricked at him. He took a breath. What could he tell her?

"We demolished your papa," Attie informed her belligerently. "Now everyone knows he's a thief and a liar!"

Judith went back on her heels. "Oh." Her expression chilled. Langford put a reassuring hand on her shoulder. Judith lifted her chin as she covered Asher's hand with her own. "I must go home and check on him," she said. She didn't sound angry, nor did she sound overly concerned. She sounded . . . drained.

Then she looked around. "Where is Francesca? I thought she would be here by now. Packing her things shouldn't take that long."

Packing? Orion went cold.

Perhaps I shall return to Italy.

Perhaps you should.

Oh no.

"I told her I planned to marry you, Judith. I told her she should go home." He swallowed hard, blood racing and his gaze scanning the faces of the others. "She wouldn't really . . . would she?"

"I would!" Attie and Judith affirmed simultaneously. Behind Judith, Asher nodded at Orion, his expression pitying.

A world without Francesca?

A world without her light, her laughter . . . her love?

I love Francesca.

Love?

Yes. It was as simple as that. In the blink of an eye, former convictions shifted sideways. Suddenly, with vision refracted through the prism of Francesca, Orion saw the world in all of its wonder and magic, at last.

"I love Francesca." He said the words out loud, in marvelous awe.

Attie rolled her eyes. "He's a genius!" Then she hit him on the arm. "Are all men so thick?" she queried Judith. Judith bit her lip, but Asher nodded again.

Orion straightened. "I have to go."

Attie grabbed his sleeve as he turned to depart. "What about your triumphant assumption of the throne?"

All of his ambitions seemed trivial next to the thought of losing Francesca. Science was wonderful. Francesca was *everything*.

Orion pulled his notes from his pocket and thrust them into Judith's hands. "You do it."

Then he kissed his little sister on the top of her contrary head and ran for the door, for Blayne House, and for Francesca.

INSIDE THE HOUSE, forced to fend for himself without a bit of assistance from a single of the useless creatures in his employ, Sir Geoffrey used his walking stick to guide himself along the wall. Finally, he reached the refuge of his study and the relief he would find in his special cupboard.

He lurched forward, his head now pounding, like his fists on the seat. He removed his watch fob and singled out the small key that would save him.

There was no time for tea.

With shaking hands, he snatched the decanter of brandy, poured a snifter, and wrestled with the lid that kept him from the contents of the special jar. He thanked God he'd had the presence of mind that day to grind additional whole pods in the laboratory and replenish his supply! He doubted he would be capable of such focus in his present state.

His fingers twitched violently but finally loosened the tin lid. He then proceeded to dump the entire contents into the brandy. After a quick swirl, and without a care for the consequences, he drank every drop. What did it matter? He was finished. Life would not be worth living with his reputation as shredded as the carriage ceiling!

Sir Geoffrey felt the liquid burn his throat. Feet planted on the carpet, he braced himself on the cupboard, waiting for the rush of liberated thought and complete invincibility to suffuse him.

"Yes!" He lifted his face to the ceiling, sensing the return to his true self. But he was interested to find it did not stop there. The concoction swept him higher, higher, until his mind was a cascade of superhuman thought. He knew what was to come. He understood everything. He could do anything.

It was so clear now. They all had conspired against him. Orion Worthington wanted his laboratory—he even admitted so the day he arrived!—and enlisted everyone in the household to assist him with his debauched plan. Every soul was in on it, from Pennysmith and Eva down to the lowest scullery boy. And Judith, of course, too timid to find herself a duke, too frail and lazy to be of any real use to him! And that outlandish brat Francine, or whatever his inept half brother had named her—she must have had a primary role in all this, with her sneaky, foreign ways. That unusual girl and her filthy rodents had made his life a living hell!

Enough!

He sucked a huge gulp of air into his lungs and stood tall, prepared to do what had to be done. Now that Worthington had ruined him, Sir Geoffrey could not allow him to marry Judith and profit from his evil deeds. The mere thought of such an outcome brought a wild hatred roaring through his blood.

Would Orion Worthington become heir to the Blayne scientific dynasty? Would he lie his way into Sir Geoffrey's chair at the Fraternity? Would the blackguard be allowed to steal the fruits of Sir Geoffrey's life's work?

Not bloody likely.

He snatched the brandy decanter and the nearest candle.

"Pennysmith!" Sir Geoffrey hastened down the hall in search of his indolent butler. How dared he not be there to greet him upon his return?

"Pennysmith!"

He shoved open the rear door of the house and reeled into the garden, suddenly unsure as to his original purpose in coming outside. He took a swig from the crystal decanter and then saw it. The fountain? Was that his destination? Well, why not?

He stumbled his way to the Italian marble, set the decanter and candle on its edge, and unbuttoned the flap of his breeches. The relief, the sheer pleasure of pissing in his own bloody fountain simply because he bloody could! To hell with them all—he was still a man at the pinnacle of his power!

In midstream, Sir Geoffrey let his gaze wander to the laboratory. *His* laboratory. One that would never fall into the hands of that sniveling Worthington! Ha! He would rather see it burned to the ground than belong to a man so unworthy.

Sir Geoffrey was suddenly struck by a flash of pure genius. He had everything he needed, right at his fingertips, to follow through on his spectacular plan. As all of the world's wisest men knew, desperate situations called for desperate measures.

With his flap still open, Sir Geoffrey ripped the cravat from his throat and began shoving it into the neck of the decanter. He was careful to leave fabric protruding from the top for use as a wick. He grabbed the candle.

His chest expanded with purpose, and his legs churned relentlessly, carrying him to the laboratory in a matter of seconds. Sir Geoffrey smiled with satisfaction as he lowered the candle flame to the brandy-soaked cravat and it caught. It was strangely hypnotizing, that flame, and with every bit of superhuman strength he possessed, he hurled the fiery decanter against the wooden laboratory doors. It exploded with a deeply rewarding shatter of glass and a *whoosh!* as the wood succumbed to the flame.

Sir Geoffrey reared back to avoid getting singed. "Aha!"

he cried, clapping his hands in joy. "Take that, Worthington! You will never best the Great Sir Geoffrey Blayne!" He turned, giggling uncontrollably, nearly falling as he lost his footing, yanking at his drooping breeches. He pressed on, ever the knight, fist raised to the sky. The smell of smoke was delicious in his nostrils, which caused his giggles to blossom into full laughter. With one hand grasping at his breeches, he laughed, and laughed, and laughed . . .

They all hated him. They were all out to get him. But he beat them at their own game! The thought struck him as hilarious.

Sir Geoffrey staggered along until he reached the cutting garden, where he tripped over a row of gladiolas and landed on his arse in the middle of the poppies.

Poppies!

Sir Geoffrey tilted his head back and roared. He continued laughing until his sides hurt, and then three words passed through his agitated mind, clearing a path and leaving a purity of understanding in their wake—*multicolored unicorn feces.*

"Unicorn feces!" he cried aloud into the night, stretching his arms wide. He heard his own laughter grow harsh, then breathless, then transition into a series of uncontrollable sobs that almost immediately became laughter again. Nothing made sense to Sir Geoffrey, yet the laughing ripped at his lungs and the sobbing doubled him over.

Oh, the bittersweet agony of it all! The tenderness! The terror! Sir Geoffrey decided that the loss of one's mind was a strangely fascinating experience.

His awareness dimmed. The last thing he sensed was his cheek hitting the damp, plowed earth.

Chapter 38

THE smoke began to thicken dangerously in a matter of seconds. Francesca had backed as far as she could from the burning doors, but the pollution had already filled the upper portion of the high-ceilinged laboratory and was pooling lower every minute.

For the first time thankful for her own short stature, Francesca kept low and tried to think past the panic simmering in her blood.

She had tried to leave immediately after hearing the shattering of glass as it impacted the large wooden doors, but the metal latches were already sizzling hot to the touch. Still, she had pressed as close as she dared, shouting for help with increasing alarm. Then she'd been forced to scramble back from the burning substance spreading from beneath the door.

Next she had tried the windows. It hadn't been difficult to break the glass, but the heavy grilles framing the panes had been made to discourage thieves from helping themselves to the priceless laboratory equipment. She was not strong enough to snap them, even after snatching up Judith's heavy gloves to protect herself from the broken glass.

The airway provided by the broken window pulled heartily at the black smoke, funneling it to the outdoors. This made it impossible to breathe the fresh air as she had hoped to do.

The stone floor was still cool and the air there relatively pure. Francesca crawled beneath one of the marble laboratory tables and hugged her knees to her chest.

Someone would come. Someone would see the rising smoke—except that it was full night outside.

Someone in the house would spot the flames—though Sir Geoffrey and the others were still out and she'd sent all the footmen on luggage- and rabbit-related errands!

They would surely return shortly, but fire was a swift and dangerous creature. It killed quickly, by asphyxiation if not actual burning.

She began to cough, even as low as she was. The smoke tore at her throat and lungs and made her eyes stream with tears.

The flames had consumed the doors and were now climbing, licking upward, always upward, until the ceiling and beams had caught eagerly.

Francesca stilled the overwhelming panic that swept her. She had to find a way to get clear air, or she would not survive long enough to be rescued.

Something like a tube, or a pipe, that she could put through a window—

With shaking hands, she began to rip frantically at the gleaming copper distillation device. Wrenching with all her might, she managed to disconnect one end of a yard-long stretch of piping.

She put one foot against the device and yanked with her entire body. The pipe came free.

With her pipe clasped in triumphant hands, she began to move toward the windows, but the black smoke hung so low in the room that she could not find them. All she could see were the flames above her head.

Instead, she crawled across the floor to the drain set in the paving.

It was no wider across than her spread hand, but if she could get the cover off, she could push the end of the pipe down the drain, into cool, clear airspace.

Someone will come. All I have to do is survive until someone comes. She wrapped her hand around the pipe, then began to feed it into the open drain. The last crook of the pipe refused to go into the hole. Francesca compromised by rolling into a ball on her side and putting her lips to the pipe.

Dank, cool air filled her lungs. It smelled of pond scum and earth. It was wonderful.

The brightness of the burning ceiling made her turn her eyes away. She pressed her cheek to the stone floor and threw one arm over her face to shield herself from the scorching heat from above.

She could breathe, but how long could she bear the heat?

No one was coming, were they?

Orion, I need you. Please come.

Please hurry.

IT HAD TAKEN Orion far too long to obtain a hackney cab on the Strand outside Somerset House. A steady stream of Fraternity members poured from the hall, some furious, some still laughing at the fall of Sir Geoffrey Blayne.

Orion beat out two fellows who had paused to reenact the bit about the "doltish perambulators" by ducking around them and frankly stealing their ride home. *Terribly sorry, chaps, but I have a woman to kiss!*

He smiled as he gave the driver the address of Blayne House and settled back into the worn velvet cushions of the carriage. His lovely Francesca awaited him there, with her dancing grace and easy laughter. She would be furious with him, he had no doubt. However, his plan included abject apology, followed by many, many kisses.

He would kiss her protests away, and soon her fury would be diverted into passion, and she would melt against him in the way that meant she was entirely his.

Orion didn't know what they would do after that, and frankly he didn't much care. They could go raise bunnies in Shropshire for all it mattered to him. He simply knew that if his future did not include that delicious woman, he didn't want it!

The traffic impeded the progress of the cabbie until Orion, tapping his fingers impatiently, opened the door and stepped out of the slowly inching carriage.

"Oy! Ye can't just go—"

Orion tossed the man a coin without even checking the denomination and began to run, ducking the moving carts and carriages with all the practice of a misspent London childhood.

Once he reached the sidewalk, he stretched his long legs and ran eagerly. A mile passed. Then another half mile. Then he turned the corner and passed the park where he and Judith had strolled just a few days and a hundred years before.

Judith would be just fine, he assured himself as he ran. Better to be disappointed in a possible engagement than married to someone who longed for another—and always would!

Francesca, Francesca. Her name sounded in the pounding of his boots on the cobbles. His beautiful, joyous, magical Francesca.

He took the five steps at the entrance to Blayne House in a single bound. He pushed the door open so hard, it rebounded on the wall behind him.

"Francesca!"

He ran up the stairs. Her bedchamber door stood slightly open. He burst through and stopped in the center of the room.

The luxurious gown of gold silk was displayed on the coverlet, along with Calliope's book of botanical illustrations.

On the writing desk was his quill, the bright blue macaw feather he had given her when hers snapped. Orion reeled—the rest of the room was devoid of her presence. The doors to the wardrobe were flung open, revealing empty shelves and hooks.

The message was clear—Francesca was gone, but she did not take with her anything that reminded her of Orion. The dress she wore the night she told him she loved him. The quill. His sister's book.

Gone? How could she be gone already? It took his mother and sisters days to pack for a journey!

He left the empty room behind him, running for the stairs. One place where he could always find Francesca—wherever there was food!

But the kitchens were cold and dark. Orion ran through the cookery and the bakery and larder and even ducked into the scullery.

The scullery was not as dark as the rest of the kitchens. The orange glow in the room made Orion step through the doorway and into the room to look through the small window.

His breath caught and his body froze at the sight of the laboratory. The great barnlike building was violently aflame, lighting the entire grounds behind the house with the blaze!

Orion raced from the scullery. None of the distance he had traversed this evening on foot felt as long as the mere yards out to the gardens and the laboratory—

And Francesca.

He didn't know how he knew. It wasn't logical. All her things were gone. By all the evidence, she had clearly left Blayne House, yet he knew she was there, in the center of that hellish blaze.

He stopped just short of the flames, throwing his hands up to guard his face from the heat. The great doors were gone, the charred and burning planks fallen this way and that on the lawn before the building. The opening gaped, a great flaming mouth to a burning cave.

A servant ran up to him with a bucket. "Sir, we sent some-one to fetch the fire brigade, but . . ." The young footman's voice trailed off as he gazed hopelessly at the laboratory. "Himself has lost his mind, he has. Sittin' on his arse in the cutting garden, laughin' away like a bedlamite!"

Orion wasn't listening. Francesca. He turned to the foot-man and snatched the bucket of water from his unresisting hands. Without hesitation, Orion poured half the water over his head, soaking his hair and clothing. Logic could not help him now. Only Worthington madness would do.

Full combustion, just as she had warned him.

Still holding the half-full bucket, he walked into the fire.

Chapter 39

AWN light streaked the sky. Black coals glowed red in the blackened rubble of the laboratory. The stone walls still stood, a mocking shell holding nothing but a family's pain.

Attie stood just outside that skeletal edifice, her green pupils vivid in her reddened eyes. Her skinny arms were wrapped tightly about her shuddering form, but her pale cheeks were dry. Attie didn't cry like other people.

Castor and Lysander helped Archie into the rubble, kicking aside the worst of the still-scorching timbers. "I want to see," Archie said. His lined face sagged as it never had before, having always been held up with his wistful smile.

"You don't." Lysander's voice was flat and rough, but his expression was rigid with tension. "You truly don't."

Castor held his father about the shoulders without speaking.

Iris drifted about the garden. Judith watched Orion's mother smile at a blue butterfly fluttering through a stream of smoke. She looked to where a very weary Miranda, whom she'd just met but liked very much, was seated on the edge of the fountain, her cheeks wet with tears. "Does she understand that her son is gone?"

Miranda shook her head. "She doesn't want to. So she won't see it. She has a rather special mind." Miranda held out a hand to Judith, who took it briefly. "I'm sorry about your cousin. Were you very close?"

Judith looked away, gazing at the garden instead of the blackened shell of the laboratory. "No . . . but we might have been, someday. She . . . I liked her. I simply didn't like me."

Asher, who had not left her side since she had kissed him, pulled her close to his side as if to protect her from her losses.

When she and Asher had returned to Blayne House last night, prepared to challenge Sir Geoffrey to cancel his plans to force her to wed Orion, they had found the house in shambles, the front hall sooty and muddy and strangers running through it with axes and buckets.

Following the fire brigade through the house, they had emerged in the garden to see the laboratory engulfed in flames. "Papa!"

One of the footmen heard her cry. "He's sittin' in the poppy patch, chucklin' away," the man told her with disdain. "The mad bugger burned his own shop down!"

"What? I don't believe you!"

The footman held up the top half of Papa's cut crystal brandy decanter. "Do you believe this? He shoved his cravat in for a wick and tossed it at the door."

"But he's not hurt?"

The footman stared at her. "He's just fine, if bein' mad don't count. The other bloke, Worthington, ran into the fire and didn't come out. Nutters, all of 'em!"

Judith was quite sure there was only one thing that Orion Worthington would die for.

Francesca.

She had lost them both, as had all these people around her, strangers who had become like her family in these last hours, ties forged by bonds of grief.

No one had held her answerable for her father's misdeeds. That tore at Judith, for she most certainly blamed herself. She had missed her father's public shaming last night because she had lost herself in Asher's kisses. There was no way Orion could have known how close her father's irrationality skated on the edge of madness.

I should have seen it. She held tight to Asher's hand. *I should have realized that someday he would do something terrible. The poppies always loosed his rage—and last night's debacle at the presentation hall would have brought on the rage to end all rages!*

The Worthingtons' cousin, Bliss, emerged from the house with a glass of water for Miranda. After seeing to the pregnant woman, Bliss came to stand with Judith and Asher as they overlooked the search of the rubble.

Bliss was a comely girl, her blond looks as warm and inviting as Judith's were restrained and cool. Her wide blue eyes took in the scorched rubble of the Blayne family honor with solemn gravity.

Then she looked at Judith. "Your father didn't know anyone was inside."

Judith blinked. "What?"

Bliss tilted her head back toward the house. "He's awake again but still talking about unicorn dung and flaming brandy. He's waxing quite confessional. However, it's clear that he thought he was burning down an empty lab. No one has told him differently yet."

Judith closed her lids briefly. Her eyes felt hot from the tears and the night full of flames. "It doesn't really change anything, though, does it?"

Bliss gazed at her evenly. "I would want to know, if it were my father."

Judith nodded. It did help, a little, to know that her father's failings did not include premeditated murder.

Bliss turned away with what Judith had come to think of as typical Worthington brevity of farewell. Then she turned back. "Also, perhaps you ought to consider scouring out the fountain."

Orion's eldest brother, Dade, had forged farther into the wreckage than the others. Judith saw him tossing rubble and burned timbers aside. Then he bent to pull a large slab of blackened marble up with his bare hands, his wide shoulder muscles bulging. "I found them," he called over his shoulder, his voice strained from the effort of lifting.

Asher left Judith's side, bounding over the fallen timbers to help. Lysander, Castor, and Archie scrambled closer as well. It took four men to pull away the remains of two marble tables.

Soon they were all gathered around the single nonscorched area of laboratory floor. The slabs of marble had been tented over the area, blocking it from the flames.

"Oh my, they do make a handsome couple."

Judith turned in horror to see Iris standing next to her. Her blue eyes were vague and dreamy as she gazed down at the two bodies in the rubble.

Judith supposed that Mrs. Worthington could not be blamed for her fantasy. Orion and Francesca, though soot-stained and singed, really did look as if they had merely chosen a decidedly odd place for a nap.

They lay wrapped in each other's arms on the floor, nose to nose, with Francesca's smaller form curled up like a child while Orion's longer body formed a C-shape around her. Francesca's singed hair covered both their faces.

Archie moved to his wife's side and passed one hand over his wet eyes while he held her hand in his other one. "Let's step away now, dearest. Make way for the boys to—"

Cough.

Then a deeper *cough-cough.*

The gathered mourners watched with stunned shock—all but for Iris, of course—as one of Francesca's small, soot-covered hands moved. It traveled up Orion's arm, then shakily moved to push back Francesca's hair from both their faces.

Orion's hand moved up to catch Francesca's smaller one in his.

"I think we're being rescued, Chessa."

"About bloody time," she said hoarsely from under singed locks of hair. "I need a visit to the outhouse."

That was when the shocked watchers let out varying cries of delight and celebration. Attie scrambled into the valley left by the debris and threw herself onto Orion.

"Oof." Orion gave Attie a weary squeeze, then pushed her off. With Lysander's help, he rose stiffly to his feet. Then he reached for Francesca.

She clambered shakily upright, then leaned into his arms, twining her own around his back. "Mr. Worthington, I fear our tryst has been discovered." Her voice was a dry rasp.

He sighed and held her close, although his arms could scarcely move. The two of them were reddened and scorched, and Francesca was going to have to cut off a great deal of hair, but they were quite miraculously alive. "There's no help for it, then. You're going to have to marry me."

She leaned her head back. Her smile was a white flash in her soot-coated features. "Say it again. Practice makes perfect."

His laugh was hardly more than a wheeze. How magical was a world with Francesca in it! He would face a thousand firestorms to keep her right where she was. "I love you, Chessa. I cannot live without you. Please, say you will wed me?"

She opened her lips to reply—and her stomach growled loudly enough for all to hear. Amid the laughter and the helping hands and glasses of cool water, Orion never did hear her response.

Iris came to embrace him gently. "What a pretty thing she is," she said to him. "Your children will be very attractive. Maybe they will get her eyes, hmm?"

Orion sighed. His mother was a Lamarckist.

Iris wandered off to pick poppies. Orion turned to go to

Francesca before someone else came to touch him to make sure he was truly alive.

Judith and Asher Langford stood before him. Judith's eyes were very red, and as she gazed at him, she let out a small, broken sound. She pressed a hand over her lips, but her guilt-ridden eyes spoke volumes.

Orion shook his head. "It wasn't your fault. You were just trying to help your father. You need not have to feel shame for your part in it."

"The engagement was a ruse, or rather it was supposed to be. I think when he realized how brilliant you are, he wanted to keep you around forever."

Orion was too weary to let the news disturb him. "It is my own fault I fell for it. I should not have considered such a cold-blooded arrangement."

Judith bit her lip and nodded. She began to turn away, then suddenly turned back. "I was supposed to burn the assistants' notes, once I had copied them into Papa's handwriting. I didn't burn yours. They're in my—"

"I'll get them!" Attie popped up between them. "I know right where they are!" She ran off on swift, skinny legs.

Orion ducked away, looking for Francesca. He saw her sitting next to Miranda, as she dolefully examined the ends of her hair. Then his brother Castor touched his shoulder. Orion winced. His body ached all over.

"Lysander and I are glad you both made it out alive," Castor began. Beside him, Lysander loomed silently. The entire family was accustomed to speaking for Zander. Cas went on. "But we can't figure it out. I can see that the marble tabletops protected you from the worst of the heat. It was a good idea to tent them together like that, but how could you breathe?"

Orion grinned at his inventor brother. "Copper piping. Floor drain. Go suss it out. I want Chessa."

Enlightened, Cas pulled Zander away to go examine the scene again. Orion headed to where Miranda sat, but Chessa was gone.

Dade caught him then. "It took four of us to move those slabs," he said. "It would be impossible for one man. How did you do it?"

It was strange, but Orion remembered that it had seemed quite possible at the time. He would be very sore, very soon, he could tell—but he shouldn't have been able to do it at all. Orion looked his eldest brother in the eye. "Magic."

Dade blinked. "I don't know what you mean."

Orion shook his head. Dade had never been in love. He didn't understand how a man could move a mountain to save the woman he loved. Orion gave Dade a wry grin. "Maybe someday you will."

Then he spotted Francesca finally, standing alone at last. She stood by the charred rubble, looking thoughtful. He forced his tired body to move quickly, reaching her side before he lost her again.

He put his arm around her waist from behind, out of affection and also to make her hold still. "We made it out alive," he murmured, thinking she was reliving the terror they'd felt, clinging to each other while the fire blazed around them and not knowing if they could survive the dangerous heat.

She leaned back into him. "I know. You were magnificent, heaving those tables over."

His muscles would make him pay for that for days. He smiled down into her hair. "You were brilliant, tapping into the drain system for clear air."

"That was clever, wasn't it?"

He could hear the smile in her raspy voice. When he had jumped through the flames, shouting her name, she had screamed for him as loud as she could, but she'd obviously screamed her voice away. For a horrible few minutes, he hadn't been able to find her.

Shaking off that terrible memory, Orion dropped his face into her scorched and smoky hair. "You didn't answer my question," he whispered.

"What question was that, Mr. Worthington?"

Orion smiled. His iron-willed Chessa. He hoped she would lead him a merry chase for the rest of his life. Turning her gently to face him, he took her hand in his. Then he dropped to one knee before her.

Her eyes widened. She hadn't expected it, he knew.

"Miss Francesca Penrose, it is not enough to tell you that I love you."

She bit her lip. Then the gesture transformed into a wistful little smile.

"I love that you can't go to sleep at night, just like me," he began.

Her smile widened until he felt that the sun had broken through the clouds.

"I love that you have strong opinions and that you have no trouble telling me you think I am wrong."

Orion heard a muffled hoot from Cas behind him and knew that his family was watching. It didn't matter. "I love that you name your specimens. I love that you are kind to my family. I love your bread. I love your *lasagne* and your Bolognese." He smiled softly just for her. "I love your iced seed cake."

She developed a dimple in one cheek at that.

"I love your unconquerable spirit." He kissed the tips of the fingers he held in his hand. "I love the way you dance."

He heard Iris sigh. "It's just like a play!"

Orion went on before Archie could begin quoting the Bard. "And most of all, I love the way you kiss me as if we were the only two people in the entire world."

With that, he tugged gently on her hand until she sat on his knee. She took his seared face gently in her cool, sooty hands.

"Like this?" Then, as if no one watched them at all, she kissed him with such tender passion that it made his heart thrum faster at the same time as it made the world slow to a stop.

When she lifted her head a bit, Orion had very little breath left. Just a little, enough to gasp. "Do it again. Practice makes perfect."

She laughed against his lips. "I fear I have just publicly compromised you, Mr. Worthington. I suppose I'd best make an honest man of you now."

Orion felt his family gather closer around them. Francesca did as well, for she straightened and sat quite primly upon his knee. "Yes, I will marry you."

Orion grinned at her, then glanced bashfully around at his family and hers.

Archie smiled genially at Orion and Francesca. "'Amen, if you love her; for the lady is well worthy.'"

"*Much Ado About Nothing.*" Iris sighed. "My favorite!"

"Scene one, act one," said every single Worthington in unison.

Francesca put a startled hand to her cheek. "Oh, I should get Nonna Laura's permission first!"

Archie smiled happily. "Ah, how is your grandmother, dear? I haven't spoken to her in many years."

Orion turned his head to frown at his father. "You know Nonna Laura?"

"Oh my, yes." Archie raised a woolly brow. "I studied physics under Dr. Laura Bassi at the University of Bologna. That was before I realized my future lay in literature."

Orion's jaw dropped. Laura Bassi? Innovator in physics, natural studies, electricity, and nearly every branch of science in the world? Orion shut his mouth, then swallowed hard. He was marrying into scientific royalty, and he hadn't even known it!

"She used to invite me to dinner with her family." Archie tucked Iris's arm into his as he strolled away. "I recall meeting Volta at her villa, and Charles Bonnet, and even . . ."

Orion turned to Francesca. "Your relations are the Verattis?" According to what he'd read about her, Laura Bassi had wed fellow scientist Giuseppe Veratti and proceeded to have twelve children while maintaining her professorship.

She sighed. "Oh yes. A rather exhausting bunch of high achievers. I like your family better. They know how to have *fun!*"

As if to prove her point, Archie clapped his hands and announced to everyone that they ought to roast chestnuts on the coals of the destroyed lab.

Orion took the opportunity to nuzzle Francesca's ear. "I'd rather have breakfast . . . and a bath."

She sighed. "Oh yes. I'm starving. And that bath had better be for two!"

Miraculously, they managed to sneak away from the families undetected. At least, Orion thought so until he saw Iris turn his way . . .

And wink.

Epilogue

ORION Worthington and Francesca Penrose stood face-to-face in the small stone chapel of the tiny village near the Worthington estate, awash in the sacred hush of the moment. As their gazes locked, Orion smiled with the utmost gentleness, and Francesca knew she would remember this moment the rest of her days.

They were together, pledging their love, the only two people who existed in the entire world.

"With this ring, I thee wed." Orion slipped a simple gold band down Francesca's left finger, and in the silence she swore she could hear his heartbeat.

It was her turn. Francesca took a breath to ensure her voice remained steady. "With this ring, I thee wed." The gold fit snugly around his flesh and before she could pull away, Orion grabbed her hand. He didn't wish to let go.

The couple held on to each other in the quiet. Never had Francesca been surer of anything—she loved Orion Worthington to the depths of her being, and he loved her more than life itself. Hadn't all the evidence supported that theory?

"This is taking *forever*! What are they waiting for?"

"In the theater, it is called a dramatic pause, Attie, darling."
From her seat in the front pew, Iris gestured grandly toward
the minister. "Continue with the scene!"

And so the vicar did. With a voice that rang through the
small church, he said the words for which everyone had
waited: "I now pronounce you man and wife!"

Without warning, Francesca's feet left the altar. Orion
lifted her into his arms and began kissing her senseless. It
was a scorching kiss, a possessive kiss much like the one
they'd shared on the Duke of Camberton's terrace, yet today
they had nothing to hide.

The crowd of friends and family burst into raucous ap-
plause at the minister's declaration, and when it appeared
Orion might never stop kissing Francesca, their approval
became a roar accented by shouts, stomps, and several piercing, two-fingered whistles likely supplied by Castor.

When Francesca finally came up for air, Orion gazed down
at her, unabashed joy and mischief in his dark blue eyes. "This
crowd seems a bit disorderly, Mrs. Worthington," he said.
"Shall we make a run for it?"

"Run mad, Mr. Worthington!"

Orion never let Francesca's feet hit the floor. He swung
her up into his arms and proudly carried her through the
pressing horde inside—and outside—the church. Because the
chapel had been filled to capacity, additional wedding guests
were assembled outdoors in the English morning sunshine.

Not an hour later, the newly married couple approached
the grounds of Worthington Manor, the family's large country estate tucked into the Shropshire countryside. A proces-
sion of carriages snaked its way behind them.

Orion glanced down at his beautiful, rosy-cheeked wife
pressed against him in the carriage, her hair now cut in a
short, curly bob and woven through with ribbon. She looked
positively scrumptious in the traditional Italian wedding dress
Button had created for the occasion, a soft green silk so pale

she seemed to be floating in a mist, the soft color setting off the honeyed glow of her bosom.

"We are almost there!" she cried.

He hoped the setting would be all she envisioned. It had taken much persuasion for him to agree to Francesca's plan—she wished to hold their wedding supper on the grounds of the Worthington family's estate. His concern was that having a fire-damaged manor house in the background of their celebration would bring back the harsh memories of the laboratory blaze, just weeks past. Francesca assured him she would be fine.

"Is the manor not being restored?" she'd asked.

"Yes, but—"

"Then its return to glory is a celebration of life itself!"

The grounds came into view. She clutched at the forearm of Orion's coat. *"Bellisimo!"* she cried. *"Molto bello! Favo-loso!"* Francesca looked up at him with wonder in her warm brown eyes.

A level section of the front lawn near the creek had been carved out as the setting for their wedding feast. Tables of all shapes and sizes were covered with colorful fabrics and surrounded by a wide assortment of chairs—some work chairs, some kitchen chairs, and some upholstered wing chairs. Pottery jugs overflowed with wildflowers. As his sister Elektra had reported, the accommodations had been made possible by the efforts of many villagers and most of the Worthington household staff, and by her own labor and that of Calliope and Iris. The much-pregnant Miranda's contribution had been keeping Attie out of the way.

The guests arrived, and though Francesca had herself prepared and coordinated the preparation of most of the delicacies, it took the vigilance of nearly everyone present to keep her from dishing out plates of food at her own wedding feast. The menu was not the usual English fare, but instead a combination of familiar dishes and those from a traditional Italian wedding *festa*. Several items had been shipped from Italy just for the occasion—olives, wine, and prosciutto among them. Entrées were noodles with a variety of Francesca's sauces, along with an English roast beef, venison, and veal; roasted summer vegetables; and fresh fruits. Dessert featured her specialty—dozens and dozens of her small seed cakes topped with swirls of cream icing.

Blessed with a splendid summer day and a lively crowd, Francesca and Orion barely sat during the festivities. There were too many guests to laugh with, too many family members and friends with whom to visit.

Not long into the meal, a rather breathless Duke of Camberton raced up to Orion. "Is Bliss here? I do not see her!"

Orion noted the forlorn expression on Neville's face. "Right over there." He pointed to a spot in the trees where Bliss and Calliope were emerging, likely after walking along the creek.

Neville was off like a shot.

As the newly married couple strolled from table to table, they repeatedly encountered a boisterous threesome—Attie and her little friend, Charlie Darwin, either running after or running from Herbert, the bunny. Herbert, a pretty pink ribbon around her neck, had reclined in Attie's lap during the wedding ceremony, behaving more like a trained puppy than a rabbit. Little Charlie was obviously exhausted from the running. Attie had informed Orion that the brilliant little boy spent most of his time in the library and she was trying to improve his circulatory system.

Judith and Asher believed they were being sly about it, but it was clear they could not bear to be more than an inch apart from each other. Several times they disappeared behind a large oak close to the creek, only to reappear in a state of disorder. Judith's hair and dress were mussed, but her eyes sparkled. A dazed smile had become a permanent fixture on Asher's face.

"I wonder if he's popped the question." Orion said this aloud while standing next to his brother Dade.

"And how would he manage that?" Dade asked with a chuckle. "Semaphores? The fellow doesn't speak!"

"I'm certain he'll find the right words at the right time." Francesca shot a playful grin Orion's way.

Suddenly, a chorus of female voices could be heard above the conversation, and all eyes turned to where Miranda stretched out on a wing chair, Iris, Attie, Elektra, and Calliope twittering around her.

"It's her time!" Callie cried, and the announcement had the effect of a call to arms. Iris directed the troops, and the women went into action, gathering supplies and summoning a carriage.

Orion and Dade rushed to Miranda's side along with their brother and her husband, Castor.

"I am here, my love." Cas crouched by the chair and held her hand. "Everything will be all right."

"I don't think I can do this!" The flushed Miranda began panting, fear shadowing her eyes.

"Don't worry, dear. You'll be fine." Iris stood calm among the nervous crowd, reaching for Miranda's other hand, which she began to pat rhythmically, her voice soft and reassuring. "We'll get you to the village midwife, who is quite competent. She delivered two of my eight—Elektra and Attie—and she'll see you through this."

"But—" Miranda winced with a wave of contractions. "The pain!"

"Oh, nonsense!" Iris said brightly, directing the carriage to pull as close as possible to Miranda. "It's just like falling off a log . . . and then getting run over by an ale cart. But you'll be fine."

Moments later, Francesca was pressed tightly to Orion's side as they watched the carriage take Miranda, Iris, and Cas to the village. Judith and Asher came to stand nearby, and Judith's eyes were wide with alarm.

"Heavens, that was dramatic!" she exclaimed, pressing a palm to her throat.

Orion gave her a wry smile. "On the contrary, Cousin—for a Worthington event, we have thus far an exceedingly low body count."

It was then that Francesca noticed members of the Blayne House staff assisting with the event. "How did you convince your father's staff to come all the way to Shropshire?"

Judith said, "They're my staff now, and they are quite embarrassed about Pennysmith's departure with Papa's silver trophy cups while everyone else was battling the flames and searching for you."

"As well they should be," Francesca said with asperity. "And what is the latest news of Sir Geoffrey?"

"I am told that his stay in the private hospital will be quite lengthy." Judith seemed unconcerned about her father, then smiled at Francesca. "There will be plenty of room for you and Orion to move in once you return from your honeymoon in Italy."

Orion took the opportunity to ask Judith if she would look in on Attie while they were gone.

"Of course!" she said. "I will be visiting Worthington House often for my painting lessons with Iris."

Francesca reached for her cousin's hand. "Are you quite sure you are comfortable sitting across the dining table from Mr. and Mrs. Worthington on a daily basis?"

Judith broke out into a smile that transformed her cool perfection into a warm, welcoming beauty. "You won't be the only married couple at the table for long."

The usually silent Asher choked, recovered himself, and said, "I accept."

Judith and Asher grasped hands tightly for a moment, and she hid her giddy embarrassment by gazing outward across the grounds. "It's going to be beautiful again someday. It's so peaceful here. So quiet."

Orion and Francesca turned to each other.

"It's quiet," he said.

"That's bad," she said.

"Where's Attie?" they asked in unison.

Moments later, Dade and Lysander were waist deep in the brook, fishing the floundering Charlie Darwin out of the brisk current. Orion extended his hand to Attie, who scrambled up the creek bank to muddy Orion's wedding suit. All the while, Herbert watched safely from a patch of moss, her whiskers fluffing innocently.

"You're older than Charlie," he reminded her. "You should have kept him out of the deepest water."

Attie was clearly offended. "I'm helping him. He needs to get more fit if he is to survive," she said.

Once the dramatic rescue was complete, Orion found he had lost track of Francesca, and located her at the refreshment tables, serving the last of the seed cakes. He headed in that direction, intending to retrieve her and, he hoped, finagle some cake before it disappeared entirely.

"Mrs. Worthington," he said, giving her a gallant bow and holding out his hand, "I urgently require your presence, and one of your cakes."

She glanced up at him, a smile on her lips, and snatched one of the remaining cakes. "Where are we going, Mr. Worthington?" she asked, holding the cloth-wrapped sweet in one hand as he led her away from the table.

"There is a fine botanical specimen of a *Quercus robur* on the grounds," he said, guiding her toward the ancient oak near the creek.

She smiled when she saw that particular tree. "Oh, I love botanical specimens!"

Once they had made their way to the far side of the great tree, the world faded away. Alone at last, sheltered by the huge limbs of the oak, Orion dropped kisses on her summer-warmed neck and collarbone.

"I thought you wanted cake," she said teasingly.

"Can't I have both? You and cake go so well together."

With a small smile, Francesca broke off a piece of cake with her fingers and lifted it to his lips. Bite by bite, they shared the confection, their lips and fingers sweetened with icing. When the cake was gone, he moved in for a deep, sugary kiss.

Orion brushed his lips across her cheek and whispered in her ear, "I'm glad I finally persuaded you to say yes."

"It was quite a chase, wasn't it?" She sighed happily, snuggling closer to him. "But I finally caught you."

Orion lowered his face into her hair to catch the orange-blossom scent of her, knowing that in his arms he held the greatest discovery of all.

The couple was so lost in each other, they didn't notice the black-and-white rabbit sitting up tall at their feet, whiskers twitching with amusement.

READ ON FOR A SNEAK PEEK AT CELESTE BRADLEY'S
NEXT WICKED WORTHINGTONS ROMANCE,

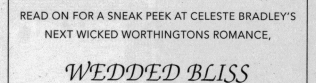

WEDDED BLISS

COMING IN MAY 2017 FROM SIGNET SELECT

"WHAT about what I want? Always such a good boy. Always doing as I'm told. So bloody careful never to offend!" Lord Neville Danworth, fourteenth Duke of Camberton, tossed back the rest of his whiskey with the awkward flair of the beginning drinker. Then he hesitated, as if resisting the impulse to throw his fine crystal glass into the hearth.

He set it carefully on the mantel instead. Then his open hand curled into a fist at his side. "Well, perhaps it's time someone worried about offending me!"

The man seated in the large wing chair by the fire didn't respond. The duke didn't really seem to want a reply, so instead he toyed with an exotically carved dagger. He allowed the candlelight to play along the blade and considered his companion carefully.

The man knew that Neville took pride in being a gentleman and a scholar. The young duke took dutiful care of his lands and his people. He danced well, when he could bring himself to ask someone, and rode well, although horses made him sneeze, and shot well, even though he had confided that he preferred not to actually kill anything that had big warm eyes or graceful wings. He spoke three languages fluently and could read several more.

Poor Neville. He was quite right to itch beneath the burden of his responsibilities. Ever the good lad. Ever the good student. Look at him now. The very thought of defying his uncle's wishes had driven him, with a little friendly urging, to seek courage in a bottle of whiskey—and the whiskey was driving him to release the bitterness he'd not even known he carried from a lifetime of performing beyond expectations in every way.

If he wasn't careful, that bitterness would push him into making a mistake.

Neville pounded his fist upon the mantel and didn't even flinch at the pain of his flesh striking the stone. He whirled on his audience of one with fury in his eyes.

"Well? Are you going to help me with this Bliss Worthington situation or not?"

As he waited for an answer, the rage turned his face red, then white. He staggered, as if he didn't know whether to stand or sit. Then the whiskey made his decision for him.

The man put away his dangerous toy and stood.

From his position on the floor, Neville blinked up at him. "Your boots are very shiny. Shiny and black, with that turned-down top. I wish I were a ship captain and could wear those boots. Or maybe I could be a legendary pirate. They have nice boots, too."

Although Neville was every bit as tall as he was, the man had little trouble lifting him to his feet and letting him fall with somewhat more dignity into the chair by the fire.

"You came home just in time, you know." Draped in a more or less upright position, Neville nodded with satisfaction. "I knew I could count on you. I knew you would help if you truly understood the situation. You'll talk to Uncle Oliver, won't you? You'll help me with Bliss?"

The big man standing over him didn't answer, but he didn't have to. He would help. He would fix everything.

"I can't do it," Neville murmured. "I cannot set Bliss Worthington aside in order to wed someone else just because Uncle Oliver doesn't approve." He blinked slowly at the fire, his gaze fixed on the blue and gold flames dancing over the coals. "After all, it isn't as though there is anything wrong with the Worthington name. I know the family is a little . . . Well, they are an odd lot—it is true—but if being odd affected one's social standing, then the prince regent would be a beggar in the street!" His own defiance of propriety seemed to startle him. He nestled deeper into the cushions.

"She's so . . ." Neville continued, waving his hand. "That golden hair, those sky blue eyes, those—" His hands rose to map a figure in the air. If one were to believe those whiskey-inspired proportions, Miss Bliss Worthington must truly be the stuff of a lonely man's dream.

Distracted by the mere thought of the feminine hills and valleys contained in the imaginary cartography of his beloved, Neville didn't even seem to notice when he passed out entirely.

The silent man stood looking down at the unconscious Duke of Camberton for a long moment. Gangling and unfinished, Neville's limp body slithered down the fine leather of the seat cushion, flopping over the chair arm like an unfettered marionette.

He had been a boy once, too, the man thought. He had dreamed of unlikely and unattainable things, just as Neville did. The difference was that when a man was a bastard instead of an heir, the unlikely remained just that, and the unattainable swung forever just out of reach. The world wasn't designed to help bastards, but it did look favorably on those of unlucky birth who behaved more like gentlemen. Perhaps this was a task only a bastard could do.

*   *   *

THE RAIN SLASHED at the rickety Worthington carriage like a wet hand slapping at a pest. Bliss Worthington was aware of the vibration of the storm against the old lacquered wood surrounding her. She realized that the seams of the vehicle dripped somewhat, and that the damp was making the horse-hair-stuffed cushions smell a bit more mildewed than usual.

None of these things dug a single furrow into her determination. Not the midnight storm, not the plight of the poor horses pulling her along, not even the probable suffering of the driver up on his bench seat with only an oilcloth slicker for protection.

"'Wishing clocks more swift,' dear?"

Bliss focused her gaze upon her aunt Iris, who sat across from her. Iris Worthington seemed just as unperturbed by the horrid London weather as Bliss was. In fact, she seemed to be enjoying it immensely. Of course, Iris always did like to indulge in a bit of theater, even that of a natural variety.

"That's from *Winter's Tale*, pet. Act one, scene two."

"Yes, Aunt Iris. I know." Dear Iris. Bliss loved her devotedly, and knew she herself was loved in return, but if ever there was a more useless woman than Iris Worthington, Bliss had yet to meet her. Iris lived in a world filled with fantasy and theater, where William Shakespeare was a constant companion.

However, Bliss was entirely undeterred by the weather, or the time of night, or any other single thing. If the narrow London streets flooded, she would hop from the carriage and swim herself to the chapel.

After all, she was about to marry the man of her dreams!

Bliss smiled contentedly to herself. Darling Neville. He was handsome, in a youthful, bookish way. He was very rich, which would be more pleasant than being poor. He was titled, although Bliss could honestly plead no interest in that, unless his social clout came in handy to further the interests of her dear Worthington relations.

No, truly, it was Neville himself she preferred over all other men. Neville was gentle and kind and good-natured and thoughtful. He was a good and fair master to his dependents and a most diligent landholder. As the Duke of Camberton, despite his mere twenty-seven years, he was truly beyond reproach.

His scholarly bent did not dismay Bliss. She was quite accustomed to people who studied and read and piled books here, there, and everywhere. Worthington House was a riotous, slithering torrent of books and brilliance and occasional accidental explosions. It was an exciting existence. But Bliss was through with excitement. Neville's propensity toward quiet reading would be positively refreshing.

Bliss knew that Neville adored her right back. As well he should. Her appearance was quite fetching, she'd been told, and she knew her figure was on the riveting side of generous. She was fashionable without being intimidating, and her taste was impeccable. She was patient, even-tempered, and intelligent. She would make an outstanding duchess and an exemplary wife.

She'd never been terribly romantic, which was just one thing that differentiated her from most of her Worthington cousins. Despite her basically practical nature, however, she was naturally eager to pursue the upcoming pleasures of marriage with her handsome husband.

With a slight easing of her perfect posture, she leaned back into the musty cushions with a very small sigh. The storm was slowing her progress toward her future, which was unacceptable. Yet she refused to become frustrated. With each grudging clop of the horses' hooves, she was getting closer to the moment that would change everything.

Neville had become duke at age twelve. The great responsibility had made him dedicated, painstaking, and, best of all, predictable.

In contrast, Bliss had been left to grow up in the sheep-infested county of Shropshire in the care of a foster mother, while her busy, wealthy parents continued their exciting, separate lives in London. All her life, she had lived day to day, never knowing when her parents might come, waiting for weeks or months, and sometimes years, before one of their fine carriages would jingle its way from London down the country lanes to her foster mother's cottage, when a well-dressed footman would leap from the top seat and flip out a small folding step made from filigreed brass, then hand down either a veiled and silk-clad woman or a stout and silk-clad man.

Mama and Papa were darlings, and of course their lives were terribly busy and important, but all in all, Bliss would have liked a bit of warning once in a while. To wait, and wait, and ever-loving *wait*—and then, of course, inevitably they would arrive while she was elbow-deep in stove black, or disheveled and sticky from berrying, or, worse, in the middle of a very good book! She learned very young that the best thing was to remain "just so" at all times.

In short, she had spent her entire life waiting for someone to come home.

Now she was in London at last, and had been residing for months quite satisfactorily with the dear Worthington clan. That was how she'd met her perfect, wonderful Neville.

Neville didn't care for travel. Long carriage rides made him ill. Neville wanted to stay home and study his butterfly collection and sit in his study to write long letters to naturalists around the world.

For the rest of her life, Bliss would always know precisely where Neville was. Like a beetle stuck to her board with the pin of matrimony, he would never leave her all alone.

No more lonely waiting. Never again.